Ooh La La!

Ooh La La!

Contemporary French Erotica by Women

Edited by Maxim Jakubowski and Franck Spengler

Translations by Paul Buck and Catherine Petit,
Maxim Jakubowski, and Noel Burch

THUNDER'S MOUTH PRESS • NEW YORK

OOH LA LA!

Contemporary French Erotica by Women

All translations by Paul Buck and Catherine Petit, with the exception of "Tarot" and "Lies" by Maxim Jakubowski, and "Eyewash" by Noel Burch

Original stories initially appeared in *Troubles de Femmes*, 1994; *Passions de Femmes*, 1996; *Plaisirs de Femmes*, 1998; *Désirs de Femmes*, 1999; *2000 Ans D'Amour*, 2000; *Fantasmes de Femmes*, 2001; *Femmes Amoureuses*, 2005.

Published by
Thunder's Mouth Press
An Imprint of Avalon Publishing Group, Inc.
245 West 17th Street, 11th floor
New York, NY 10011

AVALON
publishing group incorporated

Compilation Copyright © 2006 by Maxim Jakubowski and Franck Spengler

First printing, November 2006

Library of Congress Cataloging-in-Publication Data is available.

ISBN: 1-56025-908-6
ISBN-13: 978-1-56025-908-4

9 8 7 6 5 4 3 2 1

Book design by *Ivelisse Robles Marrero*
Printed in the United States of America
Distributed by Publishers Group West

TABLE OF CONTENTS

INTRODUCTION

A recent best-selling book postulated that French women don't get fat. Another French myth—or is it an urban legend?—is that all French women are both particularly sexy and uncanny experts in the amatory arts. Maybe—but then the editors of this anthology are married to a Russian and a Belgian, respectively, so we must both draw a discreet premarital veil on our past knowledge of Gallic pulch-ritude . . . Nevertheless, there is no doubt that, in the public imagination, France and sex have long enjoyed a fascinating rapport, a situation encouraged, fostered, and confirmed by the vagaries of history, social customs, and, of course, the cinema. From Marie Antoinette (actually an Austrian), famous courtesans, and models to the more recent charms of actresses ranging from Brigitte Bardot, Jeanne Moreau, Emmanuelle Béart, Sophie Marceau, Ludivine Sagnier, and on and on, standards of female beauty have long been closely associated with French women.

And the erotic arts and literature have long been associated with French artists and writers. Need we remind you that the Marquis de Sade was French, and that he spawned a tradition of erotic writing that also aspires to literature, a discipline that, at one time or another, has been taken up by a whole legion of well-known French authors and poets, sometimes pseudonymously, at other times with brazen openness: Paul Verlaine, Nicolas-Edme Restif de la Bretonne, Guillaume Apollinaire, Louis Aragon, André Pieyre de Mandiargues, Bernard Noël, and so many others. Writing explicit stories has never been considered a menial endeavor among French literati—in fact, the practice has often enjoyed both recognition and respectability. And when Dominique Aury wrote *The Story of O* as Pauline Reage, she opened the floodgates for women authors to tackle sexuality in an even more daring and brazen manner. French erotica by women has, since *The Story of O*, been a fascinating arena for self-confession, the unveiling of deep-seated fantasies, and a meticulous exploration of the self and the blurred borderlines between Eros and Thanatos, much more than just a clever exposition of sexual hydraulics and combinations. And few male writers, even in France, have matched its intensity. French female erotica comes from both the guts and the brain, and often balances philosophical dilemmas with an almost scientific dissection of the most outré sexual practices.

Emmanuelle Arsan's *Emmanuelle* series, much bastardized on the silver screen, was not just a pioneering work but a splendidly honest tale of a woman who embraced unconventional sexuality and, as such, can even be considered a protofeminist of sorts! And *Emmanuelle*, published by Eric Losfeld, a most unconventional and courageous publisher who persisted, despite fines and occasional token prison sentences, to encourage the writing of taboo-breaking erotica (alongside Jean-Jacques Pauvert, another early defender of the faith), was just the beginning—French women writers have almost taken over a murky territory until recently mostly dominated by male writers, and have brought to the field a crude honesty and a depth of emotion seldom encountered in "dirty" books before.

To such an extent that, today, women dominate French erotic writing and have achieved an acceptance that Anglo-Saxon writers can only dream of. Following Losfeld's retirement from the erotic "wars,"

Introduction

Régine Deforges set up L'Or du Temps, the first publishing imprint to specialize in erotica, and there are now a handful of such publishers in France—all thriving.

Some of the more prominent female writers of erotica of the last few decades have only patchily been translated into English. They include Jeanne de Berg, the wife of leading author and filmmaker Alain Robbe-Grillet; Alina Reyes; Régine Deforges; the fascinating Vanessa Duriès, whose *Le Lien* (*The Ties That Bind*) was another heart-felt shocker on the theme of submission and dominance in the grand tradition of *The Story of O*, but who sadly died in a car crash shortly after its publication; the sulfurous Florence Dugas, whose extreme trilogy (of which only the opening book *Dolorosa Soror* has been made available to English-speaking readers) explores depths of depravity and passion that defy the imagination; and, on an autobiographical level, Catherine Millet, of the notorious memoir *The Sexual Life of Catherine M*.

But there are literally dozens of other French female writers of erotica who have since bloomed, young and old, from all classes of society, and what they all have in common is the ability to make explicit and sexual private feelings and private lives, with both elegance and a clever manipulation of the art of arousal, to the extent that this school of writing is now making waves across Europe and inspiring similar writers in Spain and Italy, among other countries. Unfortunately, many of them have so far stuck mainly to writing novels: Mélanie Muller, Agnès Pareyre, Elizabeth Hergott, Clarisse Nicoïdski, Marie Gray, Aurélie Van Hoeymissen, Ariane Larsen, Virginie Despentes, Nadine Monfils, Anouchka D'Anna, Marie-Laure Dagoit . . . and we have thus been unable to include them here.

However, the stories we have selected for your enjoyment will, we strongly believe, arouse you, fascinate you, enchant you, and disturb you. The writers we have assembled come from France, Belgium, French-speaking Canada, and even Africa, and form just the tip of the iceberg in an important new literature of sensual writing for modern times.

So, in conclusion, maybe French women don't get fat, but they certainly can pen a sexy story . . .

Maxim Jakubowski & Franck Spengler

THE MAN FROM ALBUQUERQUE

Julie Saget

The first time I heard about him, where was it exactly? The man from Albuquerque . . . His real name was never uttered, perhaps no one knew it; that was what he was called: the man from Albuquerque.

Yes, the first time, where was it exactly?

Surely in a city with a harbor, those are the only ones he visits. What he looks for he finds on the wharves, along the docks; inland towns don't interest him, he keeps to the edges of the continents; from there it's easier to escape, to vanish.

That is what I was told: he disembarked one beautiful day—in Valparaiso or Liverpool, Tampico or Hamburg—and no one even knew he had landed, for he was only a shadow haunting the ports. And then someone boasted of having seen him, and the news spread; it was the only thing people talked about. On the gangways of the cargo ships berthed at the quay, his name, like a rumor, passed from mouth to mouth, and along the counters, too, in the bars for sailors, which smell of sour beer and men's sweat. They spoke of the man from Albuquerque with dread, admiration, disgust, and envy. I can still hear all those voices talking about him. I started to look for him, and what each voice revealed pushed me forward to meet him.

That's what I remember from the first time: it was in Barcelona, in that hotel room with a rancid smell, where I had been dragged by two Russian sailors from Novorossisk, who were wandering, like me, in the alleyways of the Barrio Chino. We had drunk too much, as if each of us wanted to lose some of our life in that bad drunken state. We made love, the three of us. They rode me, shot all over me, soiled me with sperm and piss. Dawn surprised us, limbs entwined, in sheets soaked with urine. My teeth were chattering, my lips and tongue swollen from far too many bites, a taste of salt and ashes in my mouth, too much sperm swallowed. I was shaking.

It was at that precise time, in that bleak light of early morning, the time for ultimate confessions, that one of the sailors mentioned the man from Albuquerque. I realized immediately that I had to find him. That now my life had meaning. I had to reach him, the elusive man, whatever the cost. He was a cloud pushed by the wind, a stench; he brushed against the black walls of warehouses, a vague silhouette in the fog drowning the pier, barely alive, barely real. We were the same, he and I.

I wasn't always like that. I was married to a powerful man, wealthy, very wealthy and influential. I was an ornament in his house, I was refused nothing. In exchange I had an obligation: to know how to behave, to spare my husband the least scandal. I loved another man. It was a passion approaching madness. Under the pretext of being looked after, I demanded to be split up. In reality, it was to be even closer to the object of my desire. That lover taught me the mysteries of my body, he pulled my body apart, he offered me to others, he fucked me alive and dead. I came for him, in front of him, I came because of him, he crucified me in anticipation of his goodwill ...Then death took him away from me. For days and nights I howled like an animal for its food—my lover's flesh, which I would never taste again. My husband offered to help me. I started to hate him. I bought my freedom for the price of my silence and total disappearance. As a result of his upbringing, if not fear that I would prostitute myself in order to survive, his ruthless generosity forced him to provide for my needs. I accepted that condition, for I was free then to take all the men I wanted without thinking about money. I would give my bush, my tuft to eat to anybody I fancied, and if I felt the desire, I would pay—with the money of the man whose name I bear—rough men who, however, don't ask for anything other than fucking the woman who offers herself asking nothing in return. At the beginning I sought those men at the gates of factories, the men who worked by night. I waited for them in the early morning, I chose one at random. Some were frightened by my offer. The money scared them, they feared a devious trick. Others, fortunately, agreed to make the most of that godsend. They allowed me to slip my hand into their fly, forage around until I pulled out their naked penis, which I masturbated until it went stiff. Standing against the factory wall, I let them work me, but none managed to calm my fury. Like a crazy bitch, from my throat sprang the growls of a trapped animal. I ordered: "Deeper, deeper, smash me!" Then, with a nasty laugh: "Are you scared? Are you scared I'll swallow you and your prick, and your balls, and all your shit? Scared I will gulp you down, drain you of your blood, drain you of your life? Fuck you! Go deeper, deeper than that! Do as I say!" They did their best. I could see in their eyes desire mixed with fear in the face of such rage. In the end I found those men too servile; they stunk of machine grease and obedience. I was aiming for something else. Men of another consistency—but their bodies always had to be dirty and their cocks had to stink—men whose language I would not understand and who would not hear my words, men coming from the four corners of the earth, with no home, no homeland, like myself. I knew I would find them in ports. Makeshift crews, they arrive from every part of the world, all races mixed, embarked for a mere pittance of a wage on tankers so decrepit that no repairs can save those floating monstrosities from disaster. Indians, Malaysians, Yemenites, they feed on spicy stews and raw onions; they have foul breath and their sweat reeks. It's them I want, them I need.

So I left. Gibraltar, Tangier, Alexandria and then, as I said, Barcelona and the two sailors from Novorossisk . . .

I went up north, ready to scour all the ports on the Baltic. I ended up in Hamburg. In the evening, I wandered in Sankt Pauli. Girls in their windows, boxed in tackiness, with an air of decent housewives displaying their asses. Not one worth fucking, but men were there, strolling about, eyeing them. My God, they looked like first communicants walking slowly to the altar to receive the host! Monumental hard-ons because that one shakes her tits under their noses and they imagine themselves stuffing their pricks in the holy of holies! You bet they haven't grown one inch since the time when, as adolescents, they shut themselves in the toilet to jerk off out of sight of their mommy's eyes! Men's desire disgusts me.

It was certainly not in those alleyways with no dark corners, where the gaudy pink neons filter, that I was going to meet the man from Albuquerque. It was down to the wharves I had to go . . . . I hung about between the angular shadows of the container stacks waiting to be loaded. I moved toward the ship I thought was the most rotten, an old tub with the look of a rusty scrap heap. I took the gangway that hadn't been lifted, a useless precaution anyway. Where could they go, the crew, those poor guys with no papers, with no money? I hadn't walked three steps onto the deck when a voice came out of the shadows to stop me.

"What the hell are you doing here?"

I answered:

"I'm looking for men."

"Men. What for?"

"For fucking."

I heard him sneer and saw him come toward me. I thought he must be the captain.

"You're in the wrong place. Do you know what the men down there look like? For three weeks, since we berthed, their wages haven't arrived. There's nothing to take here, fuck off!"

"You've got it wrong. I'm the one who pays."

He grabbed me by the sleeve, and there I was, in what must have been the steward's room. He and I sat in front of a glass of bad whiskey.

"So then, you are the one who pays? Tell me more."

I told the captain the woman I had been before, before knowing myself, before knowing who I was. I talked about the deceased lover who had taught me to understand who I was. I told him about my taste for filth and abjection. That what would seem a descent to hell in the eyes of the uninitiated was for me the path to the absolute. That I was not crazy. That I had chosen and that I had to go all the way, till the end of what I had decided to accomplish. And that it was for that reason I was looking for the man from Albuquerque.

The captain remained silent for a moment before blurting out: "Port Sudan, in a month's time."

He showed me how to gain access to the holds. As I went in, I had difficulty discerning the dozen men sleeping on the bare floor. I slipped between them. The heat was stifling. The first body my hand encountered was half-naked and sweaty. I touched the damp torso and the sleeper woke up, muttering in an incomprehensible tongue. I quieted him by placing my mouth on his. His breath was repugnant and my tongue plunged into a cesspool. At the same time I undressed and lay down on top of him. I became an undulating reptile. My belly rubbed against his and when I felt the hard swollen penis, I undid the man's sarong and, opening my thighs, I violently forced his penis inside me. There was a long moan, like a powerful note on the barely audible chords of the breath of the other sleeping sailors. My movements became more rapid, more violent, to make the man cry louder and wake up his companions. The first to wake up lit a hurricane lamp and moved closer. I beckoned him to come even closer. I undid the belt that held up his rough cotton trousers, I took his penis in my mouth. I started to suck him as if I was going to draw out the substance in his balls. The one I was riding let out an anguished rattle and I felt he was coming with all the power of a male deprived of women for ages. All the others were now crowding around the three of us. Each wanted his turn, now. I gave myself to all. I offered them my cunt, my lips, the furrow between my breasts, my armpits, my hair, all the places in my body where their come could pour out. I think they were laughing and crying at the same time. It lasted quite a while. Dawn was already breaking. Each part of my flesh was pain and pleasure at the same time, as if I had just gone up the Via Dolorosa on my knees with a crown of thorns on my forehead and the weight of the cross on my back. Transfiguration through abasement, with voluntary suffering. Before coming out into the open air, I threw them a bundle of banknotes, which the men rushed for, with the greediness of famished dogs.

As I walked down the wharf where the first dockers were already at work, I heard the voice of the captain shouting:

"You're really going there?"

I nodded. He added:

"Perhaps we'll see each other again!"

We were too far apart for him to hear my reply:

"I doubt it very much."

He must have seen, though, that I was smiling at him. I knew that was the image he would keep of me.

Port Sudan. When I disembarked, I was challenged immediately by a native in uniform who was probably acting as harbormaster, customs officer, and commissioner, the symbol of all authorities. He was fat and sweating heavily under his cap. The air was a furnace, no relief to be expected from the sea, no sea breeze, earth and water an inferno. I followed the representative of the law into a shack used as an office, where the blades of a decrepit fan stirred the fire, no more. He wanted to know the purpose of my visit.

"I've come to wait for a friend."

He appraised me suspiciously, the same way he had examined my papers earlier.

"I keep your passport," he stated in bad English. "You come get it when friend here."

Used to all sorts of traffic, he was calculating what gains he could obtain for himself from my presence. It was he who found me a place to stay. In a rickety jeep driven at breakneck speed, he took me to an old woman who spoke only Dinka. The house comprised two rooms. I would occupy the one at the back, the old woman's bedroom.

I lay down, naked, on what was nothing more than a litter stinking of rags and the sour smell of old people. I was exhausted, like someone who has just accomplished the final stage of a race. Sleep! . . . Between my half-closed eyelids, I caught sight of a hand pulling the curtain that was supposed to give some intimacy to my room. I saw the eyes of my landlady, full of curiosity, a black and greedy look whose only intelligence was that of an animal, the eyes of a rat. She came closer, attracted by my nudity, and her bony hand traced the whole surface of my skin. I was too shattered to push that hand away. The caress was soothing, in a way. The fingers lingered on the fleece of my pubis, appreciating its abundance and thickness, then they plunged inside me, digging into my depths, exploring both orifices. It was the hand of an expert who knew what it was to finger a woman, and pleasure rose in me until the combustion of orgasm. The old woman lifted her fingers to her nostrils, sniffing the traces of her exploration. She looked like she was inhaling a delicious perfume whose fragrance she had herself lost a long time ago.

How long did I sleep? When I woke up night had fallen. The old woman and I shared a stew she had prepared. Then, through a series of signs, she explained that she was going out, that she would be back soon, and that I should wait for her. I stood on the doorstep. The sky was nothing but a huge, jet black cavity dotted with stars, an oppressive cover imprisoning each portion of that godforsaken place. I realized that if there was a place where I could find the man from Albuquerque, it was Port Sudan, and nowhere else. One only lands here to run aground or die a slow death. Here everything is wrecked: men and ships.

The old woman came back, as she'd said she would. She had brought with her an adolescent boy whose eyes were lined with kohl—the eyes of a gazelle—a mouth with thick lips, and the skin of a girl. I said to the old woman, no, I was not interested. But she got upset, took me by force back to my room. She threw herself backward onto the bed, lifted her skirt, and, legs spread wide, opened the edges of her cunt and forced me to look. In place of the clitoris there was a long scar, the mark of excision. No need to speak Dinka to catch what the old woman told me:

"You're lucky, my girl, to possess that bit of flesh that provides woman with a pleasure even more intense than the one given by the bludgeons of men. It's your pleasure, not that of the male, so enjoy it!"

I let the ephebe with painted eyes put his head between my legs. His tongue came to get me, first pointed and wriggling like a lizard's tail, then wide and flabby—the tongue of a licker savoring his favorite dish with wet lapping noises. Finally the thick-lipped mouth caught me, sucked me in. I felt my clitoris swelling, my whole body condensed into that single growth, there where the alpha and omega of my woman's desire resided. I became dizzy. I grabbed the frizzy hair with both hands to make sure he wouldn't escape, his mouth wouldn't leave me before I fell back disheveled and shattered. The orgasm left me burning and unsatisfied. I wanted the penis of my lover, I made signs that he should penetrate me. That was when the old woman burst into laughter and lifted the young man's *gandoura*, showing me that he had been emasculated. They both laughed, the madame and the ephebe, as if they had played a trick on me in their own way. Afterward, they asked me to pay them, as was only right.

On the third evening the commissioner came to fetch me.

"I think your friend arrived. You want I take you to him?"

I didn't even ask how he knew that it was precisely that man I was waiting for. I climbed into the jeep and we drove in the direction of the port. The moon was full and its light, a phosphorescent lactation, radiated the sea, changing it to mercury. At the far end of the docks, a few warehouses still stood, the last remnants of a time when Port Sudan had countless fleets mooring there. The jeep stopped in front of the last shed. A man was there. He walked toward me. At first I saw only his teeth, gleaming like snow, brightened by the whiteness of the moon. The face had no outlines. It was as if he wanted to melt in what was still blurred, in that nocturnal part that the reflections of the moon hadn't been able to reach. The deep voice made me bet the man was handsome. One couldn't imagine ugliness associated with that voice.

"I know you're looking for me. In fact I was told a while ago, and I was wondering where we would finally meet."

As he pronounced those last words with an ironic smile I saw his teeth, so white in his carnassial mouth. He took his time, pulled a cigarillo from his shirt pocket, and lit it. The acrid smell of tobacco suited him. His voice grew louder:

"I know you're looking for me. But what I don't know is why."

I answered simply:

"Snuff movies."

"You're a client? You need that to come?"

"It's not what you think."

The voice spoke with a falsely innocent tone. It was a way to make fun of me.

"But I don't think anything! And I don't care what others think! It's none of my business."

"I'm not a client. I just want to be the next."

There was silence. The man threw down his cigarillo. He took his time to crush the stump.

"I never do it with women. A question of principles. I work with men perfectly aware of what to expect. Most have no more than six months to live. Tuberculosis or that type of shit . . . Their life is not worth more than that of a dead dog. They think that with all the dough they're going to earn, they can provide their family with a living, back here. You see, those men agree. It's a proper contract. I don't know what you are looking for exactly."

I explained what I was looking for. The stigmata on my body, which were nothing but purification, the come of all those men I had taken and who had come on my belly, breasts, and face, and which was like spit on Christ's face. Redemption, redemption! The martyr had to reach her end, like Christ crucified. Then I would finally be freed, liberated from the weight of my organs, saved from suffering. I wanted that ultimate orgasm and I wanted him to obtain it for me.

"Go home! I'll come tomorrow night and let you know."

All the next day I waited like a fiancée on the eve of her wedding. The next night he was there. He came into the bedroom. I undressed, and, once naked, I undressed him. His skin was like amber, smooth and golden. I ran my tongue over his torso to get the taste of that skin. He took my breasts in his hands to hold me captive. I knew that this first approach sealed the pact and that he had accepted what I had asked of him. I knelt in front of him, religiously, for my mouth to take his penis. I didn't want to hurry anything. I wanted that night to become a bountiful eternity.

With incredible slowness I swallowed the man! He had taken my head in his hands to transmit the rhythm he wanted to my movements. There was no impatience in our gestures. With infinite gentleness I came out to the tip, for it was the most vulnerable spot—there, the envelope is so thin that the flesh appears in all its transparency.

"Come here," he murmured.

He hauled me up. I wound my legs around his loins, my arms around his neck, and he plunged inside. For him I weighed no more than a small child. Again he set the pace of the ebb and flow. So strong, so manly, yet so attentive to my pleasure, as if it was the only thing that was important to him. When he realized, from the paleness of my face and the violence of my moans, that I was about to reach orgasm . . . he allowed himself to ejaculate, so that we came together.

Rolled into a ball, I remained gasping on the floor while he got dressed. He wrapped me in the old woman's sheet and carried me out to the jeep. I knew where he was taking me. Still in his arms I crossed the threshold of the shed, like a bride. Was it not the case after all, tonight, of celebrating a barbaric wedding?

In the shed, a big lamp was lit, making a luminous halo, a circle of crude light defining the stage. I saw a pulley there, suspended, where chains could slide. He tied me to them, my arms stretched toward the ceiling, as high as possible. My feet just touched the ground.

Two men in hoods appeared. I recognized one of them as the commissioner. They whipped, burned, lacerated, and mutilated me. They dug into my insides with their blades. My blood flowed abundantly. They had taken precautions to cover the ground with sawdust. Don't worry: only the first gashes really hurt. Afterward, the pain becomes so intense that one no longer feels it. The spirit escapes from the matter to float in an elsewhere where nothing can touch you.

I'm almost certain that the fat commissioner had an erection like a donkey. But not the man from Albuquerque. His eye was riveted to the camera, filming my agony. He was just doing his job.

The angel of death.

He spread his wings—that was my last vision—and, taking me once again in his arms, lifted me up and took me away. I was finally in flight.

Her last thought was that she had made him promise to send a copy of the film to her husband. He would not hesitate to pay dearly to recover the original and destroy it.

"Thanks to me," she had said to the angel, "you'll have a lot of money. Perhaps you can even stop."

The angel had placed his lips on hers (a good-bye kiss, gentle like the down of a fledgling) and, with a smile, replied:

"It's my life, you know!"

She had smiled back at the angel. And that was how she departed.

THE GARAGE

Astrid Schilling

According to her circle of friends—mainly men—Aline was an impulsive, extroverted, warm, and pretty woman.

Ever since she was young, she'd known how to combine good sense and opportunism. Thus, after the untimely death of her mother when she was sixteen, she left her village to settle in Reims, in a lawyer's home, in exchange for some work.

It wasn't long before Aline succeeded in seducing the lawyer, the good Octave Raguinet. He fancied her straightaway, for she had found the way to flatter him while still keeping her words pure and simple. Just a few days after starting her job, already bored by the smallness of her bedroom, Aline, with youthful boldness, entered Octave's room and slipped beneath his duvet. There she paid the lawyer the honors he deserved, and poor Raguinet nearly lost his papers.

It was also in Octave's arms that Aline discovered her power over the male gender. In his naïveté the lawyer contributed to the young woman's sexual education, bombarded as he was by her incredibly lewd questions.

She talked to him as to her confidant and Octave couldn't help adding to his secrets a few spicy anecdotes that he had experienced himself. He told her how he had nearly compromised his career when he seduced a girl who, like Aline, was still a minor.

"Was she good at making love to you, that girl?" asked Aline.

"Not as good as you. She didn't play with my prick. You, you handle it wonderfully. What about sucking me, my dear?"

"What will you give me in exchange?"

"Advice."

"On how to make you come, Octave?"

"On how to make all men come!"

"Oh, yes, yes, tell me."

Aline took such good care of Octave Raguinet that he decided to give her everything, except his money: much of his time, penis, dreams, and desires. He bought old erotic books whose eroticism was old-fashioned but amusing; garters to dress her as if for the Feast of Saint Eustace; and geisha balls in ivory, which he ordered, after much hesitation, from a mail-order catalogue.

The lawyer couldn't keep his secret for long, and his bragging—in bad taste—helped determine the young woman's destiny. People were quick to distort Octave Raginuet's words and sweep them like a gust of wind around the whole of Reims. Soon people were singing a little song with a suggestive rhyme about Aline: *Aline loves pen . . . is.*

It was certainly true that she liked them and it wasn't long before she stopped concealing that fact. She left Octave Raguinet, who, in a last-ditch attempt to keep her, offered her marriage. She refused and took a small apartment overlooking the cathedral square, above a garage.

It was there she welcomed her lovers, seven of them, one for each day of the week. Recruitment was easy enough, for the salacious comments of the lawyer had generated a good degree of lust in the town.

Aline's lovers were brutes. They made love to her till she fell asleep, exhausted, and often she didn't even hear them leave the apartment. In her sleep she imagined she was still making love. She was the type of woman who never stopped wanting more sensual delights and, in her dreams, she invented impossible sexual positions that she then tried to re-create during her lovemaking sessions. Aline liked, for example, what she called "the bow position on the double bass." She placed her forehead on the pillow, stuck her legs in the air, spread them wide, and asked the men to make their bow vibrate deep inside her. The open pussy of the young woman attracted the penis like a magnet, and the man became a talented musician, focused on making Aline's moans swell and surge like a lament.

She was attracted only to bodies, the dance of members, and the delight of the whiteness exposed in the hollow of her thighs. For her weekly lovers she had only one demand: that they always be ready, whatever the circumstances. She especially enjoyed having lewd exchanges with them, and at the same time feeling their penises swell beneath her fingers. She squeezed them a bit to make the blood flow in the vein, then planted herself on their throbbing cocks.

George, one of her "regulars," as she called them, was her favorite. He always came to her with greedy eyes and his prick bulging in his trousers. Each time she looked at him, Aline burst into laughter, for she knew the pleasure she would have during intercourse, and, in order to contain too obvious a joy, she peppered the flabby cheeks of the garage mechanic with kisses.

This time she was once again not disappointed. He opened his fly and produced his stiff and fleshy cock. Unaware of their panting, he started to work over her as if he were doing a beautiful repair job, taking the extra care he would if he were given permission to work on an exorbitantly expensive foreign car.

"Push harder, George!"

George pushed his prick in even further, made it come and go at a quick pace.

Aline, beneath the violence of his thrusts, tipped over backward, propelled to the back of the sofa. Her hair in a mess on the gaudily colored cushions, Aline let herself be swept into an ecstasy that ravished her. George continued working hard on her with the rough tenderness of a man in his fifties and the bliss of a pleasure with no hassles.

In the depths of their revels, they barely heard the seven strokes from the cathedral belfry, the call to mass signaling dinner and the need for George to go back to his family. He shafted Aline with even more eagerness, then emitted a raucous cry. Aline held her lover inside her until she came for the third time. Desire having died down, they parted with an idle kiss.

As soon as the mechanic had left the apartment of his mistress, someone knocked at the door. A woman in her fifties, with craggy features and simple clothes, stood on the threshold. She came into the living room and sat heavily in one of the armchairs. While recovering her breath, which prevented her from speaking, she looked the young woman up and down with contempt. Then she launched in:

"I've heard so much about you that I don't feel anything now that I'm here."

"Who are you?" asked Aline.

"You're a wretched woman," she said.

"What do you want?"

"Is George here?"

Taken aback, Aline replied quickly:

"No. Who wants to know?"

"Me. Since he's known you, George only thinks about sex. And when one thinks about sex, one cannot walk straight. I'm warning you, if you see him again, you'll regret it."

"Are you his wife?"Aline paused, then resumed. "George doesn't come here. He works downstairs, at the garage. You're on the wrong floor!"

"Everybody knows what you do to men. There's no place for a whore like you in this town."

As the woman was consumed in hurling abuse at her, Aline quietly walked to the window. She exclaimed:

"Look who's coming across the square!"

"Is it him?" the woman asked anxiously. She rushed to the window.

Aline looked at her maliciously.

"He just came out of the church. He's been praying for your salvation, so that you'll let him have a little bit of pleasure away from your sad and dry cunt."

Speechless, the woman didn't know how to reply. Aline carried on:

"I'm going to do you a favor, because I quite like you, or rather, I like the beautiful hot prick of your George. This is the best advice I can give you. Step back."

The woman didn't move.

"Step back or you'll never know. Do as I say."

Furious, the woman rushed toward the door.

"I don't need advice from a—!"

She opened the door to leave.

Aline stopped her.

"If you stay a few more minutes, I promise I'll no longer see your husband . . . There, good. Go and sit down now. You deserve my advice. You'll be able to make use of it all your life, even if your George no longer loves you."

Leaning against the windowsill, her splendid body surrounded by a halo—the first light of the night coming from the cathedral—Aline lifted her large woolen skirt above her knees.

The woman stared at Aline's movements, hypnotized.

The young woman's hands went up her stockings, toward the dark and wet place she revealed by pulling at her clothes. Her pussy, with its thick black hair, was big and shining. It seemed to hide Aline's fingers like a forest.

Aware of the spectacle she was offering as revenge, she started to moan.

"It's terribly good, these caresses. You should do it, too, unless you're ashamed!"

With incredible indecency she spread her sex, revealing, beyond the fleshy labia, a clitoris of impressive size.

"It's washing day for whites! All that come from your George! He shot so much in me!"

She shoved two fingers into her vagina and withdrew them, covered in sperm. She started to lick them meticulously.

"There's not one drop left for you! It's really good to masturbate. I wonder how I still can! He made me come three times."

Saying that, Aline started to knead her clitoris like a breadcrumb, to frenetically tickle her button to make it swell with explosive desire. Her fingers ran like thieves of pleasure over her gaping sex, skidded on her plump labia, and vanished in one swoop into her crack. Unable to contain herself any longer, she came in bursts just as the front door slammed with a simultaneous bang.

The following week was terrible for Aline. A thousand times she felt like going down to the garage to see her lover. She refrained, wondering what his reaction would be. Had he heard about the visit his wife had paid her?

Opting for caution, Aline chose to rely on her "regulars" to pound her. They were not as good of performers as George, of course, but they were stiff nonetheless. The young woman made them feel good, for she gave them all the tenderness she couldn't offer to her favorite. She made love passionately, sucking their dicks till they were as red as embers, offering to be fucked before any other play, and screaming the filthiest words she knew in the heat of passion.

But Aline continued to watch for George as he came and went from the garage. She even thought she recognized his voice, mixed with the noise of the engines. It was him she needed. The other men were meager consolation.

She imagined she heard him one morning climbing the stairs. She recognized his heavy step and, heart full of hope, immediately opened the door to call his name. Nobody answered. She went downstairs. The side entrance to the garage, opening onto the passage of the house, was locked on Sundays. She tried to open the door; a thin light filtered from underneath. Her efforts were rewarded. As she went in, she bashed against a pot of paint left near a Peugeot. The noise made her jump. She moved through the garage congested with cars and instinctively walked toward the lit space.

"George?" she called anxiously. "Are you there? Answer me."

She heard a sucking noise, another noise, indefinable rustlings, like some kind of struggle.

She came closer to the workshop office and put her face to the window to peer inside. She saw the powerful back she knew so well. Even the blue overalls couldn't conceal the striking muscles of her lover. Touched at seeing him, she entered the office.

He was in raptures. His strong arms were clutching those of his wife, stretched out on the desk. He was working hard on her and the filly in heat was swaying her head from side to side to get the most out of the thrusts. She was enjoying herself tremendously. That is, until, with one of her movements, she caught sight of Aline. She snarled so hard that her husband stopped in his tracks. She screamed:

"I'm going to kill her! George, what's your whore doing here?"

And to Aline:

"Bitch! Slut!"

Aline left the room in tears. She couldn't stand seeing her lover in his wife's arms. She slowly collapsed against a Renault. The woman leaped out of the office with George in her wake, totally confused, divided between an instinctive tenderness for his mistress and the restraint of marital duty. He could only mumble to his wife:

"Suzanne! Calm down! Suzanne!"

But Suzanne had grabbed Aline by her hair and the two were fighting on the bare floor. George tried to separate them, but their bodies were so entwined that he couldn't distinguish one from the other. At times he could see a sneer of hatred on Suzanne's face, and then Aline's sharp nails tearing at his wife's blouse. Aline took hold of Suzanne's nipples and pinched them brutally. Suzanne screamed with a pain that resonated through the garage.

Suzanne had only one thought on her mind: to kill Aline! For the humiliation she had suffered, for having taken her husband away from her.

In the struggle, the two women spat in each other's face and uttered streams of filth to reinforce their strength.

George grabbed Suzanne by her clothes and pulled her away from Aline's grip.

"Suzanne, that's enough! Aline, you too!"

George's grip was firm. Suzanne was his prisoner. She calmed down a little, though she continued to hurl abuse at her enemy and glare at her with hatred.

She looked at her husband. She had never seen him like that before. A cold rage had taken hold of him. He tightened his grip.

Aline stood up slowly. Her blood boiled, and sweat formed beads on her forehead, along the hairline. She touched her face: nothing was broken.

George had gone berserk.

"You both deserve a good beating! Who decides, the man or the woman? Well, for me, it's the man! Aline, come here! Closer!"

Aline jumped.

"What are you going to do?"

"Shut up, you'll see! Just keep quiet."

Aline edged forward.

"George, you're not going to hurt me, are you?"

George let go of Suzanne after making sure she would obey him and crossed to one of the cars. While the two rivals avoided looking at each other, he took some rope from the trunk, then came back to his mistress. She was shaking. She repeated:

"You're not going to hurt me?"

He didn't reply. He tied her wrists to one of the pillars of the hydraulic ramp.

Suzanne couldn't help saying:

"George, let me have a go at her."

Exasperated, he turned on her:

"I'm the one who's going to have a go at her. You, come here."

He took his wife by the hand and made her sit in a damaged Fiat placed on the ramp. He shut her in after two unsuccessful attempts at closing the dented door, then started the mechanism to lift it. Slowly, the ramp went up in the air, at the same time stretching Aline's bound arms.

The mechanic stopped the machine when his mistress's body was stretched to the limit.

He ripped away her skirt and struggled with her panties until he tore them to shreds.

"I really feel like slapping your beautiful slut's ass. How exciting it is like this, everything on offer!"

Up high, Suzanne, in a state, glued her face to the window to see what her husband was doing. She screamed at George to take revenge. Her words reached them like a muffled war chant.

"George," whispered Aline, "take me. I want you so much. My pussy's on fire!"

George put one, then two fingers in Aline's vagina, and moved them around. She wriggled with delight.

"You like to be spread wide? You must like big cocks!"

She didn't reply. She was terribly aroused.

"You're all wet. I love it! You know you make me really stiff?"

"Take me!" she begged. "I can't wait any longer."

"You can scream all you want! Especially as I'm going to stretch you right to the limit!"

George withdrew his fingers from Aline's cunt. He heard Suzanne up above screaming at him to hit her, to punish that slut. She saw him wetting his whole hand, and lowering it toward the base of his mistress's back. She couldn't see the rest of the show.

George ordered Aline to spread her legs wider. She obeyed, trembling.

Holding them tight to make them look like a bobbin, he slowly inserted all his fingers into the narrow passage. Aline was gasping under the terrible pressure.

"I'm going to put in my whole hand, even if I have to tear you!"

"No, George, you're hurting me."

"I'm going to make you come like you've never come before."

He penetrated even deeper into her cunt.

"Now for the hardest bit! Where my hand's at its widest!"

He pushed ferociously to stuff the rest of his hand in Aline's cunt. She screamed as he invaded her entirely. She looked down at her pussy and saw that she had devoured it all. Only the hairy wrist of her lover protruded.

"How soaked you are!"

As she came, the young woman emitted deep and cavernous screams. She begged George not to move one millimeter, for her cunt was burning like a torch, fit to burst.

When he judged that his mistress was fully aware that she belonged to him entirely, George gently withdrew from the sheath of flesh, and Aline's head flopped onto the mechanic's solid shoulders.

"George," she moaned. "George!"

He took Aline's face between his thick palms and kissed her passionately.

"Will you untie me? I'm shattered," she murmured.

He carried on kissing her before his wife's convulsed eyes, as she hammered with her fists on the window of the car's blocked door. Then he slipped his fingers between Aline's thighs. She screamed:

"No, please, it hurts too much, it's burning!"

"I won't touch your pussy, since you don't want me to. But I need to come too, now, and you're going to make me."

George opened the fly of his overall and pulled out his cock. He rubbed it against his mistress's buttocks, then, forcibly spreading the two white lukewarm globes, he fucked her in the ass.

"Can you feel how hard it is in your ass? I had no difficulty going in." He screwed her slowly at first, so that his cock could adapt to the sheath, then rammed her without paying any attention to Aline's pain. Gradually gaining a taste for the torture, she began to follow the to-and-fro rhythm in her ass.

"How hot you are!"

Aline shifted her buttocks and, like a belly dancer, swayed her hips around the swollen post. She took deep primitive pleasure in being penetrated in the ass for the first time. Her orgasm was incredible. Her scream pierced the air and soared up the ramp. George released his thick and heavy semen almost immediately.

"I gave you a good load!" he said, looking at her with pride mixed with tenderness. He untied her, and she curled up in his arms.

"George, I'm all yours," said Aline, a little sheepishly.

Giddy from so much pleasure, the young woman's legs gave way beneath her. George caught her just in time.

"Whoops-a-daisy, gorgeous! I'll lay you down." He carried her in his arms to the open trunk of a car and lay her down inside it. Aline groaned when she touched the frozen rubber.

"Are you mad at me?" she asked.

"Yes, I'm mad. You shouldn't have masturbated in front of Suzanne. I shall never forgive you for that."

"Don't say that, George, don't say that."

And with a little frail voice:

"What are you going to do? I would like to go on like before. We'll go on like before, won't we? It was so good."

The mechanic looked at her carefully but didn't answer.

"Like before, like before," she repeated, as if to ward off her fate.

"Have a rest while I'm gone. I'll take care of you later. In the meantime, keep quiet and regain your strength."

"You're not going to punish me?"

Without a word, George walked to the hydraulic ramp. Aline sank into the trunk, docile and exhausted. He started up the descent mechanism with a casual flick. Suzanne, furious at having been left locked on the platform, tried to anticipate the move. Her right arm hooked on the steering wheel, the left gripping the back of the seat, she braced herself and pushed strenuously with her legs at the bashed door until it finally gave way. But, though furious, she had to sit down again, as she was unable to stand up on the edge of the platform. George took her in his arms as soon as she was at his level. Suzanne started to hit him with anger and spite. He asked her to calm down.

"Me, calm down?" she screamed. "That's a good one! Bastard! Bastard! What did you do to her to make her scream like that? Did you bang her? Did you shove your cock between her legs?"

"That's enough."

"No, it's not enough. I won't calm down. What did you do to her?" Suzanne screamed, out of her mind. "You shagged her, right?"

George, fuming, gave her a good shaking.

She carried on.

"I'm not afraid of you! You're unhinged. It's those women who did that to you! They're going to your head. You've lost your brain, you're just a prick. Poor bastard! Go to your slut!"

George hit his wife across the face to shut her up. Then he carried her to the car, put her down against the rear bumper, and shook her gently to make her recover consciousness.

Aline sat up and pushed her head out of the trunk.

"George, what are you going to do? Is she here? Let me go. Let me out."

"C'mon, move over! I can't hold her up like this much longer!"

Aline looked at him, anxious and puzzled:

"Move over? Where?"

"Do as I say!"

"But . . ."

"Move over, for God's sake!"

Aline moved back into the trunk, grumbling:

"And what if she wakes up? I swear, George, if she touches me, I'm going to let rip."

He put Suzanne down in the trunk beside Aline. Aline shouted violently, "What are you thinking? When she comes around, you know what's going to happen? I want to get out. Help me out."

The mechanic looked at her, annoyed.

"I'm fed up with you girls, you and your fuss! Fuck you!"

"You're crazy!"

"You two are the ones making me crazy! It's time to cool down."

With a sharp jerk he slammed the trunk, leaving the two creatures imprisoned in it.

Whistling, George opened the garage door. He looked at the empty square and contemplated the towers of the cathedral for a while before making up his mind. It was fine weather, perfect weather for a trip to the countryside, perfect weather for a day off.

He let the engine warm up before he set off. The sun acted as an accessory to his contentment: his two women would enjoy the ride with him, and without bothering him. At the beginning he heard some muffled sounds, even a few screams, like kids who cannot stay still, but that was not going to ruin his day. No way!

As he drove, he remembered Aline begging as he pushed his whole hand in her cunt, and Suzanne's spasms when she swayed on his cock as he was making love to her on the desk.

Moved by those memories, George listened for sounds in the trunk. He thought he heard some noises again, weaker though, stifled. On the road he passed the lawyer's car and waved to him.

George turned on the radio, sang along with Elvis's "Are You Lonesome Tonight," stopped at a gas station to buy a Coke. He took three, the girls would probably be thirsty. His wife and his mistress . . . George thought that he was, on that sunny Sunday, a happy man.

He got back on the road, still whistling, turning off farther along at a crossroads and discovered, at its end, a pond in which a few ducks were splashing about. The spot was deserted. George got out of the car and had a good stretch. Collecting the Coke cans from the front seat, he thought about his future and wondered what he was going to do with his two women. Perhaps he would be forced to leave one. That idea was unbearable. Suzanne was a courageous woman and absolutely necessary to endure life's hard knocks, while Aline allowed him to satisfy his sexual desires. One could not replace the other! George resolved to postpone that decision and went around to open the trunk, singing:

"Coke for both!"

Then he saw them. They were dead. The two women had engaged in a merciless fight and mutilated each other atrociously. From Suzanne's tattered clothes, through her bra, protruded a bloody mass. Her breasts were nothing more than a shapeless pap. The left nipple had been torn away savagely and was stuck between Aline's teeth. She seemed to be smiling at her rival's frozen mask.

Before being strangled, Suzanne had taken her revenge. Between the stiff fingers of her hand, stuck together with blood, clung a wad of Aline's pubic hair, with, like a bird in its nest, the swollen clitoris of the young woman.

The spot was deserted, the pond handy.

TAROT

Florence Dugas

Noon was gently moving toward two o'clock. As it was already summertime, no one could tell: somewhere in the world it's always noon.

It was as if the sun had given her a sign, and she didn't return to work.

The sound of her heels against the stone of the road and the sidewalk is like a clamor of victory. She supplies a rhythm to the city, and her long, thin legs move, map, and order its topography, like a defiant army marching ahead under the newfound sun, celebrating the coming of spring. It is good to feel the heat spread across her skin, caressing her knees like two warm hands, even moving up between her thighs now no longer under the protection of nylon. The sun almost draws a crown of gold around her head, as if she were a chosen being. From time to time she even swings her head from side to side, like a racehorse in heat. Saying yes and no to her invisible mount while her heavy stream of hair undulates across her back. She straightens her back, holding her stomach in, and the flow of her hair swims gloriously in motion.

She walks as if she were leading a victory parade.

Parade. The very word echoes across her brain, to the rhythm of her heels, and it amuses her to invent more meanings for it. To parade is more than just to walk at random, no mere promenade where you never know where the next step leads. "To parade is to move like God across his garden," Brisset used to say. It even makes her look a little drunk, dizzy from her newfound freedom. Walking along, parading, as if she were about to become the heroine of some medieval ballad sung by a troubadour beneath the window of a captive king. So much sun is unusual. Walking as she is, head high, she can no longer hear Paris surrounding her, just the sound of her heels clicking along; nor can she see the cars and passersby, just the winged *Génie* of the Bastille, flying high up there close to Icarus. She is on parade: she's come out of her shell, the whole world is on offer, her steps are conquering space, taking her into a wholly new dimension.

The clock on the Gare de Lyon betrays an impossible hour, which even the sun denies.

"The next train? Well, you've got the Paris—Vintimille, in ten minutes. Seats? Oh, as many as you want. Nonsmoking? Isn't the weather lovely? The sky is so blue. Yes, I understand."

The railway guy sitting behind the immediate departures window is actually not bad-looking at all.

It's true, there are few people on the train. In her compartment, just five men: four of them are playing cards, while the fifth, farther down, appears to be sleeping already, with just his neck and short, graying hair visible from her vantage point.

With all those empty seats available, she chooses to sit on the right-hand side, so she can enjoy the sun for the rest of the afternoon.

She feels blandly happy, sunny, watching all the cows outside pass by.

The train does not stop before Valence.

* * *

She walks out onto the platform to move her legs. A two-minute stop. Up in the sky, the sun hasn't moved at all, but the heat is now more oppressive, a sign they are farther south, in the Midi. She can feel the sun rising ever so stealthily up her thighs, so much more aggressively than in Paris, and this metaphor first makes her smile, then makes her feel dreamy.

She shakes her head. "I'm getting delirious," she thinks.

But on the other hand she feels ever so free.

She returns to the compartment from the other end and walks down the rows of seats as the train begins speeding up again. She sways dizzily between the wooden seats.

The man with gray hair is not sleeping. He is watching her navigate the passage, struggling against the train's increasing motion, as if he were looking through her. The thought that somehow between Paris and Valence, on this stolen afternoon, she has physically dematerialized amuses her. Is the man not really looking at her? He is quite handsome, in a prematurely graying way. His eyes are the same color as his hair, pale grey veined with black—a man of marble. As she passes him, she gazes at his hands, laid out flat on the table. Quite beautiful hands that, in her imagination, she is already placing within her intimate theater, the hands of a pianist, or perhaps a surgeon's hands ready to sew someone's wound up, or even a pair of warm and dry hands alighting on her knees, sliding up her skirt, moving into her underwear and grabbing her butt cheeks, hands capable of measuring her ass so much more than the sun outside.

She shakes her head, both amused and annoyed by her own cliché fantasy.

The four men are still busy with their card game. As she passes them, she sees it is a tarot deck, the same high numbers and cards, but something catches her attention: the images on the cards aren't the ones she knows, the turn-of-the-century scenes so familiar to the tarot. She slows down imperceptibly, still moving ahead, and turns back to look again, not quite brave enough to stand still. She's right: the characters on the cards are mostly naked, unlike the images she's familiar with. The man nearest to her, an ebony-colored African man, still holds four cards in his hand—two small squares as well as an eleven and a twelve. On the first one, the characters are sitting around a picnic scene imitating *Le Déjeuner sur l'Herbe*; the seated woman is naked, but the man lying down is also, and another man, who is leaning toward her as if to bite her breasts, is getting undressed. She has difficulty seeing the other card, obscured as it is by the man's thick black thumb, but again the woman in the boat is nude. On the twelve, she can see only the upper half of the card: a ball somewhere in the background, but on the right-hand side the image of a man seemingly offering his cock deferentially to two sitting women whose clothes have been partly pulled open. One of the women is thrusting her peach glove—covered hand toward the imposing virile member. The man whose cock it is has gray hair, and it makes her think right away of the silent passenger in the seat a few rows back.

The black man throws the twelve down, and another of the men adds the twenty. She just has time to glimpse the image of four men sitting at a table playing cards, all in the buff, while a woman under the table is seemingly sucking off the player on the left. The illustrator had frozen the scene just as her mouth is about to devour his mushroom head and her cheeks are delicately deformed by the intrusion.

She shrugs. Scenes from a brothel, she reckons, no doubt a belle epoque set of cards.

She walks back to her seat and distractedly watches the landscape roll by, sky moving between white and blue. The Rhône river flows heavily by, moving between nuclear power stations. At any rate, the stations do not affect the area's luminosity.

* * *

She senses a movement to her left and turns. The man with gray hair is there, looking over her shoulder. And as earlier, he has the same distant and detached look, as if his eyes are fixed on a point some ten centimeters behind her.

"May I?" he says, sitting next to her.

He has a vaguely English accent.

He calmly pulls up the arm separating their two seats, deliberately abolishing all distance between them, or any form of misunderstanding.

"May I . . ." These are the only words he says, and her quiet agreement, as she does not object, is all he needs for approval, as if those two words and the unspoken answer will justify all that will follow.

The man's right hand skims by her neck while his left hand takes hold of her knee. His skin is just as she expected: warm and dry.

He allows her just a few seconds to imagine what is about to happen. His fingers tread ever so lightly across her skin, as if he were caressing water without creating a stir across its surface.

His fragrance is both pleasant and discreet. She doesn't know why, but his smell reminds her of Louis XV furniture, burnished wood pieces.

For a while he doesn't move, his face just inches from hers, his hand almost motionless on her knee, his fingers delicately skimming her neck.

The dark clouds inside his gray eyes make him look like a phantom.

And finally he bends slowly over toward her and kisses her.

She holds on to him, slides her own hands under the fashionable gray jacket he is wearing, takes hold of his shirt, grabs his tie . . .

The hand on her knee begins a slow and deliberate journey upward along her thigh and cups her cunt, forcing itself against the already wet silk. The man pulls the thin panties to one side of her gash, his fingers lingering against the soft and delicate lips with assurance. "With a sense of contained violence," she thinks aloud. And the mental image of her cunt in his grasp makes her smile and hold herself even more open. She allows her hand to slip under the man's belt, and through the thin material of his trousers grabs hold of his hardening virility, an initial contact that surprises her by its brazenness. She pulls on the zip of his fly and extricates the jutting cock now pulsing against her fingers, just as she leans her own body slightly backward so that the man's hands might have easier access to her stomach and, she hopes, her ass.

They caress each other for a few minutes. He inserts two fingers deep into the swamp of her cunt, two very long fingers with short, invisible nails, deep into the pit of her belly, exploring her with even more avidity than his cock could, seeking what she desires with an almost feminine science.

He has no need to change the pressure of his fingers against her neck. She leans over of her own accord toward the cock now surging through the folds of gray material and takes it into her mouth. It feels fresh, almost cold. First the thick, split apricot, which she surrounds with her tongue and bathes in her saliva, then the rest of his mast, as far as she can take it. Three-quarters of it almost, her mouth spread-eagled by this meat of desire, to the point of gagging against this dangerous weapon heading straight for her innards. She retreats to catch her breath and impales her mouth anew against the blood-engorged tip of his cock, torn between the need to suck him forever and forever, to fill herself with his wooden citrus flavor, and the sheer craving to feel him flow wildly inside her mouth, waves breaking against the back of her throat, and the freedom to drink all of him in.

The man then pulls his fingers out of her heaving cunt and, taking advantage of her position leaning back, moves them, still coated with her vaginal secretions, toward her ass and digs them both into her sphincter. She buckles, rears against the fingers now stretching her wide and, doing so, opens herself even more to his rough caress. And when the man's thumb at the front now starts applying pressure to her clitoris, she comes violently, feels her asshole spasm against the fingers now burrowing deep inside her, and only the cock now embedded in her mouth prevents her from screaming.

He allows her to enjoy the moment. His fingers are still digging deep into the very fundament of her ass. His thumb is held hard, unmoving, against her inflamed clitoris. He gently pulls her by her hair and allows her face to rest against his chest while she gasps for air.

Once the contractions slow down, he slides his fingers out of her and pulls her up against him as he moves onto the seat in front of her, between her splayed legs, and forcefully pulls her down onto him. Initially she fears she won't be able to accommodate him, that she's not open enough—he's so much bigger than anything she's had inside her before. His cock is still growing as he breaches her, his head brushing her labia aside as his shaft sinks deeply into her. Inside the hot furnace of her cunt, the man's cock feels as cold as ice. She bites her lips to keep from screaming when she feels the cock assault her back wall, and she takes hold of the top of the seat facing her and, seizing it desperately, allows herself to sway wildly, allowing his cock to plow every inch of her insides as she holds back her pain. The man, his hands gripping the sides of her ass, helps her rise and then again and again brings her down onto him, every time deeper and deeper, as if she were a cave with no end.

A few meters away from her, she can only glimpse the heads of the other four men every time she rises above the seat: they are still playing cards, oblivious to what is happening to her.

For a brief moment she realizes she would like to feel him flow inside her, mingling his sperm with all that is floating within her; then the thought is violently abolished because she comes again, ferociously, wantonly, literally screwed onto this cock that is splitting her apart, piercing her very heart.

She is gasping for breath when the man's hands let go of her butt and move under her shirt, partly freeing her breasts from the push-up bra, lengthily caressing her hard, sensitive nipples, enjoying himself, then pinching her breasts hard to bring her back to reality from her swoon. Through the waves of ecstasy she is also confusedly angry at him for having discovered she enjoys the combination of pain and pleasure.

The man withdraws from her, settles to her left, and folds his still-bulging cock so wet from her secretions into his trousers. Will she ever know the taste of his sperm, or just this lingering smell of wet rosewood?

His smile is muted, almost affectionate, but distant again as he moves back to his seat, and the last thing she sees of him is his straight neck and his short gray hair.

She frees herself from the wet panties now cutting into her crotch and shudders, face against the windowpane. She watches the Rhône outside. An old piece of poetry by Victor Hugo comes into her mind: "The noisy river flows, a fast and yellow flow . . ."

The heat of the sun, the cool of the glass against her cheeks, and the dying vibrations inside her belly now peaceful, moving away, drying up . . .

She doesn't wake up in Avignon, nor in Marseilles. When she opens her eyes again, she can still hear the echo in the air of the voice that has just announced their arrival in Saint Raphaël. It is now evening, and only the sporadic lights of the approaching station puncture the darkness.

She had thought of going to Nice, but why not Saint Raphaël; she's never been here before.

She is now alone in the compartment. She rises, still unsteady on her legs—she fell asleep in an awkward position and her left foot has fallen asleep—and moves forward with a slight limp, gracelessly, toward the exit, and almost topples over as she walks down the train's steps. Blood flows back into her brain, the vertigo fades . . . she takes a few steps forward on solid ground and the dizziness returns.

"I must be hungry," she thinks. And the act of thinking it makes her hungry. She walks toward the station's exit, figuring that, like all train stations, there must be a bar nearby, a bistro, some Arab grocery.

But all there is nearby is a Rolls-Royce parked close to the pavement, a very old model with the driver's seat open to the air and the back shrouded by dark opaque windows. The chauffeur, holding his cap in his hand, turns toward her.

"Mademoiselle," he says, "we were waiting for you. Would you please . . ."

She is so surprised that she allows herself to be led, just two meters of pavement between freedom and the green English leather seats of the luxury car, and the door closes silently behind her. Immediately, it's night behind the dark windows, which banish even the glow of the streetlights, barely allowing pale haloes to survive, just like the mad stars in Van Gogh's skies.

The car is totally silent; it could be stationary, just a hint of vibration betraying its motion. They drive for a long time, and the young woman, who is hungry and thirsty and badly needs to pee, is now in a bad mood. They stop for a red light and she tries to get out, but the doors are locked from the outside. She raps her knuckles on the glass separating her from the driver. The man's neck doesn't budge.

The Rolls-Royce leaves Saint Raphaël and takes a small, winding road that rises above sea level and leads deep into the hinterlands. A long time. Hunger. Thirst . . .

At last, the car slows down as it runs parallel to a high wall that leads them to an intricate metal gate topped by a mess of white metal arrows. The door opens by itself, no doubt electronically controlled, unless there is an invisible caretaker in attendance . . .

Crunching across a gravel path, the car drives up to a small castle, one of the many modern-style monstrosities that the Côte d'Azur has given birth to over the past century, and comes to a halt in front of its steps. The stylish chauffeur gets out and ceremoniously opens the door.

In a rush, the sound of the early cicadas of spring invades the Rolls-Royce.

She alights, intrigued, worried, still angry. A man stands there, on the second step, and, astonished, she recognizes the gray-haired stranger from the train. How in the hell could he have reached this place before her?

"Please accept our apologies," he says. "You must be quite tired?"

He ceremoniously takes her hand. He is now wearing a smoky gray lounge suit, the same color as his eyes.

"Come," he says. "We've prepared some food for you."

She agrees to enter the castle, although she also knows this might be a mistake, that maybe she shouldn't, now that the falling sun has retreated with all its elementary seduction and the menace of night is ready to take over.

Once inside, she glances back—intuition or ultimate temptation. The moon is full and shines over a freshly mowed lawn at the heart of which stands a white marble statue, maybe of Venus, or even Diana the huntress without her slings and arrows, the languorous shape of the goddess bathing in the moonlight.

The young woman turns back and, with quiet determination, enters the house.

"If you wish to freshen up," the man says, pointing to a door.

"Yes, I'd like to spray my war paint on again," she jokes, repressing the anxiety quickly rising inside her throat.

As she washes her hands, she gazes at the reassuring image in the mirror: she is still pretty, still looks fresh despite all those hours on the train; some would even say the darker shade below her eyes was an added bonus.

"What a face," she says nevertheless, almost out of habit.

A snack? On a small table at the center of the Art Deco living room filled with delicate furniture, she can see all the things she likes: patisseries, fruit, finger-sized delicacies, lemonade—she is still at an age where you are allowed to enjoy sugary things. In the meantime, the stranger is busy starting a fire inside the big fireplace, kneeling in

front of the first orange flames longer than he normally would, expos-
ing his slim neck to her gaze, no doubt aware she is full of questions
and in no hurry to supply answers.

He finally rises from his prone position while she finishes biting into a
thin slice of an exquisite tart.

"I will take you to your room," he says. "You'll find something you
can wear for dinner. Take your time. If you want to take a bath, just tell
Nora, and she will arrange it."

With his hand, he points to a corner of the room where a young
mulatto woman in a domestic's uniform is standing, straight and
silent. She has pale gray eyes, shining in the light of the nearby flames
like the eyes of a cat.

She hadn't even heard her enter the room.

"We dine at eleven," he adds.

They walk up a wide, pink, marbled set of stairs, a bit too ostentatious
for her taste. Then, after passing through a red vestibule, down a long
corridor punctuated by doors numbered 1 to 9. At the other end,
there is another set of stairs, probably leading up. They stop at number 7. The maid opens the door and stands back to let her go in.

The room is spacious, tastefully furnished. Not one piece of furniture is contemporary; every single piece, from the straight geometry
of the dresser to the vanity table with its crystalline mirror to the bed
shrouded with delicate linen, appears to be brand-new, although they
all obviously were made in the 1920s.

On the wall, a Millet-style print: three farm laborers resting in a
field, enjoying a drink, while a woman awaits them, sitting against a
haystack; it's unclear what she might be waiting for, as, unlike any
character in a picture by the Barbizon artist, she is totally naked, and
when you take a closer look, her hands, though held against her knees,
are tied with a thin piece of string.

This sets her thinking again of the four men playing cards on the train, the same sense of discontinuity between the image you expect and the more disturbing one . . .

"Do you wish to take a bath?" the maid asks.

There is no trace of the Caribbean in her voice.

"Yes, please . . ."

The bathroom that connects to the room is huge, all green marble, all three walls covered by mirrors, as is, curiously enough, the ceiling. Exotic plants, suspended from shelves and metal stands, spread a delicate perfume of wet earth and heavy flowers throughout the room. The bathtub, carved out of a single piece of dark marble and held up by sphinxlike feet, is positively enormous.

The maid runs the water, pouring in perfumed oil that rises in bubbles, the strong fragrance of which blends easily with that of the green plants in the room. The perfume rising through the steam now obscuring the mirrors transports her back to that sense of dizziness she experienced on the train; it's like feeling slightly drunk on an empty stomach.

The maid comes toward her, unbuttons her shirt, unhooks her bra and then the skirt. She does not remark on the fact that she is wearing no panties. The young woman allows her to do so, suddenly assaulted by tiredness, or at any rate using the tiredness as an excuse to surrender to whatever is about to happen to her.

In the water, it feels to her as if she is swimming in the immensity of the tub. Above her, she sees the shrouded reflection of a young blond woman in the misted-up mirror, her skin ever so pale, like a white mummy floating inside a green marble coffin, the blue gray of her eyes lost in the distance. But the steam rises and finally wipes out this lazy landscape of curves.

The maid allows her to soak for a long time in all the fragrances the heat is now breaking up. Finally, she comes back and hands her a Japanese robe, pale green, embroidered with birds of paradise.

"Do you want me to give you a massage?" she asks. "The bath will wash the journey away, and the massage will wash the bath away. Afterward, I shall apply your makeup. The commander has given me very precise instructions."

She lets herself go, agile fingers skimming across her skin with exquisite softness, slowly untwisting her nerves, polishing her muscles, effectively providing her with strength again after her energy has been sapped by the bath. The maid has her lie down on a folding table once she has slipped out of the robe. First, lying on her stomach, she is massaged from her neck down to her heels, unavoidably feeling something stirring inside her when the long, brown fingers knead her ass and thighs. But she'd rather believe it's just a feeling of comfort. She almost falls asleep anyway, listening to the gurgling sounds of the emptying bath.

She is then turned round. Above her, the mirror is clearing up.

The young Creole woman is working her shoulders, the beginning of her neck, grazing her breasts whose tips are hardening, not that she notices as her hands lower themselves toward her midriff, before moving back to polish her nipples from time to time. Her brown hands make the extreme winter pallor of her pale skin appear almost indecent.

The young woman looks at herself in the ceiling mirror, and from her perspective, the mulatto girl massaging her appears closer to her than she in fact is, as if it were her mouth, her lips massaging her, and not her fingers. But very soon, it *is* actually her darker lips that are now attaching themselves to her taut nipples, licking then sucking on her hard tips, racing across her tremulous skin, her pretty café au lait face soon ensconced between her thighs. All she can see is the back of her head, a mass of short, dense curls when the maid's mouth alights on her cunt, and the masseuse's tongue separates the delicate lips of her opening, skimming across her dilated clit. She feels as if she wants to come that very moment, if only to release all the tension building up inside her since she walked into the house. With her hands, she grasps the short dark curls and pulls the girl's face hard against her stomach—black against white—her lithe tongue butterflying over her clit now feeling more forceful, more incisive.

The young maid pulls her body down toward the edge of the table, both her legs now winging over the sides, the indefatigable tongue squirming around her red-hot button, plunging down into her wet vagina, tiptoeing across her anus and delicately forcing it open—she has never had the courage to tell any of her previous lovers how much she would like to be sodomized by a hard, burning tongue, all this while her long bronzed fingers keep on playing with her breasts. Finally she comes, no longer able to restrain her voice, flooding the mulatto girl's face with her juices. The maid rises, wiping her mouth, her chin, and her nose with a towel and, curiously enough, smiles not at her but toward the mirror on the ceiling. The thought that someone has just witnessed the whole scene through a one-way mirror dawns on her with absolute certainty. What other traps are to follow? She slides off the massage table, pulls the young maid by her hair as she had done earlier, forces her to kneel before her, and presses her face against her cunt, the heavy-lipped and violent mouth against her small blond bush.

"Drink," she says.

And she slowly pees into the open, willing mouth that doesn't miss a single drop, still watching the ceiling as she does so, now smiling at the mirror, pleased to be conveying in such a way to the master of the house that by defiling his slave, she is resisting his will.

She is then made up by the maid, slowly, a bit too gaudily for her taste. Then she is given a long evening dress, a glossy couture piece with classical lines that Madame Gray would have appreciated. Once inside the formal dress, she feels like a marble statue sandwiched inside a skin of blackness, the exquisite pallor of her skin enhanced by the nocturnal black of the material.

No underwear or lingerie underneath the dramatic dress. The silk adheres to her breasts, her ass, and her stomach; the sudden crispness of the wrap awakens her nipples.

"You are beautiful," says the young mulatto girl. "I'm happy the commander has brought you here."

Once again the stairs. The maid guides her from one door to another. She hears a bit of conversation; she knows that very soon she will be told where she is. She is both curious and worried and slows her steps.

The mulatto girl swings the door open and invites her in.

She is greeted by intense light. There are four or five men in dinner jackets and six or seven elegantly attired women; they all briefly fall silent and watch her walk toward them. Meanwhile the gray-haired stranger moves in her direction, takes her by the hand, and smiles, putting her at her ease.

"You are quite ravishing," he says. And he truly looks as if he believes it.

She smiles back, still cautiously, but holds on to him, surrounded as she is by all these unknown faces.

"Friends," he says, with a semicircular gesture of his hand. "All charming people, as you will see."

Why does he not introduce her to anyone? Why isn't she even provided with a name, a surname?

Just then a servant attired in quite incongruous Louis XV style calls out loudly that dinner is served, and they all march into the immense dining room, where a very long rectangular table dominates the proceedings.

The plates are exquisitely sober; the silver knives and forks and crystal glasses shine wildly under the glow of the candelabras.

The gray-haired man is at the head of the table and indicates she should sit to his left. Facing her is a very beautiful woman whose splendor has however seen better days, a thousand wrinkles smiling, a thousand small pains betraying her long and cruel past.

On her left is the youngest man in the room; he is younger than her even, his face and skin barely out of teenage years, radiant, almost effeminate. He is all smiles and his conversation is artfully banal.

The meal offers all that Provence can supply, from the most refined to the most colorful dish. Her taste buds sing along. Stylish servants see that their glasses are never empty and provide the right wine for each course: a sublime Cassis white followed by a racy Gigondas from the Aix vineyards, and soon champagne, small bubbles adhering under her gaze to the shape of the cut glasses. Very soon, she experiences a new kind of drunkenness, like an aggravated echo of her dizziness on the train. The feeling surrounds her like a scarf; she feels she is burning up, her legs are like cotton wool, her breath is short. Her breasts rub anxiously against the silk of the dress, her nipples harden again under the black material, becoming quite visible. She has the impression that everyone present is watching her, evaluating her, judging her, as if the woman facing her, eating her strawberries and drinking her champagne, is already promising her a whole set of caresses and indulgences. She feels as if her stomach is incandescent, a combination of fire and water, and the wide smile of the woman across from her indicates she is aware of it, that she recognizes the torment inside her body, that behind the combined fragrance of the wines and the food spread across the now crumpled tablecloth, she has caught an early whiff of the purple taste of her inner juices. Right then, a foot deliberately brushes against hers, caressing her ankle, gliding across her leg and the silk sheathing her. She isn't sure if it is the smiling woman or her attentive host, or maybe the gauche young man on her left. The champagne bubbles float upward to the surface of the crystal glasses, and her eyes are transfixed by the thin rising columns, as if she were the one drowning inside the glass and her oxygen was running out . . .

When they all rise to make their way to the living room, she stumbles.

"Come," says the woman, holding her arm, "are you feeling unwell? You must lie down for a quarter of an hour, allow all that alcohol to settle . . ."

Together, they climb the monumental stairs.

"I'm in number 7," she stammers.

"No need to go that far," the woman says. "I'm in 1."

The room is predominantly green, with an array of heavy brown curtains; the bed is covered with a dark green satin quilt, which feels so wonderfully cool when she settles her cheek against it and allows herself to relax. The woman helps her lie down, pulling her shoes off, caressing her thin ankles, taking them into her hands as if she were about to handcuff them.

But the girl is still overcome by dizziness and knows she will allow anything to happen.

She tries to overcome the feeling, she turns her head around, sees a painting on the wall, attempts to focus on its image, to capture some sense of reality from the shimmering fog in which the painting floats.

It's a small canvas, like the country scene in room 7, in which a court jester is offering a rose to a comedic maid—the very image of card one in the Tarot—but the woman here has pulled her skirt up and is displaying a regal, sculptured ass to him. On closer inspection, it appears that the jester is actually not about to offer the rose to the young woman, but is preparing to pin the thorny flower straight into her satin globes. It even looks as if he has begun punishing her: a long, pink cut already crisscrosses her right ass cheek, petals lie on the ground following the first blow, and the girl's face reflects pain and submission.

This is when she realizes that the older woman has folded her dress back up all the way to her thighs, and is now twirling the blond curls of her pubis with her fingers, even briefly inserting a finger into her gash, then smelling it with half a smile before licking the wet finger clean and returning her hand below to stroke her swollen cunt.

The woman suddenly stands and walks over to the wall, where she rings a call bell. Then she leans back over the prostrate young girl, lips grazing her mouth, skimming the breasts barely concealed by the crumpled silk of the dress, lingering over the uncovered stomach and the thighs that part automatically under her caress.

There is a discreet knock at the door.

"Come in," she says, without looking up.

It's one of the servants who had served at the dinner table; he has a peasant's wide and tawny features, which she had earlier found almost comical beneath the powdered wig he is now no longer wearing. But he is still attired in the Louis XV outfit meant to emphasize his thin waist. On him it has the contrary effect, highlighting his thick muscles, the incredibly wide shoulders, and the lack of neck. He is a heavy-set man; his ferocious eyes remind her of a dog's.

"Come here," she says. "Take your uniform off. That's good. Show us your cock, now. So, what do you think, my dear?"

The object emerging from the salmon-colored silk pants is just like the man himself: short and massive. Sitting on the edge of the bed, the woman takes hold of the purple glans between two fingers, just as earlier she had been handling the strawberries. With her nail she gently pulls on the cock's crumpled surplus skin and the shaft begins to grow. Short but very thick, no more than fifteen centimeters long, but so thick she has to use both hands to circle it. The prone young girl sees it all as if in a cloud; the painting on the wall is the focus of her attention, but another part of her is also aware that she is about to be breached by this almost unreal object. The mushroom head is dark purple, the blue black veins bulge, the hard brown shaft is pointing toward her, emerging from dirty pink boxer shorts—the whole thing seems more animal than human.

"Fuck her now," the older woman orders.

The domestic positions himself between the girl's thighs, spreads them wide, and places her feet high up on his shoulders, his thick shiny cock lurking at her entrance. He gradually forces himself in. Slowly, his cock plunges in, her diameter expanding obscenely as if it were literally sucking in this monstrous cock, and she finally feels its head butting her inner walls as the silk of his trousers and the rough touch of his pubic hair rub against her thighs. She comes immediately—the tension was too strong, the expectation too intense.

Now the domestic methodically plows inside her with brute force, and she cries out repeatedly, the inebriation of her orgasm blending with the alcohol vapors, thrusting her ever higher on the scales of sheer pleasure. She can't help crying, throwing her body forward, impaling herself even deeper, opening herself wider. At the same time, she feels ashamed to be enjoying this weird cock so much, and the shame doubles her pleasure, as if her being whored in this improvised way gives her latitude to scream as no other man has made her scream before, to give herself like she has never given herself before.

Prompted by the woman, still sitting close to her, the domestic withdraws from her and, with two sharp movements of his wrist, jerks himself off, long, creamy jets streaming across the now forever soiled black dress, thick snail trails of sperm jetting from his bursting cock and landing all the way up to her neck.

The woman dismisses him with a single gesture.

Once again, she leans over toward the still breathless girl, who is on the brink of tears as her orphaned cunt still gapes open, mumbling under her breath like a fish out of water, begging for the return of the cock that stretched her so, and she kisses her. The taste of her tongue is sharp, warm, and clever.

* * *

She then guides the girl to the nearby bathroom and undresses her. "Arms up," she says, as if to a child. Helping her out of the long, soiled sheath of the dress, pulling it over her head, and then the blissful feel of water running unendingly down her neck, her back, her breasts.

Then she brings her back to the large bed of crumpled satin, her body so deathly pale against the green surface, and dries her, methodically mapping every contour of her body, drying behind her ears even and between her splayed toes . . .

The woman indicates the silk dress, now all crumpled up at the foot of the bed.

"Won't be much use again," she says.

From a dresser, she pulls out a maid's outfit, almost the same as . . . what was her name? Nora? was wearing earlier. A straight black skirt, a black shirt, and a white apron with an embroidered pocket. Before she is allowed to slip the uniform on, the older woman helps her roll on a pair of hold-up opaque black stockings and, finally, hands her a pair of small, dainty, zippered boots.

The woman quickly separates her hair into thick plaits and arranges a faultless chignon, with just three or four hairpins, almost a work of art.

Inside the apron's pocket, there is a key.

"It's a pass," the ageless woman explains. "It allows you access to every room on this floor or the next. Come, girl. It's all up to you now. You must prove to us that we can trust you."

And with a gentle slap on her butt, she dismisses her from the room.

In the corridor, the young girl hesitates. Should she walk down again?

With the pass, she opens the next door, number 3.

It is empty.

On the wall there is a painting depicting a city scene with three young women wearing fancy hats, all holding each other by the arm, all totally naked. Somewhere behind them, another woman seen from the back is walking away, same hat, same nudity. She appears to be following a soldier whose silhouette can be glimpsed in the distance.

The three women are aligned by height, from left to right. Curiously, the shortest one sports the heavier breasts, the next one's are pear shaped, well proportioned, and the tallest woman's are barely the size of two small apples, high on her chest, tiny.

"The tarots," she says to herself.

She leaves the room just as another identically dressed maid comes running.

"Ah, there you are, hurry. Number 20 has called again."

Off they go; she follows instinctively, entranced by the madness of the place, down the corridor, up a spiral staircase, then through another passageway where they come across two other maids, one of whom is Nora, the only one whose name she actually knows, standing outside the door marked 20.

"What took you so long?" Nora asks.

She knocks on the door and turns the handle while doing so, just as a loud "Come in!" reaches their ears. Inside are four men playing cards, with a fifth man watching them—the gray-haired man from the train, the commander.

The girl barely has time to register the fact that these are the same four men, one of whom is black, the tarot players from the Paris–Nice TGV train—was it just this past afternoon?—when the gray-eyed man calls to them:

"Come, girls, come!"

Flabbergasted, she watches as her three companions go to kneel before three of the men and, without even being asked, burrow inside their respective trousers and quickly gobble up the still soft cocks they discover there.

"Come here, young one," the man insists.

And now she finds herself on her knees by the black man, but the cock surging through his fly is already hard. It's like a long ebony stick, shining like polished wood under the light of the room's lamps, its skin taut like bark, an endless mast whose girth is fortunately moderate, so she doesn't have to dislocate her jaw to take it all into her mouth. However, the cock soon reaches the very back of her mouth and brings tears to her eyes, a sudden burst of nausea she represses as she moves her lips back down to the cock's head. But soon she finds the right rhythm, the adequate depth.

"Keep at it," says a voice.

The man exudes an animal smell, strong, tenacious. It occurs to her that she could well be sucking a horse or a wild beast. With the hand that is not holding onto his cards—none of the men has stopped playing—he occasionally applies pressure to her neck, precisely communicating the changes in rhythm he wants her to follow. He holds her by the chignon, forcing her to first slow down and savor every one of the centimeters she swallows and then relinquishes her; then he makes her speed up and suck faster and faster, as if he were about to ejaculate in ten seconds, each time assaulting the very back of her throat, fiercer every time.

All of a sudden, there is a clap of hands. The black man pulls her away and slides his cock out of her mouth. Fascinated, she looks at the glazed, obsidian member. He pulls her up, flips her round, and throws her down on the table, pulling her skirt up at the same time. She is face-down on the table, as are her three companions, heads aligned next to each other; her cheek touches Nora's. The black man bends over her and with no word forces himself inside her. His saliva-coated cock plunges deep into her asshole, quickly reaching the bottom, and never before has she felt so deeply impaled. Like an iron bar reaching for her heart, then retreating, before digging into her again. Never has she been fucked in the ass so hard, so deep as by this harder than hard ebony-colored cock, this iron cock, this cock from hell.

On the table, right beneath her eyes, is the last hand of cards, and the courtly smile of the excuse card, and his mandolin.

Nora turns her head in her direction and kisses her, digging her tongue as far as she can into the girl's mouth, holding on to her tongue, both women grasping each other with the energy of despair as the continuous thrusts burrow through their asses, kissing and crying as the table shakes beneath them. There is a scream, a deep guttural roar, and the black man stops, still planted deep inside her ass, and she feels his come pouring out, burning her. She distractedly visualizes the powerful white jets irrigating her guts, like an unholy, boiling enema. Nora pulls herself away from her mouth and screams in turn, a shout of triumph as her flesh welcomes both pain and joy. But instead of withdrawing, the black man comes and goes a few more times inside her ass and she climaxes yet again, maybe because of the angle of the table pressing hard against her clit or the influence of the many orgasms occurring all around her. She swims in a sea of lust.

There is a pause. Then she hears hands clapping, slowly, in the background, ironic; the commander is smiling, complimenting them all.

"Excellent, ladies. Thank you. Now you may go."

And specifically to the girl:

"You're awaited in room 4," he says.

She knocks on the door; there is no answer, but she enters anyway.

There are two men in dressing gowns sitting on either side of a table, talking. The first thing she notices is that they are identical twins, although one already sports white hair, as if he has aged prematurely. She wonders what sudden emotion one day caused his hair to turn so white. He can't be much older than forty. She recognizes the two men, they were at dinner earlier, but they were seated at the other end of the table and she hadn't really noticed them.

The man with the white hair is handing a piece of paper to the other man. The heavy dressing gown's belt is loose and uncovers his right thigh, a heavy-set leg which she didn't expect from his cultured facial features.

The other man, not even acknowledging the presence of the visitor, is reading aloud: "They caress each other for a few minutes. He squeezes two fingers into the swamp of her sex, two very long fingers, nails cut short, into the deep of her belly, exploring her so much better than a penis could, his almost feminine scientific intuition aware of her innermost desires . . ."

He stops.

"Not bad. But why 'sex'? Or 'penis'?"

"Why indeed? What would you have written?"

"I don't know . . . pussy and dick? A sex, it's so anonymous."

"What would a woman say when referring to her sex? 'Vagina' is too scientific, 'uterus' is too medical. In this present context, maybe 'pussy' is too vulgar. Or it might depend on the woman. Anyway, I'd definitely cut out the 'swamp.' Reminds me too much of the worst of Henry Miller. In *Quiet Days in Clichy*, doesn't he write of 'a drooling pussy that fitted me like a glove'? No, 'pussy' just won't do. So we're left with 'sex'."

"And 'penis'?"

"Still too generic. Its so-called exploration is no more than a continuous series of thrusts into the pit of her belly. Too prosaic for what the male member is capable of."

"Why not use a metaphor?"

"Which? A split apricot? A dick-shaped mussel? A mustachioed wallet? As it is I'm uneasy with the 'swamp,' although I do enjoy its muddy, soaked-earth quality, a combination of liquid and hard matter."

"And her cunt? Just call it a cunt? Do women really think of their parts that way?"

"There's just a surfeit of metaphors. You can't just string too many of them together. 'Her cunt's swamp': it just feels wrong, too strong an image."

"The truth is you don't like metaphors."

"That's true. So, what would you suggest?"

" 'He slides two fingers into her divine gash, all the way down her magic walls, exploring her so much better than . . .'!"

"You're getting funnier all the time. But not very practical. Laughter and fucking, you know . . . Many years ago, when I was still fumbling among the amatory arts, at the beginning of my literary career, I was writing erotic stories with a friend; we were trying to use every expressive resource we could, we wanted to avoid all vulgarity, to retain a dash of poetry about it all. We tried everything: the subjective point of view, long sentences and little punctuation, like James Joyce in the midst of tits and ass, if you see what I mean, then more subtle metaphors—'under his fingers the flower of her love garden blossomed . . . at the end of the path the labyrinth of Cytherea . . . exploring her so much better than all the previous arrows of desire had punctured her . . .' all rubbish of that kind, a compost heap of mythologies. But all it proves to us is that metaphors, however deceptive and clever they might be to the intellect, just pour cold water over any hard-on; a man who thinks too much just disconnects, if I can put it that way . . . But why don't we ask this girl . . ."

He turns toward her. She's been standing there silently, surprised that they hadn't even acknowledged her presence until now, seeing they had summoned her here.

"My dear, what do you think? How do you refer to your sexual organ?"

She is somewhat taken aback, but replies: "Actually I seldom refer to it by any sort of name."

"But if you had to?"

" 'Hole' or 'pussy,' most often. No, not really. It sort of depends."

"On what?"

"On the situation. Sometimes I will enjoy shocking myself by using dirty words. Especially when it comes to the rear. I seldom use 'sodomy,' too biblical in essence. 'Fucked in the ass,' that's what I say, when it's about me. But that's mostly when referring to the act, not when it's actually happening."

"What do you mean?"

"Well, 'I'm being fucked in the ass' occurs so often figuratively speaking, that I can't really use the expression properly, if I think about it . . . But 'I want to be fucked in the ass' presents no ambiguity."

"And right now?"

"I've just been fucked in the ass," she says. "By a very well-endowed black man. His come is still inside my ass. See how useful the right words can be . . ."

She emphasizes this as the two robes both open like a theater's curtains and two honorably sized cocks are standing to attention, like twins, ever so slightly curved, thick-veined, helmets shining between the folds of the material.

She moves toward the men, gets on her knees, and caresses them both, although neither of her hands can grasp the full girth of the cocks. Slowly, delicately, she jerks them off; then, moving her head from side to side, she alternately sucks them both. They taste the same, smell the same . . .

But their reactions are different. Very soon, the man with the white hair lies down on the bed and pulls her on to him and positions himself deep inside her. As this happens, she feels the other man's hands spreading her ass cheeks and a cock, identical to the one fucking her, forces its way into her anal opening. She screams as he tears her apart, and realizes she has never been filled this way. Just a moment later, all three are motionless, she is impaled on their twin cocks, and feels they are surely about to breach the thin membrane that separates them and merge into one single hammer. One of the men is gently biting her breasts; the other scratches her shoulder. She flexes her whole body, offering her crotch even more fully, tightens her sphincter muscles and feels the cock's swollen ridge move deeper inside her, while the one in her cunt almost slips out. The invading cocks are burning her alive, but still manage to penetrate deeper within her, and as the one in her ass settles for a second, her cunt gapes open fully.

They all come almost at the same time. The ever so slight time delay allows her to experience the stream flooding her ass, and then the waves breaking inside her belly. Then the cocks lose some of their hardness, dilate and soften, and pleasure now takes a firm grip of her own body; she whimpers and squirms while still breached by the hot twin cocks and, in a moment of panic, she seeks the mouth of the man with the white hair.

They have not even undressed and, as soon as she leaves the bed, she is once again the image of a perfect, if somewhat crumpled, maid.

All of a sudden a telephone rings.

One of the brothers—they are both lying flat out on the bed, side by side, breathless—rises and picks up the antique set from the bedside table.

"Yes?" he says.

She looks around her. Inevitably, on the wall, there is a painting. This one shows two men sitting, discussing literature, on either side of a small table, the man on the right-hand side holding a sheet of paper. Close to them, a naked woman, kneeling, visible only from the back, her long blond hair reaching down to her waist, is seemingly sucking off the man on the left, the one with the white hair.

"You've been summoned," the brown-haired man says. "Room 6."

As she leaves the room, they are already deep in conversation on either side of the table, with the sheet of paper held by one of them. She hears only the final words, read out by the white-haired man:

" 'She flexes her whole body, offering her crotch even more fully, tightens her sphincter muscles and feels the cock's swollen ridge move deeper inside her . . .' "

The other protests:

" 'Sphincter muscles.' What about 'Sybil's hole'?"

"The artist's entrance?"

"The purple flower?"

"Saint Luke's grotto?"

The door closes and she can no longer hear them.

Room 6?

The sperm poured into her is running down her thighs.

The scene in the new room is almost symmetrical to that in the previous one. Two women, both naked, are sitting on either side of a table, their positions, their dark red hair held up in chignons, not unlike creatures by Rossetti: the heaviness of their breasts, the exaggerated length of their nipples, the pale complexion of their pink skin and haughty, almost disdainful, facial expressions, all striking features including, as she moves closer to them, the color of their eyes, gray changing into green.

However, this time around, they are not identical.

"Come, my dear," one says. "Come."

They ask her to stand still, between the two of them, and four hands quickly undress her, throwing the maid's outfit aside. They only allow her to retain the stockings, which emphasize the pallor of her thighs. The pale hands roam across her even paler skin.

"Look, she's just been fucked . . ."

"In front and behind," says the other. "There's a small stream of come emerging from her ass . . ."

"She's been well fucked," the first one says. "She is still very dilated."

"So it seems," the other calmly declares. "I could push my finger into her ass without even touching her edges."

The girl is momentarily shocked by the contrast between their poised appearance and the filth of their language, and particularly the clinical way in which they are describing her, as if they were conducting an autopsy.

She stands between them and, suddenly, the two women get down on their knees and without a word begin sucking her cunt and her ass, licking up the drops of come drying on her skin, biting the delicate flesh, digging their tongues into the still bruised openings.

The girl feels dizzy. The two women are so artful, even their violence has a touch of elegance, teeth assaulting her lips, fingers sliding deep inside her . . .

No man has ever sucked or penetrated her like this. The first one then the other, thrusting two then three fingers inside her cunt and her ass, withdrawing them and then occupying her again but this time with four digits, as if their hands were becoming slimmer, thinner, and soon she has a whole hand inside each of her openings. She moans when the hand forces her doors, but now her cunt and ass tighten around the invading wrists and she feels delirious.

Inside her, two hands are searching her, carving her innards apart, parallel hands as if in prayer, as if she were the object of a terribly ancient cult, being honored and consumed by the members of her sect . . .

She has never experienced a vaginal orgasm this strong. Her sphincters are seizing up so hard they could cut the hands off at the wrists, to hold them captive inside her forever.

"She's really enjoying this, the bitch," the first one says.

"You're right," says the other. "It feels as if her ass is breathless."

"She'll never want to come any other way," says the first one.

They gently pull their hands out and the pain is atrocious, not just the initial one in reverse, but the very thought of losing them, to be confronted once again with the terrible void inside her, the emptiness of her life . . .

"Don't worry, my dear," says the first one. "We have many ideas where you're concerned."

"Do you want to take her to 15?" the other asks.

"You were thinking of that, too, weren't you?"

Both women slip on almost transparent negligees, those spiderlike clouds a star of the silent cinema would wear, and move forward with the grace of goddesses. But as for her, they leave her naked, they just slip a dog collar around her neck and lead her all the way down the corridor and up to the next floor on a leash. She is herself surprised at how obedient she has become, so unlike herself. Or maybe they recognized this docile streak within her, the desire to submit to a master's orders, the repressed craving for slavery and the whip.

Had she known her tarot better, she would have realized that in room 15 she would find a photographer, and one of those old-fashioned devices standing on a single leg, and under the black cloth of which the operator must dive to ensure he is focused correctly on his subject.

The photographer is waiting for them. He is dressed in Second Empire attire, a short blouse and crumpled trousers, with a thin mustache and small Napoleon III—type beard. Next to him is the young man she had met at dinner: now undressed, she can see he is no more than sixteen years old at most. He sports the thin and curvy shape of a classical catamite, a lazy if gracious body spread over the bed, distractedly playing with his half-erect cock as they enter the room.

"Hello, darlings," says the tired adolescent.

"Hello, asshole," says the second woman. "How are you?"

"So-so," says the young man. "He's only fucked me twice since night fell. Do you think he no longer likes me?"

"Don't you like him any longer?" the first one asks the photographer.

"He bores me," says the photographer. "So what are you bringing me here?"

"Don't you think she's pretty?"

"Very," the photographer says. "I so enjoy such pale milklike skin."

He examines the young girl all over. She blushes at being so exposed.

"Her eyes are so shiny," the photographer says. "Have you just made her come?"

"Insanely," says the second woman.

"Sit down on the bed," the photographer tells the girl. "Take your stockings off, please. And you, little fag, come here."

She sits herself down on a short square of black silk, in the same pose as Rembrandt's Bathsheba. It all feels like a dream. The photographer moves his heavy apparatus and disappears under its black cloth. She hears the muted sound of his voice, commanding her:

"No, thighs apart. Good, yes, like that. Lean backward, steady your arms, breasts to the front, perfect."

He reappears briefly:

"You," he says to the young boy, who is pretending to be terribly bored, "come and suck me off while I'm working, it'll keep you busy."

"Yes, uncle," says the young man with a touch of irony in his voice. "Right away, uncle."

The photographer again disappears under his cloth, and on his knees facing him, the boy, with obvious dexterity, pulls out a remarkable cock, disproportionate in places, whose fat and swollen helmet emerges triumphantly from a dry, nervous stem. The boy licks it quite methodically and witnesses the bulging fruit thicken even more under his ministrations.

"Swallow," says the voice under the black cloth.

Obediently, the young boy opens his mouth wide and, jaws wide apart, devours the strange and monstrous fruit.

All the while, the photographer is taking picture after picture, only making appearances to change the plates and sprinkle more magnesium into his flash, just his voice emerging from beneath the black sheet.

"Yes . . . now each of you suck one of her breasts . . . like that . . . ah, a hand on her thigh . . . open wider, my pretty one . . . against that black silk background, you are just sublime. Throw her backward, now. One kissing her, the other licking her . . . yes . . . more profile, please, I can't see your tongue . . . no, don't look at the camera . . . very good, head thrown back . . . and you there, suck a bit better than that or I'll have you whipped right in front of these ladies . . ."

"Oh, yes," says the catamite, interrupting his labors.

Together with her two new friends, he has her adopt the most lubricious poses, ever on the lookout for the moment when she comes. Under their tongues and fingers, she experiences a whole series of orgasms, until she totally forgets where she is. Only the bright explosion of the flash, from time to time, reminds her that a man is taking photographs of her while . . .

Is it the caresses that are generating her pleasure or the fact she is being photographed? The orgasms, the flashes of light, one or the other or both are levitating her out of her body. Every time her mouth opens on a silent scream, the flash of the magnesium betrays the fact that the photographer has captured her moment of selflessness, stolen yet another parcel of her soul, her life . . . it's as if she was being emptied from the inside, as if her very substance was now flowing down her thighs, captured by the photograph, disfigured, transformed . . .

The sound of the door opening . . .

A bit later, a cock thrusting up her ass, another forcing its way down her throat, the room is now full of men and women, all the guests from dinner, each and every one fucking her in every way, and from orgasm to orgasm she feels herself grow wider, dilate until she is just a set of openings, of holes, deep abysses where cocks are ejaculating before being replaced by larger cocks or more numerous ones. Now they are penetrating her two at a time, in her cunt, in her ass, they come in twos to tease her mouth, and innumerable pairs of hands roam across her body, pinch her, sometimes spank her, and above it all the voice of the photographer encouraging them, and the brightness of the flash, and that anxious feeling that she is now no more than an empty space being furrowed, a nothingness full of come, devoured, eaten from the inside by a horde of vampires. Soon there will be nothing left of her, just some long blond hair matted with sweat, a white expanse of flesh torn apart by caresses, a set of pale eyes she holds tightly closed while all of her is being impaled, and only the violent flashes of light make their way through to her dead eyes.

* * *

Suddenly they all abandon her. From one moment to the next, it seems to her, there is no one left. She runs her hands in front of her eyes as if she were blind. The commander is standing in front of her and watching her: the same cold marble eyes, the same early taste of the tomb. He gently applauds her, as he had earlier, but now there is no sign of irony on his face.

"Very good, my dear, very good indeed. I knew we could rely on you."

He comes toward her, takes her hands, invites her to rise from the deeply soiled bed of black satin.

"Come," he says. "There is one final thing for you to do."

Together they walk down the stairs. There are so many rooms, so many passages she will know nothing about, whose anonymous numbers will not be revealed. What masked ball or orgy in room 12, what improvised concert in room 8? They find themselves on the steps outside the castle. The cicadas are now silent, the night is still far from morning, but she hesitates. The moon has moved across the roof and a wide geometrical shadow now covers a whole section of the lawn. All that emerges, on the frontier of darkness, is the statue of the goddess, even whiter in the light of the moon.

The commander leads her to the statue. The grass is mown short and feels hard against her bare feet. She shivers, not because she is cold, as spring down here already has a touch of summer, but because of the anxiety that always strikes toward the end of a night's party, when all is over and loneliness is about to knock on the door again and all you are left with is memories . . .

"Get up on the pedestal," he says. "Yes, like that, with your eyes facing the eyes of the goddess. Take her into your arms—very good, now your hands on her ass, yes. Now, don't move."

Methodically, he ties her to the statue with thin string. He ties her tightly, the rope biting into her flesh, her breasts crushed against the stone breasts of Venus—or is it Diana—and then her legs are pulled up against the legs of marble, ankle against ankle, until she can barely move an eyelash, her face pressed against the stone head.

"They're the same color," says a female voice.

"That's true," says another man. "Maybe it's the statue that's actually tied to her."

"Predator and prey," jokes yet another.

Are they all there?

"Let's begin," someone says. "It's time to end all of this."

The sharp whisper of the first lash precedes by a microsecond the blow that lands on her rump. She screams, or is it her tortured flesh that screams under the assault of the whip? But she is not surprised; she is already resigned, abandoned, punished because she is innocent. Innocent of what?

She screams, tries to wriggle out, but she is tied so tightly that the marble bites into her. She cries out as the whip keeps on finding her, with every new blow her skin opens up, like paper under a knife. Soon her ass, her back, her shoulders have become the mad canvas of a mad artist, blood spurting in lines and blotches, spreading, merging. The blood now turning her flesh dark, woman of bronze tied to woman of stone. Pain begins to anaesthetize pain, she is an open wound, furrowed, overtaken by heat, by fire irradiating from the very center of her belly, and she is aware that this unbearable heat rising toward her heart will soon kill her as surely as the cold poison killed Socrates. She no longer screams, just feels the heat rising, the whip opening up new valleys, Venus watching her in silence, and when the time comes a ray of moonlight reaches out to seize her in its grasp, and she dies of unbelievable pleasure, part and parcel of the immense fire of the whip.

The moon finally moves behind the house, the darkness drowns the statue and its victim. They leave her tied there and walk back to the house in silence, satisfied.

There is but a bare sketch of dawn. A gentle breeze weaves across the park, though the wind is not strong enough to lift the bloodied strands of blond hair now slowly drying.

In an hour or two, the cicadas will begin interrupting the silence again.

Noon, Gare de Lyon. The young woman with brown hair, captivated by the sun, has walked on the first train. She will pay for her ticket on board, too bad about the likely supplement.

There is almost no one in the compartment. Further down the aisle sits a man with steel gray hair, but she can only see his straight neck. Closer to her are four men playing cards, already well into their game. One is black, very black. When she walked past them, she noticed they were playing with tarot cards, and the black man was about to throw down a fifteen: a photographer, head buried under the cloth of an old-fashioned camera, is shooting an undressed model, a pale-skinned woman with long blond hair. At his feet, an effeminate young boy is sucking him off with studious application.

Conversation (A Tribute to Alberto Moravia)

Claire Yeniden

My publisher, a warm and tolerant man, has given me the opportunity to tell a very strange story that happened to me recently in the Métro. The penis of a man talked to me, and if I hadn't read *The Two of Us* by Alberto Moravia, I would have fainted with surprise on my seat. It spoke to me at the station called République.

"Hey you, the blond there, it's you I'm talking to! You can answer me discreetly, without opening your mouth. I can read your thoughts as if you were saying them aloud. Until today I haven't managed to find a woman who can hear me on this line, so now I'm determined to continue this conversation."

"But who are you? I don't think you're very polite, talking to me in that tone of voice."

"Listen, a man's penis is rarely polite, and I'm the penis of the man sitting opposite you on the jump seat, the one looking out the window. He's mad at me because he can't control me. Yes, that's true, it's me holding the reins. He can't get used to it, the poor guy. I obey nobody, I've neither god nor master. I'm the absolute anarchist. Though I'm concealed in his trousers, under his cotton underpants, in reality, I'm the power behind the throne; in a nutshell, I have power. He obeys me and gives in. My owner submits to my law. Which do you prefer, briefs or underpants?"

"I'm not sure I want to answer that question in the Métro, and besides, I've no idea, it depends on the man who's wearing them."

"OK, I can see you're one of those women who doesn't know what she wants, or you do know, in reality, and what is important to you most of all is me, and not what I'm wearing?"

"Perhaps, though the mind, too, counts a lot . . ."

"Of course it counts, my owner is almost as intelligent as me, except that I have genius, of course, or I wouldn't be here talking to you. Do you think every penis can talk? I'd like a real conversation, I'd like to know everything about what women think of me, because he doesn't want to tell me anything. He's mad about having an intelligent penis. He would have preferred a submissive cock, which would obey him, be at his beck and call. Get up, lie down, back to your kennel! He imagines he would be happier if he ordered me around. He can't bear that I escape him, that I submit to impulses and even to secrets that come directly from his brain to me. I'll give you an example. He likes brunettes, but I penetrate blondes better. He prefers buxom bosoms, but I adore being squashed between two small poetic breasts. We don't have the same tastes, but he is compelled to yield to mine, because when he follows his fancies, I don't do as I'm told. I refuse to submit to his will. He can beg me all he likes, I stay cold as stone."

"Why do you do only as you please? Why do you talk to me so much and in such an arrogant tone? Couldn't you be a little more humble?"

"On which planet do you live, sweetie? Have you ever seen an erect penis that was not arrogant? And would you like it to be humble on top of that? May as well ask a flamenco dancer to wear a pair of sneakers! You must be crazy. Surely it's not what you expect from me, humility!"

"No, you're right, but I don't understand why you need to show that you are the strongest and the most handsome. It gets on my nerves."

"It gets on your nerves? But you don't understand anything. It's an intrinsic phenomenon! It's linked to my nature, to my essence, to my inner being! I'm only happy if I know for sure that nothing will cut into my force and my will. Do you admit that sometimes you feel like stripping me of my pride and arrogance because you are jealous? Because you possess a kind of cave with threatening cavities, a not very nice sort of thing that my owner imagines to be dark and dangerous, covered with hair that only serves to conceal a yawning chasm to make the blood run cold. Obviously I tried to explain to him that the female sex is not so dangerous, that it's all warm and cozy inside, with walls oozing sweetness. But he wants none of it. He only trusts what he sees, and not me, who knows the subject so much better. A woman's sex sometimes plunges him into an irrational dread. He's afraid it could happen to me, that I would become like that dark gap, through an operation by the Holy Ghost. That's why he only keeps company with women cautiously, and he is certainly not ready to get married, not at all. He dreads being imprisoned, being smothered, and, in the end, being changed into a woman, too, by contamination."

"But that's absurd, a lot of men are married, and very happily, too. He never looks around?"

"Yes, yes, precisely. He looks, he observes, and that doesn't reassure him at all. He thinks that his married friends make too many concessions just to stick their little pricks into a warm place from time to time. He thinks they lose their integrity, their pride, their arrogance. He refuses to succumb to the same fate. I may tell him that he is scared to love, that's all; he believes obstinately in what he says, and, after all, I must confess that it suits me, as long as I'm not too old."

"Your owner hasn't met any macho husbands?"

"Oh, but he's a clever guy, he's not impressed by that superficial arrogance. He claims one shouldn't be fooled by appearances."

"So he's scared of women? But when I look at him, he seems calm and confident."

"Enough about him. He's scared for me. Like all men. Let's go back to the subject, and talk about you and me. I'd like to know what a woman finds attractive in me."

"I cannot answer you, I can't see you, you're in his trousers."

"Stupid cow! What a silly stupid cow you are! I am the archetype of male sexual organs, the male sexual organ *par excellence*; you don't need to see me to tell me what you like in me. Concentrate on your past and present experiences."

"Present? I don't have a lot of present experiences."

"What? That's just my luck! I've spent an incredible amount of time looking for a woman who can hear me in the Métro, I've been calling for months. Nobody answered; all the women who take the Métro are focused on themselves or on their daily worries, and when, finally, I find one, she's incapable of talking about her lover's penis because she hasn't currently got a lover."

"You have to realize, if you don't mind my saying so, that it's perhaps the reason why I heard you . . . I am more receptive, probably . . ."

"But, tell me, you are missing me a bit then, aren't you?"

"I'm not only missing sex, for me it doesn't happen without tenderness . . ."

"What, you wouldn't just desire me? You still need something else? For me, it's enough to penetrate you, to bring pleasure to my owner, and then leave on tiptoes and roll on, freedom!"

"So you only see my vagina as a prison? It makes me sad that a man only wants to take his pleasure and leave."

"You just have to do the same and everyone will be happy."

"Not everyone behaves that way. A lot of men appreciate staying with a woman and finding happiness."

"Yeah, probably, but that's because they don't listen to their penis, which would surely prefer to explore new horizons. But in my case my owner listens to me and only does what I want. I dictate his behavior and I order him to leave, in most cases. I have no disposition for married life."

"So only superficial relationships interest you?"

"Excuse me! Relationships don't interest me one bit. Only penetration interests me. You haven't answered my question. What do you like about me?"

"When you are erect, or . . . ?"

"What a stupid question, of course when I'm erect! When I am not, I sleep, I rest, I reflect, I don't act, I think about something else, I recharge my batteries, I leave my owner alone. Well then, what do you like in me?"

"Well, you give me a feeling of strangeness. You are so different from me. It's as if I've taken the plane without knowing my destination, to find myself projected into a land which fascinates me with its customs and beliefs, so remote from mine. It moves me deeply that something so strange exists so close to me!"

"So close or so far away? Make up your mind!"

"Both. I am overwhelmed by a man's erect penis, in the intimacy of a bedroom, I mean, in private . . . you know what I mean?"

"I feel like a creature from outer space invited for tea by an aristocratic English lady. No, to be honest, I don't know what you mean! What about my physical appearance, then? My force, my beauty, my power! For Chrissakes, my physical power! What about it?"

"Yes, of course, it all combines for the effect, but faced by an erect penis, what I experience is an upheaval. I am overwhelmed, let's say; I am fascinated because I don't possess such a member and, at the same time, I can feel the man's vulnerability when he's stiff. I keep quiet most of the time, for fear of scaring him. Yes, I'm impressed by its power and at the same time I fear seeing it vanishing, I perceive its fragility. I'm moved and I want it to enter me."

"Finally, an interesting word. But hey, girl, a man's penis is not that easy to break. I'm much more solid than I appear."

"That's what they say about babies . . ."

"Fine, forget it. So when I penetrate you, what happens?"

"The most extraordinary moment is right at the beginning, when you enter and my flesh spreads open to let you in. It's an exquisite sensation, as long as you're not too big and you don't hurt me. My whole body feels warmed up and my entire being concentrates in the belly to receive you and feel you. I open up, I absorb you and I adore to have you there, deep inside me."

"Ah, you understand now why I like to be free again. I don't want to stay imprisoned in that. A little time, OK, half an hour perhaps when I'm well aroused, but after, quick, the open air and light! My owner is always worried that a woman he sleeps with won't give him back his penis, in other words, your servant here. And that's not without reason. That has happened before, in the real as well as the figurative sense. There are women who want to cut me off to keep me in the real sense, and others who want to cut from him everything that resembles me to keep me in the figurative sense. And he is right, one has to be careful . . ."

"I can't stand men who are suspicious and scared."

"But all of them are suspicious and all are scared; you'll have to get used to it, otherwise you won't be able either to be careful, or to reassure them, and then, good-bye hanky-pankies! From the toughest, the most macho, to the dimmest, the funniest, they are worried for me, their most precious possession. Obviously they don't want women to know that I'm the one giving the orders. For example, when they don't use me sensibly, when they are overawed by the situation and my independence, they try to forget about me with their jobs, their politics or religion."

"Yes, you're right, I had a lover who was a politician. The worst lover I ever had in my whole life. He had an enormous organ and he used to ejaculate less than a minute after penetration. He had been married for twenty years and made love like that to his wife. He was absolutely certain that he was excellent in bed. It lasted two minutes, after which he spoke politics. It was horrendous."

"Aha, you're through with the fascination you talked about earlier. That I'm erect is not enough for your happiness, then? That I experience pleasure is not enough, either? And if, on top of that, I'm too big, madam doesn't like it?"

"How silly you are! What an utter fool! Of course your pleasure is not enough, you need dexterity, tact, gentleness, patience. We women are not set like clocks, except for those who have been making love with the same politician for twenty years, and always in the same way. No, no, the others, those who really like you, we need tenderness, gentleness, that you caress our inner walls with your velvety flesh. And if you are too big, we don't feel much as you take up too much space. Anyway, that's a personal point of view."

"What a job, all those demands! I don't know if I'll have the courage to hold back each time. It's the only point on which my owner gets very angry with me, if I let go when he wants to control me to give pleasure to his mistress. I'm lazy, and it requires some effort to give a woman sexual gratification. Of course, he is so thrilled when he manages to control me that it's worth it for me to be patient, but in reality, it's to make him happy. If it was for me, I would give way to orgasm, and . . . cheerio!"

"A charming attitude indeed. You obviously have no respect for your owner. You don't want him to experience that feeling of joy and triumph when, thanks to you, he made a woman come, and satisfied her? How could you be so selfish? Can't you see his happiness is at stake? A man is much happier when he makes a woman happy. It's fundamental . . . and you, with your fancy talk of freedom and I don't know what other nonsense, you would deprive him of that joy?"

"Ooh la la, what eloquence suddenly! But she's getting all worked up, she gets on her high horse. It's obviously her own happiness she's defending."

"It's a certain idea of love I defend. If you dictate selfish behavior to your owner, you isolate him, you cut him off from true love. All the more, for being a good lover is not sufficient to make a woman happy in the long run. Availability and reliability are also needed."

"What? But that's the House of Horrors you're describing! And what else now?"

"You are not happy because you're no longer in control. It's the heart and the soul that are going to dictate feelings to your man, and not only his penis."

"My word, you're playing again the old conflict between body and soul. How very boring."

"No, what is utterly boring is when one or the other alone governs the life of a man."

"You're wrong, because in my own way I'm quite spirited, and I only have in mind, if I might say so, the well-being of my owner. And he's grateful, too. It's me who determines his being, his life, his mood, his desires. It's thanks to me that he's a man."

"How pretentious of you! You believe that the mere fact of owning a penis makes a man out of a human being?"

"It helps, you know. You can get angry with me but it's a fact."

"I'm angry about your illusions. It's not the penis that makes the man. All men have a penis, but not all of them are men."

"You play with words now, you create syllogisms backwards, you give a different meaning to the word *man* when it suits you, you play the clever dog, you're argumentative . . . You don't want to see reality: it's the penis that makes the man, and when a man stops being a man according to your obscure criteria, it's very often because women have interfered, believe me."

"But without women, there are no men!"

"And vice versa!"

"It's true. Let's make peace."

"So, now, are you going to answer my questions?"

"I'll try. Perhaps I'm not the right person to ask, because my relationships with men are difficult."

"How many times do I have to repeat that relationships don't interest me?"

"All right, all right, it's no use raising your voice, you really are quick-tempered!"

"I'd like to know what you feel at the moment of coming, when I'm inside you and suddenly it starts."

"I wouldn't say it starts all of a sudden . . ."

"But what triggers your pleasure?"

"You want to know so many things! As if it was easy to explain that in two little sentences, just like that. It depends a lot on the situation."

"Situation? Don't I adapt to all situations? Situations, I can't see myself declaring that to my owner. Don't worry, their pleasure depends on situations. He's going to send me packing. He wants real answers. We've made a truce, me and him: I stop chasing all the pretty women long enough to bring him a few answers to help lift up his spirits. I didn't tell you why I decided to carry on with this conversation: he's anxious, he's sad, he reproaches me for being interested only in immediate sexual gratification, and for not helping him build a loving relationship."

"You see, he's an intelligent man."

"Of course, as soon as I bring grist for your mill, you're pleased. Well, those situations? What's it all about? What situations bring you to orgasm?"

"You don't get it at all, it's not the situations that bring me to sexual pleasure, it's the words, the things that happen during those inti-mate moments."

"The words, the things? But he is going to skin me alive him such vague answers."

"OK, what I like most is to be desired. And it's not arousal, but a desire. When my last lover stopped desir still sexually aroused, but I was deeply unhappy."

"I lost you there. He was still getting stiff?"

"Of course."

"So he was desiring you, period."

"No, his penis was stiff and ruled him like you do with your owner, but he no longer desired me."

"I don't understand a thing. You mean he no longer loved you?"

"Not exactly. But it's linked, surely. If I think about it, it was no longer me as a whole he wanted, he was aroused and wanted my vagina to find a very physical immediate gratification, but his mind was elsewhere. I could have been any other woman, he didn't really pay attention. As for me, I could have an orgasm, but an orgasm ten thousand kilometers away from my body, and which didn't have anything to do with real pleasure. I no longer wanted to make love to him."

"OK, I still don't get it, but it doesn't matter. Let's talk about the previous situation, the time when you experienced a real pleasure. Where did it come from?"

"He desired me and I was unique. His whole being was stretched toward me, not only his erect penis. When he had an erection, I felt his desire so strongly that it sent little erotic shivers through my whole body. My sex opened up to welcome him and words of desire came to our lips. The same words pronounced only with sexual arousal or with an intense desire don't have the same effect."

"I sense that I won't win over my owner with information of such little use. Couldn't you be more precise? For example, at the beginning, before feelings or false and true desire were part of the picture, how was it?"

"From the start, his desire gave me great pleasure. I screamed when I came in his arms, especially when I felt him close to coming, or when he had just come. It's strange, a man's orgasm, if it doesn't appen too quick, it often triggers mine. Just before or just after, metimes at the same time. Anyway, I was screaming with pleasure."

And that didn't scare him? Because it's a bit shocking, right?"

on't know. No, I don't think he was scared, otherwise he would have told me, or I would have felt it. I relax by screaming, but I could control myself if I wanted."

"Wait, I'd like to understand. When you masturbate, do you come a lot?"

"Yes, sometimes."

"But your lover isn't present then, so it's not his desire that increases your pleasure!"

"You don't get it at all. When I caress myself, the moment when I have the most pleasure is when I remember his desire. I think about the happy period when he used to desire me totally, and I re-create, in an imaginary way, my past happiness."

"What a disaster! Nothing concrete is coming out of this conversation. The mystery remains whole . . . If I say to him: it's true desire that increases a woman's orgasm, he's going to interrogate me: what is true desire? And why put the word *true* in front of the word *desire*? Is there a fake? No, I'll answer him, it's to establish a difference between mere sexual arousal and true desire. Then he will answer, with his usual logic: in that case, let's talk about arousal and desire, let's keep it simple."

"He's right, a man's sexual arousal doesn't touch me much, but his desire moves me."

"Oh, God, things are getting worse. What makes a woman feel desired?"

"What makes a man desire a woman?"

"Ah, that I can answer precisely. I am in the right position, for Chrissakes. My owner desires a woman all the more if he doesn't feel me threatened, because then I agree with everything he asks me. He thinks that I function wonderfully, he feels no reticence from me, and off we go! Let the music begin!"

"Hold on, I thought relationships didn't interest you."

"I'm not talking relationships, I'm talking penetration. My owner is satisfied when he feels my contentment, when he understands that I'm about to get stiff and penetrate his mistress without a hitch."

"That shows that the woman counts, that the relationship is valued, that desire exists and that, in this case, intercourse is nothing else but a manifestation of it. Your owner desires the one who threatens him least, you said? The one who makes him feel like a whole man? The one who is like this or like that? The one who is unique in her own way, for him, is that it?"

"And what do you do about the men who can sleep with almost any woman as long as they are attracted to her, physically at least?"

"Those men ignore desire, they only know sexual arousal, and I wouldn't want to be one of them for anything in the world."

"It seems to suit them, though. Besides, my owner is rather like that, he never desires a woman for a very long time, if I put it your way, but he is still aroused."

"And didn't you say that he was sad and anxious?"

"Perhaps . . . listen, this conversation is coming to a deadlock. I still don't know what I shall report back to him from your nonsense."

"Say to him that desire is not intercourse, that it's something else. If a man wants me, I feel pleasure; if he's only aroused, sexually speaking, I can, at most, reach orgasm. It all depends on what one is looking for, and the level of requirement one has."

"What if all women are not like you?"

"I don't pretend to speak for all women. But is it not to me you've posed your question? Am I not the only one who heard you? Don't I have that particularity, that unique character that made me aware of your request?"

"Ah, there we are, unbelievable, the arrogance of women! Immediately you want to show me how absolutely necessary you are. But you are wrong, I can easily do without you."

"I have no doubt, but in that case, why have you been so desperately seeking answers for months now on a Métro line where no one answers you? Why isn't your owner satisfied with his aroused condition? What else does he want?"

"Alas, I fear he only wants what I alone can't give him; he wants a woman to desire him to death, he wants to hear her losing her mind in orgasm, he wants to make her faint when he's making love to her, he wants her to drown when he penetrates her, he wants to be taken through the vertigo of desire so much that he forgets me and that I become the instrument of his power and his pleasure, while he rubs me between his mistress's breasts, maps out a burning path on her spinal column, while he sticks me inside her, looking her straight in the eyes, and discovers in those eyes an intoxication similar to his, and then he kneads her body and her breasts, while gently plunging in her as deep as possible, after having spread open her thighs with both hands."

"Really?"

"Really."

"But then, you do know what I'm talking about. You know that one cannot reach that experience, that exchange, if one doesn't give a part of oneself, if one doesn't risk everything in a relationship. After the excitement of the first meetings, one can only keep that magic going if both partners want to share that abyss, if each commits their being in that sharing. If one proves to be selfish and seeks only sexual gratification, all eroticism vanishes and the love life, so rich in emotions, disappears, too. The only thing left is sadness for the one who has been abandoned, plunged into a painful dereliction. Doesn't the man you're talking about know all that?"

"Yes, probably, but he fears your demands."

"What more can I do, except keep quiet?"

The man's penis didn't answer. I almost felt a touch of bitterness as I climbed the Métro stairs leading to the street and the lights of Paris. Hadn't I already experienced the sadness and the mourning of a desire that had turned away from me? Let's forget that.

I would like to meet a man whose penis would talk only to me

A Plot Forever

Laure Clergerie

I had neglected the gestures of love, let my body escape me. I stuffed it with food, locking my desires deep inside my guts. I was no longer affected by them. I had given up any encounter as lost. The last went back so far that I had forgotten how it felt. I had never come, as referenced by the writers and poets prolific in erotic literature. Always never-ending caresses where one pulls at the nipples, sucks them occasionally, hand in pants and crumpled clothes. I always clenched my teeth until they discharged laboriously. The ritual question followed. I nodded with a smile, impatient for them to leave.

In the depths of winter, a torrential rain fell on our town. People took refuge under the bus shelters, scorning social conventions. A woman in her seventies muttered bad words about a teenage boy. A man pressed against the bottom of a woman bedecked in jewelry. Young people swapped addresses. I flattened my buttocks against the glass, leaning on it. I turned around. Someone was staring at me from the entrance of a café. I hesitated. I nipped out and ran over to the place. My breasts bounced about miserably. My hair got soaked and my suede shoes were ruined.

We eyed each over. He grabbed me by the arm. The warmth of his fingers spread to my limbs. I was fascinated. Barely twenty, he had piercing emerald green eyes. His aquiline nose parted a face with high cheekbones. His black curly hair made me think of a cherub crossed with a devil. His white shirt opened to reveal a bronzed hairless torso. He dragged me toward some paved alleyways. I was clumsy, perched on heels too high. We stopped beneath the dirty sign of a hotel whose light flickered intermittently. A narrow corridor led to an employee filing mail behind the counter. He held out the keys, after looking at us with disgust through bifocals that hid the greenish rings around his eyes.

A pernicious coldness made my senses freeze. A bed with bars stripped of paint occupied the place of honor in the sparse room. An orange blanket with a missing fringe gave off an unpleasant smell of sex. The stranger pushed me toward it with no consideration. He instructed me to get undressed, as if my body was repugnant to touch. My enormous breasts, the folds in my belly, and the fat on my hips made me blush. I blessed the darkness. I lay down. He spread my arms and thighs. He tied my wrists and ankles to the posts. He gagged me. From a cupboard he took out an implement. When it got closer, I recognized a whip. He caressed me with its cords. Suddenly he lashed me violently. Insensitive to my stifled prayers, he struck me more and more. He heaped abuses on me. His ardor increased with my sobs. He pushed back the rolls of fat of my distended and opalescent flesh to penetrate me. I barely felt his penis. It was lost in my cunt, flooded with juice. He withdrew, he lacked experience. He had to start again, before ejaculating. He groaned like a child. Without a word, he left. With each effort to move, the ties cut into my skin. Through the latticed shutters a starless sky discharged its tar. Numbed, I fell into a painful sleep, blurred with visions.

Children were masturbating in gardens, aroused by a dog mounting a bitch. A woman slashed her wrists, then licked them greedily. Some men fucked each other in the ass. I swam in the Acheron, swept along by currents of sperm and juices, passing bodies emaciated and broken.

A knock at the door woke me. I was foaming, on my way back from Hades.

An ageless woman stood there, looking at me lewdly. She had deformed hands with large rings. She sniffed at my cunt. She introduced a finger, examined the mucus. A serpentlike tongue came from her pinched lips. She darted it at my clitoris. I could not escape her assaults. She applied herself to licking me, penetrating my vagina and anus. She fingered me. A wave of contractions swept over me. I came too fast.

The days went by, barely distinct from the nights. I had lost my identity. I was no more than a body, the one in room 13. Forced to diet, I lost weight. I held myself again as before my culinary orgies. I felt the lack. My mouth became dry, used as it was to some food. The time before sexual frustrations was lost in the origins of time. I accepted my new condition irreversibly. What to think about if not the wait for the next to come and abuse me with my consent?

In the darkness I struggled to distinguish the faces. Heavy and greasy faces, dry and blotched skins, delicate china features revisited my sleep in a carnivalesque parade. I adopted the shape of their bodies as an illusive way to get rid of myself. Their words were reduced to a minimum. *Suck me, open your cunt, spread your ass.* I never replied. My gestures were automatic. I got used to pain. It proved I was still alive.

A thought tormented me, that of the chosen one, the one who would make me die of pleasure. My clients didn't care about my pleasure. When one had a drooping penis he accused me of being responsible. Then he gave me a good thrashing.

An older man entered one day. He kept all his clothes on. He undressed me extremely slowly. He examined each part of my body. He lingered on my lower abdomen. He blew on my pubic hair. I felt a delicious tickling. He licked me with much care, after having spread open my lips. He massaged my clitoris with dexterity. He interrupted to apply more mucus to it, plunging his tongue in deep. As the pleasure increased, I started to lose consciousness. Everything converged on my cunt. I screamed. A thread of saliva trickled from my mouth. My eyes cried. Spasms rolled, unfurled. I no longer moved, abandoned on a shore unknown until now. The old man darted his prick into my anus before unloading on the sheets. I shook him violently. He was dead, his eyes showing their whites. He was so ugly that I felt nauseous. His emaciated body and his crazed eyes pursued me long after they took him away. A smell lingered in the room, heavy with indecency and agony.

I was falling apart. My life had never had any meaning. Changed into prey, I had the hope of the helpless. My mullioned window reminded me of the crosses of the church where I used to pray as a child, begging for trinkets. From my bed, I stared at the posts as if obsessed. The sunsets bathed their blood on those rows of bars like an ephemeral shroud.

My pleasures became vulgar through pretense. I became accustomed to the torpor of hurried intercourse. I felt no hatred toward my clients. I judged them indulgently. I offered my body as a communion host, aiming for a hypothetical redemption.

I hoped for a priest to fuck me in the ass, to burn me with crucifixes. As for confession, there was nobody to hear me. I had lost the use of speech. I was superb in my saintly muteness. The ascendancy over my body made me possessed, ready for ecstasy.

My room, open to anyone, was nothing but a place for atonement. The torn wallpaper, the iron bed, and the creaking springs bordered on the sordid. The unpleasant smells of sweat, juices, and sperm would have made more than one person vomit. I gorged on those organic liqueurs. I enjoyed the debaucheries that sharpened my senses. I despised the outside world with its wistful echoes.

I heard the echo of those waves through the window. During storms I gazed intensely at the lightning. The rain battered the windows with such violence that a little water trickled through to the floor. I regretted not being able to go out naked under my coat, to feel the puddles lapping beneath my feet, to lean back against a tree. I would have screamed my pain of being.

Some men would have raped me on the sodden earth. They would have tied me to an oak tree. I would have cried with delight and fright. I would have taken off my loosened bonds. I would have lost my way in the forest. I would have come across a pond, haloed with mist. It would have offered itself to me. I would walk through the reeds. A teenage girl's body would be lying there, blood between her thighs. Her limbs broken, she would represent a dislocated doll. A swarm of flies would circle her pubis. The murderer would have strangled her. I would caress her budding breasts and her tangled blond hair. I would enter the water cautiously. A snake would disturb the surface before fleeing toward the bank. The silt would rise to the surface.

I would come back close to the corpse. I would raise its eyelids, lick its wet orbs. I would grab its hand to arouse my clitoris. I would hurt myself because of its long purple nails. I would hit it with all my might. The softened flesh would elude my blows. I would tear away the last bits of clothing to wipe myself. I would drag the body into the water. It would sink quickly. The hidden sun would burst through the clouds offering a blinding halo, then disappear. A gloomy silence would petrify me. The murmurs of the forest would be a long time coming. I would come back to my senses when a cloud of cawing crows flew over me.

The visits became more frequent. Pricks barely felt seeped into my orifices. Their overflows were poisoning me. I was lost. An endless task, like the Danaides pouring water through sieves, I continued to consent to the game with greed. Desire tore at my entrails. If I had been freed, I would have stayed.

My last client wore a mask from a Greek tragedy. Two tiny holes showed mournful eyes. The opening at the mouth let me discern two rows of even teeth. Thick hair and a luxuriant beard completed the face with its extremely classical features. His naked body offered an abundance of hair on his torso, shoulders, back, and legs.

He was dancing. His movements were jerky. It seemed to me as if the features of the mask changed with the light of the shutters. Too weak, I could not accompany him in his dance of death. He masturbated conscientiously. He smeared me with his sperm. He took a knife from his tunic. He slashed himself. His chest ran with blood. He held the weapon out to me, pointing at his penis. I sliced the penis, then the testicles. He collapsed on the floor in terrible convulsions. His throat rattled before he came to rest.

I removed the mask. I discovered a face destroyed by fire. The cartilages of his nose had melted. The eyelids were shapeless. The lips could not be distinguished from his skin. I grabbed the organs. Still warm, I kneaded them vigorously until they were unrecognizable.

Other men would come, but I would be dead, for want of having loved any man. It was a direct way from here to hell, caught in the trap of the burial plot forever.

CHALAD'ORO

Marie Boman

I was born in Italy with a special gift that caused me more grief than joy. Puglia and Calabria, colonized by the Greeks, were very prosperous during the Middle Ages. Toward 1900, the weather conditions and the Mafia considerably damaged those regions. As a result, most of the inhabitants emigrated to France or the United States. The village of Corato, situated inland, near Bari, was the cradle of my youth. In the middle of the main square a statue occupied a place of honor. The vox populi entrusted it with special virtues. It represented a Greek warrior, naked, standing upright, carrying a helmet and a shield. It also used to have a spear, but that had disappeared. On the pedestal was an inscription to attract the eyes of the passersby.

> *To what do you not drive human hearts,*
> *cursed craving for gold?*
> *—Virgil*

The dull face didn't especially attract attention; on the contrary, the strength of the athlete was quite apparent in the green bronze and the graduated shadings of the various browns. The particularity of that statue resided in its solid-gold phallus—majestic, virile, and erect—which excited young and old alike. No resemblance whatsoever to the prepubescent penis covered by a tiny vine leaf of the Greco-Byzantine ephebes. The artist had provided an independent and provocative personal touch.

The inscription by Virgil was feared by the superstitious villagers. None ever dared to steal the tiniest fragment of gold, despite their inner demon coaxing them to do so.

The young mothers used to pass by quickly, holding their hands like shields in front of their young children's chaste eyes. Their subsequent curiosity would only be exacerbated by it, but morality was saved. Teenage girls used to hide in the adjacent alleyways to perfect their education, for the Chalad'oro anatomy conformed to reality. Teenage boys grinned, then compared their willies to that of the statue. Even grown men on a drunken night would engage in competitive bets. Dionysus would be their judge: "Who has the biggest?" Chalad'oro or some pretentious man who would come to bitterly regret the ridicule of the situation? The superstitious Italian women soon came to beseech the statue when their husbands experienced various failings.

In the village, a very unhappy and pious woman spent long hours in the church, praying to the Virgin Mary to give her children. She had been married for five long years and lamented with her husband their sterile union. A bizarre idea, though one of absolute clarity, was breathed in the darkness of their bedroom. She declared later that a holy voice had suggested she devote a novena to Chalad'oro. For nine days and nights she moved around it unrelentingly, and, each time she passed in front, she stroked the prodigious gold phallus. With no sense of shame, she said her beads, mixing prayers to the Virgin Mary with pagan supplications whose aim was the much-desired fertility. On the tenth day she rested. On the eleventh she prepared a feast, brought out her best stoneware, the height of refinement, laid out a gingham

tablecloth and invited the master of the house to honor such a sanctified belly with his semen. On the thirteenth day she went to thank
Chalad'oro, sure of the germination of the little seed.

I was born nine months later, a beautiful baby boy of seven pounds,
with jet black hair, already curly. The day after my birth my proud
father took me in his arms, a rarity at the time. Newborn babies were
usually women's business. In his love and hurry, he knocked me against
the edge of the cradle. That is when he heard a characteristic noise,
despite the large square of wool that swaddled me tightly from head
to toe. The tinkle of gold, no mistake about it.

"Wife, why do you hide coins in the child's swaddling clothes?"

My mother was forced to admit to my anomaly. My little willy,
barely bigger than her small finger, was made of solid gold. A supple
metal at the temperature of my healthy baby boy's crotch.
Consternation. Sorcery. Malediction or luck? Nevertheless I was bap-
tized Valoro.

The square with its miraculous statue became a pilgrimage site
known across Italy. Sterile women came in procession and moved
around the Chalad'oro, begging it to grant them the joys of childbirth.
The local café expanded, and the front window was painted red.
Golden letters invited the men in for *vino d'oro* (golden wine), while
sterile women took their procession around *il Chalad'oro.* Day and
night, it was all but invocations, while the husbands drank the bitter
local wine. By the fourth glass they found it excellent and gave up
keeping a close watch on the devotions of their pious spouses. The
belief in the infallibility of the statue increased with the number of
miracles created and pregnancies declared. The Vatican was already in
a state. The women said that at night Chalad'oro got down from his
pedestal to make love to them, spreading his fertile semen. That was
the mark of a great prodigy, for they didn't feel anything but a wave of
warmth, then the flow of an unctuous stream deep inside their bellies.
A few spasms of a warm feeling and that was it. Nothing to do with

the sanctified orgasm of the marriage relationship they shared with their husbands. A light fertile breath, the active intervention of the divinity would modify their destiny and announce a future maternity. The bad-mouthers said discreetly that, once they were completely exhausted, those poor women collapsed on the ground, and the village layabouts surreptitiously took advantage of the situation. The Vatican become more cautious, but processions carried on.

At three, I started kindergarten. Stumbling along on my little legs, I often fell over, emitting the characteristic sound that promptly made the nursery teacher come running to me. She thought she would quietly pocket a few coins. When she saw "the object," she made me giggle with her "innocent" tickling. I discovered early on the irresistible attraction to gold. What would a school inspector have said at that sight?

The more I grew, the more that golden rod distinguished me from my comrades, and the more it got in the way. There was no football match where I was not noticed, no rugby tackle during which I didn't pleasantly tinkle in everyone's ears. Moreover, that anomaly was now spreading to my balls. Two golden balls were added that tinkled like sleigh bells. I had to wear overly tight pants with elastic that bit into my skin. A real torture.

I passed my primary school certificate. My parents wanted, naturally, to send me to a boarding school. An education on a level with my capacities was necessary.

Oh, they were not wealthy, but they sacrificed themselves working on the terraced slopes. Though they managed seven hundred meters of variation in height, the barren chalky soil didn't sustain more than a few rickety olive trees, some citrus trees, and grains. Their small farming was barely sufficient to feed me and my two sisters. Girls are a curse in this country, for one has to marry them and, above all, to provide them with a substantial dowry. They wanted me to become a lawyer, a soldier, or a priest, the only three professions that measured up to their ambition. Was I not already a gift from heaven?

At boarding school I had few friends, I was an extremely solitary child. However, I made good friends with Julio. We spent our days studying, talking, listening to Chopin or Liszt, and running in the woods. I was happy to be like other kids at last. Alas, one night, I awoke with a jolt. Julio, armed with a pocket knife, was trying to grate my penis to extract a fine layer of gold and buy himself a few cigarettes. That was the end of our friendship. After that I couldn't sleep. I lost weight. And my anxious parents took me out of boarding school.

Back in the village, the priest agreed to complete my education. With his vow of abstinence I almost felt I could trust him. Almost . . . I was a bright child and I quickly made enormous progress. I was allowed to borrow books from the church's library. I read them avidly in the evening by the light of a flickering candle. While my sisters were told off for sewing at night, I was never accused of uselessly burning hard-earned candles. That's the benefit of being a male in Italy.

At puberty I discovered the delights of masturbation. My golden phallus became warmer in my hand, its volume doubled, and I held a rich rod that gave me much pleasure thanks to its softness and metallic brilliance. From my first jerks shot a nectar with the taste of honey, an ambery color oscillating between copper, bronze, and pink gold. I often admired myself before the wardrobe mirror, finding myself even more attractive than the Chalad'oro in the square. If the village girls had been aware of my mystery, they would all have thrown themselves at my feet. My value was increasing with age. But the girls from Corato, poor village girls, mainly uneducated, didn't interest me in the least. I was keeping myself in reserve for bigger projects.

Despite my parents' tears and recommendations, my youth had to shine. I left for the capital, my heart light and my head full of ambition. My mother had given me all her savings with her blessing, but my pouch seemed very light to me. "Valoro," she made me swear, "do not ever cut into 'you know what.'" I found a little hotel in Rome and went for a stroll in the artists' quarter, the streets of antique dealers, the odorous covered markets. There was a whole life whose existence I had not been aware of. It was a daily revelation, a constant wonder. In the evening, in bars welcoming poets, musicians, painters, girls of easy virtue intoxicated us with their perfumes, the arch of their backs, their round buttocks. They were not wild, and willingly accepted the sonorous slaps we gave them in thanks for their services. That joviality, that camaraderie, made me dizzy. However, I remained chaste, unwilling to have the wealth of my crotch discovered too soon. I was a young man of twenty, in the prime of life, and never would my virility be as great as it was then.

One evening, though, I succumbed to the advances of a little brunette who, for a few days, had been disturbing my lonely dreams. Taking things in hand, she undressed me skillfully and slowly, playing with her lips on each bit of my chest and neck. Her divine tongue slid on my lips; she bit my ears gently; and then, like a little cat, she lapped down my hairless chest, sighing with pleasure. That little hussy liked to make love with refinement, you could sense that in every one of her gestures. I had a terrible hard-on and my golden rod had taken on a considerable volume. How great was her wonder when my treasure sprung out of my open fly. She didn't cease in her exclamation, caressed it like a wonder of the world, swore on her life never to have seen such a perfect work of art. I glimpsed the unimaginable fantasy in my power. *What do you think, ladies, of the rigidity, the texture, the warmth of a golden rod deep inside your vaginas, wet with desire?* Ornella, for that was her name, ran her ecstasy up a crescendo of a scale invented in honor of my golden cock. It possessed nerve endings that felt all the variations of temperature. Gold is the most malleable and the most ductile of all metals, as well as being an excellent conductor of electricity. I felt the vibrations with an intensity that no other man could ever know. Ornella had cold extremities but a bubbling heart. I trembled beneath her cool fingers, hardened, tensed up, and her soft warm breasts delayed me in a way that delighted her. My solid-gold phallus slid wonderfully into the lubricated jewel case of her silky sex. Impaled, having become a demon, she didn't pretend to come and confessed that magnificent fireworks exploded in her brain at the moment when a shared orgasm had made me delirious. I was finally happy to be able to exploit that gift from heaven. She didn't seem venal and loved me sincerely, for who I was . . . But men are sometimes immeasurably stupid in the face of the perfidy of women and their own complacency. For me, love, harmony, and even solicitude were going to be inaccessible dreams. I was on the point of realizing that.

Emboldened by that experience, overflowing with a vitality restrained for such a long time, I wished to lead a more debauched life for a while. Marriage seemed premature to me. But I needed money, and I no longer had any. I spent a few painful nights looking for solutions other than the one I had squarely in my hand. I had promised that I would never touch it, but the best rules are those one gives oneself the right to transgress. In the early morning I took a sharp knife and decided not to cut a slice of my penis, but instead to taper it, knowing that its diameter would vary only slightly. I was surprised to feel no pain whatsoever. My penis didn't show any wound and, at first glance, I was the only one who could see a slight difference. I went to sell my thin layer of gold and as a result could live for a few days in an opulence I had never known. How quickly one gets used to luxury!

Sprawled on maroon silk sheets, my eighteen-carat-gold prick was rubbed against the big breasts of a fleshy prostitute. She had just discovered its sublime and precious roundness. I could already see in her eyes, shining with greed, that she was calculating its value. To be honest my cock was worth its weight in gold . . . She was stroking it with her silky hair. An infinite languor, certainly due to the French champagne brought in by the headwaiter, clouded my brain. Suddenly she confessed to a fantasy I did not share.

"I would like to feel the taste of gold on my lips, to polish your wonderful organ with my saliva, to venerate that glorious pleasure tool . . ."

Until then I had always refused fellatio. But that deep-seated fear was curiously decreasing beneath the woman's expert fingers. How could that witch have convinced me so easily? I'm still surprised at it. All men's weaknesses are concentrated in their sex. Samson studied the truth of that way before me. The lessons given by history are only understood when we experience them ourselves. Her lips hastened to gobble the well-polished jewelry. She greedily sucked its metallic flavor. A dash of copper, a bit of silver, zinc, nickel. All in all, I retain a delicious memory of her mouth around my golden erection. With my dazzling organ, I fornicated in her welcoming throat. Never had a woman given me such a sensation. My massive cock was roused by the tips of her nails, then kneaded, caressed frantically, sucked with delight. Before each intake of breath, she murmured:

"Mamma mia, mamma mia, mamma mia . . ."

Who hasn't sucked at their delicious christening medal? In the past, they used to bite gold coins to be sure they were real, and that was not done without some relish. My jewel was burning, my balls were knocking against one another with melodious tinkling. I was caught liking myself. The cajoling prostitute seemed to enjoy seeing my confusion. She had guessed it was a first for me. With slow and diligent movements of her tongue, she went down until she felt my jewel knock against the back of her throat. She stayed like that for a moment, not breathing, then went back up, unfurling her lips on the pole and the glans. All anxiety had dissipated. I was moaning with pleasure, shaking my muscular buttocks. Eyes closed on a supreme happiness, I had reached the paroxysm of delirium. A roar of pleasure was already coming from my throat. Imminent explosion, ecstatic apotheosis . . . Then, suddenly, the bitch bit me and took off the tip of my "ladies' pleasure." She had a slice of gold around one centimeter thick in her mouth. Her eyes were ablaze with a perverse joy and she quickly took flight, leaving me dumbfounded by her felony. I never saw her again, and I knew from that moment on that girls of easy virtue would not count among my mistresses. That bit of future revealed in the present should have put me on my guard. I had a few other experiences, with Fiorella, Lucciana, Sylvana, and others, which proved to be frustrating, as my anxiety was so great. And each time, they stole particles of gold. Forbidding them to take me in their mouths, their nails, often very long, would be filled with the precious metal.

That theft of my person filled me with horror, but my erectile nature, inherited from Chalad'oro, wouldn't leave me in peace. Bucolic and insipid days slipped by. I saw again my little Ornella, who seemed to love me with a love that had become platonic. I no longer wanted to diminish the size of my genitals. But I still had recourse to remove a few thin slivers, for they gave me the money I needed to carry on with my life of leisure. Men are weak faced with life's futilities.

I was desperately alone, I missed women, I dreamed every night of the pleasure of that last fellatio and, at the moment of ejaculation, the nightmare would start again and the castrating bite would wake me in an indescribable state of anxiety.

In the end I submitted to Ornella's love, I trusted her. I appreciated her. I believed in omens. Didn't she have, like me, a name that contained the golden word *or*? Ornella and Valoro sounded like a full purse. She didn't ask for anything, she waited for her time to come. We took long strolls together like lovers, and one evening I ended up asking for her hand. I truly thought then that a loving wife would never dare emasculate me. I innocently thought that three elements were primordial in the life of a couple: sex, good food, and children. I had omitted the essential: money, or rather gold.

As a proof of love, but also to pay for a decent wedding, my parents being incapable of affording such a thing, I decided to inquire at a goldsmith in Rome. I commissioned him to engrave along the length of my penis the name of my beloved, an illuminated *O* near the base, and the *A* at the tip. The artist gave his all and the name decorated my penis like a precious tattoo. He chased a few erotic artifices around the *O*, embellishing the work, giving it an undeniable sensual power. The residue, sold immediately, allowed us to start off on a comfortable married life. Our wedding night was unforgettable. Ornella was moved to tears while I paraded my phallus erected with her name.

We had three children. During those few happy years, when I found a job in a bank, my future seemed secure.

My wife, rather prudish at the beginning of our married life, became bolder and invented a thousand fantasies to make our sexual life even more attractive. She venerated my penis even more than the Madonna.

Once, taken by sudden desire, she raped me.

"I couldn't wait any longer. Your big golden cock filled my head . . . and my sex was overflowing with irresistible desire."

Another time, she implored me to let her shave my crotch and anus. Body hair is synonymous with virility and animality, and its absence often verges on repressed desires for femininity. As an Italian macho, I was sometimes surprised by her boldness. In our country, it is men who make the decisions, men who know the best techniques in bed. Attentive female lovers only have to be in raptures under our caresses. Are we not the best lovers in the world? But this was part of "modern" eroticism, a civilized, rather innocent way of thinking. I loved her inventions, being by nature rather calm and passive. She liked hairless men with small penises, she claimed. I was happy to be loved. She became greedy, lewd, and knew how to give me pleasure in an unbridled way, shamelessly, for there is no such thing as sin between spouses, is there? Ah, those Roman women were much more profligate than the women of my native Corato.

That day was diabolic.

With me standing against the wall, she started by sucking my golden cock while delicately scratching my balls with her nails. I could only resist thanks to a few psychological or mathematical artifices, such as counting the floor tiles. I felt lustful and told her to enjoy my body however she wished.

"Lie down on the bed, I'm going to tie you hand and foot with bits of cloth."

She spread my legs wide with the help of a broomstick. The cloth held my hands tight to the bedposts, but without hurting me. I was at her mercy. She blindfolded and gagged me.

"I'm going to inflict terrible tortures on you."

A fear, mixed with great trust in my wife, made me perspire, in addition to exciting me terribly. I knew of her irresistible attraction to gold. But I thought she was incapable of betraying me. The bedroom was becoming unreal, strange, disturbing. Its dimensions seemed modified, the noises muffled by the scarf became difficult to identify. A hot breath moved across me. Then I felt a wet tongue going up my legs toward my penis. My darling hussy wanted to conquer a different territory, though. I stiffened. Hadn't I given her permission? A truly fine psychologist, Ornella had guessed a powerful fantasy of mine. Naked, offered, with no wish to rebel, I felt ashamed. She was exploring my scrotum, rubbing around my anus, going up the delicate furrow. Then, boldly, as if she was going mad, she plunged one, then two fingers into my carnation. I felt it expanding, blossoming.

"The gold of your penis is taking on an amber color, *amore mio*."

That sublime excitement transported me to a new world. For the first time in my life, I was made to feel the sensations of being penetrated. Becoming a woman, a whore, an object of crude concupiscence. Her insidious splaying made my buttocks arch. She succeeded in making my ass bloom. To my surprise, I begged:

"Spear me, drill my ass."

My legs lifted toward my shoulders, my ass offered, I waited. The bonds had given way beneath the force of my desire. She had taken hold of a small cylindrical object. I later learned that it was a tube of aspirin. She crouched and impaled herself on my penis, one hand firmly holding the object, oscillating on my belly. I experienced a rare dual sensation, feeling myself both a virile penetrating male and a little ponce fucked in the ass. At that time I still had stupid prejudices. Innocently, she had revealed a fantasy to me which would become obsessive. Ornella had had the cunning idea that as a couple we could do without my genitals. She had given it a go, and the results were more than conclusive. I was in a torpor of total bliss. I dozed off when I felt, in my dream, a slight bite. My own wife was granting herself little morsels of gold during my postcoital sleep. I grabbed hold of her hand violently and discovered a piece the size of a chickpea. My world collapsed. The *A* of her name had disappeared with my blind trust. The following years were difficult. Her abuse tormented me, but I finally forgave her. Our relationship was calmer after that.

Not long before our fifth anniversary, I found Ornella in tears. I didn't know how to comfort her, for I was unaware of the cause of her sudden despair. In bed that evening, while she was fondling my golden rod, she admitted that she now found my penis a bit too voluminous and that it hurt her sometimes. On top of that, she wanted a fur coat for our anniversary. I quickly understood the hint: having a golden goose and being deprived of so many things. Greed has no limits!

"Do me a favor. I've never asked you for anything since that day when I lost my head. I was very sorry afterward."

She was right, she made me happy, our children were superb, well-behaved, clean. I sliced off a bit of my penis and offered her the much-desired coat. I sacrificed an *L* from her name. Alas, as soon as you give in an inch, an avalanche of needs becomes immediately irrepressible. The bids were higher. We bought a new house: *EL* was disposed of. We bought furniture and china. The children needed new clothes: *N* disappeared. Their education became more and more expensive. I was left with only a little stump a few centimeters long on which one could still read *OR*, a sad play on words. Ornella assured me of her extreme pleasure rubbing her clitoris on it. She was still coming fabulously, but I felt dispossessed . . . My love was being distorted along with the inscription.

And then the drama started. The economic conditions and the war made me lose my job, even though it was not a very profitable one. Ornella strained her eyes at needlework, but it was barely sufficient to ensure a proper plate of spaghetti Bolognese. Three meats are necessary for such a dish: beef, pork, and horse. Otherwise, the taste is bland: cooking fit for English and American tourists! One day, the bailiffs paid us a visit, for Ornella had contracted various debts. To pay them off I had to sacrifice the *R* and a testicle. The second one followed soon afterward. In less than ten years, I had allowed myself to be castrated. When I was left with the illuminated *O* alone, it was the war, and she decided—for security reasons?—to go back to her parents in her native village. The children, of course, went with her. I gave her half of that O. I was feeling hollow. I didn't have a penny left. I was no longer a man. I remembered bitterly the inscription on the Chalad'oro pedestal. It had sealed my fate implacably.

> *To what do you not drive human hearts,*
> *cursed craving for gold?*

I was in hiding, I had barely enough money to live. The war over, I was a wreck. After a time of depression and wandering, I had to make up my mind. I could not spend the rest of my life lamenting my fate, a thoroughly well-deserved fate. I dug out the last centimeters of gold kept at the cost of great sacrifices. I had in my hand a part of the fateful *O*. It was going to decide the rest of my life.

Various choices presented themselves. To go back home with my tail between my legs—that was one way of putting it. To set off for a dream country where eunuchs are respected and happy. As a keeper in a harem, I could invent tales every day: "From the thousand and two nights to the . . ." in which I would mix my own story with other spicy stories I had often listened to on the sly in my childhood and debauched youth. The last solution was to become a prostitute. My aborted adventure with Ornella was tormenting my body. No longer having a penis, I desired anal penetrations. An unconquerable desire pushed me to buy a one-way ticket to Paris, the city of debaucheries. I vaguely felt I had to go to the end of my decline. What would be the fall? I didn't know; I let myself be guided by my impulses.

Insatiable and ready for anything in order to achieve the most shameful pleasures of sodomy, I was a godsend in the shady areas of Paris. I was still the young handsome Italian that Frenchmen are fond of. But time quickly makes the most beautiful flowers wither, and I grew heavy. My skin hardened and took on a granular look.

I solicited mainly near a bridge. I stood facing the Seine, which I watched flow past, indifferent. The man would quickly dig into my trousers, find no sign of a male, barely question it, take out his dick stiff with contained excitement, and fuck me in the ass. He would shoot rapidly, after two or three thrusts. He sometimes called me a "dirty faggot," slipped me a banknote, and left without turning back. No human connection, no conversation—except for the price of the fuck—no intellectual ecstasy. The effervescence past, I felt annihilated in such sordid places. Being is more important than the act, in the sense that to be fucked is insignificant, and yet I still felt duller and harder. Now the life of those passing strangers no longer interested me . . . Mental decline.

My joints were getting stiffer, I found it hard to move. I was only in my early forties. What was happening to me? I saved up enough money to go back to Corato. Nostalgia for my village, its twisted olive trees, the smell of bergamot, bore into me. To return to my roots had become the sole aim of my extreme physical and mental misery.

Beneath a blazing sun that dried everything up, I arrived in the little square. The same men with chiseled faces and cracked skin sat motionless, chins resting on their walking sticks. The air was vibrating, burning, just as in my childhood. Nothing had moved. Old women embroidered complicated and immaculate white lace. The pot-bellied priest was mopping his face, perspiring under his cruel black cassock. Only the statue of Chalad'oro had disappeared, though the pedestal and the fatal inscription were still there. After the theft of its golden phallus, the statue had been melted down to make bullets during the war. Like me, it had been submitted to destructive outrages. I spent one night in a little inn. My parents' house had been demolished. They were dead. My head was becoming heavy. I had great difficulty putting it on the pillow. I also had to grab my legs with both my hands in order to stretch them out. My heart was slowing down, my blood seemed to flow more slowly. I was not in pain, but I felt very stiff. What was happening to me?

In the early morning I looked at myself naked in the wardrobe mirror. Involuntary gestures placed me in the position of the Chalad'oro. How I looked like him—if it hadn't been for the gaping hole where once there had been a golden phallus! A few hairs had grown back, giving the illusion of a woman's genitalia. An hermaphrodite, a being both ridiculous and attractive. At the time of the siesta, as the village was dozing off, when not even a bird was chirping, I went down and approached the pedestal. A slow transformation was taking place in my body. The quotation by Virgil had vanished and a new one had appeared. One could now make out:

> *Nobody, as women say,*
> *escapes their destiny.*
>
> —*Plato*

The message was slowly carved in my very fiber. Valoro would occupy the place of Chalod'oro. I had a lot of trouble climbing on the plinth. I remained motionless, almost reduced to a statue.

Around five in the afternoon, the children, quickly followed by the adults and the old people, surrounded me. All mocked my absent penis. They held out their arms, roaring with laughter. At the café, the legend of the Chalad'oro was told again. Some declared that "he" had returned. I spent the rest of the night standing on my pedestal in the most perfect state of immobility. In reality my limbs refused to move. My heart had almost stopped. My fingers, now stiff, were almost set. I could no longer stretch my arms. Only my spirit was slowly wandering. In the early morning, the cockerel gave the signal for the sudden arrival of young people. My skin, bristling with small grains of limestone, was cold. My fingers inert, my feet stuck to the granite, my hair stiff in its curly harmony. The young people approached, shouting names. One of them, who had seen me arriving in the village, dared to touch me. He recoiled in horror, declaring that I had become a statue of stone. Incomprehension aroused fear. Some women would perhaps have knelt and cried "Miracle." The young generation was more violent and destructive.

With an outburst they threw themselves upon me, tipping me over. I fell, shattering into a thousand pieces.

Eyewash

Michèle Larue

The three of us sat in the backseat of an Ambassador, bumping along the road from Madras. Our reward was to be Mysore, where the Indian driver ultimately dropped us off. One of my friends, big-boned and Irish, led us into the first hotel that came along, the Sapphire, next to the bus station. Corrupted by Indian fatalism, we let her make all the decisions. At dawn, the bus drivers tested their engines beneath our windows before venturing out onto the streets. Kate, the Scot, lit her first bidi. Our skin was oily, our hair lusterless, we were haggard and marked from the road. We needed to move upmarket.

Built for some British vice-consul, the Lalitha Mahal Palace was the best hotel in town. In a dining room done up in the manner of English pastries, Kate began finding fault with the waiters' baggy trousers. She came from a family of penniless aristocrats and had latched on to the Irish Laura, who didn't seem to mind paying her way. They both had the same scapegoat: the English. Kate was into women, but Laura paid no attention to her overtures; she was a man-eater who couldn't go three days without a fuck. Whenever sex was in short supply, her personality changed.

Then the bonze came in and our laughter froze on our lips. Athletic-looking, holding his shaved head high, he looked the diners over with mischievous eyes as he strode to a table of Americans. A childlike shoulder protruded from his saffron robe. Kate and Laura commented on his physique and asked my opinion.

With tears in their eyes from the spicy food, they went over the games they might play at his expense. Kate would lift the sacred robe with her teeth—"100 percent cotton, soaked in musk!"—Laura would tickle him with the feather tips of her earrings—"Only ten quid at Harrod's, darling"—and finish with his bare feet, so appetizing in those sandals, with their well-cared-for toes. Then, together, they would lick his buttocks—"Butterscotch, dearie, but zero calories." The texture of his skin was anybody's guess.

The program included exploring his anus with a finger, and Laura held out the copper green nails she'd stuck on with Krazy Glue. Kate would make comments on the boy's expressions while Laura burrowed into him with her ring finger. Would he keep that serene expression that they both envied? One thing would lead to another, and the next vile act would be tasting his anus. They would suck their greedy fingers right under the bonze's nose, and soon a makeshift dildo would take their place, such as the penlight bulging through Laura's pants pocket.

They finally decided on a banana; Kate would stick it in, but in which orifice? They argued. First the mouth, to get it wet. No, no, the asshole first. "It's so much more humiliating, dearie!"

My religious sensibility kept me from taking part in this deluge of pornography. Whenever one of them sought my approval, I would answer with a cowardly nod. To keep the fantasy alive, Kate kept ordering fresh pots of tea from the waiter. Beyond the range of their cocky voices, the living statue shone forth.

Later I learned that the monk lived in a nearby camp of Tibetans. He was a political messenger, pleading the refugees' cause to foreign benefactors. Kate led the way out of the restaurant and managed to touch the saffron robe. A flicker of amusement lit up the lama's pupils. Surely that dazzling sparkle was meant for me . . .

Out on the street, I put my hallucination down to collective hysteria. Kate resolved not to wash her hand for the rest of the day.

En route to Blue Valley, we passed an elephant with her baby, then a busload of Japanese. An Indian army colonel was waiting for us on a wildlife preserve, in the middle of the unspoiled savannah of my dreams. The camp included a few permanent bungalows. During dinner, an officer wearing a blazer told us of the elephants' mating season and their sexual excitement, the musth, when they trampled everything in their path. Late that night, in spite of the fire in the ditch, a troop of them destroyed the lamps outside and beat on the walls of our bedrooms with their trunks.

The next part of my dream materialized the next day. Perched on the back of a tame elephant, I photographed wild animals in their natural state; the idea of wild beasts terrified my two friends, and they kept to the camp day after day. There was a private courtyard, safe from prying eyes, where they could strip to sunbathe. In the end, they got an urge for colonial nostalgia, just like their English "enemies," and set off for Oloon, a tea-growing town in the hills. After a week of safari, I'd had my fill of bears and buffaloes, and set out for Mysore, where we were to meet up again.

The windows of my hotel looked out on a ruined palace in an unattended park. By noon, the heat was stifling, and I went for a swim at the Lalitha Mahal Palace. Feeling relaxed from the pool, with my hair still wet, I glimpsed a saffron robe turning at the end of the hallway. I met my rickshaw driver at the entrance. As we drove slowly over the dry lawns, the bonze appeared and waved to us. He was taking an elderly monk to the bus station. Sitting down in the middle of the seat, the young lama took advantage of the first turn we took to put his arm around my waist. At the bus stop, I loaded sweets into the old man's bag and we helped him to his seat.

Lobsung, for such was the bonze's name, came back to the hotel with me. No sooner had he come into the room behind me than he'd seized upon a pair of binoculars lying on the bed. Braced against the balcony railing, he was peering at the ruin across the way when he burst out laughing. I took my turn at the binoculars and saw across the lawn a tiny monkey hanging by its rear legs from a children's swing. It was holding a kitten coiled in its long tail and fucking it as it swung. We could even hear the feline mewing. The monk's laughing mouth blew cool air on the back of my neck. He pressed his chin into my flesh, began rummaging under my blouse with one hand while the other stroked my belly with juvenile awkwardness. I was dying to slip my fingers inside his robe, imagining the warm gap between his cool skin and the cloth.

I showed him how to kiss. After that, I had to slow him down. He'd have licked my tonsils, so hungry was he for a woman. He peered down my cleavage: the virgin wanted to see everything there was to see on a female.

He sniffed me and I did likewise. He had a sharp, woody smell; his skin tasted salty. He gave me the impression of someone who'd been told about sex and was busy checking out his secondhand anatomic knowledge. His breathing was slow and abdominal. "Working on his chi," I said to myself while his girlish hands stroked my thighs.

The moment the idea of chi entered my mind, all my thoughts focused on Lobsung and his breathing honed in on me. His mauve lips chanted weirdly into my vulva. The buzzing of a fly. Or sometimes the throbbing of a trombone. He blew his breath into my sex and sucked it out, humming all the while. He drew muted sounds from my nether parts, cavernous echoes of his own melody. I had become a Tibetan bagpipe. Blasts of hot air, gusts of wind, a Buddhist hurricane, blew my dress away like a hot-air balloon.

Now his rangy body emerged in turn from the folds of orange. His legs grew thin at the ankles and his penis hung pointing at the floor. Without further ado, he sat down on top of me and began rubbing his perineum and buttocks against my belly. Then he entered me from above. Only our internal muscles moved, exchanging a series of voluntary contractions.

He was attentive to my sensations, and waited until the time was ripe to move his organ in the proper way. My pleasure peaked each time he stopped. Orgasm was not a goal in itself but a point of no return, a killjoy both of us were determined not to reach.

To make the pleasure last, we drew apart. He lay on his back and worked on his energy, breathing slowly through his nose, not breathing at all for long stretches of time. Propped on my elbow beside him, I watched.

After our first "climax of delight," we began to explore further. With this man, pleasure involved different levels of intensity, stages to be negotiated. It was my turn to sit on top, with my legs wrapped around his hips. My belly shuddered electrically and I opened for him all the way. He lay with his eyes shut, motionless inside me, his firm hands resting on my shoulders. Then he withdrew. Wrapping a towel around himself, he went to the window, had a look at the monkey, and giggled.

He wanted me to sit on him again, but the other way round, facing his feet. This time there was a whole succession of tiny movements, and muted vibrations rose to my skull: the will to pure pleasure by osmosis. A Bengal light began to sizzle in my head. Nirvana lasted a long time, but in the end I couldn't keep up with his tantric apprenticeship and collapsed on top of him, worn out before I could come. Lobsung muttered something in his language, more like onomatopoeia than words, and went to sleep with a smile on his lips.

In the cool of the morning, I went looking for my two friends near the bus station. By telepathy or bush telegraph, the desk clerk at the Sapphire predicted that "the English ladies" would be a day late.

Back at the hotel, I saw Lobsung in the ruins across the lawn, weightlessly leaping between the windows. He did a double somersault, landed on his feet in a martial stance, and went on to do forms. Then he levitated on the veranda steps. I remembered Kate's horrified expression when a child stuck his fingerless hand through the car window for a cigarette, and Laura's cynical remark: "Eyewash!"

I was on my way back to the hotel when I saw two silhouettes hobbling up the road with familiar-looking giant-sized suitcases rolling behind them. My friends were on the verge of exhaustion. From a distance, they'd taken me for a boy in my baseball cap.

The Oloon–Mysore "express" had broken down in the middle of the wildlife sanctuary. Neither Laura nor Kate had left the bus for fear of elephants. They'd been terrified to see several passengers actually go off into the bushes to answer the call of nature. And when they opened their sponge bags, a horde of monkeys had swarmed into the bus through the open windows and made off with their cosmetics! At the Sapphire, they asked the desk clerk for their old room back.

The final blow fell later that evening, when they came to see me in my hotel in a state of extreme nervous fatigue. The peace and quiet, the panoramic view from my window, made Kate hysterical. She took it out on Laura for having chosen the Sapphire, but Laura wasn't listening, she was gaping at the saffron robe on a chair.

My head bounced off the wall from the slap she gave me. She grabbed me by the hair and Kate pitched in with a kick to my kidneys that knocked me to the floor. Then she kneeled on me and squeezed one of my breasts in the crook of her elbow. They dragged me over the linoleum and called me a hypocrite.

When they finally left me alone, I looked for the bonze's robe. It was gone. The bathroom door was banging in the evening breeze. On the windowsill, a tiny monkey with knowing eyes stood swaying on its paws. I thought to myself: "That wasn't fair: two men ganging up on a girl."

THE MAN WITH NO FACE

Alina Reyes

At the moment of dying, I experienced an incredible feeling of being in the present. People say that at those moments one sees one's life unfolding as in a movie, but sped up. I was in the film, and everything unrolled in slow motion, or perhaps it was very fast, but in such a clear and detached fashion that each microsequence was loaded tenfold with dramatic force. For the first time I could see the face of the man I had loved passionately for months and, in dying, I was living again each of the meetings, the anxieties and unutterable pleasures he had brought me.

The first night he had appeared standing in a garden, perfectly still under the yellow light of the moon. Leaning out of the window of an unfamiliar house, I contemplated his silhouette, tall and slim, like that of an adolescent. He was wearing the trench coat of a private eye; perhaps he was naked underneath. Although his face was turned toward me, I couldn't see it.

That very simple dream left me with such a strange feeling that when I woke up, I wrote it down. Then I forgot it, until he came back, seven days later. I was still at the window of that unfamiliar house, in the light and shade of a full moon, but there was nobody in the garden. I wanted to whimper like a cat, for I desperately wanted to see him again.

I stepped through the window frame, legs like scissors, and found myself in a forest of foliage like in a painting by Henri Rousseau, growing denser and darker to the point that I felt my way in almost complete darkness. Still racked by desire, I cast off my clothes as I walked and let the ferns gently caress my thighs. Finally, feeling a breath on my neck, I turned around and it was him. My hands recognized the slim and firm body I had glimpsed in my previous dream. We fell into the grass, and he plunged his unseen face between my spread legs. A sexual pleasure sharper and longer than ever awoke me.

I stayed in bed for a long time, unable to move, exhausted, stunned with happiness.

He came back every night. I watched for him at the same window, hoping he would come and meet me. But he never showed up, and instead I went to meet him among the deep, always dark thickets. Sometimes the terrain got rugged and, in order to meet him, I had to make considerable efforts through the tangle of sloping and mysterious forests, like those in old engravings. I was gripped with anguish, while a more cruel vegetation scratched my body, until the sudden and unexpected moment when I collided with his warm limbs. And each time, mouth to sex alone, we drowned in each other's sensual delights.

And when the sensations reached their greatest intensity, I woke up, panting, next to my real-life partner, slightly worried now about my nocturnal and solitary jolts, all the more because I was slowly turning away from him, filled with love for my fantasy dream rendezvous.

The man with no face, perhaps he was a ghost, gave me such rare and sweet pleasure that I no longer desired others. I found myself lying down at any time of the day, as soon as I had the chance, in the hope of falling asleep and finding the unparalleled sensual delight that he alone could bring me. The more my daily life and my connection to real life fell apart, the more I felt like sleeping and dreaming.

But the more I dreamed, the longer and more arduous the path leading to my phantasmic lover became. At times I happened to wake up, worn out, after wandering among the branches, without having been able to meet him and enjoy his favors. Frustration exacerbated my passion, and those times—increasingly rare now—when I managed to reach him, I went into a delirium of love, kissing his toes, drowning his sex in my tears while quivering beneath the gentleness of his tongue. I convinced myself that if I could see his face, I could hold him more easily. But the moonlight didn't reach into the thickets where we fell, and he didn't let me discover his features with my fingers. We spent almost our whole time together head to foot, vertiginously head to foot.

For just one of those sensual delights, life was worth living. Did it matter if my partner was drifting away from me? If we were separating? If I was no longer interested in those I loved? To whom could I have spoken about my new love? Others are always so conventional. I was too. And the conformist in me sometimes rebelled, refused to be consumed by an imaginary being, even if that intangible man gave me real sensations.

I think that those sensual pleasures drove me crazy. I started to stride around town convinced that my dream lover would be there, incarnated somewhere, and that I would eventually find him. My days tracking through the streets resembled my nights of pursuit in the depths of the garden. Each time I caught a glimpse of a silhouette similar to that of the man with no face, on a sidewalk or in a café, with all the boldness that desire gave me, I worked out a stratagem to accost him and seduce the one whom, in my delirium, I identified with my nocturnal love. But as soon as we had slept together, the mystification revealed itself and I had to start all over again. Even handsome and gifted (and they were not all like that, for desire sometimes made me blind, to the point where I would pick up anyone), no young man was capable of making me die of ecstasy like him.

At the end of one night when I hadn't fallen asleep successfully, and thus had not met up with the only man who really made me orgasm, I found myself, I don't know how, despair probably, on the emergency turnout of an oily and poorly lit highway. In the early morning drizzle, a truck driver stopped. I didn't give him the time to pull away. I provoked him immediately and outrageously. We made love there and then, in his cabin. My attitude had aroused him so much that everything went fast, too fast. Out of spite I started laughing, making fun of him. He tried to push me out, but I hung on to him, to his powerful arms, much more powerful than those of my beautiful love, and continued to make fun of him, with nasty words, the nastiest I could think of.

He put his giant hands around my neck to silence me. He squeezed and squeezed. I could no longer talk, but I tried to keep that defiance in my eyes. Then I started to die. I entered a long white tunnel and, in the light at the end, I recognized his silhouette. He was there, arms outstretched. He was waiting for me, he was calling me. I carried on walking toward him, radiant with peace and happiness. He was looking at me, his face exposed, the face of an angel, as handsome as his caresses were gentle. I had tried so hard to see his features, all those nights, and all those days. But at that moment, the driver gave up trying to kill me. He had regained his self-control and relaxed the grip of his fingers on my throat. He opened the door of his truck and this time managed to push me out, back into life.

THE SPRINKLER SPRINKLED

Maïna Lecherbonnier

My profession as a psychotherapist sometimes leads me to play a role in my psychological research and in studies with certain characters or patients. I know for sure that my looks and curves often attract lustful eyes and sometimes trigger unusual adventures in which, without my realizing it, I end up being the "victim." Here is my diary entry from December 12, 2003.

Christopher is a photographer who has always admired me and shown me respectful adulation. I don't know him very well; he cannot be part of my circle with his slightly bohemian, rough-shaven look, jeans and leather jacket. He's not really compatible with my friends or my social position, although he is a rather handsome man, tall, fortyish, green eyes, his hair in a ponytail. He looks a bit like Jeff Bridges. I met him at a photography exhibition in 1999. I had noticed his rather original work on female nudity. He often pays compliments to my looks and considers me his Egeria, while I like to show him my total lack of interest, a slightly haughty and disdainful indifference. Secretly infatuated with me, he has often offered his emphatic help:

"If you ever have a problem, you can count on me, I'll come right away."

I live on the Boulevard Malesherbes in Paris, and I often spend my weekends at my parents' house near Fontainebleau. It was the beginning of winter and, on that Friday, I had to have an echography in a clinic in Fontainebleau. My car broke down! It was impossible to postpone the appointment, which had been arranged two months earlier; and there was no time to rent a car. After calling a few acquaintances, all "unavailable," I remembered the photographer's proposition. He accepted with enthusiasm.

He was crafty; he took advantage of my trouble to suggest the possibility of taking a few pictures of me in the forest. I thought, why not, I can do him that favor, he's been waiting long enough! He helps me out, and I have the whole day free after the echography. It was a sunny day, blue sky, cold, dry weather.

Leaving the clinic, he proposed to have lunch at an inn on the edge of the forest. I have to admit that we drank quite a bit, which made me somewhat merry. We played guessing games. It had been a long time since I'd laughed so much. Those games were a pretext for rather mischievous penalties! For the first one, I had to remove my panties under the table in the middle of the lunch. Luckily we were the last customers . . . For the second, I had to agree, after lunch, to pose in the forest partly undressed.

A pressing urge was beginning to take hold of me! At the clinic, I'd had to drink two liters of water for the echography. I'd tried to go to the toilets at the inn, but unfortunately part of the restaurant was being renovated, including the toilets. I thought of relieving myself outside!

Because of my pressing need, he insisted on taking pictures of me urinating! Shocked, I replied with a categorical *no*, sending him packing with, "Are you mad? You need to see a psychiatrist!"

Disconcerted by his proposition, I'd instinctively pulled away from him. I was walking fast when suddenly I heard a dull thud, followed by swearing. He had stumbled on a root and fallen flat on his face. I burst out laughing. Christopher read my stupid laughter as an acceptance of his request. Taking into account my swollen bladder and his presence, I didn't have much choice. To save face I gave one condition: "That you take only one shot, and that my face is not visible." Happy as a child, he accepted!

We were two hundred meters from the forest. That distance seemed too great. I started running and felt my bladder ready to burst. I was afraid of urinating while running and soiling my stockings. The photographer indicated a wooded area, where he perched me on a small rocky mound before placing himself in front of me, down a little, on a lower level, for his shots. I was wearing a dark brown, loose-fitting dress in thick cashmere, which reached my calves, with woolen stockings that went up to the groin, attached to coarse suspenders that I had shortened to their minimum on a 1950s corset. My grandmother had given it to me, specifying: "If you want to lose five kilos on your waist, wear that!" It was the first time I had worn the light brown Weston boots given to me by my parents for Christmas. In order to avoid splashing them while urinating, I had to crouch and open my thighs to the limit while at the same time spreading my feet. Before relieving myself, I cast a quick look around the place, worried about hikers. I was itching to let go. I was trying my best to contract my perineum. The urge was too strong and the urine started to seep over the top of my stockings. I cursed Christopher, who was already shooting. He must have noticed the ring on my stockings and taken advantage of my handicap. He was on his starting blocks, his eye glued to the viewfinder. He was hoping to see me produce water like a fountain. That pee stop seemed to act like a powerful aphrodisiac on him!

The wine I'd drunk at lunchtime had put me in a state of euphoria and excitement! Once I crouched down, everything sped up in my head. I no longer distinguished between the limits of my upbringing and that indecent exhibition before him, where excitement was predominant. I thought: "It's a game, we're in a discreet, isolated place, and it's nothing but a little moment of madness!" But Christopher's lens pointed at me and his eyes, popping out of his head with lust, paralyzed my bladder! Embarrassed, I didn't dare look at him! Suddenly I felt dignified again, I wanted to get up to hide behind a tree and urinate in peace. But my urge was becoming unbearable! I thought, if I get up, my bladder will burst with no warning and I'll soak myself without being able to control it. So I closed my eyes and emptied my head, and all the muscles of my pelvis relaxed immediately. I was so ashamed that I lowered my head between my legs. I heard the photographer coughing to stifle the noise. Apparently he was as embarrassed as I was! Then we both started to laugh uncontrollably! Making the most of that moment of relaxation, he came closer, nearly between my legs, and asked me to prop myself up with my hands behind and to open my thighs at an angle of almost 180 degrees. Still ashamed, I allowed myself to do it, I complied without thinking. In reality, he was trying to show my sex to advantage! I was offered like a sacrifice. I imagined the vision I offered that voyeur, where my open sex prevailed over my whole body. It was like inviting him to fuck me! That extreme exhibition aroused me terribly, in spite of the icy little wind nipping at my labia and penetrating my gaping cunt.

And the show started; I felt the warm liquid flow between my buttocks fast and furious, while the photographer frantically took as many shots as he could. Bowing my head I could contemplate my gush rising vertically like a fountain of youth. My eyes stopped at Christopher's fly, where I spotted a protuberant shape. That bastard had an erection. His very tight jeans showed the thickness of his penis to advantage! That cheeky complicity started to have an effect on me and, delirious, I let myself go completely. I was undulating my pelvis, trying for a performance. I saw my stream reach a distance whose length I underestimated. It extended to such a degree that I was pissing on the jeans and shoes of the photographer. Surprised, he stepped back.

The show was at its height for both of us! Emotion changed the rhythm of my breathing, my heart was beating irregularly, I was panting, letting out little cries of pleasure in spite of myself. I was getting unusual pleasure by exhibiting my intimate parts to a guy I barely knew!

Because of my behavior, I allowed him an open door, like an invitation to take me. His attitude had changed, too, his movements had become hesitant, as if he was no longer in control of the situation! Suddenly he stood up in front of me, his legs apart, his eye still glued to the viewfinder, his right hand holding his camera and the other playing shamelessly with the bulge in his trousers. He plunged his hand into his pocket to adjust his painfully constricted penis! Removing his hand, he succeeded in extracting from his pocket the head of his penis capped with the lining of his trousers! Was he trying to impress me, or only to ease his member? Whatever, the head of that cock emerging from his pocket proved he was hung like a donkey!

The atmosphere had got the better of my taboos and my modesty! In my head images aroused me, and I imagined his big arrogant cock erect like an Easter candle, the glans freed of the foreskin, with his heavy balls hanging like ripe figs! Was I becoming an exhibitionist? My eyes were constantly switching from his penis to my stream! Was I hoping he was going to lose his head? Was he going to unbutton his fly and take out his impressive device?

No! He kept shooting! Why so many pictures for a rather static pose? I realized later that he intended to make a montage, like a video clip, to make a better appreciation of that ceremony and the rainbow of my micturition!

My bladder wouldn't stop emptying, and with the cold a very visible steam was cast against the light. At times the sound of my fountain became intense, for it fell on a little puddle of frozen water contained in the rocks between my feet! That addition of urine formed a little pond that overflowed and rushed down to the photographer's feet. He was gesticulating so much that he was actually paddling in that mud! To my astonishment I was incapable of reacting when, without hesitating, he drew his left hand close to my stream and lifted it to his mouth to lick his fingers smeared with it. I couldn't help it, I shouted two words: "Dirty pig!" I must have aroused him by insulting him, for he repeated the offense, drank a mouthful of my urine as he smeared his face with it!

That was too much. My mind was no longer in control. I was now vulnerable, and completely dependent on the situation, unleashing desires throughout my whole body!

Christopher's triumphant and arrogant look betrayed his satisfaction. He was standing in front of me, imperial. He was gloating, contemplating me like a submissive in that filth! How could I have fallen so low? Why had I agreed to this stupid game? I was caught in my own trap! Another anxiety took hold of me! With what was I going to clean and wipe myself? He was making no move and didn't anticipate anything to help me! He could have gone back to the car to get water and tissues!

He was drinking in that humiliating situation right down to the last dregs! Having left my bag in his car, I didn't want to beg him for help, so I decided to sacrifice my white silk Hermès scarf to wipe myself.

Back at his car, I sat behind him and pulled on my big sunglasses in order to hide.

I didn't say one word, despite his flatteries. He confessed that he had experienced an unforgettable moment, he thanked me for the special instant I had given him; he said that his admiration and devotion would remain intact. I half-believed him. I was thinking and trying to get rid of my guilt! On further consideration, I had an inkling of a psychological benefit. He had acted on his fantasy and, as a result,

I had discovered a real sexual pleasure in exhibitionism. And that still stimulated me in the car, especially when we drove out of the forest to go down a little shady and chaotic road with big cobblestones which hammered at my pelvis, arousing my clitoris. Exhausted and frustrated, I felt like a bitch in heat. I would have liked to have finished with a cock, to calm myself down! After all we hardly knew each other and I didn't think I would ever see him again!

Once we reached my place, I left his car without looking at him or responding to his "good-bye." I undressed quickly and threw myself under the shower to be rid of that abandon! After that I wrapped my body in a warm bathrobe. I was recuperating morally, despite the flashbacks, which haunted me! I put on a CD, Chopin, and stretched out on my bed to relax.

Appeased by the music, I sank between waking and sleeping. Distraught by my experience, I felt a need to rejoice. My erogenous zones were prey to an unsatisfied yearning. A violent desire to caress myself took hold of my mind.

Without my realizing it, my right hand stroked my breasts and my belly down to the pubis. Reaching the perineum, I felt, with the tips of my fingers, a sticky liquid flowing from my sex. I suddenly remembered the dildo I had hidden under my bed. An impotent lover had offered it to me so that we could have fun together.

To the naked eye, the aspect was quite striking—it looked like a real cock! As for the feel, the texture conveyed a realistic sensation, thanks to its shape and all the details of the veins! It was made of elastomer. The instructions, in English, specified the dimension (twenty-four centimeters) and that the mold had been made from a real penis. I went into the bathroom to get a tube of lubricant.

Having found the dildo, I felt like sucking it. I tried to put it in my mouth but I almost dislocated my jaw. And I have a big mouth! Now I felt like having the dildo in my vagina. Lying on my back with my legs lifted, to make penetration easier, I placed my feet on the wall behind my head so as to increase the visual pleasure on both sides. In front of me, slightly to the side, was my pivot mirror, reflecting my image, increasing my pleasure even more. As if on a dare, I took the dildo with both hands and made it enter my body. I forced the penetration despite the vaginal resistance. And despite my arousal, my sex wide open and naturally lubricated, the enormous head of the dildo penetrated with difficulty, millimeter by millimeter. Barely four centimeters in, the pain made me lose patience! I decided to remove it for a fresh attempt, to introduce it better! I dipped my finger in the Vaseline pot and smeared the dildo from top to bottom. My thumb and index finger barely circled it at two-thirds of its length, so thick it was, specifically at the end where the testicles would be (imagine the diameter of a can!). I had another go at penetration, hoping this time to introduce it entirely! The ceremony lasted quite a while before I saw that powerful dildo disappear within me, up to the hilt! In that acrobatic position I remained for a while in ecstasy at the sight of the performance. I contemplated my ass at work in the mirror. I was captivated to see my sex so dilated and plugged up this way! I thought I was a work of art! I thought, how could I have swallowed that monster! I experienced the incredible impact of that foreign presence inside me! I gently withdrew it from its nest and the easing eclipsed all that painful constraint. The dildo fitted my cunt like a sheath made to measure! The dance of the coming and going no longer offered resistance and, as I pleased, I increased the rhythm with small jolts and quiet moments followed by frantic jerking! I enjoyed myself withdrawing it completely, then plunging it in deep, brutally, to the limits of my vagina. I heard the sloshings of the wetness, I flowed with arousal. Metamorphosed by everything I had experienced that afternoon, I had to release myself with an orgasm!

I rejoiced; my breathing became uncontrollable. I moaned my pleasure, unleashing a colossal orgasm followed by an explosion of screams whose echo penetrated every floor of the building. But that day was simply destined to frustrate me, for my pleasure was spoiled by my next-door neighbor thumping with her fist at my door.

(Thanks to Christina Peter for her editorial help.)

In Memory of a Cock

Sandrine Le Coustumer

Can one love a man for his cock?

I think I loved him for his cock. I knew it straightaway. Afterward, I looked for other reasons, as if that reason was too obscene to even be conceivable. Still later, when our story had ended, I found that essential reason, the pure and true reason of my love for him. His cock.

I don't know, in reality, what attracted me to him when we first met. The face of a weak man, with flabby outlines. A body too bulky for his age. He was spineless, in an almost repulsive way. But there was a call in his eyes.

He was not even ugly—there is an ugliness as fascinating as beauty—no, he had even been a very attractive young man, but gradually his face and his body had been permeated with his true nature. And the work of the personality was still shaping his whole person, acting like a developer, in the photographic sense.

I remember experiencing a second of panic when I came to terms with the evidence of my desire for him. "I don't know what is happening to me, I'm attracted and I don't understand why . . ." was the admission I barely dared to formulate. Fat has always inspired me with a quasi-obsessive disgust. Whether it had to do with food or the human form, I almost systematically applied a kind of aesthetics of thinness. I liked bony bodies, emaciated faces. So my irresistible attraction to that overly heavy body, that flesh in which the fingers probably sank, seemed incomprehensible and, to be honest, frightening!

I liked the way he looked at me. I was intrigued by the wary confidence he put into it. What I must have perceived, beyond the disgusting aspect, was there, concentrated in his eyes. It was a way of telling me, "I have something you're going to like . . ." And if it's true that our faces bear the stigmata of who we are, his beautiful cock was there, filling his eyes, mouth, cheeks, forehead, and chin . . . as if already he was only that alone for me: a cock.

On the first night, I didn't notice it. He was too busy concealing his body. His hesitations were in fact indicative of a lack of confidence in his capacity to seduce. I led him to my bed. It took him an eternity to kiss me. I think he was scared. Scared to be rebuffed? Or perhaps aware that what he was about to unveil could disgust me? I had to finally place my lips on his to give him the signal. And, even at that moment, he was not entirely sure he was authorized to go any further. I was so impatient I ended up getting undressed myself. It was still a long while before he joined me under the sheets, and then he turned off the light.

He wanted to see my face as we made love. The flame of his lighter briefly lit our bodies. I saw his enormous belly—at least it appeared enormous to me—on top of me and I had the anachronistic feeling that I was grappling with a Buddha. That body so overlapped mine that it could entirely cover me, crush me, smother me. I had the strange feeling that something was happening outside of me, that it was an act in which I didn't really take part, whose surprised spectator I was at the same time that I was filled with disgust.

Next morning he repeated, endlessly, "Why me?" with a voice that suggested the gratitude of those who have been given something they were not entitled to. As if I had done him a favor. I've always felt a certain contempt for men who, after the first night of love, are full of gratitude toward the woman who has *given* herself to them. Can't they imagine that it's not a gift at all, but an act lived like a communion? If the woman gives in, it's to her desire, and not to their—so often obvious—little manipulations.

I didn't think it necessary to respond to that anxiety, but I attributed to it the bad performance of that incongruous lover. I decided to give him another chance to show that he deserved the honor I was supposed to have given him.

The second night, I discovered what I had not been allowed to scrutinize the night before.

Though his body, in its entirety, was flabby, and his skin dull, at the bottom of a belly formed of several folds was the most beautiful cock I had ever seen in my whole life. It was not so much its length or its width that made it remarkable, as the impression of harmony and strength the appendage gave off. It seemed to exist for itself, claiming its independence from the body to which, however, it belonged.

The dark brown skin bore a scar, like a little seam at the base of the glans, a few centimeters long, the reminder of a surgical procedure that had made it a circumcised cock. Its texture was extremely soft, silky, velvety.

Immediately I felt like taking it in my mouth. To feel it swelling and vibrating and quivering was extraordinary. I felt like keeping it like that in the warm moistness, indefinitely, without moving, for the sole pleasure of thinking it was mine. That night, the cock, and above all its owner, behaved, if not more elegantly, at least with more restraint.

In the following months, I grew more familiar with my lover's cock. I was slowly taking possession of it. My first impression was confirmed: it was a brisk cock—sometimes a bit too brisk—almost always hard when offered to my eyes, reacting promptly to all sorts of solicitations, displaying pride, even self-respect—the absolute opposite of the man with whom it shared its existences. It looked like it had been unfortunately grafted onto an inadequate body.

He himself seemed embarrassed by the cock, whose demands he could not always satisfy. Did he at least have some control over it?

I realized the love affair was a mistake, but I couldn't give it up. He was a coward, he was stingy, he was an opportunist. He was never really clean, and he lived under the influence of an abusive mother— quickly nicknamed the ogress—who made sure he remained a little boy. Did she know that if she had given him permission, her son, the possessor of an exceptional organ, could have become a great lover? If she had known, she would have done her best to prevent it.

It was an interesting case of castration—a kind of crime. She had succeeded in weakening the virility of a man endowed with a prodigious member, a quality of authority inadmissible in her son. If she had wished to put a spell on that cock, she couldn't have done it any differently.

My sense of smell was never fooled. Just by smelling him I could tell whether he had washed. That mixture of perspiration and various secretions had a disastrous effect on my desire. I knew how to convince him to rectify his negligence.

"If you don't wash, I'm not sucking you."

It was a sure way to force him to scour the nooks and crannies, all the orifices that he tended to forget during his macerations in filthy bathwater. I noticed that flabby bodies like to bask in the cloudy water of their own dirtiness. Is it to feel lighter that they surrender to that hygienic aberration? Is it a chance to forget the gravity to which they are doomed?

Even thoroughly washed, the cock still had a slight smell, a sickening perfume that intoxicated me as soon as it approached my face.

One day, when he had managed to drag me to his country house, I masturbated him in his bath. With his body relaxed in the hot water, almost entirely covered in foam, I had the illusion I was alone with his cock. I was holding it as one holds a living being ready to escape. I saw it alone, paid attention to only its reactions. It was the cock that was moaning, sighing at the rhythm of the movement I was imposing on it. And when it surrendered to that interminable caress, I thought it was going to detach itself from its unworthy body.

During the night, I happened to lift the sheet and, in that moment of secret intimacy, I devoured it with my eyes. It always lay across the right thigh, offered. I used to touch it furtively, afraid to wake him up. It quivered and barely swelled. He was a heavy sleeper, as was his body. It seemed that he didn't feel anything of those stolen touches. It was a kind of parallel relationship. Some people lead a double life with a lover or a mistress; I was having an affair with his cock. I think I endured the man and his body to be able to take full delight in his cock.

During a trip to the Greek Islands he found a rock. Of an ideal shape and polish, it was the exact replica of his cock. The object had the length and thickness reached at certain moments, moments that tended to become rarer. Had my repeated complaints prompted him to look for that stone? That natural dildo had the delicate color of a stone; it was a unique and original piece that delighted me. The same evening we experimented with it. Using such an accessory is not so simple. It is only through various trials that one succeeds in adapting it to the female anatomy. The main problem encountered was the problem of temperature. We hadn't thought the stone would retain so much of the heat of the water we used to make it wet. Penetration had to happen very slowly; in fact, it was more about the vagina opening itself to allow the object to take its place inside. The density of the stone gave to that coitus an unprecedented roughness. The pleasure mostly came from the situation: the man using an accessory supplementary to the symbol of virile force itself, the care he took in his manipulation, and his eyes following the progression of my emotions. The rock was always hard! By what erotic transmutation did it give the cock its stiffness and vigor? It was as if it wanted to measure up to its mineral double. It knew then to show an unusual inspiration and stamina.

The cock also provided a substance whose taste was unique,

though changing. Coffee, for example, gave it a bitterness making it almost unfit for human consumption. But usually it had the salted flavor of an inexhaustible sea.

"Sometimes I have the taste of your sperm in my mouth!"

Today I realize how that cry of love unleashed one night in a street in Paris was addressed to the object of my adoration, and not to the man.

"It's nice to feel a cock, even soft, against one's buttocks when one falls asleep." Those few words, heard at nineteen in Jean Eustache's film *The Mother and theWhore*, have echoed inside me for years. They've returned regularly to my mind like an enigma to be solved. And now those words, uttered by the sad and flat voice of Françoise Lebrun, took shape in my story. The cock instinctively flattened itself against my buttocks, or embedded itself in their crack. Even in deepest sleep it didn't allow itself to rest, it kept a stiffness I never knew in any other cock, as if it were already ready to penetrate one or another of my orifices. My ass and my pussy were made for that cock. Alas, neither my spirit nor my soul were compatible with that man.

In that floating period that precedes every breakup, the time for love placed in parenthesis, when we play for the last time at pretending it is still possible, I had a very instructive dream. As with all of my dreams, this one was full of complex developments. But its outcome seemed to provide the key to a relationship that had lasted far too long.

I was having sex with my lover when strangers suddenly appeared, warrior types from another era, armed with spears, and in a display of mute violence, one of them cut off the cock planted inside me. They removed the body of the man I no longer loved and left me alone and appeased. Far from inspiring me with horror, as it should have, that act satisfied me perfectly. When I awoke, I realized it was all I would keep of him, his cock.

LIES

Geraldine Zwang

It was past four in the morning when I opened the door to my flat, hesitant as a thief. I felt dirty, exhausted by what I had just been through. In the hall mirror I quickly noticed the darkness surrounding my eyes, as well as a look of exaltation I had never glimpsed before. In the penumbra of the hallway, the mirror was showing me the very image of a loose woman, so far from the conservative and restrained bourgeois fifty-year-old image I tried to adhere to.

I was silently making my way to the bathroom when I heard my husband's voice from the corridor.

"Do you know what time it is?"

Unwittingly, he was saying the exact same words my father would throw at me whenever, as a teenager, I returned from parties at my friends'. A wave of fear coursed through me, a fear that quickly turned into anger. Anger at the proprietary male, the accountant in our couple. I'm anything but a submissive woman, far from it, but there has always been a part of me that makes all women of my age her husband's woman.

As a soothing April dawn neared, I knew I no longer wanted this relationship and that from now on I would lead a new life according to my own will.

Lies

"I've just been fucked," I said, enunciating the words carefully, with an assurance that surprised me.

Sometimes silences can feel endless, but this one lasted an eternity.

"Is that your idea of a joke?" my husband asked disbelievingly.

I knew for a fact that his voice was not that of someone who had just woken up. He had been waiting for me. I wasn't surprised when he appeared at the door fully dressed. His eyes alternated between wrath, incredulity, and consternation. The ironic tone of his earlier question disappeared as soon as he looked at my face. I really did look like a woman who had been fucked. Eyes tired but grateful, lips ever so swollen by kisses and bites, and an overindulged body that had lost its remoteness.

The "where have you been?" triggered an avalanche of questions: Who had I been with? What had I done?

The more he spoke, the more he was overtaken by fear. Without even answering him I was already assuming a dominant position, watching him shrink with every passing moment. I was no longer afraid and could observe this man who was my husband with detachment, even with curiosity. How could I have been physically content with this man for so many years? I was now resentful for all the cold years when physical desire had faded to just a memory. So, in a spirit of vengeance, but also to test him, I decided to tell him everything, with nothing left out. I beckoned him into the living room and ordered him to sit, facing me, behind his desk.

I confessed that I had had an adventure with two men I had met at an art gallery opening.

My husband's face froze, and I was unable to read any of his feelings right then. It was as if he was discovering a new woman he had never truly known. All of a sudden, all his certainties were falling apart. His voice muted, he continued his interrogation.

"But what actually happened, you didn't go with them together, surely?"

"I did, one in my cunt and the other in . . . my mouth, then . . . in my ass."

My honesty and poise affected him even more than it would have if he had witnessed the act. I saw him tighten his fists but, visibly excited, he still wanted to know more. I knew from that very moment that power had shifted from him to me.

"Did you know when you followed them, what they were expecting?" he stuttered.

"Of course. Each one as they rubbed against me whispered into my ear what they would do to me. I was both embarrassed and flattered by their lust."

"What did they say?"

"The first man was just about thirty years old. He was short but well-proportioned. He hadn't said a single word before he moved against me. I could clearly feel the tip of his cock against my leg. I'd noticed him a few times already moving around the art gallery and had found him handsome. I don't know what came over me but I pressed hard against him to confirm I could feel his cock and didn't mind him rubbing against me."

"But what did he say to you?"

My husband couldn't contain his excitement.

"He said: 'I'd love to split your luscious middle-class ass open while you're sucking my friend off.' His lips barely moved next to my ear, but the faint breath that came from him was already making me wet with desire. He rubbed himself against me even harder. 'Once you've expertly lubricated him, he'll slide underneath you to fuck you.' There was a smoothness and a lack of aggression to his vulgarity. Without even thinking, I asked him: 'Where is your friend? I'd like to feel his cock against me, too.' "

My husband's patience exploded.

"Sophie, how could you say something like that?"

"I wanted that man, so why not his friend, too, if he was pleasant enough? Why be a hypocrite and wait for another day to give myself to the other man?"

"It's disgusting."

"Why should it be disgusting to provide pleasure to two nice young men and get some in return? Do you consider it healthier to masturbate while watching your porn tapes?"

Once again I'd defeated him, and he would rather suffer and know more than order me to be silent. I continued:

"Jean-Marc introduced me to his friend Yvan. He was a very young man, not quite twenty. He was quite beautiful and his youthful features were fascinating. I could have been his mother. I was proud of the fact they desired me. I felt young and was entertained by the envious looks of the other women around us. Yvan moved toward me, his two arms outstretched as if he was about to lead me onto a dance floor.

" 'She looks really hot; we're going to have great fun. You warm her up a bit more and then come and join me at the bar,' Jean-Marc said.

"Yvan took me in his arms as if he had always known me. I didn't even try and avoid the hard bump of his cock as it brushed against me. I could feel he was hard. As much in defiance as in provocation, I swiveled shamelessly against his young cock. His voice was very soft, still tinged with echoes of childhood, but his erotic vocabulary was way beyond his age."

"So what was he telling you?" my husband interrupted me.

"Do you really think I should tell you? You're already so upset."

I could guess that my husband, sitting behind his desk, was touching himself, but I pretended to ignore the fact.

"Yes, Sophie, tell me everything."

"OK," I sighed, "but you asked for it. Both Yvan and Jean-Marc were whispering sheer filth in my ear, like, 'You'll chew on my balls to get me hard again after I've discharged into your clammy hole.' These salacious words, that they'd probably said to hundreds of women before, no doubt, were making me crazy. For the first time in my life, I felt like a slut and I kept on pressing my parts against his cock. Yvan said that if I continued he might even come right then and there, and as a precaution moved slightly away from me. We joined Jean-Marc at the buffet table.

"Once we had reached the table, he took my hand in his and positioned it against his cock and said quietly in my ear: 'Look how hard you've made me, it's full of come, all for you. We're going to feed you well, you pretty slut. You're going to love it.'

"His impudence was electrifying me and I daringly pushed the envelope.

" 'I'll have you spitting into all three of my holes, you pretty things. You'll throw up a white flag once my tongue gets working on you.'

"Yvan smiled in admiration and caressed my ass. I did not stand back when he moved one of his fingers into my asshole, pushing the cloth of my skirt into it. I groaned, still holding on for dear life to Jean-Marc's cock, indifferent to all the people around us in the room who meant nothing to me any longer.

"Jean-Marc indicated it was time for us to go and we were soon in his car. Yvan sat me in the back. As soon as we drove off, he kissed me eagerly and took hold of my breasts in both his hands. My own hands took his cock out and I began steadily jerking it off while playing with his youthful balls. Jean-Marc loudly encouraged me.

" 'Milk that dong, you fat cow, suck his cunt juice out.'

"His driving was erratic, he was in a hurry for us to get back to his place. I could no longer hold back; I had already swallowed Yvan's cock to the hilt a few times while fingering myself. I felt like a young girl again, all excited, with her very first lover, my lust flying in all directions.

"In the elevator taking us up to Jean-Marc's flat, I caught a brief glimpse of myself in the mirror and I looked decidedly beautiful, young and flushed. They placed me roughly between them and took turns rubbing their cocks against me. I moaned wordless sounds, begging for them to take me. We got out of the elevator, the men pulling me out each with a finger stuck inside me.

"Once inside the apartment, I rushed at Yvan, whose cock was sticking out of his trousers. I crouched on all fours so that my ass was well exposed and sucked him with savage glee. Jean-Marc brutally pulled up my skirt and viciously pulled the elastic of my garter belt aside and let it slam back against my thighs; it wasn't that painful, but the sharp sound it made was exciting. I heard him undress behind me. I wanted him to take me with no warning, just to feel his hard sex penetrate me before I could even feel the approach of his body. Yvan pulled his cock out of my mouth, about to come. He left the room, leaving me there on all fours. Jean-Marc forbade me to look back and ordered me to 'polish your cunt to warm yourself up'."

Having reached this part of the story, Sophie was increasingly overcome by excitement; she couldn't help rubbing her legs against each other in search of further pleasure. She was living the evening all over again and had banished me from her world. I had already come in my trousers. Feverishly awakened by my ejaculation and my wife's violent story, my own cock refused to lie down as I listened to her with fascination.

"He handed me a bottle of rosé wine, a long and cold bottle, and I was summoned to fuck myself with it. The initial contact with the icy neck of the bottle saw my flesh contract and only served to increase my frenzy. Yvan had come back and was encouraging me: 'Yes, fill that pretty pussy, cool it down for me.' I had only introduced a few centimeters of the bottle into me when Jean-Marc sharply pushed it in even deeper. I felt as if I had been split open, gaping in a way I had never been before. I screamed with pleasure, with shame and joy blending exquisitely in my mind and body. I felt Jean-Marc spitting against my asshole and spreading his saliva across the pucker of my hole. I was scared; I hadn't had much anal sex. He entered me with one single push forward, despite the bottle still filling my vagina. I was in heaven; my body had come to life thanks to the cock now plowing my innards. Yvan was masturbating himself in front of me and I held my head high to eat him, milk him. All I could see was that dark column of flesh that I couldn't reach, and I begged him to let me have it. He found it amusing to tease me, to move his cock to the tip of my lips before withdrawing it again out of reach. I was going crazy and was impaling myself farther down on the bottle, spreading myself open even more. With a thrust of his cock, Jean-Marc pushed me toward Yvan's member. Yvan had now sat himself down in front of me. He pulled the bottle out delicately and positioned me onto his friend's cock. They must have done this before, as the maneuver was rapid and expertly done. I came at the very moment that Yvan's glans pushed its way past my outer lips and again when he reached the pit of my cunt. Each thrust from the two men inside me had me screaming. As I felt Jean-Marc's sperm flooding my ass, I shouted to Ivan: 'Come in my cunt, come, come . . .'

"And he did.

"The three of us collapsed in a pile and it took some time for our energy to return.

"I needed to pee and asked where the toilet was. The two men accompanied me and asked me to pee in the bathtub with them present. Like a madwoman, I did so. Initially embarrassed, I soon let myself go and spread my thighs wide so that they might enjoy the view. Once I had finished urinating, their cocks had become hard again and I felt like sucking them. First I sucked Yvan off while Jean-Marc caressed my breasts.

" 'Now I feel like peeing,' said Yvan, 'but I'd like to pee on your pretty whorish face.'

"He had barely said the words when a warm and bitter jet invaded my mouth. I gagged but nonetheless continued to guide the stream of pee toward my face as if I were taking a shower. I had never felt so wet, inside and outside, my slit was dripping and I managed to insert four fingers into my cunt while Yvan shook his last drops against my tongue and I swallowed them.

"Jean-Marc joined me inside the bathtub and mounted me doggie style. He parked himself deep inside my pussy and began peeing inside me. I roared as the hot liquid created a whole new feeling.

"Later, they both sodomized me slowly until each came deep inside my ass.

"The three of us took a shower together, still fondling each other wildly, and then they escorted me to a taxi rank.

"There you are, I've told you all."

As soon as I'd finished my story, my husband leaped on me, his cock harder than I'd seen it for a very long time. Without a word, he threw me onto the settee and forced my lips apart with his girth. His lust pleased me; my husband wanted me again. His erection was a gift for me and I sucked him off as if my very life depended on it, forcing him to spit out a torrent of come that I swallowed like a divine offering. He roared his pleasure.

I gazed at my man with love, as if I was discovering him anew:

"Oh, the sort of things you have me imagining, my love."

"Thank you, *mon amour*."

THE HORSEWOMAN

Brigitte Lahaie

The steam that rose from the stallion's body evaporated into the persistent mist of that autumn morning. The neck and back were soaked, but Everest, the dark horse with the lively gait, now walked with a quiet step, glad for that moment of union with its beloved rider. There was a special complicity between them. The horse, which had a reputation for being highly strung, had accepted that uncompromising woman immediately, as if they had recognized each other the very first time they measured their strength against one another. If it can be said that horses are man's best conquest, in reality, it is women who have the most success in taming the wildest horses. That, anyway, was what Claude enjoyed saying at the business dinner parties she was obliged to attend.

On that morning Claude was up very early, for she had a busy day lined up. The rider hadn't spared her mount, just like each time she'd had a conflict with the male of the species. In a way Everest allowed her to wash herself, body and soul. Her hips melted into the saddle to accompany the back movements of the brown bay. In those moments of wild galloping, she no longer knew who guided whom, whether it was animal or woman who determined the gait. Such strength emerged from the horse that she felt carried away, lifted straight off the earth. Her eyes closed, and deep inside her belly, she started to feel tinglings announcing sexual delights. Sometimes, when she really succeeded in letting herself be carried, when her loins didn't present any resistance and, on the contrary, adopted the flowing movement of the animal perfectly, she reached ecstasy. An ecstasy that didn't have anything in common with that experienced in a lover's arms, an ecstasy at the same time more intense and gentler, longer, an ecstasy that took hold of her body, starting at the level of her perineum and climbing up her backbone, radiating as far as her brain before slowly fading away. The young woman would have found it difficult to say if the starting point was located inside her body, or if her pleasure took its source externally, but anyway, the sensual delight took hold of her in successive waves and always left her appeased. For a few moments, even minutes, Claude felt inhabited by a new strength. Was she still part of the human race? She was an integral part of Everest, so close to the chirping birds early in the morning, so close to the surrounding nature and, above all, so far away from Paris, its aggressive lights, noise, and pollution.

Only then, as if to reward the kind animal for that moment of eternity it had allowed her to reach, she gave it back its head and let it return to the stable at the pace of its choosing. Most of the time Everest turned its head toward its rider, looking for a treat. He looked at her with his bright eyes and seemed to understand their complicity. Today the stallion walked at a good pace and the young woman gently regained the reins. It snorted, it was virtually trotting on the spot.

"There, boy, don't be in such a hurry to go back."

The soft and reassuring voice of its friend had an immediate effect. The brown bay slowed its step and shook its ebony neck. As if in mimicry, Claude shook her own long black hair. The pair returned to the horse riding club, where several horses were already working out in the sandy arena. Having a bit more time at her disposal, like some other early-rising owners, she took the opportunity to work with her horse. A chestnut mare that was jumping a combination with exceptional ease attracted her attention. The animal had style, its forelegs folded with swiftness and its back rocked with suppleness. As for the rider, he followed the jumps with grace and ease in spite of the relative height of the obstacles. Claude was intrigued, all the more so for she didn't recognize either the mount or the man on its back but, in order to conceal her growing interest, she decided to remain in a far corner of the arena. The horsewoman set Everest at a gathered gallop, the stallion willingly consenting to her demands. A final jump on a particularly demanding combination put an end to the work session and the young man dropped the reins and patted his mare's neck before moving along the track in a relaxed manner.

Claude took Everest back to his stall, but her curiosity was aroused, and she promised herself to inquire about the identity of that new pair, who seemed close to her instructor. Her passion for horses went back to her childhood. She undoubtedly took after her grandfather, who lived in the countryside with his shire horses. Her parents were not overly enthusiastic about her taking up a sport they considered dangerous. They would have preferred for her to play tennis or golf, sports which, all things considered, were much better suited to middle-class children. Fortunately, a rather serious fall had forced their daughter to abandon competition show jumping. These days, she divided her time between working in her father's business and escapades on the back of the stallion she'd bought on a whim. It probably reminded her of earlier dreams—when she had seen, like many children her age, the film *Black Beauty*.

Every time she observed the riders jumping obstacles she felt a pang. Yet the few months she'd spent lying still on a board hadn't filled her with the desire to take up jumping again. Now Claude was scared, even if she was too proud to acknowledge it. Everest, too, was afraid of the bars, and that's why she had wanted to buy him from his blundering owner, who hadn't been capable of slowly teaching him the rudiments of the discipline. The brown bay had enormous potential, but that accident, in its fourth year, had made it reticent. From time to time horse and rider took pleasure in stepping over a tree trunk lying in the middle of a path. It was a true feat for both of them, bringing them even closer.

Claude took care of her friend, rubbing him down with straw. He nestled his head in the young woman's chest, half knocking her down. She burst out laughing, then hung on his neck, breathing in his wild and musty smell. Her face was beaming; she closed her eyes for a moment, the better to enjoy that instant, but the stallion gave a jump and neighed. Claude let him go and, opening her eyes, met those of the rider, still mounted on his small chestnut mare. She realized they had been there for a little while, watching them. The man was probably in his thirties, attractive despite incipient baldness. His green eyes sparkled with mischief. He smiled and, with a very strong Russian accent, said:

"Excuse me, but my mare finds your horse very much to her taste."

Claude appreciated the compliment, but the idea of being caught in a moment of intimacy with her companion upset her, too. She retorted, somewhat curtly:

"That's fine by me, but Everest doesn't like red bays."

"Pity for her, but I adore brunettes. Can I buy you a coffee before you leave for work?"

They agreed to meet at the clubhouse after attending to their horses.

Within a few days, Sacha and Claude had become friends and confidants. From equestrian meetings to social gatherings, they graduated to a relationship. For Sacha, their first sexual intercourse was dazzling. Never had a woman given him such a feeling of belonging. In his heart he felt so strong, but also so vulnerable. His life changed dramatically that night, taking on a different direction. Suddenly his past objectives seemed laughable. His existence gently took on another flavor. The young woman, however, kept her distance. His muscular male body, the symbol of an all-powerful virility, gave her the kind of voluptuous orgasms she'd never thought any man capable of offering her, even though she knew it was out of the question to place her destiny in the hands of her lover.

The young Slav could spend hours massaging the body of his mistress, caressing parts of her body so far from her sexual organs that she felt a frustration rise deep inside her belly, clamoring for him avidly. He left her wanting it, sadistically enjoying his concentration on her neck, loins, the hollow of her elbow. Thus, when their sexual organs finally united, intercourse always seemed too brief for Claude, who suddenly sensed danger, so dependent was she on that pleasure.

Sacha was not particularly possessive, and his frequent travels left Claude with much freedom. She seized the opportunity to see Everest and enjoy their voluptuous complicity. But she could not always reach her former ecstasy now. Sometimes, at the crucial moment, the face of her lover appeared to her. At first she was deeply annoyed by that, but gradually, she began to savor those moments when they were three. So when she was in her lover's arms, she now dared to tell him of her escapades with her stallion. He smiled, seemed to understand her, and loved her even more for it. For him, too, horses had for a long time compensated for his lack of love. They had undoubtedly helped him not to lose his mind when he lost his mother at ten.

Then, one beautiful spring morning, Claude sent Everest into a full gallop, but nothing happened in her body. It refused to give itself to the horse, as if it was keeping itself definitively for her lover. That day she realized she was a woman in love. The stallion must have felt it was no longer her favorite, for it became slightly more capricious. It even turned slightly aggressive when Claude was grooming it in its stall. Her instructor, to whom she had disclosed the slightly threatening attitude of her companion, suggested that perhaps it needed to be castrated. Claude rejected that notion immediately, feeling the mutilation within her own body. That same evening, Sacha remarked that she had been taking much less care of Everest lately. How many mornings had she preferred to stay in bed to recuperate after their torrid nights, leaving her lover to go alone at dawn to take care of his mare? The competition season was approaching; it was necessary to prepare Ines, to get her ready for competition, and, of course, Everest wasn't going to compete. However, the few minutes spent letting off steam in the training area couldn't replace hours of complicity with its rider. The young man dared to ask his girlfriend if he could mount the proud stallion. For the three years that Claude had owned him, nobody had ever had the right to climb on her horse. She liked to think that nobody else could tame the fickle brown bay. But Sacha's proposition seemed reasonable. After all, he was an excellent rider, and she had to acknowledge that Everest was getting bored.

The young woman accepted, but on one condition: she wanted to be present at the first session, to be sure that her companion accepted Sacha. He accepted his girlfriend's demands willingly, without daring to ask for which, man or horse, she was most worried!

The following Saturday morning they left together for the club. While Sacha was working Ines, Claude prepared Everest. She took particular care in grooming him, and the stallion felt that something unusual was happening. He was once again very affectionate, play-biting the sleeves of his rider's jacket, and she enjoyed their renewed complicity. Finally she took the stallion to the entrance of the arena and held it still until Sacha was mounted. The rider gave the horse its head straightaway. Everest was quivering, worried to discover some-one different on its back. But he slowly relaxed, increased the pace, and lowered his neck. As soon as Sacha realized the stallion had started to trust him, he broke into a trot, taking care not to pull hard on the bit. The stallion was quick to stretch its reins. It lifted its head and raised its stature. Claude was full of admiration. Everest showed all his power and grace, but also a certain lightness. Other riders watched the pair. Sacha ignored the various recommendations of his mistress and allowed himself to experience the sensations. The horse was ready to give itself, to offer its fabulous energy and generosity. The young man asked for a galloping start and spurred the animal to gather it a bit more. The neck rose, the haunches lowered. Everest was leaping, totally submissive to the orders of its new companion, happy to finally belong to someone who could draw the best out of it.

Sacha decided he had worked enough for the first session and moved toward Claude, slightly anxious about her reaction. She welcomed them with a smile, putting an end to all his anxieties. After copiously patting the horse, she kissed her lover warmly. Then she proposed:

"Why don't you try jumping a bit, since he seems to accept you so willingly?"

Sacha had never thought he would jump a few bars. The couple sometimes argued on that subject, for she thought he was asking too much of his mare, while he was trying to explain that horses adored jumping, on the condition that everything happened harmoniously. He forgot that Claude had the desire to see how far Everest would accept its new trainer. The horse hadn't jumped for three years, and the last session had been catastrophic for the rider who had been on its back that day, but Sacha was not worried; he had felt the power and goodwill of his new mount. He answered right away, trying to conceal his enthusiasm:

"All right, but if it goes well, you'll let me train him for the competition season."

That ultimatum, in other circumstances, would have shocked Claude, but she was definitely enamored of her lover and, if he succeeded in completely taming Everest, she would only have more pleasure to surrender, body and soul, during their moments of intimacy.

Sacha was ready to jump the first obstacle. Claude trembled, she could not have said if she was afraid for her lover or for her horse, but to see them like that, united, ready to accomplish what seemed to be a great feat, gave her a strange kind of pleasure.

The stallion was moving at a gathered gallop, the rider, with a discreet motion of the reins, lifted its nose. Everest pricked up his ears and, seeing the crossbar, accelerated slightly to jump the obstacle. He made an excessive jump, but it didn't impress the rider, who brought him around more calmly. Within three jumps, the horse was settled. Claude progressively raised the bar. Everest seemed to have a taste for that exercise, which had been fatal for its first owner. The young woman admired the ease with which the brown bay flew over the oxer fixed now at one meter fifty. She appreciated the riding qualities of her lover, who was one with the faithful charger. To finish off the session, Sacha jumped the other obstacles set out around the arena, one after the other. The horse yielded to the demands of its new master, just like its owner the same evening, who experienced intense sexual pleasure when Sasha finally devoted himself entirely to her.

Sessions with the obstacles occurred regularly. The horse proved to be particularly gifted, and Sacha started to talk about it as *his* horse, almost forgetting to allow any time for Claude to ride it. Everest was changing, he was getting stronger, more vigorous, more agreeable to mount, but also more demanding with the rider on his back. In a way he accepted the mistakes of its rider less. The horse that used to be so docile when Claude gave it its head became too brisk when she was no longer holding the reins.

One morning in April, a drama unfolded. The young woman wanted to ride Everest, despite the session Sacha imposed upon it. While he was riding his mare, she took the stallion out for a ride. The ground was still slightly hard, and conditions were not ideal for starting with a wild gallop on paths still marked by winter. But Claude wanted to be elated, and, above all, to take control again of the friend who had given her so many sensual delights in the past. The horse felt the slippery ground under its hooves and didn't really respond to its rider's impulsive demands. Everest held back, not through lack of generosity but more through survival instinct, perhaps to protect itself but also to protect she who had been its companion for so many years. However, Claude forced it to go even faster and, as the horse was holding back, she repeated her demand by aggressively giving its flanks the spur. Everest neighed, reared, then lifted its back and kicked its hind legs in a new form of violence, sending its poor partner onto a stump lying along the forest path. The horse, now free, rushed for the stable at a wild gallop, abandoning Claude on the ground, unconscious.

Claude recovered consciousness in the ambulance. Sacha was at her side, holding her hand. She met his eyes and read there all the anxiety of a man in love. She felt her body. A throbbing pain in her shoulder suggested a nasty break. Claude already knew she would have to spend weeks looking after her body, patiently waiting to regain her autonomy. For a moment, she hated Everest and his fiery spirit.

In the hospital, the surgeon diagnosed a broken shoulder. Two months of immobilization would be necessary before she could resume any sporting activity. Sacha proved to be a very present companion during those two months, attentive, adorable, as if the failing state of his mistress made him all the more in love. Claude accepted his invitation to stay at his house, but she didn't really feel ready to share her lover's life. For sometimes she judged him to be responsible for her accident.

In the meantime, Sasha rode Everest to make him even more docile, so that he would never again harm his beloved. He took pleasure in telling Claude of the horse's progress. Competition started, and Everest proved particularly successful. On the last Sunday, during the grand prix, a potential buyer introduced himself, interested in acquiring the proud stallion. Obviously neither Sacha nor, even less, Claude could think of parting company with a horse with such a promising future. The young woman should have been overjoyed. She had found a man worthy of her, in love, handsome, respectful of her personality.

And yet their nights of love seemed tedious. She was getting bored with her lover's caresses. Sometimes she finished herself off while dreaming about her proud stallion. She could picture herself galloping for hours in the forest, her body dripping with sexual pleasure.

The doctors finally gave her permission to ride again. Sacha was not particularly delighted with that news, for Everest was enrolled for the coming championships and the pair had every chance of winning, on the condition that the stallion remain focused. However, he realized that Claude counted more for him than all the medals in the world, and he refused to confide his fears to her. He even proposed to accompany her early the next day to give her a lesson in the arena. He firmly opposed the idea of letting her go alone into the forest.

It was on those conditions that the rider mounted her horse. She quickly overcame her apprehensions and experienced once again some agreeable sensations. The weather was good; a light wind caressed her face. She changed pace, and the horse trotted with ease. He began well, and responded perfectly to the least of her requests. Sacha encouraged her to become more demanding; he insisted she accept taking control of the reins. Suddenly Everest grew bigger, she felt the incredible strength of the beast, which had become much more powerful, more mechanical. Claude realized the horse was better trained, "better set" as the professionals say, but it didn't seem to communicate anymore; it seemed to have lost all initiative. It responded almost like a machine to the demands of the person on its back, and anybody could have obtained the same results. She didn't doubt the equestrian talents of her lover, but at that moment she hated him for having stolen Everest's soul. Using the pretext of pain in her shoulder, she climbed down. Sacha, only too happy to be given back his jumping horse, didn't notice the veil of sadness in the eyes of his mistress. Claude watched them moving around the arena. They really understood each other, and she felt excluded. She no longer existed for them. It was at that precise moment that she formulated a diabolical plan.

A few days later Sacha was rehearsing for the last time before the big day, making Everest jump a delicate combination. The horse still had the tendency to extricate itself from that type of difficulty. Claude was seated on the rail around the arena, right next to the triple that the pair was about to jump, when her cell phone rang. She had set up, a few hours earlier, a ringtone that imitated the cock's crow. Everest had just successfully jumped the first barrier. His ears were pricked up, directed at the second, a particularly important oxer, when it heard the shrill sound that reminded it of former traumas. The brown bay pulled up. Sacha, feeling his companion stiffen, thought it was worried about the width of the second element of the triple and, without hesitation, gave pressure with his legs to send the stallion toward the exit of the combination. The horse, though disturbed, had the heart to respond to its companion's demand, and tried to set off in spite of its fear. However, it had lost the impulse required to clear such an obstacle. The poor animal reared and gave a good kick with its legs to attain the top of the bars, but it was too late. The horse toppled, kicking its forelegs, which got entangled in the bars, its hind legs pedaling. He crashed into a forced landing, his head hitting the ground first. His neck broke. As he fell, the rider was thrown on the posts and his body was smashed.

Claude rushed toward her two loves, not knowing which one to help. Everest tried in vain to clamber up, but the worst was to be expected. Sacha was lying still, lifeless. He had not worn his riding hat and his head was bleeding profusely. Claude started to scream. She had to be taken away from her lover by force, away from that lifeless body that had given her so much pleasure.

For hours on end she whispered:

"I didn't want that."

The horse was put down. Sacha remained in a coma for many weeks, and he was never able to properly ride again. Nobody imagined that the horsewoman was responsible for the accident. Everybody had heard that in the past Everest had a tendency to become dangerous, so what was more natural than that the stallion had done it again! Claude alone knew that the horse had been broken in on a farm, and that the cock's crow still reminded it of the maltreatment it had endured in its early life. Claude kept her secret, ravaged with guilt. She looked after her lover like a true woman in love. Would they ever get married? Time alone would decide.

A Stroke of Luck

Françoise Rey

Daniel is stretched out on his bed. He's reading the paper and smoking a cigarette. He is careful, for his mother doesn't like him smoking in bed. The other day he made a hole in his pajama bottoms and burned his thigh with the glowing end. Not that he felt anything. From the waist down Daniel is totally insensitive, completely dead. Since his accident. A car accident. Daniel rarely traveled, except by car. Not by motorbike, his mother thought it was dangerous, nor on a bike: he was not fit enough. Mind, he was fit enough to practice archery. Soon he would be able to start practicing again, in his wheelchair. How lucky! said Dédé, who always hit the nail on the head. Yes, lucky. Daniel liked to go fishing, play chess, go to the movies . . . He didn't chase girls, couldn't dance, detested jogging, rarely went skiing, and spent hours in front of his computer. In the hospital where he was stitched back together, they never stopped rejoicing and encouraging him. Here was a life that could just carry on like that without too much reshuffling! That was not the case for the poor guy in room 111, a professional ice skater who had fractured his spine. Talk about a wrecked life! And that swimmer, what a drag, when she dived! Without even mentioning the rugby player in 128, or the bricklayer in 114! Imagine that, being a bricklayer, hey, and having to build your wall sitting down! Daniel's father seemed the most convinced of the venial aspect of his problem. A trifle, after all, to be deprived of those two legs! Daniel even began to wonder why he had never thought of being amputated earlier, it all seemed so simple, almost simpler than before! "Those wheelchairs are much improved now," his father said, adding: "It's lucky we live on one level." Lucky, indeed! "Don't worry about your work, I went there to measure the elevator and it's wide enough. The manager is very nice, he's ready to reorganize your office. And even to ask for adapted toilets." Great! Adapted toilets! Daniel hadn't explained to his parents what he had to learn to be able to enjoy that kind of convenience. Daniel is a decent guy . . .

He hadn't tried, either, to destroy their confidence when they declared: "Nobody said you can't get married! You know, there are perfectly nice girls who marry boys like you." (Four months after, and they still couldn't bring themselves to say the word *handicapped*.) "You have a good job and, thank God, your faculties are not impaired!" Thank God, thank you God, for having left my faculties intact, though my head is a bit messed up, inside, with lingering migraines, a massive anxiety I don't always talk about, and vertigo. They say it's normal, following several impacts: the accident, the operations . . . but, hey, the external envelope was untouched. That was true. A round and regular face, not bad at all, rather pleasant to look at in fact, but let's not exaggerate, blue eyes, black hair cut very short (it's finally growing back, it's been shaved several times for various scans), glasses, same as before, unbelievable, the double roll didn't even break them. So yes, perhaps one day, a nice girl would be interested in this rather gentle-looking quiet intellectual, with broad shoulders and long arms, a bit thin for the moment, but that will soon change with archery. In return, that damsel would do better to have no desire whatsoever for that thing under the belt, that's obvious. Daniel couldn't raise that with his parents: "But Mom, Dad, I no longer get hard-ons and I will never get one ever again. What girl, however nice and decent, would be tempted by that?" He had nodded several times, yes, yes, getting married, why not, he'd think about it . . .

At the hospital they had started "re-education." A big word, meaning in reality that someone moved Daniel's legs to maintain the flexibility of his joints, and a bit of his muscles . . . and, as everything was fine, he was allowed to go back home. "Hospital at home," his father had decreed jovially. "The physiotherapist will come every day. You'll be like a fat duck!"

He could not have said it any better. Daniel is like a fat duck. A capon, yes, in the congealed fat of forced immobility. He doesn't feel he has the right to complain too much. After all, it's true, he was no flamenco dancer, no marathon runner, but, nevertheless, sometimes he is fed up. Already. And his half-life is only starting. The physio comes at around eleven in the morning. A tall, strapping fellow, not very talkative, in tight jeans and T-shirt, beneath which one can make out each part of his body: the pectoral muscles, punctuated with tonic nipples, the biceps, triceps, backside . . . One can even spot much more intimate details. Daniel always looks at him when he comes in and thinks: "If he has a hard-on in there, either he crushes his prick or his fly will burst open."

Today, the physio is late. Daniel stubs out his cigarette, folds his paper, does a few rotations of the shoulders with his arms stretched horizontally. Ah, a car! A diesel, in fact. The physio has changed cars. The door opens. The physio himself has changed: it's a girl now. Ponytail, glasses, no makeup, a floppy sweater over pants, flat shoes: absolutely plain. Daniel has never been a womanizer, but he does appreciate beautiful women, and has sometimes vibrated with solitary fever when browsing in those special magazines where adorable goddesses exhibit their charms with no regard for drafts. Since returning from the hospital, he has found his magazines again, hidden under his mattress. But the spell has been broken, his imagination, too, is crippled! He is left with his eyes (intact, thank God, what luck!) to appreciate dispassionately the physique of those glamour models.

This lady, who moves toward his bed, has nothing smashing about her, that's quite certain. There's something wrong with her left eye, she has a cast. Her loose sweater makes big, graceless beige waves roll down to her buttocks. She says: "Hello! My name is Isabelle." She looks a bit better when she smiles, except she has a broken tooth in the front. Not much, a chip, but it looks untidy. And Daniel likes things to be tidy. And then "Isabelle," honestly! A romantic name, suggesting long blonde hair . . . hers needs a good wash. Daniel answers "Hello," like a well-brought-up boy, he even adds a certain cordiality to it. "What do we do?" asks Isabelle. What do you mean, what do we do? If she doesn't know, he's not going to teach her. She realizes he is puzzled. "Usually," she specifies. "My legs are moved around," he says. "Not by me, I cannot move them." "Ah!" she nods. She understands. She puts down her bag, comes close, grabs Daniel's pajama bottom. "I'll make you comfortable. Are you wearing underpants?" Luckily, I am, Daniel thinks. Without waiting for an answer, she quickly takes off his trousers. He's there with his bare legs offered to the stranger's gaze. She touches his tibia. "My hands are cold," she says. "I can't feel anything." "Ah!" Nevertheless, she rubs her hands vigorously, then grabs one of Daniel's legs at the ankle and carries out small back-and-forth motions, exactly like a rolling pin flattening out pastry. The amenable leg moves at the rhythm of that movement, the foot sweeps the space like a windshield wiper, left to right, right to left, the thigh follows, rolls on itself. "The other now!" says the young woman, placing her hand on the second ankle. "It's quite supple!" She then folds the knee, unfolds it, folds it again, conscientiously, at length, with the edge of her left hand in the popliteal hollow, and the right hand at work. She leans on Daniel's folded leg and works on the joint of the hip, thoroughly, in a circle. Daniel feels he's taking part in medical care that does not involve him. He has crossed his hands behind his neck, he's waiting for it to be over. He doesn't even look at the exercise of his lower limbs, that humiliating kneading he suffers without feeling it. The physio has folded the other leg; she works at making the joint of the other hip supple, with a full, smooth twirl. Suddenly Daniel's eyes wander to his blue underpants, and . . . "Oh!" His amazement draws this exclamation from him. The girl has followed his eyes. She sees the object of his surprise, the reason for his cry, that revolution under the cloth, that uprising, modest but nevertheless indubitable, those little moving jerks of an animal still asleep but that is, gently, coming back to life. Daniel is blushing heavily, his cheeks feel like they're on fire. He hesitates between dying of shame and yelling with joy. The physiotherapist is astonished at his emotion: "This has never happened before?" "Yes! Yes! Often! Before!" he stammers absurdly. "Yes, but since your accident?" "No, never, I was told it was finished. Forever. It's the first time." He rejoices visibly. "You know," she says in a very sensible voice, "it's not a miracle. More like chance, an uncontrollable connection, probably just fleeting. Not everything is explained in paraplegics. There are always little mysteries." He feels like slapping her.

Little mysteries! You bet! Now he has a real puppet show in his underpants! Look! He even forgets to be embarrassed! "Do you feel what I'm doing to you?" asks the nasty squinty-eyed jokester. "No! Nothing! Nothing at all." It is neither what she's doing to him, nor the idea he has of it. It is . . . incomprehensible, unexpected, rather comical. But he no longer feels like shouting victory since she has given him the cold shoulder. He just observes from afar, as if elsewhere, that part of him that dances and bows, while she, unruffled, carries on working.

She is gone. She said: "See you tomorrow!" He keeps his erection for another fifteen minutes. Afterward, he looks for the magazines under the mattress. Of course, in vain. He risks a shy and reluctant hand under his pajamas, finds a bit of limp meat, desperately dull, the same he lines up several times a day with his tube in order to piss . . .

He tries to create stories for himself under his tightly shut eyelids, thoughts about Cathy, their best moments . . . to no avail. Perhaps their best moments were not so good, after all, as he'd suggested at the time. He used to make love to her in the dark and come too quickly. She'd barely sigh. He thinks about her soft and tight pussy, she didn't get wet easily . . . puh! . . . even in his head he can't get an erection.

Isabelle is back. She works on his ankles, knees, hips. Daniel's underpants have started to jerk around again. It's as if she possesses, in her physio bag, the puppet strings, and she enjoys pulling them, casually. She looks like she's a bit mad. She obviously wonders if he's not pulling her leg. She asks to see his file. She reads it standing in front of the window. She says: "Talk about it with your doctor."

Daniel already had an appointment. He had insisted on the urgency of the situation when he phoned. The consultant had kept him all morning at the hospital. X-rays, tests, exercises. He made very eloquent sounds with his lips, little implosions that meant: "Nothing new under the sun." He said: "Listen . . ."

Daniel knew what he was about to explain. He had seen him twisting his mouth and raising his eyebrows.

"There is no physical reason," he started.

"And psychologically?" Daniel interrupted abruptly.

"Neither. You are not connected as far as the nerves are concerned. In principle, the current no longer flows. Switch on a lamp whose lead has been cut . . . it's the same thing."

"Yes, I know," said Daniel. "It's that girl, the way she handles me."

"Try with someone else," the doctor advised. "The same handling, by somebody else, and you'll see."

"I tried," said Daniel.

"And?"

"And nothing."

"But that girl, in your head?"

"Nothing."

"You see! It's not connected. Your body jerks. For no reason. It's flesh moving, why, how, I'm incapable of explaining."

"But . . ." Daniel protested.

He looked unhappy, really unhappy, for the first time. Doctor Blancodini, who had been looking after him for months, had never seen that sad and tormented mask of a face.

"Do you remember," he resumed, "that I offered you a solution? If the situation is unbearable to you, I mean your impotency, there is a very simple remedy. A stake, sort of. It's accepted, people are quite happy with it."

A stake! What would that look like! No, thanks. Daniel prefers corpses to lie down, it's more decent. He is offered a permanently stiff mummy instead of his poor dead thing, which at least has the merit of being authentic. Dead flesh, yes, but his! And then, sometimes, the deceased wakes up, he has seen it. He is thrilled by that adventure. If it stands to attention, it's nevertheless finished, there will be no miracle, never again will it move. No, thanks, no stake. Daniel is an adult, and is responsible for his own life. He is in charge, like a big boy, even if in his wheelchair he has lost half a meter; that fifteen centimeters definitively erect won't give it back to him.

Isabelle has washed her hair today and thrown away her horrible green elastic band. Her blond hair waves prettily around her face. She is quite cute, actually. A shame about her eye! As she doesn't ask about his visit to Blancodini, perhaps she doesn't care. Perhaps she's embarrassed . . . She has started the session as usual, or almost. "You aren't taking off my pajamas?" Daniel asks. She has forgotten. She remedies it right away, silently.

Ankles, knees, hip. It doesn't fail to work! The girl has a power. Daniel has lifted himself on his elbows, he's feverish, talkative: "Miss! Isabelle! Miss Isabelle! The doctor said it's impossible! Or, it's a fluke. But a fluke every time, do you believe it?"

Her movement remains suspended, she has hold of his pajama bottom. "I'm going to send you somebody else!" He lets out a shriek of anguish and, with his eyes brimming with tears, says, "No, don't do that, I'm begging you!"

She comes back. Still wearing her old baggy sweaters, but no more ponytail. Her eye is getting better, it seems. On Easter weekend he is alone in the house. He had insisted: "Mom, Dad, please go, it's OK, I can look after myself! It's very important for me to learn how to do that!"

When she opens the door, she finds him in the dark. He has pulled down the blinds, drawn the curtains. A small bedside lamp spreads a pinkish gleam. "Are you all right?" she asks. "Yes, but . . . I have something to ask you. Something special." He breathes in hard and throws himself in at the deep end. "I would like you to use it!" She hesitates before understanding, keeps silent for a minute, taken aback, then says: "No!"

"But why?"

He looks like a vexed little boy.

"Because I don't feel like it!"

"Me, neither!" he declares, stating the obvious.

"But why do you want us to do something neither of us feels like doing?"

"I don't want it, physically speaking. That desire, I shall never experience again. What I would like, it's to know that someone . . . a woman . . . you, Isabelle, has used me, has had their pleasure thanks to me."

"As with an object?" she interrupts coldly.

"Yes! Entirely! I don't mind being an object. I want to make you happy! The house is empty. We have all the time in the world."

"I don't," she says.

"The time you need, and if you find me repulsive, no problem, I turn off the light."

He switches off the light. The room is in complete darkness . . .

She performs a few gestures in the total darkness. "What are you doing?" "I'm taking my clothes off." It is not true, she is cheating. She has only removed her sweater, to have naked arms, just in case he brushes against her. "Don't forget your manipulations," he whispers. "I won't forget." Ankles, knees, hip. "So?" he asks. "So, that's it, you're doing fine. I'll take off your clothes." She does that, at least. It isn't much. Pulling off the underpants, she feels the young man's penis oscillating, tonic like a spring. She climbs on Daniel's legs, astride, a bit higher, on his thighs. "Can I touch?" he asks.

"No, no touching, no looking. We agreed on that."

"OK, but you'll have to tell me what you're doing . . ."

She begins her deceptive story. "I'm holding your penis in my hand."

"How is it?"

"It's big and hard. I caress it from top to bottom, and vice versa. It slides. With my other hand I'm touching myself."

"Do you like it?"

"Yes, I'm getting wet, soon I'll be ready. I'm going to take you inside me."

"Describe your position."

"I straddle you, my thighs on each side of yours."

"Naked, your thighs?"

"Obviously. And now I'm placing you, you're penetrating me."

"Easily?"

"Not really, no. You're too big, it hurts a bit."

"Wait then, touch yourself a bit longer."

"Yes, I'm waiting. I only inserted the tip. I make myself wider with it. I'm going down. I swallow you gently."

Isabelle mimes her ballet, ten centimeters from the object she describes. For the noise on the mattress, for the vibrations, he needs to feel her plunging, and going up again, so that he really believes it.

She has kept her pants on, even her shoes. She continues with her parody, calling herself crazy, in reality feeling confused and ashamed.

"I'm impaled on you, right down."

"What do you feel?"

"I'm really excited. You're going deep inside me. I go back up again, leave you, you slide, all sticky, the tip . . ."

"Yes?"

"The tip of your penis is on the edge, right on the edge, and I'm turning around."

"You like it?"

"Very much! I suck you in very gently. I eat you with my pussy."

"I'm still hard?"

Isabelle moves to check on the thing.

"Yes, more than ever. You are even bigger than before."

She has placed her hands flat on Daniel's chest and, unconsciously undulates with her pelvis to the rhythm of her commentary. Daniel has grabbed her wrists, he strokes her arms now. "And your breasts, Isabelle, can't I touch your breasts?" "Wait a minute!" She leaves him hastily, and, next to the bed, she pulls off her clothes as if they were burning her. Hopefully he won't notice anything. "What are you doing?" "I still had my T-shirt and bra on." Quick, quick! She rids herself of her shoes with a furious kick, her trousers and panties with the same urgency, the T-shirt flies, the bra doesn't resist, either, though she pretends to fight with it in order to gain time. "The hook, I can't undo it!" What a liar! What an actress! Where did she learn to lie like that? She didn't know she had that talent, that passion, that desire to please, to intoxicate, to make someone happy. She returns to him. "Touch them." He puts his soft and rapt hands on the globes offered to him, quivering, and he draws himself up on the bed, moves his mouth closer and drinks, bites, suckles that exquisite melting flesh on offer.

"And down there?" he asks suddenly. "What's happening down there?"

"I'm fine, I'm fine," Isabelle whispers. "Your prick is a velvety masterpiece."

"You no longer hurt?"

"No, I'm all wet, I'm sliding around you, I'm eating you, I'm hot everywhere, electricity everywhere, you open me completely, you're fucking me exactly like I want it."

"Can I touch, Isabelle, please?"

"Yes, yes, touch!"

She is the one taking his hand now. He can feel his prick, the root of his prick solidly planted in a torrid and soaked thicket. He puts his finger in, into the fabulous hole that beats and swells, and the hole gobbles up his finger, too, and just with that aspiration, with that rhythmic pressure around his finger, that increasingly rapid and greedy mastication, he imagines what his penis would have experienced if it hadn't become deaf and blind in that fucking accident. He thinks: "With Cathy, or any other girl, I would have come already . . ." His heart beats very fast, his finger is still stuck there, in the blaze, it is as if he was touching the coupling of a woman and a man who is not him, as if he was invited intimately to their union, as if he was a very special witness, a very indiscreet witness to their wedding night. He feels the delightful stiffness of a vehement rod against his finger. It is his own prick, he finds that hard to believe, and that prick goes up and down Isabelle's extremely wet cunt, which palpitates like a beating heart, which dribbles a warm juice, which pumps more and more voraciously. He withdraws his finger, he turns around that magnificent and delicious meeting with the tip of his finger. He can feel the stretched labia, separated, swollen, filling up around his mast, the pubic hair like a halo, all around, bathed by the adventure, as far as the asshole, which takes part, too, which seems to call for attention. He ventures in, penetrates it effortlessly. Isabelle moans and crushes his finger. In her ass he still feels his prick, fully erect, all long and round and hard. He accompanies it, flatters it, outlines it through the thin membrane, which plays the game. Isabelle moans louder, he is sitting, his left hand can't stop marveling, how her breasts are beautiful, and heavy, and alive! . . . He whispers: "Call me, say my name." She murmurs: "Daniel! Daniel! I feel good, I feel so good, but I'm not there yet, not yet, I take time, you know . . ." Ah! He doesn't care! What luck, what a stroke of luck, he will be able to offer her his insensibility like a real present, as long as his prick agrees to stay stiff, as long as the miracle will hold, he will encourage her to take advantage of him, to run at full speed, to go up and down, to ride him and then to slow down, to stop and start again, to dance around, to churn hard, to screw fast, to fuck and fuck some more. He puts his finger in again, he explores the wonderful terrain of their meeting, he plows the suave and gaping slit, finds the clitoris protruding. He plucks at the petals of the flower, pulls at them, pinches them, rolls them, joins them and parts them, stretches them. How good that is, that woman open on top of him humming, breathing fast, with her mouth closed, commenting on the sensual pleasure he's giving her! "Isabelle? Can I turn the light on? Isabelle, can I?" She doesn't say no. The pink light flashes, making a magic halo around her. How gorgeous she is, with her hair a mess, her moving breasts, her round shoulders, her hips in a frenzy, and her open cunt, the color of intoxicating carmine on her golden wet hair!

She is leaning backward now, she is resting on her hands, pushing her chest forward, lifting her chin up, looking upward with glazed eyes, and in the gaping hole of her thighs that great thing appears: his own big cock, well oiled, nicely erect like a steeple, and Isabelle banging away on it, blindly grimacing and galloping faster and faster. "Ah!" she screams: "Ah." She is coming, she is riveted on him and she is coming with an open face and open eyes. She no longer has something in her eye, only a radiant and terrible fire, she's still coming, she says again: "Ah! Daniel!" Her cheeks are very red, her mouth in ecstasy, her adorable little cunt still pumping like mad. "Ah! Daniel." "Ah!

Isabelle." She is the most important woman in his life, at that moment, and forever, he knows it now . . . She breathes noisily, she looks like she's in pain, but she's smiling, beyond that dear and resplendent pain for which he is responsible . . . "Ah! Daniel!" The treasure of her dazzled eyes, of that shortness of breath, of that half-open and self-satisfied mouth, he wants to keep all of that forever, it is his, his, fuck, destiny owes him that, at least, and those two beautiful breasts, so round, and that belly, that belly . . . She places her hand on that delicate bulging belly. She contemplates Daniel with tenderness or something similar.

"Isabelle, marry me!" She smiles gently, sighs seriously, she still has little spasms, like a kid who has cried for a long time. "Marry me! I have a good job, I'm about to win my lawsuit. I'm going to get a lot of money, my parents are nice, they will leave us the house and you give me an erection, Isabelle, look, I'm still stiff . . ."

It is true, his penis hasn't softened. He could cry for joy. Isabelle leans on him, kisses him affectionately on the cheeks, leaves the bed.

"And you," she says. "Have a look at this!"

She is standing up. She has placed both hands on her belly, arching her back.

"You've noticed, right? Nearly four months now."

Four months? What is she talking about? No, he hadn't noticed anything else but sweet, pretty, round, full, tender . . .

"Four months?" he asks. "And the father?"

She makes a gesture, kind of disillusioned, while reaching for her T-shirt.

"Oh, the father, when he realized I wanted to keep it, he ran away as fast as his legs could carry him!"

Daniel doesn't believe his luck. As fast as he could! Oh, the bastard, the sublime bastard, on his formidable deserter legs, running away like a bastard, leaving behind, all ready, all warm, all alive, the divine little belly of the divine Isabelle! What luck! "Isabelle, come here!" She comes closer. He takes her in his long arms, places his cheek on the comfortable hill of her belly. "Isabelle, you see, I could take him in my arms and rock him, hold him tight against me. I'm left with my arms, my heart, my chest, and, thank God, all my love to give. A lucky break, isn't it?"

The Black Swan Hotel

Nathalie Perreau

I have the silly habit of never reading the names on envelopes I find in my letterbox. I opened that one like all the others and my attention was immediately caught by the handwriting: it seemed to be disguised. I could not identify it, but it was somehow familiar. I was about to go out. It was hot and I was wearing nothing, or almost nothing, under my silky black dress. That is what I was thinking about when I opened the letter. A thick vellum paper, a heavy handwriting with looping strokes in black ink, which read:

I just had to meet your eyes to realize. You are mine as much as I want to be yours. I imagine the moment you will surrender to my desire. I want you to wear your red silk dress. You won't wear anything underneath, apart from the gold chain with the little seahorse. I will be waiting for you on Thursday at 4 at the Black Swan Hotel, room 9. Don't be late. Don't wear any perfume. I want to breathe your own wild scent.

I want you to know why you will come to that rendezvous: to be ravished, to give me your body without restriction, to submit to my whims, to all my fancies. You have been feeding my fantasies for so long now.

The moment has come to pay for the desires you provoke. Whatever I ask you to do—and some of those things perhaps you have never dared agree to—remember that I love you. You are the only one I want to love now.

Othello

In a state of excitement, I folded the letter back into the envelope. I was seized by a feeling of dread mixed with curiosity: who could the mysterious Othello be? He knew intimate details: my red dress, the little golden seahorse hanging on a chain I sometimes wore around my waist. How dare he propose to meet in a hotel, as if I was some cheap call girl? If he was one of my acquaintances, how could he think that I would give in to his request, to his summons? I was married, I lived in a milieu in which women avoided anything that could jeopardize their high social position, at all costs. If I had done crazy things in my youth, for some time now I'd been leading a decent, irreproachable life, within the strict boundaries of freedom that my husband Renaud and I had agreed upon: he had a mistress he was seeing once or twice a month; I had a lover, Yannick, who helped me to work off my sexual energy once a week, at most.

My youth! Was he one of my ex-partners? Julian, the pervert, who almost raped me as we were leaving a country dance. He had pulled up my clothes on the grass and, for the first time, a burning tongue had licked my yearning pussy.

Vincent, the glamour photographer, who wanted to make a star of me, but only took me to his bed? Vincent had spread my body wide and his penis had split me apart, making me moan like a demented bitch.

Pierre, the stallion, who drove me crazy for a whole summer in Saint-Tropez? That one succeeded in turning me into a real bitch, giving me incredible pleasure with his monstrous swollen penis, its glans protuberant like the head of a snake. Or Yves, married with children, who had taught me a few perversions unknown to me at the time . . . He had forced me to masturbate some truck drivers in a highway parking lot, and the well-built guys had poured the overflow of their virility onto the blue raincoat, which still bore the whitish traces of their ecstasy.

It was useless going back that far. None of those men could know about the red dress, nor the golden seahorse. No, I was in the grip of a maniac, probably a pervert spying on me for weeks now, someone on the lookout . . .

I turned to the window. The towers along the Seine seemed to look at me. Perhaps he was there, hidden behind a window, binoculars in hand. Perhaps he was watching me . . . An image appeared in my sub-conscious of a middle-aged man, leaning against a wall, masturbating slowly, pulling his foreskin back as far as he could, all the while watch-ing me. A shiver of arousal went down my spine . . . That was a fanta-sy I was familiar with. Sometimes I imagined that scene when Renaud made love to me and I had difficulty coming.

It was Thursday and it was already three in the afternoon. I left my apartment, called the elevator, then changed my mind. My heart beat-ing, I ran to my bedroom, took off my black dress, and slipped on the red. Then I pulled it up and, contemplating myself in the mirror of my dressing-table, my tanned and glistening stomach, my depilated pubis, the pink vivid notch of my pussy, I attached the chain with the small golden seahorse around my hips. I called Renaud at his office. I needed to talk to him, I needed him to come to my rescue. His secretary informed me that he was out at a meeting. I had completely forgotten: it was the day he saw Barbara, his regular mistress, an ex-dancer with a sculptural body, whose beauty I couldn't stand. Renaud often related in detail how she licked his balls from behind, in front of a mirror, so that he could see her squatting on the floor. I hung up with the bitter feeling of being abandoned. Too bad for him.

It was only in the parking lot, sitting in my small convertible, that I became aware of what I'd just done. I was giving in to the desire of that stranger. The old demons lying dormant within me had been freed by that infamous letter. Curiosity tormented me and another desire already overwhelmed me: attraction to the forbidden. The pride of accepting a challenge unacceptable to all others. As I started the car, a man came out of the shadows and walked toward me. I saw him approaching, a shiny black silhouette—he must have worn matching leather jacket and pants—which unleashed unbearable visions of rape. The man was about to pull out a knife, to threaten me with it, perhaps to place it at my throat. About to force me to unzip his trousers, take out his dick, caress it, take it in my mouth despite my entreaties. He would force me to go all the way, to wait for my throat to be filled with the sticky milk of his pleasure.

The man went to the car next to mine and climbed in, giving me a rather charming smile. My thighs were wet. What could Othello want from me? And first, why Othello? The drama of jealousy? Othello was jealous, sickly jealous. He had followed me to my lover's. He had managed to catch me in my intimate embrace with Yannick.

My lover had the habit of tying me, blindfolding me, before making love to me. He sodomized me slowly, pushing his pubis right up against my buttocks, his penis planted deep within my loins, right to the hilt, without moving. Othello had surprised us like that; he was sick of it and wanted to take revenge by blackmailing me. But in that damned letter, that I had crumpled, and that I read again at the first red light, there was no allusion to blackmail.

He was in love with me. Perhaps he was going mad with a true passion for me? Was it his only way to make contact? He was going away, far away, forever. He had no time. He wanted me.

My heart racing, I stopped in front of a tearoom, ordered a coffee, ran downstairs. In a phone booth I hastily consulted the directory. Black Swan Hotel. A little street near Montparnasse. I plucked up courage and dialed the number. A nasty, rough voice answered:

"Black Swan Hotel, how can I help?"

"Can you put me through to room 9, please?"

There was silence, then the voice again.

"There's nobody there. The key's on the board. The gentleman is not back yet."

I mumbled a few inaudible words and hung up after saying thank you for that useless information.

The little street was lined with shops and the hotel wasn't much to look at. I drove past slowly. The door was half-open, as if to invite me to come in. I parked a street away and came back. An indescribable nervousness overwhelmed me. I had to go to that rendezvous and, at the same time, that desire disgusted me in my heart of hearts. I wanted that man to take me, fuck me as he wanted, as I wanted now as much as he, and at the same time the arousal that made me wet literally terrified me. If he was a maniac, he could kill me without anybody coming to my rescue. He would demand that I make humiliating poses, that I offer him my spread cheeks, my open thighs, that I present my breasts to him, that I put out my tongue as if to suck an imaginary virility. He would make me kneel on the dubious-looking carpet, eyes closed, mouth open as a sign of total submission. He would want to make me his slave, to whip me. I would scream. He would ravish me, and, soon after, he would be violent, if he was a criminal . . .

I went into the dark and empty hall of the hotel. A dusty counter, a threadbare carpet, a yellowish lampshade. An indescribable smell, a mixture of tobacco and cheap perfume floated in the oppressive heat. Above my head, I heard laughter, then little moans. I waited patiently, two, three minutes, then, frantic, I took the risk. It was just after three-thirty. I climbed the stairs, which creaked beneath my feet. I reached a narrow landing. The door to room 9 was at the end of the corridor. I could still turn back, leave, run away. But I moved closer, unable to resist. I listened carefully. The silence was only broken by the moaning coming from room 7 and the distant sound of cars passing in the street. My heart pumped so fast that I restrained it to decrease its pulsations. I wanted to give myself to that man, to surprise him, to catch him in his own trap. I hesitated, then decided to knock on the door. I threw myself back against the wall. If he opened, I would run away down the stairs. If he tried to catch me, I'd cry for help.

Nobody answered. I went back to the hall. The key was still hanging under the number 9. I was going to enter that room, would take off all my clothes, lie on the bed, and adopt an indecent pose when he opened the door. I would raise my hips so that he could see my whole intimacy offered to him.

"Hello," I'd say. "I'm Virginie. Take me."

As I was about to take the key, the door to the hotel opened behind me. Instinctively I flattened myself against the wall, behind a drape, and held my breath. A hand stretched toward the key to Room 9. A woman's hand, an elegant hand. I was surprised, I turned to the mirror to find out who the woman was. Totally confused, I recognized Adeline, my best friend. She lived on the same floor as me. I didn't understand. She climbed the stairs slowly, somewhat anxious. I left the hotel and ran back to my car. Then suddenly I stopped, dug into my pocket, took out the crumpled envelope which I still hadn't looked at. It was addressed to Adeline Rastier.

A simple mistake: it had been posted in the wrong letterbox. Adeline had a red dress, and she had bought the same golden seahorse with me. Breathless, driven by an uncontrollable force, I went back to the hotel, slipped through the deserted reception where the phone rang tirelessly, and climbed up to room 9.

The door was still half-open. Adeline was kneeling on the carpet in front of a naked man whose back was the only thing I could see in the darkness. Her head came and went between his thighs and her imploring eyes looked up at him. The man stepped back a little and masturbated with delight on the face of my gorgeous friend. Suddenly he stiffened, clutched his cock, approached her delicate face, and sprinkled it with his sperm, big, heavy drops, which soiled her hair, eyelids, nose, and chin.

"That's nice," said the voice of Renaud, my husband. "You're such a good bitch."

OF HIGHER JOYS

Jeanne Decize

I said to myself: stop,
no one see you:
And without the promise
Of higher joys.
Let nothing put you off,
Sublime retreat.
                    —Arthur Rimbaud

The sky is dirty for Baptiste's burial. Lightning and thunder flash and rumble in the stiff clouds whose ominous grayness makes you feel so sad you could die. Faces are embarrassed, attitudes awkward, some even seem anxious for the ceremony to come to an end. When the man reading the Epistle to St. John declares that one has to love with action and not with words, my neighbor and I burst out laughing. The others look at us, incensed, their indignation makes us step back a bit. Unnoticed, we withdraw and, without talking to one another, leave the cemetery. He informs me that he is the one who discovered Baptiste's body.

We step into the first café we come across. He holds the door open courteously, stands aside to let me pass. As soon as we are seated he orders two whiskeys. I try to avoid his eyes. Something dark which reminds me too much of Baptiste dances around on his face.

"I'm Albert. You're Jeanne, right?"

I smile.

"You're Jeanne," he decides.

My heart beats from wanting to know, for I know nothing. I've only received the notice announcing his funeral. I remember letting myself slip to the floor at the letterbox, loosening Baptiste's scarf around my neck and biting the silk to prevent myself from screaming. I certainly hadn't cried, for I never cry.

"Was it you who sent me the card?"

Albert smiles.

"How? Tell me, Albert."

Albert hesitates. He gestures to the waiter to bring two more glasses.

"How? Tell me, Albert."

He swallows his whiskey in one gulp.

"We were going to have dinner together. The door was ajar. I entered the apartment. Baptiste was hanging, stark-naked, the handle of a whip stuck in his ass. He looked like a happy cockerel, with a fine leather plume in his ass. I won't describe the state of his body. His face was inaccessible, as if bewitched. He was breathing an unusual joy, really. Incredibly dazzling."

Albert holds my trembling hands in his. My eyes are dry like stones. I close my eyelids, it's night.

It's night, two years ago. It's summer, the weather's nice, it's warm. Baptiste and I are walking back to his street.

"What a boring film!" Baptiste says. "I don't like horror movies at all! Jeanne, we'll never go to the movies again!"

He climbs to the third floor two steps at a time. He always whistles when he ascends the stairs quickly. He hates staircases, landings, elevators, corridors, bus stops, Métro platforms, and stations. They are unbearable, too. He prefers speed, passing landscapes and people. I am much slower. I've barely entered the hall and he's already in the living room.

Baptiste doesn't turn on the light. He collapses on the sofa, unbuttons his shirt, spreads his long legs in front of him. He lifts up his hand, his open palm offered in the darkness.

"Come, my Jeanne, hurry up. Come quickly. Speed is beautiful, you know. Show me your pretty ass for my cock to wank in. Quick, let's drain the cup."

I come closer, bend a knee between his legs, which spread open. I rub it gently and Baptiste's cock is slowly set on fire. He grabs my hips, turns his smile toward my breasts. His mouth wets my stomach through the material of my dress. I touch his neck, brush his shoulder, and become wet immediately. He lies down the other way, takes my rounded ass in his hands. Baptiste hums the tune of a world slowly vanishing. I undo the buttons of his fly. I brush against the pole, which stiffens as I imagine a heart swells with the visions fed to it by the brain. Baptiste rolls the silky material, in little waves, up my loins. He pulls my panties down over my thighs. I see them flying across the room. Baptiste pushes down the base of my back, stops for a second while I grasp his cock. I caress the veins stretched beneath the tight skin. I follow the beautiful blue one with my tongue, the one whose blood, I like to think, fires his balls. His lips fastened on my asshole, Baptiste no longer sings. Silence follows. I am puzzled; tonight Baptiste hesitates. Tonight Baptiste lies by omission.

"Baptiste, do it," I whisper, not knowing what he has in mind.

"No, I wouldn't do it with you. Suck me, my love. Suck me better than that. Be a bit more slutty, my Jeanne."

I stuff his cock as deep as I can in my throat. His legs stiffen, the sea of blood seething in his dick swells, burns a liquid there heated by the words he doesn't pronounce.

"Baptiste," I insist, "do it."

He laughs. I push a finger up his ass, then two, he moans, at three he screams.

"Baptiste, do it."

I push without thought or consideration, dig, furious—the flower tightens and opens in jerks around my fingers.

"Baptiste, do it."

He frees himself, gets up. On my knees, my ass pointed at the ceiling, my face buried in my hands, I hear his hesitant step coming back to the room. His tall silhouette is planted in front of me. I discover his shirt open to the waist, his trousers, out of which his cock stands, and also the stirring mess of his hair. I don't move, I just smile at him to celebrate his sensual allure. He's holding a whip against his cheek, which he lowers to brush against my shoulder. He takes off his trousers, lies down on the sofa, his naked thighs framing my hips. I can see, a few centimeters down, the bluish veins that bring the blood to his feet. Baptiste pushes the whip on my neck. I tilt toward his balls, lick them. The smell of wet earth they exude immediately intoxicates my mind. Baptiste brushes lightly again my soaked crack. He caresses me with little strokes, arousing me, unnerving me, making me move my hips in a manner that I suppose is obscene, but obscenity loves everyone.

The handle plunges into my rosebud, its leather lianas slide across my swaying buttocks. Baptiste moves the delightful whip, pushes it even deeper, even more brutally. Pain makes an iron cage around my temples. Baptiste's tongue goes down on my fur, drinks at its banks, becomes a thin dagger inside, withdraws to drown even more. I breathe in with more ardor in order not to think. I think about nothing, I think about nothing else than Baptiste's cock in my mouth, my ears humming with the wet sounds of his kisses. He suddenly grabs my hips brutally, marks them as if he had metal fingernails. I shiver, I close my eyes, I hope to dampen my mind in order to love only the sensations. To give pleasure to Baptiste, to savor his sperm on my palate, then burn my throat with it afterward. My ass lifts itself up.

He moves the whip around, right to left, his tongue brings little suns to my rain. The lashes of the whip probably brush his face lightly, give him little dry slaps. Baptiste bursts out laughing. Baptiste is afraid, because he always laughs when he's in a panic. Now he handles the whip with such violence that he must hurt himself much more. He hurts me but I keep quiet, for I hear the leather strips hitting hard at his face. His cock grows bigger in my mouth, bigger than it ever has before. He screams his pain from the lashings he inflicts on himself. Don't I suffer atrociously, too, split like that, horizontally, by hard, cold wood? I stroke his balls tenderly.

"Harder, my Jeanne, harder. Hurt me, I'm begging you."

I plant my teeth in his flesh. Baptiste howls, takes forever, agonizing, his whiteness sticky in my throat, the bitter and peppery tip makes my cry hoarse. I want to withdraw, but Baptiste sits my ass on his face.

"Do you want . . . do you want to piss?" he mumbles, madness in his voice.

I feel his body shake more violently than other nights. Now and then a jolt lifts him up. He suffers when his red stripes are inundated by the acidic gush I piss on his face. Arousal torments him, unsticks his loins in jolts from the sofa. He's on his way to heaven, I imagine. He flies away, his eyes wide open on an ecstasy he gives himself, which I don't see.

I turn to him, the wooden handle hurts my asshole more. I feel my blood forming beads. Each drop falling from it digs a hole in my heart. I take his face in my hands. He's bleeding from some slashes, tears stream from his dark pupils. He is sobbing, shivering and trembling on my shoulder.

"Thanks," he whispers. He is very pale.

His skin is freezing with fear, his shame burns my cheek. He doesn't know how to breathe. He needs new darkness. Below us linger the dregs of piss, shit, come, salt from childish tears, an undertow brought back to his grown-up eyes. Baptiste turns me over on the sofa, rests his head on my stomach. He is still shaking with sobs, with solitary sorrows, with silences that torture, which he abandons between my thighs. His nails scratch at my breasts. I bite my lips to stop screaming, to stop suffering, to avoid scaring him even more. He spreads my crack open, wipes his eyes in it, his cheeks, hits his forehead on the frame of my ass, smears his face with my come. Panicked, I call him, Baptiste, I grab him by the shoulders, bring him back to me, Baptiste. His hallucinating eyes appear, seemingly observing something far away behind me, which is impossible for me to see.

"I would like to really come just from what I imagine."

A migraine begins to bore into my head and thumps at the back of my neck. My hand is shaking on his stomach, where a taut snake warms fingers suddenly turned cold.

Baptiste says he wants to be subdued like a rag doll.

He says children are cruel with their toys.

He says he wants to be thrashed before being brushed at length with sharp implements.

He says he wishes I was the woman wounding him by accident, for I wouldn't properly see the effects of my gestures.

He says that when he saw me removing my contact lenses the very first night, he got a hard-on straightaway.

He says he is madly in love with my shortsightedness and adores the idea that my eyes sometimes encounter only emptiness.

He says he dreams more than anything of seeing his flesh suffering beneath my blurred gaze.

He says that desire dazzles him so much that it wakes him up at night.

Baptiste wipes the sweat from his brow.

"And then?"

"And then I think I could never look you in the face again."

I bite his shoulder violently and, in my hand, his cock springs to life immediately. I dig my nails into his back as deep as I can. Oh, how his balls swell. I squeeze his neck and his cock moves furiously inside me. I throw my legs around his loins, his hand brushes the emptiness, lifts my lower back, withdraws the whip from my rose-bud to place it in my hand, open on the armrest. He moves, back and forth, caught by terror and speed, mouth open, eyelids quivering. At each caress of the leather on his back, Baptiste shivers, bites his lips till they bleed, grinding his teeth. Foam pours from his mouth, flows down his chin, and wets my stomach with a heat that flattens Baptiste against me.

Softly, he brings his tongue close to my eyelid, stretches it like a shell-less almond whose sadness one soaks up. A fear mingled with horror overtakes me. A suspicious fatigue on the lookout for Baptiste's imagination. He pulls away abruptly.

"You know, my nightmares . . . they're horrible, Jeanne . . . My nightmares are really my dreams. I can see myself sliced by your teeth. I would be torn apart, like a piece of meat with which you would play, yet at the same time I would be alive enough to see it, and you, too shortsighted to see it. I would look with all my eyes, I know I would come in the most perfect way."

I suddenly experience a horrible anxiety. I step back, his eyes become more and more opaque, withdraw to a remote horizon from which I am absent. Terrible landscapes open up before him. I can hardly see them, they slip away from my overly clean indecency. Baptiste half-opens his mouth. He wants to speak but his tongue is silent. He gives up. We just look at each other, as if we were saying good-bye without wanting to.

I discover his back mottled with thin snakes of blood, the softness of his skin has varnished. He carries the whip with him like a kitten perched on his shoulder. His gracious silhouette disappears at the end of the corridor.

I have to say good-bye to Baptiste, to bow, to kiss his forehead, to look at him dressing in the hall, to kiss him from afar. He's concerned only with his own bewilderment. He leaves, spellbound, for somewhere else, where the forests are full of tree whips and the bushes crowned with solid teeth that will spoil his flesh better than I can.

My hand fades along the sofa. A ridiculous embrace, a final kiss, a last caress dies in silence on Baptiste the wonderful, who leaves to adore the abysses.

I open my eyes. Night is falling on the cemetery. Albert watches the sad snail of Baptiste's friends move along the pavement.

"You string of gloomy cunts, you make my stomach heave," he murmurs.

The street empties. Before long there's no one in sight. Albert smiles.

"Come, Jeanne," he says, taking me by the neck.

We are alone before Baptiste's grave. Albert crouches. He touches the stone for a few seconds, then grabs my anxiety at my ankles, drags it to the sheaf of roses laid on the slab. The heel of my shoe stabs a flower. Albert parts my cunt and masturbates me like I've never been masturbated before. His fingers get sticky beneath the menacing sky, black with storm. My eyes are thrown back, I see the clouds spinning around. I have to force myself not to scream beneath his hand soaked with my come. I lift Albert. He is sobbing. We cry on Baptiste as the rain lashes tears on his grave.

SUITE 2502

Julie Turconi

The young woman looked confused as she stared at the contents of her closet; it was too full. She hesitated, she no longer knew what to choose. The doubt only lasted a moment, and then she abruptly made up her mind. That short, asymmetrical, sexy black skirt she had bought recently and that he hadn't yet seen would do the job perfectly. So would that little black top, very cute, with two adorable white cats on one of the breasts. She closed the door and pondered the question of underwear. Should she put on a pair of panties? Yes, but a thong then, satiny and delicately lace-edged, with gray, slightly bluish tones. And a mauve bra, almost lavender, a play of transparency and lace, too. And fishnet stockings, obviously. That was unavoidable. He adored them. To complete her battle dress, she put on her knee-high black boots, high-heeled and laced at the front. Then she made herself up, lightly. Just enough.

She was ready.

He was at work, like every day. In front of his computer screen, files scattered around him. From the twenty-fifth floor of that tower downtown, he enjoyed a beautiful view over the city. Everything seemed so small from up there! He liked to relax while watching the toy cars playing cat and mouse down below, the lights of the city turned on one after another at the end of the day, the big towers lost, some days in the blue of the sky, other days in the mist or the rain. It was his way of escaping the stress of his job: to marvel regularly at that familiar yet constantly changing sight while letting his spirit wander toward other images. He thought about a woman's soft skin, the magical curves of her body, her intoxicating smell . . .

She wrapped herself in a long black coat, left her apartment, her heels clicking down the stairs, and arrived at the subway, where she took the direction of the city center. Impatient, she was burning, already quite aroused. She felt good, confident in her seductiveness. Men's gazes turned frequently toward her in the crowded car at that rush hour. Bodies pressed against one another, everyone had to get home no matter what, and not be stranded on the platform. At each station, she felt pushed farther toward the back by that tired human tide. Tired but full of lust, at least the men. She felt the insistent weight of their gaze, and the contact of her body with others was not solely due to chance. She was aware of that and enjoyed the power she had over others. The weaker sex. Suddenly she felt a caress on her hip that slid toward her buttocks. So soft and light, she almost thought she had dreamed it. Until the wandering hand came back, a bit more precise this time, a bit more insistent.

He looked at his watch. Soon it would be the end of the day! It was already dark outside and the city's face had changed before his very eyes.

Winter and cold weather were approaching fast. It would soon be the season of weekend cuddles under the duvet, the proximity of bodies and heat, cocooning. He was looking forward to it. He thought about the woman who would come back to him after the big energy drains of her busy summer as a festival organizer. The woman who would come back to see him more often, to take advantage of his body and recuperate her energy. The woman whom he had seen so little of recently. He dreamed of slowly caressing her body, her animal curves, of skillfully undressing her, of taking her generous breasts in his voracious mouth . . . He felt his erection stretch the material of his trousers, it was embarrassing. He shook his head, cleared his throat, and immersed himself in his work again. He would call her later.

She grew imperceptibly tense under the touch of that bold hand, but she didn't move away. The car was full to bursting, and she couldn't go far anyway, but she took pleasure in that little game, an almost innocent game. It was a man's hand, wide and slightly callous, that she felt now going up her thighs, stopping for a second at the edge of her stockings, to go in better, between her legs, slightly parted to help retain her balance. She smiled and spread them a bit more, all the while pressing against the man's body, who continued to caress her like that, confidently. She began to move her hips gently to the rhythm of the jolts and vibrations of the train, lasciviously. It wasn't long before she felt a tremendous erection against her cheeks, and the hand resumed its move toward her avid wetness. Skillful fingers stroked her through the thin material of the thong, but she didn't want to go any further, it was only a game. Luckily, the next stop was hers. She suddenly pulled away from the stranger and stepped quickly from the subway train, leaving him no chance to follow. She felt somewhat intoxicated with pleasure and power. She thought about her man, high up there in his tower, who didn't even know she was on her way.

He lifted his eyes, the noise of his neighbor packing up for the day had broken his concentration. That was it: time to go. The office would soon begin to empty, calmly. He hadn't finished yet, but he was left with little to do. Another ten minutes of work, he thought. Then I will be able to go home. Perhaps she will come and see me, if I invite her tonight? In one of those scanty little numbers she wears so well. Something sensual, alluring, which would make him crack up completely. As usual. He daydreamed about the contact of his hands on that satiny material, of his body against that of the woman who had bewitched him. He fantasized about what he would do to her, the caresses, the intercourse.

She was in the elevator, which had been going up for ages. One floor after another. Sometimes it stopped, then started again with a calculated slowness. Then it hiccuped, jammed for a split second, before releasing itself with a jolt, and took up its ascent once more. She was startled. This was not the time to be stuck, not now. She finally reached the twenty-fifth floor, left the elevator, turned right, and moved without hesitating toward Suite 2502, right at the end of the corridor. Instinctively she readjusted her clothes, smoothed down her skirt with a firm hand, and reached up to ring the bell.

He sighed, relieved. Finished! He only had to tidy the piles of files on his desk a bit. He vaguely heard the bell but didn't turn around. He had his back to the door and wasn't expecting anybody. Somebody else would go and open it. He leaned forward, grabbed his satchel at his feet . . . then suddenly stopped in his tracks when a high heel violently forced the bag to the floor. Bemused, he slowly looked up.

In front of his dazzled eyes, two legs in knee-high leather boots, tightly fitting and laced up at the front, outlining the curves of those unknown calves, fishnet stockings—one slightly frayed on the left thigh—a black miniskirt that revealed the top of the stockings on one side but concealed it on the other. A delicious shiver ran through him, head to toe. It was her, he would swear to it. Nobody else could play such a game. He felt his body become taut, ready to jump on her, but he forced himself to sit up again very slowly. Then he stopped moving altogether. He looked at her and waited.

She was planted in front of him, a devastating smile on her face, her eyes sparkling. Gently she freed the satchel from the hold of her heels and came close. She saw from his face that he was really surprised, then read the slightly perverse excitement growing in his eyes. She was provoking him, she knew that, and in his office on top of it. But he played the game, right away. He was waiting. She knew that some of his colleagues were still there, even if none of them had a direct view into his office. But they'd all seen her arrival, and their gazes, full of lustful desires, followed by whispers of admiration, had accompanied her entrance. She wanted all of them to know that she had come for him. She was standing up facing him, one leg on each side of his knees; he was still sitting on his swivel chair, motionless.

He could no longer resist this femme fatale. He held out his hand, let it run along her endless thighs, up underneath her skirt. The other hand rested on her cheeks, brushed them lightly, feeling them. His fingers paused for a moment on the thong, savoring the silky texture and the intoxicating proximity of her wet labia. He moved the thin material aside and gently caressed her hot crotch flowing with sensual delight.

She closed her eyes, arched her back, let him do it for a short while. She put herself through agony. A terribly exhilarating sensation. But she hadn't come for that, not really. She interrupted him, aware of the gazes that didn't leave her for a minute in that not-entirely-empty office. She pushed him back gently, then went down on him, knelt, spread his thighs. She took her time in spite of the unbearable desire to strip him of his clothes and take him there and then. Instead, she caressed him, started to unbutton his shirt, kissed his torso, his stomach, which in turn stretched then withdrew beneath her lips. Then she started to work on his fly, stopped for a while on his blue underpants, her fingers lightly brushing his glans, increasing his monumental erection. She took him in her mouth, tickled it with her expert tongue, swallowed it, sucked it.

He had closed his eyes too, ecstatic. His head thrown back, breathless, he moaned softly. She was incredible! With his hands he touched her hair, her neck. Then he grabbed the armrests of his chair, squeezed tightly. His whole body was stretched, his senses on edge, but he held back. He certainly didn't want to come already, the pleasure was much too intense to be stopped so quickly. He concentrated on her movements, her long hair tickling his belly.

She stopped her little game abruptly and abandoned him, got up and turned heel with a provocative look. Follow me if you dare! She left him stupefied on his chair, slowly coming back to his senses. And she moved toward the exit, after winking at the envious colleagues who were brave enough to do overtime tonight. But her eyes discouraged all those who felt like following her. She slammed the door, walked to the elevator, which she called before leaning back against the wall. She was waiting for whatever would follow.

He recovered slowly from what had just happened to him. He was shaking slightly. My God! That woman was a real bombshell! He came back to earth, his penis hurting, swollen with desire. He got dressed as best he could, his fingers trembling. He got up in a hurry. He couldn't let her go like that, she wouldn't get away with it. All the more because she was as hot as he was. He ran across the office, forgot to slam the door, and reached the elevator, breathless . . . just in time to see her disappearing. He jumped in after her. The doors closed. He caught his breath.

Suddenly he realized they were not alone. Another man was standing at the back of the elevator, stiff in his three-piece gray striped suit. An expensive suit, for sure. He held a leather briefcase with golden locks in his hand. A serious and important look on his face. That stranger had his profession etched on his face. He was a lawyer, you could see it a mile away. There were so many of them in this tower! He looked away and turned toward her.

She was eyeing the lawyer up and down, from head to toe, shamelessly. She smiled at him seductively. He was rather handsome, she thought. It could be very interesting. Intentionally she turned her back on him and leaned her weight on her right boot to retie the lace, which was not, of course, necessary. Her short skirt was lifted, revealing the start of her plump cheeks to the lawyer. She stood up slowly, planted her eyes on those of her man, and smiled at him. She was provoking him again. She wanted to play, and she would go all the way.

He understood. He leaned on the wall to admire the show. She wanted him to see her with another man. Very well. Astonished, he realized that the idea aroused him. He looked at the lawyer again and caught his lustful eyes. How could one resist such teasing?

Suddenly the elevator stopped with a jolt. The violence of the movement made them lose their balance. The lights went off suddenly, plunging the cage into complete darkness. He no longer moved, transfixed. She fumbled her way, looking for a wall to lean against. A hesitant hand slipped under her skirt, another awkwardly found her breast. She didn't know who was touching her. She felt herself getting wet, aroused. The unknown hands gently caressed her breasts, squeezed her already stiff nipples poking through the material. She relaxed and enjoyed those sensual caresses. The other hand went up under her skirt, toward her cheeks, grabbed them roughly.

With a metallic *clonk*, the emergency light went on, a pallid, yellowish gleam, barely enough to discern the inside of the elevator.

He saw her, mouth half-open, enjoying the caresses of the lawyer, who, for the occasion, had dropped his precious briefcase. He still didn't move. The lawyer hesitated for a moment when the light was switched on, but his hands resumed their discovery of a body offered in its entirety. His suit was already crumpled. He smiled, opened his fly.

She moaned. She held her hand up to the lawyer's jacket and removed it without further ado. She seized his tie, undid the carefully tied knot, pulled it over his head, and threw it to her man. Without looking.

He collected the balled-up tie from the floor, stared at her for one or two seconds, then moved closer to the half-undressed couple. He started caressing her too, from behind, not letting go of his precious bit of cloth. Then he grabbed hold of her hands and, with a sharp tug, pulled them to him, tied her wrists with the tie behind her back. She was caught in a trap she had deliberately asked for.

She let out a small cry when he pulled her backward to him. She felt his erection against her cheeks, his hands invading her. The lawyer removed her tight-fitting little top, her breasts overflowed her bra, their tender flesh swollen by desire. He took them in his mouth, nibbled at them, played with his tongue on her nipples, sucked them. She moaned more and more while the fingers—whose?—lubricated by her juice, made their way inside her without difficulty. She arched her back, breasts stretched forward, buttocks pulled backward, kept from falling by the bound wrists that her man still grasped in his hand.

He couldn't wait any longer. He withdrew his finger from the burning pussy of his lover, tore off his trousers and underpants, his hard penis erect in front of him, impatient. Her buttocks were stretched toward him in mute prayer. He penetrated her brutally, in one thrust. She screamed again. The lawyer knelt in front of her and, with his tongue, took over from the fingers working at her sex. He licked her, she was wet all over him and screamed in rhythm with the rough thrusts inflicted by her lover toiling behind, his breath increasingly hoarse, his hands clutching her hips.

When he felt her on the verge of orgasm he let himself go inside her, too, ridding himself of all his energy in one last thrust and animal cry before withdrawing and resting against the wall, emptied, drained. In seventh heaven.

But she hadn't finished, for the lawyer was still stiff, kneeling, his tongue active. She stepped brusquely backward, breaking free of him and his greedy mouth, regained her balance, and pushed him to the floor with her heel. She dropped next to him, on her knees, bruising herself. She impaled herself on his erect prick, her hands still bound behind her back, her head thrown back. They moved in rhythm, faster and faster, but she withdrew just before the lawyer ejaculated in her too and, before the satisfied look of her man, she took him in her mouth to finish him. The sperm sprang out generously as soon as she touched the penis of the lawyer, who moaned with delight for quite a while.

He moved toward her and, in a gesture full of tenderness, undid the knot of the tie that had kept her prisoner. Then he helped her up. She was shaking. Her body relaxed suddenly, after the extreme sexual tension she had just experienced, and she offered herself to her man. He took her in his arms, held her tightly. She whispered in his ear: "I love you," which he didn't expect at all, and the light switched off again. Shock nailed the three of them on the spot for a moment, then the white and powerful light of the elevator came back into operation and it began to vibrate and hum. The mechanism hiccuped, once, twice, then started again, painfully.

Dazed, the lawyer dressed and readjusted his clothes hurriedly, awkwardly, trying to understand what had just happened to him. He found his briefcase in a corner, his only reassuring reference, and stepped back into the depths of the cage. As far away from them as possible.

They looked into each other's eyes and smiled. They didn't pay any attention to the lawyer's confusion.

When the elevator reached the ground floor, nobody was waiting for it. They left, the lawyer walking away in lengthy strides toward his world. His tie was still clutched in the young woman's hands.

The couple was clasped together. They set off for the subway station. They took their time. To catch their breath. She recuperated quickly, her pace became brisker, lighter too. He followed, still under the shock of that quite unconventional end to his day at the office. They disappeared into the subway car, noticeably emptier at that hour. She stood, holding on to the main pole. He leaned against the wall. They hadn't exchanged a word since leaving the building.

The train slowed down, stopped at Saint-Laurent. It was still far from his home, and even farther from hers. With no warning, she threw herself out as the doors started to close. Flabbergasted, he had no time to react, let alone to follow. He knew she'd done it on purpose, of course. She played with him like she played with all the others. And that was what held him.

Once on the platform, she turned around, looked him in the eyes and smiled, waving her hand. Then she vanished onto the escalator while the train picked up speed.

SACRIFICE

Karine Keller

"She is absolutely incredible!" The guard, like all the men present, couldn't help salivating when confronted with the sight of the woman they called "the prison tart." A prostitute? That was not exactly the right word. Prostitutes are paid for the pleasure they give. Not her. On top of that, rare would be the prostitute who would accept to relieve prisoners in an institution where the most recent member had been incarcerated for more than five years already. Let's say the cells were packed with wild loonies in heat.

But that didn't scare her off. On the contrary, she adored it!

At the beginning, she used to arrive during visiting hours—at every visiting hours—dressed in a provocative way, merely to make the prisoners salivate. She walked among the prisoners like a queen among her servants. The obscene abuse shooting from all directions didn't seem to touch her. She remained impassive, a strange smile on her face.

One evening, after one of her visits, one of the guards took her back through the corridors leading onto the cell block.

Slightly drunk, he let her entice him. She aroused him and, in front of the frenzied prisoners, she was flattened against the wall and fucked in the ass.

She returned regularly, either to give the guards blow jobs or to be fucked by several of them. And that always took place in front of the frantic masturbations of all the prisoners.

But she was not satisfied.

One day, as she was being fucked from behind in the corridor, she pulled herself toward the bars of a cell. The prisoners, more excited than ever, had pulled out their pricks, which stood proudly erect between the bars. She moved forward, still wavering under the guard's assaults. The prisoners who were closest managed to grab hold of her head and stick their pricks right into her mouth. She started to suck them energetically, until it turned into a real riot. She could not put all those pricks in her mouth at the same time!

She nearly had her head ripped off. The guards quickly intervened.

After that, unexpectedly, she returned frequently, practically every day.

But she refused to be satisfied by the guards alone; they were not aroused enough for her taste. They worked out a procedure: she would enter one cell at a time, with no more than two prisoners to start with, and an armed guard. The prisoners were warned that at the first incident, even the most insignificant, they would be condemned to go back to fantasizing with their old porn magazines.

Of course, each "session" would happen in public, before the amateur gaze of prisoners and guards alike.

Today was tryout day.

They heard her arrive. The sound of her heels echoing on the floor was known to all and welcomed with excited shouts. She arrived dressed in a tight little red dress with nothing underneath, they knew that already. Three guards escorted her. They seemed as aroused as the prisoners. They took her to the cell chosen for that purpose.

The two prisoners, notified that very morning, stared at her, their eyes popping out of their heads. They hadn't touched a woman in more than seven years.

The door to the cell was opened. One of the guards preceded her. Then the door was locked again. The prison was abnormally quiet. All were waiting.

The two elected were visibly getting hard, but didn't make a move. They were stunned to see her there, two meters from them.

In the end she made the first move. She came closer, knelt down, undid one man's trousers, and started to suck him. The whole prison went wild. Everybody was screaming, shouting obscenities. The man immediately suffered an epileptic fit and ejaculated in the young woman's mouth. He fell on the floor, spent, his eyes still wide open.

In the meantime, the other was starting to react. He moved forward while she was still on her knees. He stood behind her, yanked up her dress to reveal tender and generous flesh. He opened his fly, forced her to lean forward, and took her like that. As he was tossing her about with his thrusts, she grabbed the bars and lifted her head to see all those men getting aroused around her. She came almost as quickly as the man fucking her.

All in all, it didn't last more than ten minutes. That is why the guard allowed himself to fuck her, too.

She left the prison half an hour later.

After that she came even more often. She made them agree to let her visit cells with at least four prisoners in them. After the very first time, they got much smarter. Usually they jumped on her as soon as she stepped into their cell. One massaged her breasts, another licked her cunt, while a third took her up the ass. Their violence was so good, so sexual, that she never failed to reach orgasm while the sperm sprayed her from all directions.

After each session, she was also fucked by some of the guards, at least two. It seemed she could never get enough.

The most violent men were her favorites. She liked being thrown on the floor and seeing all those males jump on top of her, sometimes fighting to be the first to fuck her.

But she wanted to go even further. She asked to be taken to the underground jail, where the most dangerous men were kept locked up.

At first it was out of the question. But after the tacit threat that she would never come back, the guards agreed to her request.

She went down, accompanied by a single man. The gloomy corridor looked endless. From time to time terrifying screams could be heard. She shuddered. Noticing it, the guard said:

"If you want, we can go back up."

She shook her head. She didn't want to. She had to continue.

They stopped in front of one of the metal doors.

"That's Joël Waten. He's a serial killer. If you need any help, don't hesitate to call."

He opened the door.

The cell was pitch black. A nauseating smell of sweat, excrement, and stale air drifted from it. She hesitated for a split second before entering. The door closed on her with a harsh grating sound. It took her some time to get used to the dark. Most frightening was the heavy silence. No breath of life seemed to break it.

However, she had the feeling she was watched. She played on that and began to undress. She finally heard breathing coming from a corner of the room, as well as a noise now familiar to her. He was masturbating. She started to caress herself, too, aware that he was watching her even though she couldn't distinguish his silhouette.

She rubbed her breasts, leaning her head backward, enjoying it. Then she slid her fingers down inside and started to touch herself. She heard him moan. She moaned, too. He accelerated the tempo. She did, too. He came with a grunt that was related more to pain than pleasure. She withdrew her soaked fingers from her cunt and went across to him. She approached slowly. A few centimeters away from him, she finally caught a glimpse. He was curled up on the floor. She held her hand out to him, covered with her juice. He hesitated, then took it abruptly and stuffed it in his mouth. He licked it as if his life depended on it. He took it like a famished dog gnawing at a bone.

Against all odds, she felt an unknown pleasure. She withdrew her hand from the prisoner's mouth and, flattening him against the wall, offered him her cunt. She pressed his mouth forcefully between her open legs. He devoured it as he had done her hand.

What an orgasm she experienced! She held him hard against her, as if she wanted to be penetrated by him, as if she wanted to swallow him whole. Never had she been explored so deeply and with such violence. He had to continue again, and again! Oh, my God, it was so good! She could no longer stand it! She arched her back completely to open her sex further, and, with a powerful lick, he made her reach ecstasy.

She woke up on the floor, still shaking. She had probably lost consciousness for a few seconds. She looked around; everything was quiet again. He had moved farther away, withdrawn into another corner of his cell. She fumbled on the ground in search of her clothes. She couldn't hold back her feeling of disgust when her fingers met something cold and sticky. She stood at once and went to knock on the door. The guard opened it the following second. He looked at her with a smile. She was completely naked.

"Could you please get my clothes? I can't see a thing in there."

It was always surprising to hear her talk. She spoke softly in a language that didn't accord with her actions. She only raised her voice to scream her pleasure.

The guard went into the cell and came out with the young woman's clothes. He held them out to her but then stopped, looking at her. More precisely, looking at the level of her pubis. She followed his gaze and was startled to discover streams of blood running down her thighs. The guard smiled, thinking he understood what it was about. She remained still for a while. He went to her, started to dress her, taking the opportunity to paw her. She let him do it without reacting. He forced her to masturbate him and she obeyed, going through the motions mechanically, like an automaton. It was in that state that she walked back through the prison to leave. She didn't even look at the aroused prisoners.

She had found the man she needed.

She came back even more often, but she rarely stayed with the prisoners above. She contented herself with a few blow jobs here and there. Sometimes she let the guards fuck her in the ass.

She only came for him. She went down to his cell and stayed there for an hour. The guards could hear her screaming with delight. She left with blood on her legs and vacant eyes.

Then she started to come every day, but she no longer stopped for the other prisoners. Even the guards no longer received her favors. She visited him and him alone. The prisoners started to voice their displeasure. The guards decided to refuse to let her in.

That is why on that particular day they blocked her passage.

She was pale and had lost a lot of weight. Nevertheless, she was radiant. She was carrying a bag in which the guards found a Bible and a nun's habit. Immediately they thought it was for an erotic game.

She begged them to let her come in for the very last time, she promised. With treats for each she was authorized to enter.

She went into his cell.

After more than an hour, as they could no longer hear any sounds within, the guards decided to enter.

They found her lying on the floor, her nun's habit pulled up above her devoured cunt, the prisoner still relishing his finest meal. A strange smile floated on the lips of the dead. A smile, soft, so soft . . .

And so perished Sister Elizabeth, devoted to lost souls, offering them her piety.

She chose that cannibal to punish herself for her sins while continuing to give him comfort.

Poor martyr.

POOR FISHERMEN

Agnès Verlet

I met Isabelle at the airport in Marignane. She looked preoccupied, mysterious, almost anxious, but I didn't ask her any questions about her unexpected visit. She told me she had to go to the fish market. The smell of fish, which images in a dream had emitted, had reawakened in her an essential aquatic life, resuscitated a previous life in which her body had been a kind of eel, or maybe a frog, before becoming a mermaid.

She drank a cup of coffee and, to my great surprise, ordered a dry white wine, specifying she wanted a *blanc de Mâcon*. I don't know if the waiter subscribed to that oenological finesse, but he brought a balloon glass of white wine and placed it in front of Isabelle, looking intently at her. He said: "There you are, a Mâcon." Isabelle drank it in one gulp, her eyes fixed on the waiter. She uncrossed her legs, breathed deep, and, when the waiter had departed, recounted her dream.

She was in a hotel room (or a hospital room), a closed world, a room with no contact with the outside, stretched out on a bed, alone. Out of the ground came fish, big sea fish, cleverly springing through the wooden floorboards, sometimes their heads, sometimes their tails, silver, shining, and wet. Only parts of them appeared, crawled, tossed about, wriggled, and she experienced the strange feeling of a swarming life beneath her body, an aquatic effervescence, which she saw and felt, but in which she couldn't participate, for she was lying down, unable to move. The bed was made of copper and its legs were too high for her to be able, even if she stretched out her arms, to touch any of those fish that attracted her. At that moment she had an urgent desire to touch, but she noticed that she was tied, that her two hands were attached to the metal bars. "The fact of being hampered exasperated my desire: my naked body braced itself, my buttocks rubbed desperately against the sheets, my open thighs were calling. Underneath, the fish continued their dance, as if they were calling, too, or seducing me. Sirens, I heard the song of the sirens, and the bindings holding my arms prevented me from reaching for that marine life that fascinated me. Was I a siren too, who, in order to become one, had sacrificed her arms, but not her legs? My legs were real and alive, and my body was nothing but an avid sex aroused by the fish dance."

Isabelle left some money on the café table. The bustle at the fish market was intense at that hour in the morning, and I was dazed by such exuberance, slightly intoxicated by the sea and the noise. Isabelle looked determined. She wandered around the fish stalls, indifferent to the calls of the fishmongers, and carried on her way down the alleys, looking for something. Her white dress was a touch transparent in the light, her golden sandals, heavy with water, dragged some seaweed behind them. The sight of us, a couple of tourists, attracted attention. Isabelle was still looking for something, but she didn't tell me what. She was looking less at the fish than at the fishmongers, or rather, her eyes went from the stalls to the mongers, from the mongers to the stalls, and it became obvious, in the way she stared at the men who started to contemplate her with curiosity, that she was not a simple housewife wanting some fish to make soup. Suddenly she grabbed my arm: "Let's go, Marie-Ange, I don't like this modern fish market. We can't see the sea, no one is crying, nothing can be smelled, it's just cold here." Despite the heat, it was true, I noticed she was shaking. "I'm cold," she said. "Let's go to the old port."

There, on the pavement, in front of the shimmering square of water, between the stall sellers' hats, balloons, and hair accessories, the fishermen were unloading the fish that the women were to sell on the blue wooden stalls. Isabelle looked exhausted. She went directly to a white-and-green boat that had just arrived, called to the fishermen, and took out some money, in 500-franc banknotes. The boat was full of silver sardines, still alive, jumping around, a few sea breams, a box of slightly scary pink fish, which I'm told were scorpion fish, and long reptiles curled up like eels, which seemed to fascinate Isabelle. I don't know what my friend had agreed upon with the fishermen, but they helped us climb aboard, and made us sit between the boxes of fish, despite the cries of their wives on the quay, who didn't understand why the men hadn't unloaded the merchandise. As for the sea excursion, it didn't seem to surprise anybody, and the fishermen were delighted at the idea of a fishing trip with Parisian girls. Isabelle took off her sandals, caught a sardine, and placed it between her toes. She was focused, her nostrils shivering, her lips half-parted. She plunged her hand into the box of fish and, while staring intensely at the forts of Saint Jean and Saint Nicolas, which were fading into the distance, she stroked the sardines, forcing her arms right up to her elbows in them, plunging and replunging her hand voluptuously into the shimmering fish. Her left hand rested on the bench, her neck was stiff, her face tense. She was still, her gaze fixed, she seemed on the lookout. When we sailed off Saint Jean, I noticed she wasn't wearing any panties. André, the fisherman who was at the helm of the little green boat, glanced in the direction of Isabelle, who was bent over, her legs spread, focused on feet that she tickled with the wriggling sardines. Philippe had come closer to me, for, barely out of the old port, I had started to feel seasick. He took the opportunity to put his arm around my neck and paw my breasts. "It's a *pointu*," he said. "What?" "This tub, of course. A *pointu* from Marseilles, and a good one," he said, laughing aloud. "It goes fast!" Indeed, the boat started to roll on the waves and Philippe held me by the waist, putting his hand under my T-shirt. He took my right hand, placed it on his fly and shouted in my ear, because of the wind: "That too is a *pointu*, the best fly of the old port!"

Suddenly Isabelle shrieked: "Look, Marie-Ange." She lifted her skirt up to her waist and sat her bottom down on the sardines, under the astonished eyes of the fishermen. "What's that! Good grief!" Isabelle had fish between her thighs, they were jumping around her cheeks, a red mullet wriggling in her slit. She took off her dress. André looked worried: "Lie down, Miss, someone could see you." Isabelle struggled with the box of sardines, poured its whole contents on the bottom of the boat, and lay down on them, caressing her breasts, belly, and thighs with the living sardines. "More, Marie-Ange, more fish, perches, red mullets, breams, smooth and soft, especially eels, congers, mackerels, and small fry. It's a miraculous catch!"

I was feeling more and more seasick, and the stench coming from the crushed fish made me gag. We had passed the Château d'If, then Frioul and Pommègues, and the fishing boat was pitching in the open sea. Bent double, I was reeling about, around other crates of fish that I tipped over Isabelle, who was lost in sexual ecstasy. Crouching next to her, I was shaking with violent spasms, and then I vomited. Philippe came next to me, swaying like a drunken man. On all fours, holding my stomach, he was pawing me with his rough fingers. I crawled to the bulwarks and puked over the edge, hanging onto the railing. Behind, Philippe, one hand under my skirt, dived into my panties and spread my thighs. I let myself go with the flow, holding on to the edge of the boat, while he penetrated me, jolted, capsized, stood, erect beneath the sky, his trousers open, barely pulled down, his chest tanned and hairy, triumphant. The sun was fierce and the blue of the sky held an unbearable violence. The man rocking the boat overturned my body and disturbed the water, deep inside.

André had cast anchor and joined Isabelle, who was reaching her sexual zenith among the fish. Though cursing those filthy fish, he lay down on top of my friend and fucked her. I could see his cock penetrating, coming and going, shiny, wet. I said to Isabelle: "Conger eel," and tickled her ear with a dripping sardine. In the animated expression of her sexual climax Isabelle's head squashed the bloody fish, making their guts squeeze out, creating a terrible stink. Her ears were full of blood and viscosity. André stood up. "Fuck! What a stink!" and went to piss over the edge. Isabelle asked me to lick her ears, neck, and pussy, too, catfish. The pungent smell of fish and entrails made my stomach turn. The water at the bottom of the fishing boat reddened, thickened, let off a brackish odor, mixed with piss and decay. Bent double, I hurried to the edge to vomit. The bile came back in my face and stuck to my hair. I was so convulsed with spasms that I no longer knew where my pleasure lay. Philippe was seated on the bench, masturbating while he watched. He took me in his arms, hastily explored my body and its marine openings. I wrapped my legs around him, straddled him, and while he spread my sex open, in one concerted push of my loins, I sat smack on the erect prick that pierced me through, ringing in my depths till I screamed. The fishing boat was pitching and that man was making me spin, lifting my body and my cheeks, plunging into my belly, from stem to stern, and me, howling and dripping, dancing on top, riding him, me, too, salted tongue, sticky hair, surging into blasts of endless pleasure.

FRANCE

Valérie Clo

France is my whore. I've known her since I was sixteen.

One summer afternoon when I was particularly aroused because of the sweat running between my breasts, making my legs give beneath me, I had this brilliant idea: "What if I were to go and see France, the local prostitute? She might teach me a thing or two!"

I knew her only by sight. My brother had pointed her out to me one morning as she was doing her shopping at the market. I thought her drop-dead gorgeous. Around forty, nice and curvy.

She was wearing a long faded denim skirt and a low-cut top with maddening white lace. Her chestnut-brown hair, lightly waved and cut square, rolled voluptuously on her long, tanned neck. And green eyes, piercing like those of a cat. To see a prostitute so at home in the middle of the vegetable, fruit, and meat displays made me feel funny. Obviously she was entitled to do her shopping like everyone else . . . and all those eyes fixed on her, far from embarrassing her, made her even more attractive. Her gestures were rounded, gracious, a bit brisk, as it is when one is at one's best and feels looked at.

When I made the decision to go and see her, with the boys, it was a fiasco. It was impossible for me to open my mouth to be kissed. My jaws remained firmly locked, against my will. And I won't even mention the hot flushes, the scarlet cheeks, the shaking legs, and everything else. I felt like a ninny and so did the boys, apparently.

France thought I had made a mistake and gone to the wrong floor when I rang at her door for the first time. When I explained what I wanted, her mouth remained open for a long time. I told her I had money, so she let me in.

Five years now it has been going on.

I was right to think she would teach me a few things! And I can say, without showing off too much, that I have become an expert in that field.

At the beginning I shamefully placed my notes folded in four on the corner of her dresser. I don't know why that shame bought me pleasure. Now she no longer wants me to pay, she says seeing me is a kind of relaxation for her. In a way it relaxes her to caress a young and fresh-smelling girl like me.

I'd like to stay forever in her lap.

One day she let me watch a client. Hidden in the big wardrobe facing her bed, I watched the guys buttocks agitate frantically on my France, her legs spread wide, arms clutching at his neck. She made some delicate and muffled moanings, which put me in a terrible state of nervous irritation. Especially, I think, because of that look of a job well done on her face. After the client had left, I shouted in her face that she was overdoing it a bit, if I might say so. She replied:

"Obviously! Why do you think my clients come back?"

That day I slammed the door when I left, and France never let me watch again.

We sometimes argue bitterly, because of that casual air she takes. I could gladly scratch her haughty and determined little face. She says she's fed up having me hanging on her skirts and that I should find myself someone to marry.

"You're not going to end up a prostitute like me, are you?"

I tried to find myself a fiancé, really I did, but I don't know what happens, as soon as I show what I know, my suitors vanish without a trace. When I told France about that, her look hardened, then her head leaned forward tenderly and she asked me to come closer.

"By spending so much time with me, my pretty one, you've become like me. You no longer know how to keep one for yourself."

I am happy in her arms and I love it when she takes on that compassionate look. I kiss her forehead and those cheeks, always a bit too made-up. She closes her eyes and lets me peck her, smiling gently. Then she gives me what I come to get several times a week: that long, oily, and passionate kiss. I could kiss her for hours on end. But my France knows all about time. For her, time has a price.

She is so obsessed with time that in her bedroom there are two big clocks: one facing her bed, the other on its right. Around her neck she wears a little old watch in white gold on a long gold chain. There is also a clock-radio that she programs to ring almost every hour, just in case she loses track of the time!

We could be deep in making love, but if the radio starts, she stops immediately, leaving me in the lurch, in incredible states of arousal. Her professionalism puts me in a terrible rage. She shouts that my problem is that I'm too slow. Then I leave, slamming the door behind me.

When she gets ready for her client, she is simply fascinating. She dresses up, you should see her, in all her sexy, enticing underwear. All curves in her colorful lace. I could eat her alive, if only she would give me the time. Her chestnut-brown mossy triangle is always exposed. She doesn't realize that seeing her getting dressed for men like that makes me feel incredibly sad and helpless. Sometimes I think I behave like an idiot in love. Surely it's not normal to want to be with her all the time like that. Then I can see that though she's affectionate with me, she doesn't really love me. She says she doesn't want to get attached to anyone.

"They all come and go, you'll do the same. One day, you'll see, you'll get married, and everything I taught you will be for your man."

That's my France's big speech! She doesn't understand, the silly cow, that I would give anything to stay with her.

"You could teach me the job and we could settle together. We could do up the apartment, or move to a bigger one. Together we could increase the number of clients. And, since we are used to each other, we could offer threesomes where we would charge a lot of money."

She looks at me with shrewd eyes. In them flow expensive underwear, precious jewels, the high life! I continue.

"We could start an excellent business. More than the town, the whole region will come and see us."

She is easily impressed, my France. She's taken aback as she sees herself as a high-class tart, changing status. She looks at me hard, as if she no longer knows me, eyes me from head to toe, and rubs against me like a hungry cat.

"You're really not all that bad-looking," she says, grabbing hold of my breasts, my thighs. "With tits like yours, you could easily hook them."

I love it when she handles me like a beautiful filly she is proud to have found. She paws my breasts so heavily that she ends up hurting me. She puts a finger in my crack, spreads, enters, plunges deep, comes back to the pink button, and starts going in and out, accelerating my breathing. She stops suddenly, gets up, leaving me open and begging for it. She looks at me furtively for the last time and announces:

"OK, we'll try a threesome. I'll talk to a client, I'm sure he'll be interested."

That day, she didn't have anybody beforehand, so she had time to prepare me well. She made me up like a stolen truck, dressed me like a scarecrow, you should have seen it. I was crammed into ridiculously colorful and completely inane froufrous. Seems the client liked it. She looked so busy and happy getting me ready that I kept quiet.

She didn't say a word, but saved the best for last: the first garters of her sex career! Indeed!

When the guy arrived, we were both dolled up and perfumed like two tarts.

Thirtyish, his hair smoothed with soap, our client entered the room, looking sheepish and anxious. I was terrified. Fortunately, my cheeks were covered in makeup—I'd have looked stupid getting red like that in front of the client. He didn't look well, either, to say the least. As for France, she was like a fish in water. Smiling and talkative, she came toward me and delicately took off my panties, looking around at him to gauge the effect. My arms dangled, I didn't know what to do with them. Both of us now, bottoms exposed, mine framed in white, hers in red, we looked incredible. Worse was that the client seemed extremely aroused. His eyes were almost popping out of his head, and he was so red he looked like he was about to explode.

Then she made me lie on the bed, on my back, and spread my legs wide, inviting the client to step forward to see how appetizing I was. The guy was more and more excited, his legs shaking, and he turned his head away each time our eyes met. Finally France knelt in front of me, showing him her blossoming buttocks before turning around and putting them on my face. Which meant, as you will have guessed, she offered him to savor our 69.

I drank as much as I could at her burning pussy undulating beneath my wet kisses. As for her, she put so much passion into it that I found it hard to concentrate, and I felt like I was going to faint from pleasure at any moment. I almost forgot our friend, who didn't miss one bit of the action. She's a worker, my France! And work well done gets paid! That arrangement lasted for a while, before France abandoned my sex briefly to throw a discreet glance at the clock. That was just like her, my honeybee! Most important, don't forget the time. Thus, while continuing her pelvic movements on my mouth, she said:

"It's about time you give it a go, my lad, time's running out fast, you know."

The client looked at us for a bit longer, then unfastened his trousers. France took the opportunity to reverse to her initial position and offered him her vertiginous posterior and her wet and worked-up mound. She turned her head toward him again, urging him with her eyes. How she ran her little business! I hardly had time to see his erect penis than it was already buried in France. She emitted a deep sound from her throat and arched her back as he penetrated her. I felt as if he was penetrating me at the same time. Her eyes were closed and she gave me her mouth full of my cream. Just enough time to exchange one of our long passionate kisses before he collapsed on her back.

"He goes quickly, that one," she whispered in my ear.

Looking at her like that, so serious, so businesslike, I still felt like kissing her. But she pushed me out of the bed and let the poor guy fall to the sheets for a rest. She allowed him ten minutes before waking him, stroking his hair with her hands.

"It's time, my lad, I've people coming."

He rose quickly, barely looking at us, and pulled his clothes on just as fast. Taking a comb from his trousers, he pulled it through his hair stiff with soap. Then he extracted a big wad of notes from his pocket and placed it on the bedside table. His eyes still lowered, he told France that it was good and he wanted the same arrangement the following week.

Once the client had gone, France leaped on the wad and smiled her carnivorous smile, crushing my heart with one blow.

I think she's going to keep me.

THE BELL

Calixthe Beyala

All things considered, I'm totally incapable of being a willing accomplice to the ways and desires of men. Not only don't I come during their fucking sessions, but I'm unable to bear their smells, winks, jokes, so-called responsibilities, farts, and burps. I know now why I detest them so much: women. Yes, I'm totally and utterly feminine, back and front. I'm very beautiful and very aware of my splendor. I love wasp-waisted corsets and I hate boyish haircuts, jeans, and the big sweaters some broads dress up in. To hide what exactly? To demonstrate what? Every man thinks of me as a rival. I'm so fascinated by real bitches, so admiring of their spread legs, that any slightly intelligent glans finds me suspect straightaway.

This story happened two years ago. I had just arrived in Paris. I had never fucked a white man. In fact, the idea appealed to me, a kind of reverse safari where I would enjoy controlling a nice purplish cock and making it an object of pleasure.

It was lunchtime. I was seated opposite Josette. She was a beautiful, tall twenty-eight-year-old. She worked in the sewing workshop where I was employed as an office clerk. She set down her cup and said:

"I'm not exaggerating, I swear he has an enormous one, like that. It's my turn this afternoon."

And she made the same gesture that fishermen make when they're boasting about having caught a big fish.

"You exaggerate, sweetie. If that was the case, the boss would have pierced you through!"

"Your turn'll come, I'm telling you, and you'll see for yourself. All the girls have to take turns. He's a real bull! You've never noticed the bell? It rings twice a day and we each take our turn to be fucked by him. He's insatiable!"

"What about his wife?!"

"Oh, her? She's the stuck-up type, always in suits and stockings. God, she's enough to put off any penis!"

"Good for Monsieur Demis, if nature has been so generous to him."

"I could do without it, love! When it's your turn, I'm sure you'll be delighted."

"He's not interested in me! Look, I've been working here for more than two months, but he's never tried it with me."

"Monsieur Demis is class and hates scandal. He keeps a close watch on his prey before jumping on it! A true male, eh?"

"Do you like it when he fucks you?"

"No. But what can you do? I'd be out on the street if I refused to go in. I don't want to take the risk."

I knew the little bitch enjoyed it, despite her allegations. She knew perfectly well how to combine devotion and desire. I looked closely at her ultrafeminine, slightly snub nose, her chin, firm but full of contradictory desires, and her full lips. I liked those lips. When they were closed they provoked the desire to suck them as if to gorge oneself on mango juice. They opened to reveal two rows of glistening pearls and a little, rather unruly pink tongue, which delivered thoughts of the most intimate nature.

I closed my legs tight. I rose from the table, paid for my coffee, and dived out into the street. It was a beautiful December day; I had an hour to spend before going back to work.

I came out at Place Pigalle. How many times had I walked up and down that street? On Sundays especially, I went up and down that street a good dozen times. And the earthquakes that shook me during my descent into the heavenly hell of that street were equal only to my fascination for the prostitutes smelling of perfume and sperm. I knew some of the faces by heart, the Banania blacks, the spiteful whites, the tarts who solicit, those who have lived, the occasionals, the exhausted . . . Then the bundles of men, the Arabs, the blacks, the whites, and those fallen apart, wrecked. All that animal life that examines the goods, evaluates the consistency of the buttocks. I can spot the ones who've just given themselves and I wonder if they know how to take something from it. When they come down they recognize me, we smile. I pass by indefinitely, again and again, in front of that magnificence of the universe, for the sole pleasure of smelling them, brushing against them, and then, alone in my bedroom, I give myself up to the joys of the solitary vice.

But that day I could no longer stop myself. I went into a shop. There was all the gear necessary to metamorphose into a sublime whore.

I bought the lot.

Back in the office I worked with my coat on. I looked at the clock. In ten minutes, the bell would ring and Josette would go to the boss. I left the workshop in a rush. I headed for his office.

"What do you want?" asked the secretary. "Monsieur is busy. Go and wait for the bell."

"There is no more bell," I said.

She was taken aback by my assertion. She was jealous and it showed. In the past she had been Monsieur Demis's mistress. His whore, more precisely. He'd grown bored with her over time.

"Monsieur hasn't told me . . ." she began.

I cut her short.

"Monsieur doesn't tell you everything."

She capitulated, reluctantly. I was in a hurry. I went in without knocking. Monsieur Demis was surprised when he saw me.

"It's not open to all and sundry," he said. "You must make an appointment with my secretary if you want to talk to me."

Without saying a word I opened my coat. I appeared in such an erotic outfit that his pen slipped from his hands, his lips parted like those of a carp, his eyes opened wide like those of a child before a Christmas tree laden with presents.

"Oh! Oh! Oh!"

He rose from his chair. His big belly hung down lamentably. He was fifty-one and going gray. His presbyopic eyes looked at me like a madman's. The total nudity of my chest enthralled him. The bra was almost useless. The cups were so small that my voluminous breasts were entirely free, simply uplifted with supports, as if two male hands held them. The nipples were straight. I appreciated that triumphal moment of my femininity. Everything I wore was black. The zip at the opening of my underwear indicated that one could have access to my most secret parts with a little ingenuity, without pulling my garters apart.

Suddenly decided, he opened his fly. A rammer leapt out, horizontally. My face did not betray my amazement. I was truly turned on. The wetness between my legs proved it. I felt like touching myself but I remained in control. I am a bitch, and the experience I'd gotten from my fifty lovers had taught me that the best way to submit to a man occurs inevitably, through the control of one's own desire. He came closer. He took me in his arms. He kissed me. He explored my mouth with an expert tongue while caressing the intimacy beneath my underwear. Impatient, he used his forearm to sweep clean the top of his table. He pushed away registers and tools, which fell to the ground. I sat, my buttocks firmly planted on the edge of the table, legs spread wide. Feverish fingers opened my sex. Suddenly he lowered himself down, gripped my hips, and lost himself deep within my welcoming flesh. He impaled me. He slid slowly back and forth. Not a bad lover. It was obvious he had much practice with women. The thrusts of his loins accelerated. I bit my lips not to scream. I extricated the beast just when I felt it was going to die a little death. He looked at me, haggard. With both my hands pushing at his shoulders I compelled him to go down. He hesitated when I offered him my boots.

"The rules of the game have changed," I said.

He lifted his head, surprised. But the determination, deep in my eyes, dissuaded him from rebelling. He took off my boots. He kissed my ankles, my toes, my varnished toenails. Then, dropping my feet, his tongue took possession of my intimate parts. He lapped the female sap with delight and when I took his head out of my depths, his soiled features were such that I would have thought him ten years older.

"Take off your trousers," I said. "And get down on all fours."

He trembled slightly. But shoes and shirt, trousers and socks quickly flew to the carpet. I expected a little bit more resistance on the part of my lover. I was dazzled by his docility. He knelt down and waited. He looked comic with his coconuts hanging like that.

"I think I'm going to have fun," I said sarcastically. "Hey, boss, if you were in my place, wouldn't you laugh at you and your pathetic position?"

"No . . . not now . . . later, perhaps. But the moment I'm living thanks to you is exceptional. I ask only one thing, to be in this position more often thanks to you!"

"I'll think about it, you can be sure of that . . . now, on your knees! Better than that! Relax. Arch your back. Lift your ass. That's good. You're suitably obedient. I'm glad you're well-endowed. Now, let me tell you, it's not enough. What a woman wants is a big dick, stiff and hard between her legs. Come on, pull it!"

How silly, stupid, and exciting is a man on all fours! I turned him around, stationed myself behind him. I opened the valley of his buttocks. I trenched in. I stopped at the anus. I tickled it. I forced his Brussels sprouts. Unutterable sensation! I was fucking my boss in the ass! I was sodomizing him. The man was mine. The man was in my possession. He moaned, his eyes closed. He contracted his muscles . . .

"Is that the first time a woman has fucked you in the ass?"

"Yes," Monsieur Demis admitted, short of breath, eyes shut. "It's the first time ever."

"Is it good?"

"Yes," he said.

"Wait, little piggy, it's not finished."

With my other hand, I enveloped his Siamese plums. I kneaded them gently. Then I grasped the rammer firmly. My hand closed around it as if I wanted to strangle it. He grew excited, stoical, ready to burst.

"You want to come? I'm not going to stop you, on the contrary."

I knelt beneath him, my buttocks lifted high, my elbows sunk deep in the carpet.

"Come closer!" I said.

He crawled to me. He took me from behind. He was completely inside. There was a terrible thud . . . *slap*! where it was happening. A marvelous lover. He made me come three times and came as many times himself, after recharging his batteries. He repeated the assault. No, no, no! He changed location. His member plunged into my dilated sphincter, up to the hilt. His balls banged against the wet pink crack. A hand caressed the iridescent clitoris. The phone rang and my boss picked it up while continuing the anal possession.

"I'll put you through to your wife," announced his secretary viciously. "My wife!" he exclaimed, surprised. I grabbed the telephone from his hands. "Pass her to me . . . hello! With all due respect, Madame, I wish to inform you that your husband is my employee for the coming six months."

Madame shrieked. I hung up on her. My boss found the scene so exciting that he farted in long bursts. Quite marvelous!

I withdrew. I turned to him. The one-eyed one cried. I retrieved the last of the potion. I sucked. I swallowed. I lapped at the last drops. He regained his breath. "You're the most delicious mistress I've ever had. I'm at your disposal. My only hope is to be the happy slave of your whims."

I didn't waste time thinking. I took out the yellowish piece of paper, unfolded it, and gave it to him.

"What's that?" he asked.

"It's the bill for the suggestive underwear that just made you come. You need to reimburse me."

"Two thousand and fifty francs! That's too much!"

I looked at him without batting an eyelid. He nodded with his graying head and said:

"Give it to Yvette. She'll pass it through as general business expenses."

"That's not all," I said.

"What else do you want, my love?"

"Two hundred francs each time I come and see you!"

He hesitated. He took out his wallet. I heard the characteristic rustle of banknotes. I slipped them in my bra. Before leaving his office, I picked up the bell from beneath the astonished eye of my boss.

The secretary looked at me, her eyes filled with hatred. She had just realized that I possessed the key to the seven wonders. But that hatred was also part of my pleasure. In the workshop, Josette confronted me.

"Bitch!" she said with venom.

I didn't answer. I went to the toilets. She followed. She closed the door behind us.

"You have no right," she said. "It was my turn."

I looked at her. I knew she was submissive by nature, like the other girls in the workshop. I had to get straight to the point.

"I'm the one who makes the decisions now," I said. "Take off your panties."

She wavered. As always, she didn't take any risks. She obeyed.

"Josette," I said, "you want to love me, don't you? You want me to take the place of that idiot boss? Tell me."

I pushed her against the wall. I grabbed her big sweater, pulled it over her head. I attacked her breasts. I bit them lovingly. Then I went down. She was hairy, the hussy. I carefully parted her sumptuous pilosity. A long finger took care of her clitoris. Another started to come and go in her soft avocado.

"You want to be dominated, my little bitch! That's what you want . . . open, open up."

She lifted her skirt and spread her legs.

"I no longer want to see you dressed in tatty clothes, do you hear?" I said as I continued playing with her intimate parts. "I want to see you made up, in garters and stockings. Is that clear?" She nodded. She started to cry, prostrate with pleasure, while I gently slipped beneath her and my lips lost themselves in the pink slit edged with its long lashes.

Two years have passed. My bank account has perked up. Monsieur Demis died a beautiful death six months ago, during a wild session. I inherited the bell. I would like to get rid of it. I want to be a woman with no responsibilities. But nobody wants that. They take their revenge, the bitches! I do my best to show them the advantages of the bell, but they persist in refusing. They know that the person carrying the bell carries her sexuality in her head. They want me to act the savage. They pursue me. They want it all. They turn nasty. They bite me. They must like a bit of black. Isn't it a terrible nightmare to live in a world covered with white discharge?

MAKO

Marie L.

Mako is beautiful. She no longer has any teeth, but she is beautiful nonetheless. When I'm in her mouth, it's a bit like a deep vertigo, a loss of balance. I look down at her from above, she on her knees, me standing up, already long gone. It's Madame Bertrand who bought Mako back from her owner, a small, smooth-skinned man with slit eyes. It was he who, when she was ten years old, had all her teeth pulled out. So that she would suck better. So that she could be in step with the customer. In Asia, they all have a specialty; Mako's was the blow job. Once in a while I go to Madame Bertrand and pay for Mako.

I love women, I love all women. Small, big, fat, anorexic, what the hell, as long as I can fuck them. One day a friend told me that he didn't really understand me. I had just introduced him to the most recent one I had pinned and, it was true, she was ugly. But an ugly woman makes an effort. She gives her all, with her whole body, for she thinks she can't let a man escape, for a man in her case is a rare thing. Thus she gives her all, and it's that all that I steal from her.

* * *

She was called Mireille, she looked vaguely like a shar-pei, with anarchic folds, same volume, and same mess. When I met her the first time, I thought she was expecting a child, if not due soon. At second glance, I felt the child was not due yet, for there was no child, just a stomach full of fat, extremely distended, almost nausea-inducing. To lose oneself in there was a bit like going full throttle on the accelerator. Let me tell you that as a bad omen, it was scary. And then there were her eyes, two fixed beads constantly wet-looking. You don't know what it's like to look deep into a woman and see nothing there. For that was Mireille, a kind of nothingness. The more I looked, the more I was engulfed by nothingness.

I had picked her up in a bar, at the end of the afternoon. She had come accompanied by one of her friends. The friend was awesome, one of those time bombs who make you lose your head and blow the rest. You gonna ask me, why the ugly one? Because the ugly one is used to being abandoned when she goes out with her friend, so to get interested in her is like already climbing the stairs. I'm sure to lie down with her within the hour. Women are like that, they function by steps. You just have to know that. And I know it all. For all of them have been consigned to my little spiral notebook. All of them tested, studied, dated, annotated like the Michelin Guide. I even do the five stars. Just in case . . . I've met hundreds of them, and no, my nose is not getting bigger. I'm not an ace player, but my failing is that I always believe in it. What do you mean, it's not that easy? I can see you now, reading me and thinking: he's making it up, that guy is making it up, it's just not possible. You're wrong, my friend, even you could succeed.

So tomorrow, first exercise: you go down the street, and you approach them:

"I feel like making love to you, madam, please."

And don't forget "please." They might be hot bitches, but they like to think they are respected. And really, what do you have to lose?

Nothing, if not to come back empty-handed, like a novice skirt-chaser. That's it, I can sense you're getting stiff. No, come back. I was just kidding. What are you risking? That they giggle, "Oh monsieur, please," and then, you'll have dozens like that, but I can assure you that by the end of the morning, you'll bed one, for sure. Yes, it's called probabilities, my friend, we learn that at school, with black and white beads, but it's just the same. You will meet the white one, and the white one will be hot stuff, and you or someone else won't matter as long as she sleeps with one of you. Don't believe they've got haloes. They're just like us, I'm telling you, they're even worse. Impulses in them are big explosions.

Bitches, all bitches. I'm telling you. So try your luck, like animals. Do you think they ask permission? You think the dog invites the lewd bitch to the restaurant, talks to her about long walks, the weather— how pretty you are—and in the end pays with his American Express? No, he sniffs at the oozing desire and climbs straight on, in the street or the fields.

Anyway, this being an erotic little story, let's resume the "before" of "how Mireille was laid by this man, me."

I had taken her to my bedroom. *Bedroom* is the right word for it. A small room, a big bed, a sink. I keep it for the ladies passing through, those who, between you and me, don't ever stay very long.

I resume. We'll keep to the present tense, that'll inject some life, and you'll think that you are me and plunge deep inside Mireille, as if you are there. My little friend Mireille, I mean, my big friend. Well, she climbs the stairs to the apartment, ahead of me, clambering with difficulty and, one by one, each step like that, her breathing more and more resonant. I can perceive in her climb a lot of determination, as well as a strong smell of perspiration. My eyes rest on her two haunches, the color of a chicken's, which rub against each other as she moves. She knows what's going to happen, Mireille. She knows because it must be months that she's been thinking about this moment. She pinches herself, the dope, for she still doesn't believe it. And I'm already thinking: I've got to turn the light off, remember, do not slap into her with the lights on. I'm used to it, women must be taken in various lightings, so for Mireille, it will be complete darkness. The advantage of her volume is that it's impossible to lose her.

I knock her over with no consideration.

With one hand, I rake up her skirt, with the other I ply the left tit. Kneeling over her, I take out my cock, force the opening of flesh made by her lips. Now she, underneath, sucks greedily. I have to say I help her by pushing her head back and forth like a trombone. I tell her to swallow it real deep. That I want to hear my glans knocking against her glottis. That I heartily recommend her to accompany that delicate sucking work with a skillful massaging of the lower parts. That in my excitement I say to her: "And stroke my balls, you bitch." I can feel her aroused, and me ready, ready for anything to give that poor girl a bit of pleasure. I drop her head, which falls back like an overweight parcel that one can no longer carry. A sharp and dull sound. I say to myself that girl is definitely too noisy. To thank her for being so delicate, or, to be more precise, to thank her for not having scratched my dick with the disgusting stumps in her mouth, I suck at her nipple and, like one rewards a filly, slap her thigh.

It's strange how those places, in some females, can be viscous, and trembling, a bit like those jellies served as desserts in England. The bitch relaxes, opens wide, her parted legs make me think of wet tongs being dipped for gherkins. Now the call of the female. Cooings, mumblings, the olfactory resonance of seeping come. I penetrate her immediately, don't lose time on foreplay. I insert. She is here for that, so that's what I do, I insert. I especially like to hear the slap of my balls on her ass. She is tight, Mireille. That's part of the lovely surprise, so it's good, one feels good there, almost secure, like in Mommy's arms.

I close my eyes. Temptation. Oh, yes, temptation . . . one thinks, Mireille is not Mireille, it's her friend. She is good, Mireille's friend. So I grind, I grind hard. And I go limp just as fast, for that cunt, Mireille, has moved her head, and I catch her in the fire of the red dragon, I mean, the neon sign of the Chinese restaurant below, which has just been turned on.

Only one solution remains, to turn her over, like a pancake on Shrove Tuesday. Stick her head on the pillow, and relieve myself as fast as I can, in her ass, between her thighs, in the duvet, who cares, but above all I have to come fast, and make Mireille go away, far away, far, far away, even, get lost, with her accumulation of fat and her smell of grease which already clings to me, like the stench of a five-day corpse; yes, she has to clear off as fast as she can, no, she has to spread her crack wide open with her hands, shake her big ass, shake it like a belly dancer to accelerate the process and then, above all, yes, above all, she has to keep quiet, not a word, no shouts, not even to breathe, she should bite into herself hard to avoid speaking . . . or she has to die. Or rather, no, she'll have to escape my bed, crawling like an earth-worm, letting me see nothing.

Nothing at all. No, I don't know that girl. Nobody. I know nobody. And you?

Who are you, by the way? And what is that story about a woman, and that circus act, that rumpus on the stairs, it looks like something that rolls. What? Mireille. I don't know who this Mireille is. And, any-way, I never liked that name.

PASO DOBLE

Caroline Lamarche

It's raining.

I think about my grandfather, who, even when it rained, forced me to accompany him on his daily walk. We didn't go into the woods then, we just went for the other "turn," around the meadows. Standing in front of the cows, he held my hand and said to them, politely:

"Hello! You are so clean today!"

I used to reply merrily:

"It's because of the rain!"

I'm no longer a child. I no longer speak for the animals, nobody holds me by the hand. I go out when I want, and I go wherever I please. Today I took a shower. I'm clean and fresh like a cow under the rain, my lips are moist, my cheeks smooth, I'm wearing a very short skirt hidden beneath my long black coat and, inside my panties, there's a wet dew weeping through soft hair. That's where I pen my animals.

I walk fast, in the direction of the posh neighborhood. When I arrive at the building, I ring and, without waiting for a response, I push open the glass door, walk across the hall, and climb the steps two at a time, right up to the top floor.

Each time I tell myself: perhaps he won't be there, perhaps I made a mistake and it's the wrong day, perhaps he's changed his mind, he's not alone, he won't open the door. Then suddenly he's standing there in front of me, in the doorway of his luxurious loft with the sky eating the glass roof, the tree whose branches bang against the panes, and, tonight, the rain patting in short quick bursts.

"You're so big, so strong, you have strength," he says.

I hold him tight against me, thinking about her, the woman with slim ankles. Her wrists, ankles, long neck, and hips are all so narrow. You can see how narrow through her dress. There's a photo of her on the refrigerator door. Another on the living-room table.

"Paso doble!" he says, sweeping me away.

In his home there's always music. As soon as one enters, one has to sway and adopt the tempo. He is so supple. He comes and goes, and I follow him, sensual, or at least trying to be, for I must be sensual for him to fancy me, or I'll be back in the cold suddenly, in the rain, without anyone to take my hand.

"Relax," he says, "we're in Spain, the gypsies are dancing like goddesses, with their heavy breasts and their protruding pubes. Then, when they fuck it's seven orgasms an hour, a whole chain of explosions, the witches' cauldron. *Paso doble*, dance!"

He clings to me, the woman who can't dance, and the stylish living room changes into a dark cellar where gorgeous gypsies stare at me and laugh. He leaves with three of them, and I stay there, under the rain of a season that will pass like all the others.

Later, in the kitchen, I watch him eating. He's eating alone, for, as usual, I've declined: "Don't worry about me, I'm not hungry." He always obeys and never prepares anything for me. Seated opposite him, I drink a glass of wine. He's wearing one of the twenty-five shirts that the woman with slim ankles has given him. His shoulders are broad, his waist narrow, and his legs long, legs that will grip mine tight. I tell myself we're married, even if it's not true. Because I watch him eating, because his legs imprison mine, I'm his wife forever. We'll have children and take them to the meadows to see the cows in the rain.

He finishes his meal as the phone rings. It's not always raining, and the wind doesn't always push the branches of the tree against the panes, but, each time, the phone does ring. I have permission to stay, I don't intrude. I leave the table, take a book from the shelves, and lie down on the thick pile carpet. If I raise my head I can see his feet walking up and down the carpet, his shoes always beautifully polished, and his English socks. He doesn't buy them himself, she runs a men's clothing store. I imagine him sitting in a small fitting room, his feet naked, and she, kneeling, her skirt pulled up her thighs, her transparent groin exposed, drawing on the English sock, a sock as soft as a vagina.

He's talking to her on the phone. I can't hear what he says because of the storm in my head. I can only see his lips moving, begging, and his eyes seeking mine. "Stay," his eyes say when they catch mine. "Stay, you're so strong."

Afterward, he puts the phone down and slides next to me.

"Did you hear how I comforted her, how I gave her strength?"

He snuggles in my arms, fidgets like a feverish child. I ask him tenderly:

"Is she going to leave her husband soon? Will she come and live here with you?"

"I don't know," he says. "It's so difficult, it's such a long story. If only you knew! We are alone, she and I. Alone against the whole world."

And he starts crying, devastated.

I stroke his face and say, in the same obstinate rhythm as the rain, those same few words, always the same:

"I'm with you both, against the whole world."

The tree rubs against the pane, the rain marks the glass.

He has laid me on the bed. He takes off my shoes, caresses my hair, pulling it back.

"Your forehead is like a little girl's."

His fingers brush against my wrist, undo my watch. It slips and falls to the floor.

There's a lamp next to the bed. And under the lamp always something belonging to her.

The first time it was a letter with fine writing which started: "My love . . ."

I didn't read any further.

The second time, placed on a piece of white paper, a tuft of very dark pubic hair, cut with scissors.

Sometimes a wristwatch. Forgotten.

And today?

Today there's nothing under the lamp.

But when I lie down and he pulls off my skirt, when he skins me like a rabbit freshly killed, I see a shadow on the ceiling that looks like a muzzle.

I sit up. On the lampshade, there's a pair of women's panties.

I say nothing. I lie down again, wait.

He leans over me.

"Remove that!" I scream.

He lift his shoulders, stretches his arm, grabs the panties, white with their little garnet-red flowers and flat bow on the front, garnet too. He puts the panties on his face, nods slowly, careful not to drop them.

He laughs.

"I haven't washed them."

Suddenly I change my mind, apologize cheerfully.

"Leave them, it's not important."

Then I crawl, beg:

"Swear that when I come here there'll always be an object belonging to her."

"Promise," he says, putting the trophy down underneath the lamp.

He lies down on top of me. His voice is gentle now, as soft as his skin.

"I know you by heart, you're tense like a little girl, you don't move, you don't scream, you never will, not like her. She screams, if only you knew how she screams!"

He lifts himself up, gazes at me, changes my position. My left arm stretched out, my right arm covering my eyes, my legs spread but bent to make room for him between my feet placed flat on the bed. He sits cross-legged, he's naked now, a yogi meditating, then he breathes in calmly, a deep-sea diver getting ready.

He dives. His fingers are in me. Without looking at me, he focuses on the hand that spreads open, searches, lets itself be swallowed like the sucking of an octopus, then pulls out, shining, soaked like my grandfather's hand when he stroked the muzzle of his favorite cow. The other cows breathed hard, then left, seemingly anxious. But that one let him come closer, unworried, put out its wet tongue and swallowed his fingers pensively.

"She . . ." he says pensively, stretching me beneath him.

He rolls his beautiful shirt, one of the twenty-five, under my loins. "You."

His voice has changed, it's a knife that has to quickly cut the meat still warm, before it cools, before it loses all its blood.

"You," he says, "you."

He has words like that, words of power and necessity, words of the famished ogre, the surgeon averting the hemorrhage, the vampire who must finish before day breaks.

He takes me. Far. Hard. My head bangs against the wall.

"She," he says, withdrawing slowly. "And you," he says, plunging in again to kill me with pleasure.

He keeps quiet, drills his way in as a stranger, with a despair that concerns them both, he and she, two beings united, through me, against the whole world.

"Don't scream!"

I double-lock my scream, murder it, in tribute to the woman with slim ankles, the woman who dances and fucks better than me.

Then, suddenly, for being so quiet, for that docile silence like a big body letting itself be moved, I come into the immense light. And my limbs are ablaze and fly away with great flaps of their wings, while he cries out and falls back.

Afterward, he falls asleep like a very heavy child, my leg imprisoned by his. When it hurts too much I move slightly, but he feels it and, in his half-sleep, he leans harder and holds me immobile. I turn my face to the window. It's pouring with rain, channels are forming, all the waters are joining together, and the branches bang against the panes, and the cows stare at us, mooing with their dull sound.

"How clean they are today, Granddad!"

"It's because of the rain!"

LOS ANGELES SONG

Françoise Simpère

In the depths of the night, Neil's body suddenly crashes on top of me, heavily. His mouth seeks mine, wakes me up. His kiss has already deserted my mouth, takes hold of my neck, travels down to my breasts . . . He is driven by the frenzy of an ogre, devours my writhing belly, licks my cunt, my thighs, while my hands grip his shoulders, scratch him and drag his big body upward with all my might, to fit inside me straightaway, his sex in mine.

"Come inside me, I want you to." I am spread wide, and when he penetrates me, my walls, stuck to his dick, draw it in, take it all the way in. I feel my buttocks contracting to grip it even tighter. He moans under that hot and rhythmic caress, and he plunges even deeper. We are joined together in a slow coming and going where his penis explores every nook and cranny, bashes, slides, feels at home. My vagina offers him refuge, board and lodging. Later on he will devour me again, his tongue will insinuate itself into the smallest place and I will scream my pleasure. He kisses me as he fucks me, licks my eyelids, explores my mouth, both our tongues entangling. He plunges a finger in that I can feel sliding in my moistness. Neil penetrates everywhere inside me, my whole body shivers, I want him to stay like that forever, always anchored that way in each of the orifices he fills and satisfies. Then he turns me over, lies on my back, bites my shoulders, feels his way and finds the narrow route. I quiver and scream, I quiver and cry, from that so peculiar orgasm when one laughs and cries, so intense are the emotions. Sometimes, on the contrary, my body pierced by the sharp arrow of pleasure stiffens and comes to rest, silent, bewildered . . .

Then Neil rests on top of me, his faun head placed in the hollow of my shoulders. His heart beats very fast, I feel it pumping against mine. We fuck all the time, night and day, in hot weather, in the cool dawn, in the thunderstorm crackling and hammering at the shutters . . . I was about to write "we make love," for it is love we are making—I love him, he loves me—but it is also fucking, the hungry and wild fucking of a man who decided a long time ago that women were too much trouble to ever get hooked with and who was satisfied with quickies in the company of prostitutes during drunken parties, or with his hand to provide relief on certain nights. But most of the time, he didn't even think about it anymore. Neil told me all of that in one go, on the evening of Uluru's spell. As soon as we emerged from lovemaking, he sighed heavily, lit a cigarette, and, exhaling his first puff, said:

"Well, let me explain now . . ." In a monotonous drone, as if he was reading the Bible or an insurance policy, he told me about his life as a happy recluse between his mates and his plane, a life I had turned upside down without wanting to, in fact because I didn't want to, entering his life like a safe "mate," a friend who had breasts and buttocks, and would scarcely be aware of all that, and now he couldn't imagine how he lived before I came into his life. He spoke without interruption, as if trying to rid himself as quickly as possible of those confidences he was not used to, he the taciturn exasperated by psychobabble, the lover of big silent spaces who ran away from rooms full of squawking, wealthy heiresses to come here to play his own Western far from the city. For I also learned that night that Neil was the son of a wealthy family, his father in high finance, his mother a legal expert, his little sister a fashion designer; it sounded like the casting for an American soap in which the elder son was the black sheep and didn't give a damn. He had been an art student, had tried theater, had known some success among the cognoscenti, taken part in short-lived artistic experiments, and then, tired of that milieu which was even more narcissistic than he was, he'd studied for his pilot license and decided to leave the city behind and become king of the desert.

As for me, who was threatening a balance he'd reached at heavy cost, I had come into his life like a burglar, but now the man who had been burgled wanted to keep his burglar. While I caressed his back with one hand, the other wandering over buttocks whose softness surprised me for such a crude being, Neil told me serenely:

"I'd like you to stay with me. For a long time. For as long as possible."

My heart jumped joyfully. I let those words slowly enter me with infinite happiness, ready as I was to share Neil's life, as we'd been doing since I'd arrived, like a "mate," as adventurous as he, with the additional aspect of the sexual pleasure, which linked us strongly. But Neil didn't leave me time to speak. He put a finger on his lips, and added:

"Don't say anything, think before you answer. I feel good with you, we're happy together. It's the first time in a long while, and perhaps it's the last time I'll make that proposition to a woman. But if you accept, I want you to be totally mine. I'm an uncompromising man, I couldn't share you with somebody else. Not even with Alex, who's like a brother to me."

Do you remember, David? One evening as we were talking about our broken hearts, you asked me how I had been able to give up some passions. I had confided my secret to you: when I feel my heart and my body invaded by Prince Charming, in order to rid myself of his hold I just need to imagine how my existence would be if I decided to live with him only, and to renounce meeting any other man. It's not a lack of love, it's a need for freedom: I'm capable of loving passionately and eternally, but I refuse to entrust my life to a single man. As I get older, I'm even more convinced of that. Several times I thought I'd met, as one says, the "man of my life," which clearly means that several men were capable of being that man, and not one single person on earth, as little girls are told. For the world to progress, David, it needed scientists, intellectuals, bricklayers, farmers, adventurers, dancers, and even policemen and greengrocers with gray overalls and a pencil behind their ear. For a life to blossom, I think one needs various loves and one cannot abandon one's existence to a single being, brilliant as he might be. But how to explain to a man who thinks he's making you a worldly present by asking you to give up your freedom to live with him, that his present is a poisonous one? Especially when that man attracts you in a shameful way and moves you to tears?

Neil was not surprised by my silence. He'd found the solution himself:

"You need to go back to Paris, you have to go back to work anyway. You go back, you take the time to think it over and you make up your mind. I am not in a hurry, I've been living alone for more than ten years."

I had a lump in my throat, a terrible desire to shout at him: "Neil, it's all decided, I'm staying with you, we'll never be apart." I was in a state of romantic intoxication, when one thinks a chance like that, a man like that, won't happen again. Are there many men who turn to you with such limpid eyes and whisper like an excuse: "I'm sorry to cause you problems. I'd like to say stay with me and live as you want, but I know I won't be able to."

Neil accompanied Alice to Brisbane, where she got her luggage and then flew to Paris from Sydney. The Sydney–Paris flight was heading to Los Angeles. She had chosen to go back via the United States, after having arrived via Asia. Never had the Earth looked so round to her.

The Sydney–Los Angeles flight was packed. She found herself sitting next to an obese blond woman whose arm, wobbling like jelly, dipped at regular intervals into a giant bag of potato chips. The flight attendant was pulling her hair out trying to accommodate the passengers, who were unhappy for the most part about the places they had been allocated. The big lady would have liked to be next to her husband, a sturdy Texan from the same mold as his wife, but the seat was not available. The husband insisted, the hostess sighed, gesturing that she was powerless . . . Trying her luck, she asked the husband's neighbor if he would mind changing seats, and that is how Alice ended up sitting next to a brown man, nearly two meters tall, with turquoise blue eyes. He greeted her politely, then became engrossed in the reading of a financial paper while crunching on some celery sticks he extracted from a brown paper bag marked "organic food" and ate as fast as a squirrel shelling hazelnuts. The handsome young man asked the hostess for a special tray. He was served an assortment of vegetables and cheeses definitely more appetizing than the fried chicken served to the other passengers. Alice plucked up the courage to ask:

"Are you a vegetarian?"

"Yes, and an ecologist, too."

In a few sentences he told her that he was a broker in the stock exchange, an ecologist and a Democrat, a bachelor with a diploma in economy, and a lover of Romanesque churches he went to visit each spring in Europe "because old stones give Europeans a solidity that the American don't have because of their lack of history." In a word, a rare specimen of learned cowboy. After dinner Alice fell asleep. In the half-somnolence allowed by the din of the jets and the continual coming and going of passengers and crew, she daydreamed . . . Under her eyelids a group of sharp kangaroos passed by. She saw once more the ocean depths that she had explored with Neil, the electric blue starfish and giant corals. She found the smell of the air hangar in her memory, the dryness of the dusty takeoff strips. She remembered an evening when both had played poker with Neil's mates, fleecing one of them who had lost everything, including his shirt. She remembered the rustic breakfasts when Neil proved capable of devouring half a dozen grilled sausages with his coffee, and the pleasure she'd had chatting with him some afternoons while he showered, naked in the garden, letting her contemplate him with no embarrassment whatsoever. It was that man she had fallen in love with, that generous adventurer who had opened his life to her with no restrictions. It was that man she had desired, because he had appeared immense and boundless. But once they had made love, the limits suddenly appeared. The adventurer had changed into a small landowner anxious to defend his property. Alice felt sadness flooding her. To get rid of it, she tried to evoke lovemaking with Neil, to feel again the emotion of his caresses, but, funnily enough, only images from before she'd met Neil came to her mind. She sighed, yawned, and slowly sank into a half-sleep. At some point she felt a blanket placed on top of her, a soft and light blanket wrapping her in a relaxing warmth. Her head found a rest that seemed comfortable, and she snuggled up. The aisles of the plane were dark now, punctuated here and there with night-lights. One could hear slight coughs, quiet stirrings. Some passengers removed their shoes; others went to brush their teeth. They were entering that long night flight like a parenthesis out of the world, where only the crew is awake, like sailors keeping watch.

Alice opened her eyes at around two in the morning, awoken by a cramp in her calf. She realized her head was resting on her neighbor's shoulder. He had spread the blanket across both their knees and seemed to be asleep. She felt the long legs of the American against her thigh. As a dare, she leaned slightly, but he didn't react at all. She then slipped her hand under the blanket between the man's thighs and closed her eyes again. She was now completely awake and on the lookout for the slightest tremor in her neighbor, to whom she replied with as subtle a pressure. At the beginning it was imperceptible, just a touch of heat spreading from his body to her hand. Then the heat took shape, very slowly. Ever so lightly she clenched her fingers, stopped, waited. The shape was becoming more precise. It was magical, magical as if her hand was transforming energy into matter. As magical as a man's erection always is. Alice continued her progress with the same slowness, her eyes still closed, her body perfectly still. Only her fingers communicated with the prick, which was becoming more and more receptive to their messages. When it became necessary, she sent her other hand to the rescue of the first, to open the zip of his fly, very delicately . . . The American didn't move one iota, but Alice was sure he was no longer asleep, except of course if he thought he was having an erotic dream. His prick was warm and of decent size, only waiting to blossom even more. Alice caressed it first with a delicate forefinger, then with two fingers, and finally with the whole hand encircling it like an elastic and moving sheath around the missile. Her movements, coming and going, were extremely gentle and regular, in perfect harmony with the ambience of that night on the plane. Only the pressure she placed on the base of his penis or at its tip was at times more insistent. The little game didn't last long. She felt her neighbor's hips shudder, a quick undulation under her fingers and almost immediately the spurting of sperm, which drew a soft moan from the man. She spread it on his cock with little gentle circles, kneaded it in delight with her hands. The man half-opened his mouth and caressed his lips with his fingers. Alice noticed, moved, that he was doing on his lips the same little circles she was drawing at the tip of his penis, at the same rhythm, two melodies played together in harmony.

Then the American turned his face toward hers, took it in his hands, and kissed her like a passionate lover, punctuating each of his kisses with whispers that said: "Oh, love, my love, you are my love," and Alice savored the sweetness of those kisses, of those hands that were caressing her face, of those loving words that made her feel warm all over and wrapped her up in the exact tenderness she needed at that moment. They traveled through the night, huddled together, hand in hand, until the lights were turned on again, an hour and a half before landing. The flight attendant brought breakfast. Alice and the American smiled at each other.

"Hello, did you get a good night's sleep?" Both felt relaxed and happy. Alice knew that she could never give up living such magic moments.

ONE-ACT PLAY

Sonia Rykiel

Onstage the setting has been arranged.

Exactly as in the drawing.

With the sweater.

"I said it was the only set I wanted. A red sweater."

"Why red?"

"Because of the text."

"But the text doesn't count, not really."

"But I wrote it. I started it all over again, several times, in the countryside, under the chestnut tree, with the children playing hide-and-seek, and the woman, there, the one who walks across the stage. I asked her to play the part. She accepted on one condition: that she play all the female parts."

"Obviously not thinking."

"No, self-seeking."

"She was a young woman. But what was touching about her was her mobility, the way she placed her hands, rounded her arms, played with her legs. I watched her for a long time in the garden. She was picking cherries, placing them in the basket. I didn't know I was writing the text. It dropped on me like a peach."

"Why, did you find her attractive?"

"I'm not interested in women and I knew nothing about her, except that there was a man in her life, a stranger with a book under his arm who visited sometimes, but never stayed."

On the door, to the right of the stage, a sign saying, I'm Leaving.

Then the stranger smashed in the door.

She was on the floor, her face powdered very white, her lips crimson, outlined with a pencil. A pillow under her head.

She was reading.

He approached, took the book away, placed it at her feet.

"Were you waiting for me?"

"No! You can see I'm leaving."

"I forbid you to leave."

"You knew I would have to leave. That we wouldn't be able to carry on. I fall asleep waiting for you. It's true, you haven't promised me anything, you've kept your word more than you said, but I'm tired. Tired of waiting, of understanding, of admitting, tired of hearing, of living on two floors at the same time. Of course the terrace has a view over the forest, the sun shines on both sides of the house, there is fire, music, food, every type of nourishment. There is you, sometimes. But that 'sometimes' crushes me. It's like I was traveling, and I don't like traveling. I like to settle, to lie down on the sofa. I like to be touched, that you touch me, caress me. I need you every day in my movements inside my sweater. I'm dying to take it off, to put it back to front, to tear it. I can walk like you ask me across the living room, naked under the wool, with the high heels you like, my hair pulled back to show my neck. I can imagine those people all around us looking at me and you looking at them to see if they're really looking at me. You would like to have your name written across my body, on that mayor's sash you were wearing not so long ago again. You would like me provocative under the fold of that transparent skirt, like an etching drawn with drypoint."

I would be far away, out of everyone's reach.

In the story, golden candles were burning in baroque-style candelabras. The air was heavy with incense and flowers, red like my sweater, hydrangeas, staring at us.

"You've never seen red hydrangeas?"

"Of course, since I'm saying so. They would be there, by chance, cut into vases as beautiful as sculptures. Giant crimson bulbs that would contemplate us, mouths wide open."

I don't know why it reminds me of Venice, the beauty probably, the water, the oblivion. In Venice one forgets everything except for champagne with a drop of squeezed peach, and to touch each other with the tips of one's fingers first, then the hand, and the face, across the table, in Harry's Bar. But you would be there behind me, dressed up, ready to take me in your arms if I flinch, if I'm scared to walk across that room naked, under everyone's gaze. You wanted me to sit in front of that table, alone. I no longer look, but I observe. You whisper: how gorgeous and voluptuous you are!

I removed that sweater gently, lifting up my arms. I had never imagined anything like that.

I knew you were right, that I could do it and, above all, that afterward I would be able to play the scene.

That is when the incident happened.

Before stripping, I leaned back on my chair, my body rocking, arms behind me, and I swayed in the emptiness. I felt a hand grab mine, like in a slow-motion film. I let myself go. The hand stroked mine for a long while, then entered the sleeve of my sweater and caressed my arm, went still farther up, and across to my breast. I lost all notion of time. I could see only the lit candles. Everything was turning, but I felt fine. The lower part of my body was riveted to the chair. I closed my eyes and did not move. The hand didn't move, either, but the other hand slid into the other sleeve, this hand was less predictable, moved along gently, pressing on the flesh to leave its mark.

The two hands now gripped my shoulders tight. I held my breath, waiting. They were skillful and agile. They followed the outline of my body, brushing against the sensitive parts that consented to them totally.

"Come back to your senses," I told myself, "or you're going to fall like a hen into a trap."

For I had already been taken like that, hands in sweater. When we traveled by car and I was drawing in the passenger seat, he used to say suddenly:

"Lift your sweater."

And I had to lift my sweater. We avoided so many crashes on the highway. I was frantic, but he smiled and continued driving without looking at me. At other times, in a restaurant, seated in front of me, looking straight into my eyes:

"Lift your sweater!"

"But there are people around."

He didn't reply, just looked at me. I obeyed.

Once again he had forced me to take a shortcut. There were people everywhere.

"I'm not a woman of easy virtue!"

"You're a woman that belongs to me."

Nothing was left to chance. He led me by that little sweater exactly where he wanted.

He read me through the wool and the flesh, he read that I belonged to him, each stitch, each row and each stripe.

"I built you, wrote you, I gathered you in my book under the red cover with a golden binding and a bookmark with your initials on it. I inscribed your name on the back cover and I dedicated that book to 'the woman of my life.' I could draw your body freely on each page, caress it, question it. But you never answer."

"Ask questions."

"Love?"

"Not always."

"Novel?"

"Kundera."

"Beauty?"

"It's always striped."

"Making love?"

"I surrender, I don't cheat, I display it all, I gamble, I laugh, I touch, I can start all over again if you want."

"Already?"

"Again? Touch wood to exorcise, drink wine, Château Margaux in a glass with a crystal stem, lie down on the carpet, turn over."

"Sweater?"

"Venice."

"Luxury?"

"To walk across the room, rolling like a pearl."

"Pearl?"

"Fake."

"Black?"

"No rules, all that glitters is not black."

"Game?"

"Define the rule, un-define the role."

"Robe?"

"I change robes like I jump fences, with knife pleats, arms up, zip open down to the buttocks."

She was truly disgraceful.

"Dream."

It all happened as in the dream. I had only one desire, to keep those unknown hands inside my body, imprisoned in my sweater, to forget the text (which I had difficulty remembering), to start the dialogues all over again, but, above all, rule out that man dressed up to whom I belonged, to turn around to see the man with the hands, the one behind me, who kept caressing me. But I knew I would be lost if I saw his face.

"Lost?"

"Yes."

And my hand closed on his arm. He must have been tall and strong and calm. He moved forward against the chair.

The man dressed up facing me watched the scene, fascinated. He had often told me: "The strange thing with you is that I always feel like I'm in a film."

Now he was in the film, at the center of it, he didn't move. I knew he was scared but, at the same time, I could feel his desire. He moved toward me across the table and opened his arms. I leaned backward.

"Don't lie."

"It doesn't matter, I could die after that, lie or die or depart because the man dressed up will never let me go. I have no choice, except to run away."

I could really have died as I wanted at that moment on my chair, or at least disappear inside that stranger's body.

But imagine it's not a dream, a wonderful dream, more beautiful than all the dreams you ever had, a mad adventure you lived for real, one evening in Venice, in Harry's Bar.

Imagine you followed that man, because you couldn't do anything else, you went into his bed because you needed to, your life depended on it.

And today . . .

"The curtain falls."

THE ECSTASIES

Sophie Cadalen

Floriane had done some tidying up in her life, in her head, and in her soul. She had cleared her memories, sold some land, chosen her ground, and sunk permanent foundations.

Nothing could harm her efficiency, no hazard would slow down her productivity. She had disentangled herself from her marriage, ejected her lover and his perversities, which looked more and more like habits. She had scratched her exes out of her address book, the exes of a past she had put away for good.

She looked hard at her situation. She adored her job—she was a publicist—and everyone respected her. Her professional life provided her with challenges, races against time, contracts won by sheer force, success and rewards, everything coated with an euphoric fatigue that would turn to depression should Floriane quit.

She liked *that*. But apart from *that* there was nothing but deceptions, lies, unanswered calls, betrayals . . . and a few paltry orgasms compared to the troubles endured.

She was aware of her power of seduction and the handling of that fabulous tool. She adored devouring the other with an offensive sensuality that was hers alone. The confidence in her eyes grabbed the man's balls, took away any inclination to resist or oppose her plan. She opened wide the doors to an imaginary bed in which the irresistible charm of the prey thinking it was the hunter would triumph . . . and stopped at the last stage of controlling the situation. When a flutter of the eyelid was enough to bed a man, Floriane turned her back on her victory. What could the following promise or reveal that would be as exciting? A lover on his high horse because he fucked you? A husband for life and children to wipe clean? No, not for Floriane. Seduction only rhymes with manipulation. She would no longer lose time thinking in terms of emotion and affection. That almost always ended up in disillusion.

She didn't understand how a woman could pine for a man and his dick. Floriane was quite happy without. Her hand knew the preferences of her clitoris much better than her lovers—whose ability was acquired at the same time boredom settled in. Three years ago she had even bought herself a dildo, for she hadn't wanted to pay the price of frustration for her new life. She tried it once and mostly laughed at seeing herself in the mirror, laboriously discovering her new tool, like a dedicated pupil doing her homework. She hadn't needed that thing between her legs. She threw it to the bottom of her cupboard and returned to the gymnastic performance of her fingers on her button.

These were her life perspectives, the plans for a career at the very center of her preoccupations. Out of the question now for a promising pretty cock to turn her away from the strong sensations that excited her daily. Everything was fine. And would be. Thanks to her.

A female friend—as there were many in that career begging for favors and ready to do the same in return—had arranged for Floriane to be invited to a show to predict the next Parisian sensation, on the condition that as a publicist she take an interest, obviously.

That friend hadn't told her a lot about it, except that it was a song and dance act performed by two partners, the "new trend" variety turn. Floriane had to make up her own mind.

She was invited three hundred times a year to attend the "next revolution" in the world of entertainment. Her obsession with markets and budgets prevented her from getting tied up in the warm solicitude of those desperate artists. She would see if there was a way to strike it rich or not, would contemplate investing her competence if the outcome promised to be juicy.

This "event" was performed in a cabaret in Saint Germain, one of those seedy remnants of the glorious postwar period whose meager returns were provided by the well-worn numbers of tired entertainers, one of those places where darkness didn't prevent their despair from rising to the surface.

Floriane's presence had in itself dusted off and cheered up the "song cellar." Her conversion to the god Work already gave her some recognition, essential for her ascent to the top of her profession. She was thus preceded by her reputation as a fighter, the first trump of a publicist when comfort and success haven't weakened her in the battles.

She found there the usual clique of hangers-on, their exaggerated displays of affection as noisy as indifferent. The owner offered her a glass of champagne, installed her at the best table, begged for Florian's indulgence during the few numbers preceding the show.

Onstage, a succession of none-too-subtle comedians, pale copies of popular singers, and magicians burdened by hats with no rabbits.

The master of ceremonies, as dashing as the cabaret, finally announced the long-awaited moment, the attraction "the whole world is rushing to see"—the world can be kept in such a small space—the future stars of a firmament that was already warming up for them: "The Ecstasies!"

The spotlights softened the narrow stage.

To syrupy music of antiquated arrangements, a male and a female transvestite appeared, having swapped genders.

The man, or rather the woman dressed as a man, pulled apart the structure of the melody with the voice of a castrato. The woman, or the man made up as a woman, hammered that song with singularly low notes. The whole was rather curious, disconcerting, more disturbing than entertaining. Their movements, the choreography of their exercises in vocalization, were measured and rare, but extraordinarily lascivious. They set the stage afire with their attempts and restraints.

The song ended with them facing each other.

They looked at each other, took each other's clothes off with gestures of evanescent precision and a calm that held back time. Then they turned to the audience and displayed their identities: the woman become a woman again and the man a man, their bodies embraced in clothes more provocative than plain nudity. Another song followed, thick and dripping, a pretext for an excursion of their voices into still different octaves! They were at ease in every register, and their stoicism, embellished with new definitions, doubled the eroticism of ambiguity.

Nothing in that tableau appeased or reassured the spectator. The gender swap, the voices, the placid expressions, the brutal and effortless sensuality, the strangeness of the melodies in that dubious kitschy music, all was moving and repulsive, captivating and unnerving.

They resumed their strip as the last notes struck. Surprising the audience, they appeared now as two men who could not be mistaken as anything else, for they wore only skimpy pants. Their third and last interpretation was still accompanied by that gloomy music they rolled from low to high and high to low, their sonorities clashing and attacking one another as their hands caressed each other unequivocally.

The number came to an end. They faced the audience, each with his hand placed on the other's erect penis. They turned around, their other hands clutching their partner's buttocks. The light faded on their faces joined together in a full-blown kiss.

The light dragged the room out of the dark, caught Floriane in the midst of her feeling of uneasiness, which was not really uneasiness, more like a funny feeling, a strange feeling, a feeling of being in between.

She was incapable of either penalizing the show with her disapproval or praising it with her encouragement. She didn't know if it was good, or if she liked it. She just couldn't think in terms of impact on the audience. She was still in shock, a shock she didn't know if she would wake from happy, disappointed, or unscathed.

The owner, hotfooting it over to gather her reactions, came up against her unease. Without thinking, Floriane asked to meet The Ecstasies. A pointless request, which made the owner move quicker than any encouragement thrown like crumbs. He charged to the dressing room, leaving her in that indefinable mist.

The two men were seated before her in a flash, indecipherable as their faces had been during their whole act. They didn't obey the rules of Floriane's profession, which were, basically, that they were the ones who should be begging, the ones doing their utmost to win her over. They waited. They didn't show any interest, not even to be polite, didn't ask for her impressions. They waited. And Floriane no longer knew why she had summoned them. She clutched at a few tricks practiced in her job, became entangled in her discomfort, the so-called tricks necessitating an interlocutor she didn't have. She mumbled vague compliments, argued over thoughts she hadn't even had, asked questions that were met with a stony silence.

A few splutterings later, the two men, unmoved and silent, rose with the same intention. Floriane sprang from her chair:

"No, no, don't leave! We have to discuss, I have to . . . I can help you . . . we have to talk it through!"

Her "we have to" was heartbreaking, begging. She didn't give any order, she beseeched. Like their show, playing on the permutation of roles, there she was, Floriane, an efficient and pragmatic publicist, clamoring for the attention of two completely unknown artists earning their living in a seedy joint.

They looked at her for a long time. Then one of them made a sign for Floriane to follow. She complied immediately. They led her backstage, to their dressing room, a tiny room cluttered with costumes, flounces, sequins, and fake jewelry bathed in a red aura whose muted tone gave it a threatening air.

She stood in the middle of the box room, between the two men seated on the only two chairs in the place, which couldn't have held any other seat, anyway.

The man who had invited her uttered some words in a warm, deep voice, with a South American accent:

"The play on genders scares people. The one we just showed you. It's not certain that people want to see it. My name is Gabriel. I love Roberto. I love his cock, I love the little whore that he is, I love the bitch he would have been if that thing hadn't grown between his legs. And you, you like to know that we fuck each other in the ass, you like us to touch each other and show you."

Floriane tried to protest in a cocktail of exaggerated laughter and unconvincing denial. He interrupted her:

"You don't need to promise us articles for us to fuck you. But you don't know how to ask for those things. You have a guy in you who has his ass on fire, you are a bitch who hasn't sucked for a long time. Roberto, the lady needs us."

They fell on their knees simultaneously, cornered her between the oppressively close walls and their naked torsos. They slipped their four hands under her skirt, reached the top of her stockings, and rolled them to her ankles. Together they went back up for her panties, which joined the nylon at her feet.

Floriane was unable to react, think, or escape. They had guessed quicker than she had, they had beaten her to the post of her desires. Yes, Gabriel was right. That's what she wanted, those two gays to ransack her and gobble up her liberated desires.

Her skirt was pulled up to her waist, her sex and ass delivered to the lappings of The Ecstasies. Gabriel numbed her crack with intoxicating speed. Roberto devoured her asshole with a muscular and stubborn tongue. Floriane's pudenda dripped with saliva and juice, sweeping her off her feet and flooding her thoughts, an overflowing the men soaked up.

Gabriel made her clitoris explode into a first orgasm, kept the pleasure button at his mouth and tongue, kept hold of Floriane to stop her withdrawing from a sensual delight so unbearably full of tension. Roberto took the opportunity of the deflagration to poke into the asshole, the spasms of pleasure gripping his tongue tight in the vestibule of her rectum. Floriane was nothing more than a floor cloth, a derisory piece of material trying to contain the waves of an ocean.

Her nostrils were excited by highly recognizable emanations. She smelled a coulis of sperm, the cream of their glans, that rare decoction that trumpets the erection and serves as a prelude to the geyser.

The two men mastered the score with magnificent chords.

They stood. In the same movement they placed Floriane on her knees, bent her forward to their brandished penises. She swallowed the most pressing, sucked in and drank at the velvety stick, choked herself going in search of its very root. The other cock berated her neck, demanded her attention with repeated and insistent nudges. Floriane turned her head, reassured the lonely one with the same favors, while the abandoned one rolled itself snugly in the thick of her hair. The two men stuck together, simultaneously imposed their aims, pushed themselves between her lips, her cheeks bulging with their impressive rams. Floriane felt and heard The Ecstasies kissing while she retained them in her mouth, their tongues entangling and their cocks intermingling in her warm bodily fluids.

Roberto withdrew, leaving Gabriel free to swim and frolic on Floriane's regal palate. He lifted her back on her feet, demanded her ass, without Gabriel's cock being abandoned from her mouth.

Her carnation was still lubricated from previous lickings. He pointed his glans at the entrance of the anus, checked its elasticity and consent, plunged irremediably to the limit to glue his balls to Floriane's shell.

She was breathless, mouth and ass stoppered, her breath taken away, her senses reeling. Roberto and Gabriel grabbed their hands, adopted a to-and-fro rhythm, together polishing Florian's ass and buccal cavern. She felt heady from the alchemy of pleasure and the pain of sodomy, lost her footing and consciousness. Roberto supported her with a sturdy arm around her waist, keeping solid the connection between Gabriel and himself.

Roberto, still planted in her asshole, suddenly straightened her and almost carried her, lifting her legs, revealing the gap of her slit and inviting Gabriel to shaft her.

He obliged. He left her mouth and cleaved to the vulva. Floriane was taken from both sides, their cocks separated only by a thin membrane, playing hide-and-seek inside her, inhabiting her country only to chase after each other. They resumed their rhythm and alternating, one pushing forth while the other drew back, one filling her while the other left her. She was the instrument of their eroticism, the gadget of their sexual delirium, a pretext but not the object of their fantasies. And it was fabulous. She no longer felt her legs, she didn't have any strength left, she was nothing more than two holes swept like a chimney by their disrespectful monsters. She no longer decided, she no longer controlled, she was taken, battered, transported, denied, pierced, transgressed . . . and it was good, so good . . .

She lost consciousness, crushed by orgasm, killed by The Ecstasies, lashed by the revenge of a body neglected for too long.

She came back to her senses almost immediately.

She was crumpled, a pile of clothes abandoned on the floor, between the legs of Roberto being fucked by Gabriel. Roberto's sperm spurted out in her face, at the same time that Gabriel came in his friend's ass. They hadn't reserved for Floriane the dime of their desires, the elixir of their body dance. It was not her they honored, but their love that they brandished, their imagination fed on others and their unavowed lusts.

She remained prostrate, her face soiled by Roberto's sperm, her skirt rolled up and her stockings hanging loose at her heels. The two men leaned toward her. Roberto grabbed Gabriel's cock, wiped the shit and come in the mouth of Floriane, who showed no sign of protest, then dried it on her silk blouse. He rubbed himself against her, cleaned the stickiness of his gaping ass, slipped Floriane's hair in the furrow of his buttocks. She didn't protest. Didn't even think about rebelling. It was normal. All of it was normal. By urging her body to be quiet, she had to be used as an outlet. She had no regrets. Her belly was still quivering. Her orifices hesitated to close for fear of no longer being forced. Her lips already craved other cocks to clasp, to enclose with tenderness.

The Ecstasies left without a word, without looking back, plunging the dressing room into darkness and leaving her on the spot, the caprice of the night made invisible.

She rose painfully—painfully because she felt good there—and feebly readjusted her clothes before aiming for the exit.

The owner was waiting for her. His face contorted when he saw her, convinced that the abuses she had visibly been made the victim of meant the definite closure of his joint. Floriane crossed the room without saying a word to him, disregarded the call for a taxi, and disappeared into the night.

The Ecstasies never became famous. Sometimes they were the object of an allusion, quickly forgotten, never again raised. Those who crossed their path—men, women, couples—never mentioned them. The cabaret act took on the illusion of a myth that was spared its moving reality.

Floriane changed the direction of her career: she became interested in young talent, enjoyed hunting them down, worked hard at making them heard, making them exist.

Uncertainty and unpredictability regained their rights and Floriane went from delightful meetings to sexual delights. Passion stole the place of calculation, the uncontrollable took the place of the unavoidable.

Her reputation was nevertheless considerable. It was not that of the remote heights, but that of a devastating enthusiasm.

BELLE DE NUIT

Jeanne de Berg

In New York things change fast, everyone knows that. A Parisian guy had recommended his show, *Belle de Nuit*, and given me the address. To be certain, I thought I would check out the information once I was in town.

It was an ordinary building on Eighteenth Street, in a district devoid of any interest. If it hadn't been for the smaller plaque, among all the others indicating the offices, which said, BELLE DE NUIT, 10th Floor, I would have thought I was mistaken.

The elevator gave directly onto something resembling, as far as I could make out, an apartment. I should say rather, *would* have given directly, for, as soon as the door opened, I saw that the entrance to the apartment was barred by a strong wrought-iron gate with elegant scrolls, a style commonly called Spanish Lace in Louisiana. The gate was padlocked: obviously they feared unwelcome visitors (though I appeared at a very reasonable hour, in mid-afternoon). Alerted by the noise of the ascending elevator, a young woman was there, waiting, standing behind the gate. We started a conversation, she behind the gate, I constantly pushing on the button to keep the door of the elevator open, for at no time did she look as if she was going to let me enter. Another young woman came to have a quick look, then disappeared, indifferent, without uttering a single word. I asked what time the show was in my hesitant American, with such a characteristic French accent that a third woman appeared and gave me, in French this time, the information I wanted. She was curious and asked me what I was doing in New York, and what I did in Paris. She said she was French. Around thirty, a slim brunette, I found her quite attractive. When I let the door of the elevator close, she added: "Come on time Friday, it's going to be crowded."

The following Friday the gate had vanished. I entered an apartment whose main room had been hastily transformed into a kind of café-theater. A small stage with a curtain had been erected and, in front of it, several rows of benches where around fifty spectators, mostly men, sat close together the best they could. When I arrived, late as usual, the show had already begun. I sneaked in discreetly toward a bench at the back where there were still one or two free seats, just next to a round table with flaps on which a few plates of biscuits and a tower of paper cups were laid. On the raised stage, I recognized the Frenchwoman, who was heavily made up, her shoulders and arms bare, dressed in a leotard laced with shiny vinyl, her narrow garters holding up tight thigh-high boots. Crop in hand, she was whipping a naked man on his knees with his back to the audience. His face was visible in the mirror reflection that formed the backdrop. That face didn't express anything, or rather, I should say that I was too far away to know with any certainty if it expressed something or not. It was the face of a young blond man. When the Frenchwoman made him turn toward the audience, I saw that he had a slim body, not too much muscle or too hairy, agreeable really. With leather straps, she tied his wrists to a steel chain that she stretched with a system of pulleys fixed to a wooden rack and a handle that she cranked as the body stretched, arms taut and joined above his head. When she stopped, I rose a little to see if he was stretched to the point of standing on tiptoes. No, his

Jeanne de Berg

heels hadn't even left the floor. What a shame! She resumed whipping, from further away, in a wild manner that went further than the force of the blows, which didn't seem all that violent. The man started to get an erection and bit his lips, which took away the suspicion, always disappointing, that it was only pretense. Her hand was steady, her movements large, eyes cold, mouth hard, lips red. That suited the role of "mistress" that she had chosen for herself, and that suited her so well that she could have her place in comics among the spiderwomen and tigerwomen, all sisters of La Baronne Steel. Her partner, in his role as the submissive, was no less in keeping with the ideal model. When she finally untied him, and the curtain fell, the audience applauded generously. Wasn't it theater, after all?

The subject matter of that first number was, undoubtedly, whipping. That of the second would be bondage (abbreviated to "B&D" in small specialized ads).

Coming home, a young woman surprises a burglar in her apartment. He pounces on her, overpowers her easily, after a short struggle during which the two halves of her flimsy blouse, barely crossed on her chest, are parted. (She is not wearing a bra.) In order to carry on with his job in peace and quiet, he gags her, forces her to sit on a chair, to which he ties her, legs wide open, with a rope providentially found at the foot of the chair. He binds her firmly, winding and rewinding the rope in various ways, much more than is justified by his desire to continue ransacking her drawers without being disturbed and also since the young woman, as soon as she is gagged, gives up struggling (too soon, I thought). Besides, nobody was interested in the burglary now, not even the burglar. As soon as he moved back a few steps to contemplate his work, after making sure for the last time that the young woman had definitely been rendered helpless, by introducing his fingers between her breasts and the rope, then between thighs that she tried in vain to close, the curtain fell. And the audience applauded voluminously.

Acts followed one after the other, revisiting the most familiar aspects of sadomasochism. After the bondage there was the sadistic lesbians, then the fetishist shoe-store assistant, etc.

Each time the curtain fell, the audience applauded, contented.

As for me, I was not happy. As the program unfolded, the playlets were less and less convincing. The two lesbians who, apart from their youth, had little to offer, looked like two decent girls lent clothes they didn't really know how to wear. The scene with the shoe-store assistant was treated like a comedy act. The Frenchwoman (it was her second appearance), in a strict tailored suit with gloves and hat, tried on a pair of ankle boots with the help of a fetishist shop assistant who willingly accumulated various blunders. He was badly treated by the annoyed customer, who kicked him a few times. He liked it. He informed the audience of that fact, with side winks accompanied by obscene gestures. The audience, already amused, began laughing openly. As I cannot bear jokes and the gross outbursts that follow, I became more and more annoyed.

At the end of the show, the actors and actresses came back again and again to salute a decidedly satisfied audience. I rose to leave when one of the actresses stepped forward and announced, so it seemed, that the spectators were now invited onto the stage for a few minutes to use their services as well as the accessories placed at their disposal.

A young Eurasian guy rushed onto the stage, said a few words to the actress, quickly pulled down his trousers, and lay across the chair (where only his stomach could rest on the extremely narrow seat, leaving his arms and legs dangling on either sides). The actress who had made the announcement, young, plump, and devoid of grace, gave him a spanking. She did it with such a lack of vigor that it looked as if she was giving him a series of friendly pats. I wondered if she was not in need of some advice . . . I hadn't time to answer my own question before the young Eurasian rose, left the stage unruffled, and sat down again on his bench to much applause. Meanwhile, in the first row, the woman sitting next to him stood up. She was a "beautiful blonde" and she replaced him on the stage. She seized hold of the young spanker, stretched her across the chair, and thanked her resolutely, as if she too had thought to show the girl how to do it directly, not with words. Interrupted by one of the actors, who thought he should restrain her, she returned to her bench. Instead of sitting down, she remained standing, and calmly undid, one by one, the buttons of her ivory silk blouse, removed it, then unfastened her red pencil skirt. She handed it all to the man next to her on the other side, a man whose head I caught a glimpse of between the other heads, a man with white hair, visibly older than her. She appeared in a black leather bra and a chastity belt, in the same black leather, locked with a small golden padlock. I am no longer sure about the bra (perhaps it was a corset), but I am sure of the chastity belt whose padlock produced a tinkling sound when she climbed back onstage, serious, very calm still, followed by the white-haired man. She presented him with her wrists so that he could enclose them in the leather straps that hung at the end of the chain. Like the Frenchwoman at the beginning of the show, he turned the handle and the chain stretched, shortening with the sound of the grinding of medieval machinery. The woman was eventually suspended by her arms, on tiptoe, in a traditional, albeit flattering pose (and even exciting as long as the adequate bonds can avoid the use of ropes, which could dig into the flesh and wound it). The man operated the machinery with dexterity, as if it was not the first time he had used such an apparatus. Were those people "real" spectators? More than the husband or the lover, mightn't the man be the actor for a surprise act, planned for the end of the program as an encore? An encore that took no risk of tiring everyone, for, after a few whippings for the sake of it, the man freed the woman and they both regained their seats as simple spectators among those who only watched—and now applauded, of course. As nobody else seemed to want to follow, there was nothing else to do but go for a drink, a sangria (which explained the biscuits and paper cups next to me), the last of the freebies of the house, before parting. Once the spots on the stage were turned off, the sangria presented in a salad bowl was brought in. The actors filled the cups, passed them around to the audience, who, in the meantime, had gathered about the round table. It was here, in the warmth of a shared sangria, that comments, addresses, and phone numbers were swapped. The Frenchwoman, who had abandoned her imposing stage costume for a simple little dress, asked me if I'd liked it. I pulled a face: I liked her, yes, she was OK, but the others . . . ! She agreed. Questioned on the beautiful blonde and the white-haired man, she was adamant that they were not fellow performers but a couple who came to exhibit themselves from time to time, always in the same way, at the end of the show. She asked me what was happening in Paris, the addresses of dressmakers specializing in leather outfits, etc. (In spite of my denials, she took me for a professional come to check out "what was happening" in New York.) Marianne (she was called Marianne) suddenly interrupted our conversation for, she said, she had to speak to a client. It was late, and I took the opportunity to slip away.

Alone in the muggy night, I wondered about the exact meaning of the word *client*. During the taxi ride that took me back downtown, the evening unfolded again in my head. In the new, harsh light of that word that caught, *client*, the evening seemed to me to be arranged like an insidious trap that drew you in without you even realizing. Seen from that angle, the show was also, in fact, a collection of little illustrative scenes in which you chose your own model; the participation of the audience a way to incite you to taste the savoir-faire of the performers, and the charm of the accessories; the drink a way to make it easy for the most timid, in the informal closeness of the buffet and the euphoria of shared alcohol, the approach of the subjects (wasn't Marianne's simple dress, in its modesty even, more affable in a way?), and the bold decision, that of asking for an appointment. And you have become, without realizing it, imperceptibly, a client, perhaps even the ideal client: a regular.

I remembered, the day before yesterday, the gate, the surprised, suspicious girl, the comings and goings, Marianne in mid-afternoon, the wrought iron gate with the arabesques, the gate obstinately closed on the secret appointments of the *belles de jours* of New York.

BULLFIGHTING

Françoise Allain

The hair of the girls shone in the sun, the flowers decorating them were fragrant and gave off a scent heavy enough to make the boys and their fathers drunk, and slightly jealous. None of the girls paid them any attention now. Though they'd dressed in their best, the girls only had eyes for the one bowing below in the arena. He was like a god, buttoned tight in his splendid costume reflecting the rays of the sun. He was handsome, with a narrow waist, elegant calves, thighs firm beneath the satin trousers which, by chance, also clung to his balls and even the recumbent penis that could be made out beneath the fine material.

The sun was already high in the sky and blinded the audience. More than one girl was enraptured, already seeing herself as the chosen one fainting that night beneath the thrusts of that magnificent instrument. So many legends circulated around that cock, which had allegedly possessed a good number of celebrities, film stars, dancers, and extremely wealthy society girls.

He was indeed cocksure and smiled at some, whose hearts immediately beat faster beneath breasts so appetizing in their corsets. The tiers were crowded, the boxes of honor all occupied. The bourgeoisie and the nobility also flaunted their women, who, though they'd have denied it, would have loved to be the chosen one.

Only one box was empty, as it had always been, for twenty years. That was the place reserved for the most noble Amazons de Licornas family whose origins dated back to the queen of Sheba.

The current representative of that family didn't like bullfights and, though she was the owner of one of the wealthiest haciendas in the region, she had never made an appearance at a fiesta there. There was much gossip surrounding her. In particular, some which said that it was mainly women they saw at night going into the old house set back from the road, strangers as much as strange men and women. Nobody really knew what went on behind those high walls. And the mistress's servant had never opened his mouth on the subject. He was a mute.

The picadors made the first round, the floor was soon covered with flowers, all destined for the one who paraded in the middle. The first bulls were young, barely out of their herd. They were blinded by the sun and the brandished red cape inevitably attracted them. One after another they succumbed to the matador's law, and then, seized by their feet, they were dragged out of the ring to swell the ranks of those destined for the slaughterhouse.

The show became more exciting gradually; Don Juan smiled, still whirling around with his *muleta*. The organizers had promised him a quality adversary. In the meantime, he was amusing himself; the young bulls were nothing but hors-d'oeuvres. He was waiting. Once again he knew he was going to get bored.

He also scanned the crowd looking for the one who would spend the evening with him. After the kill he would have dinner with an uninteresting girl, one of those brainless birds who no longer knew how to speak once in his presence. He would do her the honor of the most handsome *toro*'s balls, a dish fit for a king, and after that he would wearily fuck her. And all just to maintain his reputation as both male and victor. He was quite blasé about it now.

Of course, if the *toro* promised was up to it, at least he could pretend to be tired if he decided he didn't like the girl or if she was stuck-up . . . He started to daydream . . . when would he finally face the one he would love to meet, to possess? Not one of those cheap young ladies, those airhead girls he was continually presented with and whom he consumed without even taking pleasure in doing so.

When would he have a worthy adversary whom he would bring to heel like the *toro* he would tame in a few moments?

The atmosphere was warming up. The crowd was more and more excited; the *toros* followed one another; the horses were restive and their riders found it harder to control them. The heat was rising. A few impatient girls fainted from the temperature, and also from tightening their belts to look their best. The others fanned themselves with increasing fervor.

It was time for an interval. Flamenco dancers invaded the ring cleaned of the bloodied sawdust. Guitars and castanets let out their frenetic rhythm.

Waiting his turn to appear in the center of the arena, he looked at the tiers, searching for his next prey, the one to whom he would dedicate the *toro*'s cock, once it was vanquished. He found it hard to choose, though he had been told about one or another young woman, attractive and high-ranking, whose name could have added further credibility to his list of conquests.

No, today he couldn't make up his mind.

The audience, too, awaited the advertised main dish. Before moving forward to take a bow, he looked a last time around the tiers and caught sight of the curtain of the empty box, which moved slightly.

Could it be occupied?

Yes, for he had just glimpsed a white hand resting on the edge of the railing. His name was chanted by the increasingly animated crowd. He turned on all sides to bow to his public. Roses fell from everywhere—except from the box.

He caught sight of a profile, pure and proud, a face partially concealed by the Andalusian shawl covering it. That face, whose lips didn't smile, whose eyes didn't look at him.

Who was that mysterious woman?

He exchanged a look with his assistant. It was her, the woman everybody talked about without really knowing her: Doña Francesca, the heiress of that old family.

Suddenly his heart beat louder. She was the one he wanted. That contemptuous woman who didn't even look at him, the hidalgo. That woman who detested bullfighting had undoubtedly come to show off, to throw her nobility in his face. He would have her tonight. She was the one he chose for the candlelit dinner, to share the love balls of the conquered animal with him as well as the bed reserved in the most beautiful suite in the old luxury inn nearby.

He threw one of his gold embroidered epaulettes in the direction of the box to signify his choice. A cheer rose from the delirious crowd. The epaulette landed right on the beauty's knees, though she didn't make any movement to pick it up.

He didn't have time to think about that insult. The *toro* had just been released.

The animal was truly powerful and conformed to all that he had been told. Its coat was ebony black, its muzzle, pierced with an iron ring, blew hot like hell. Its size was impressive. It was already scraping the ground, waiting for its adversary. The picadors set the ball rolling, the *banderillas* were quickly placed, looking like blades of straw on the animal's spine. For the moment the *toro* looked calm. The crowd grew increasingly excited at the sight of the passivity of the imposing animal.

The torero looked from time to time at the box from which no noise could be heard. The *muleta* was waved before the *toro*, which seemed to play and mock his adversary. The man began to feel bored and irritated. He turned around the animal, which shook its heavy head as if it had flies on its forehead. Why was that *toro* not reacting to the passes from the experienced man? Nevertheless the *banderillas* made his blood flow, coagulating and attracting insects. Surely it must have felt those stakes penetrating its flesh.

The man got worked up, lunged, made mistakes. Eyeing the profile of the woman, who ignored him from her patrician's box, he forgot to stay on his guard. He saw her make a sign with her hand, almost imperceptibly. He understood too late. The bull rushed him through the red cloth. It lifted the man, its left horn caught in the belt that decorated his spangled costume, and threw him in the air. A shriek of horror rose from the crowd: No!

Could it be that their idol had feet of clay? Wasn't he immortal? The spectators stood to see better the defeat of the man caught unaware by the animal.

He landed flat on the *toro*'s horns, which tore at the front of his trousers, ripping away his balls in a flood of blood. The red bollocks, like the useless *muleta*, now lay in the sun on the ground in the dirt of the arena, miserable balls of flesh, like dice cast on the casino cloth before the unlucky player.

The animal had not yet let its victim fall, despite the *peones* encircling it, trying to make it lose its grip. It threw the man in the air for the second time, as if playing with a cup-and-ball, resuming its murderous excavation. It was only when it sniffed at the balls and penis ripped away like the finger of an anatomical model in a medical school that it abandoned its prey.

The man was taken away on a stretcher. The assistants had done their best with a tourniquet on the gaping hole that replaced the male attributes he was so proud of.

He cried and murmured incoherently, looking in the direction of the box.

Its occupant had risen. She approached the wooden guardrail and jumped into the arena, throwing herself in front of an assistant who wanted to finish off the animal, now judged dangerous.

The monster calmed down instantly as it recognized its mistress. For the *toro* belonged to her, as certified by the tattoo in the shape of a unicorn, the coat of arms of her family, on its forehead, between the massive horns. It had fought valiantly and defeated the man. It had the right to live. She picked up the trophies won by the demon from the dirt, trophies that now belonged to it.

The women bawled in despair, the men stared at each other, wondering, not knowing what to say faced with the determination of that fury, so sure of her right. The bull, calm now, waited for its fate to be decided.

The judges settled it once and for all: she was right, it was the law of the bullfight. The *toro* would live in peace in the pastures where it had grown up. He had conquered, he had won the right to be the head of the herd, the king of the prairies, and the father of other *toros* and peaceful cows.

She led it away. It followed like a faithful dog. In the middle of the arena there remained a small patch of reddened sand, tainted by human blood mixed with that of the animals he had tortured.

The following day in the hospital, Don Juan, having been operated upon, now rested in a room filled with flowers, making a type of catafalque for him. He knew that his life as a womanizer was finished, as was his career.

How could he reappear in an arena, or before a woman, when every man and, above all, every woman knew he was no longer a real man and would never be?

He thought about the woman he had glimpsed at the back of that box, the one who had disturbed him to the point that he'd forgotten he was in the arena. He even had the feeling that woman and animal had acted in collusion.

What a bitch, what a whore. Why had she done that? Hatred? Vengeance? Madness?

He would never be able to pay homage to girls, women, or virgins again. He, the proud hidalgo, the ladies' man, would no longer impose on them the cock he was so proud of, his conquests praising his caliber, hardness, vigor, and stamina. He who was planning to marry into money eventually. Not immediately, of course, but eventually, for he spent everything as soon as it was earned.

If he had known he would have made his choice among all those idle rich women who always hung around and whom he had neglected, always looking for bigger and better fish. If he had known, that damned stupidity would never have happened.

He remembered his whole life as a womanizer, perused without the slightest remorse the names of all those girls whose hearts he had broken by rejecting them once the joys of discovery were exhausted. He also thought about all those bulls he had finished off, often with cruelty, sometimes with bravery, but always unnecessarily, until his own life as a man and torero terminated before that *toro* and its mistress.

What was she like, that woman he barely saw in the end, and whose gesture of death he had caught, like Nero's thumb condemning the Christians? Why had she done that?

Good God, how he fancied her . . .

As if in answer to his questions, the door opened. She stood before him. Dressed in a silk dress that clung tight to her arrogant curves, she was female to her fingertips.

He stared at her, incredulous. What was she doing there?

Her small feet, clad in high heels, tapped the floor impatiently. She sat, without waiting to be invited, in the only armchair available, peeled off her black lace gloves, and produced a small packet from her handbag.

"I took the liberty to bring them back . . . my cook has prepared them to your taste, since my bull, Hector, didn't want them. He's not carnivorous."

He couldn't believe his ears, thinking he'd misunderstood or was not yet properly awake.

She removed the paper from around a delicate old china pot, then raised its lid. At the bottom of the dish, delicately surrounded by black truffles and garnished with fresh cress, were the two love balls, until yesterday still an integral part of his being, but now swimming in an aromatic creamy sauce.

Still smiling, she took a knife from her bag and brought it close to his throat.

"Eat now, you deserve it. I think you still love life, but I'm warning you, if you shout, I'll cut your throat."

Her voice showed determination. He looked at her without uttering a word, petrified. He knew she would do what she said.

He picked up the silver cutlery bearing her coat of arms that lay next to the dish and, lowering his head, began to eat his horrible meal.

She stood over him, her eyes never leaving him, not for a second. He chewed the first bite with difficulty, lifting his head, begging her with his eyes. She smiled with disdain.

He resumed his savoring, pushing each bit around in his mouth. It was slightly rubbery, elastic . . . in reality, exactly the same taste as the other love balls he'd previously been partial to.

Beneath the dressing that concealed his wounds, he felt his cock, the cock he no longer had, the cock he saw in the dirt, a pathetic piece of bloodied flesh, getting bigger, inflating, and his desire rising and rising.

Shit! What's happening to me? It can't be real!

That woman's getting on my nerves! I'm going to call the police!

Besides, it's all her fault if I'm here. And that cunt of a bull, it wasn't even killed in the end.

But for Christ's sake I like her, I'm going to have her . . .

The bitch . . . she makes me slaver, eat my balls, and now I'm getting stiff!

Am I crazy? Am I dreaming?

The whore! What's her game?

He saw her toying with her knife, rubbing the blade against his dressings, pretending to follow the perineum bound in bandages with its edge.

She felt her interlocutor agitated. She wet her lips with pleasure, at the joy of making tremble the one who made so many pretty women's eyes cry.

She continued toying with her weapon, slowly pulling the tip across his naked chest. Vanquished, he lowered his head again, crying at his own weakness, mute before that woman he hated but desired like mad.

Soon he couldn't hold it any longer, again felt the rise in him of a huge, crazy wave . . . he felt like throwing himself on her and at the same time crawling at her feet.

Grabbing the bars of his hospital bed, he closed his eyes. His body braced itself beneath the sensation of the rising sperm. The moment of climax approached, invaded his brain, made it cloudy. He was going to explode . . .

She watched him as always, impassive.

"That's it. Come, little man, come . . .

"See how good it is. Though you're no longer a man. You're just a ball-less male, a eunuch, a slave fit for a harem.

"Come in the way that will now be the only way permitted to you. No longer able to penetrate the women you used to humiliate with your stupid cock. Rejecting them as used tissues. It's you who will now be thrown away, ridiculed, soiled, reduced to looking at women taking their pleasure before your eyes.

"You'll see, for from now on that will be your life. Looking but not taking part. Like a woman, like all those you have blighted, knocked up, abandoned in the end.

"You'll see the pleasure they have with their cunts and asses, their skin, their breasts, and every inch of their bodies. Much more than you, you poor guys who think you are above women because of that pathetic little thing dangling between your thighs. Which used to dangle between yours!

"You see, you don't need it to have an orgasm, eh, little man?"

She stroked the mouth whose closed lips exhaled a sigh. He opened his eyes again. They followed the hand that still held the knife. He felt like kissing that hand, biting it, kissing it, biting it . . . licking it so it started all over again. Feeling the cold blade on his belly, grazing lightly, drawing a bloody mark. He wanted to hear that mouth insulting him, whispering his name. To feel again that endless pleasure.

"Sleep now, little man, in a few days' time you'll be on your feet again and I shall come to get you. You'll live with the Amazons, my sisters, and you'll see what real women are like. And sometimes you'll have permission to take part in their games. At least if you prove to be a good servant."

"Yes, madam," he said, reduced to obedience.

"Good-bye, little one!"

She closed the door behind her.

He took the china pot she had left behind and licked, licked again the cream at the bottom and fell asleep, satiated, full, dreaming of *toros* and eunuchs at the feet of the Amazons.

The Protocol of La Fère

Florence Dugas

"We met at the lycée," she said. "In preparatory class, just before the *bac*."

I looked at her. She hadn't changed much, or so it seemed. If I was to believe her, she was now twenty-three years old, she'd just gained her teaching certificate, and would probably teach next year. But she had kept that very young look—it was undoubtedly not mere chance, she perpetuated her adolescence, faces talk as much as masks. Gray eyes and black hair, cut very short, with thick locks, and milky skin. Judith Salomon was rather beautiful. She beamed—though I detected signs of anxiety in that slight swelling of the veins at her temples, but that could also be a symptom of fatigue.

"We were living in Laon at the time."

Laon, its cathedral, its ramparts, its tedium, all that history gathered in a few middle-class houses and the sky of the Aisne: even when the weather was fine, something gray hung in the air, like sheets damp and crumpled in the morning.

"Doctor," she said, "can you help me?"

She half stood up from the sofa. The effect of her gray eyes suddenly full of tears was not lost.

 *

"We had an essay to write, I had to meet him. We were attending the course, sitting next to each other, the chances of the beginning of the year, when one finds oneself in an unfamiliar milieu. The weather was still nice, in September, I was wearing a T-shirt. He took hold of my left arm and wrote his phone number on my skin, just before the bend of the elbow. 'So you won't forget it.' He had a strange way of speaking, as if he always had a second meaning in the most innocuous words. I looked at my arm and blushed."

She hesitated. Her voice had a different tone now.

"My grandmother survived Treblinka," she said. "She was thirteen in 1944, but she looked older, and the SS commandant spared her—he was obviously up to something. Three months after she entered the camp, the Russians arrived and liberated them. She was one of the very few who didn't go hungry.

"She got married, ten years later, to a French soldier stationed in Germany, who brought her here. They had a daughter—my mother—who married a young engineer from Saint Gobain in 1976, a Jew, but I always thought that was pure chance."

I refrained from telling her that there is no such thing as pure chance, and that the daughter of a deported Pole marrying a Mr. Salomon is a way to recover a filiation, to go back to the tree.

"She died the following year, giving birth. One thinks that doesn't happen any longer.

"My father literally gave me away—abandoned me to my grandmother. I saw him more and more rarely. I don't look anything like my mother, but I think I am a kind of remorse for him, a suffering anyway. To make a long story short, my grandmother was still very pretty, she could even pass for my mother. Did I say I look a lot like her?

"I called him one evening. We arranged to meet at his place. Then I rubbed my arm clean. I had a lot of trouble erasing those ten absurd numbers. A trace remained. It's my grandmother who noticed: 'You've been marked with a number, too,' she smiled. Everything that reminded her of the camps made her smile. She has made a remarkable system of self-defense out of it. Sometimes there is just that smile—and I know she thinks of Treblinka, and that her thoughts are not joyful.

"She never told me anything. I examined all the photo books, the survivors' stories; I knew all the barracks, the watchtowers, the striped pajamas, the hollowed faces, the dormitories and showers. I saw all those photos. When my grandmother smiled, automatically, the pictures come back to my mind—but they are images, aren't they? Not life . . . On her arm she also has five numbers—now that she's getting old, the skin is withering a bit, and only a trace remains, exactly like that phone number badly erased on my arm that evening.

"I went to his place, no longer thinking about it. He opened the door. 'You are late,' he said. I blushed like the day before—I remembered all the more for I don't make a habit of it, and I didn't understand why his every word made me feel uneasy. He helped me take off my raincoat—it was raining, for a change, my hair was wet, he ruffled it as if to dry it. He grabbed it with his hands and pulled me toward him. I felt all weak, helpless.

"He didn't kiss me—and during those five years he never did, actually. That would be . . . how to say . . . inappropriate.

"We were in a kind of living room, cluttered with military memorabilia—his father is a colonel, today, and he collects objects, weapons, and uniforms. In his house there is even a room entirely devoted to models and armies of tin soldiers to play kriegspiel. A maniac.

"He was holding me by my hair, my legs were shaking. He made me kneel down. Then he removed my sweater and bra.

"He stepped back a little, to judge the effect. I was on my knees, in jeans, bare breasted, a bit cold. When I think about our meetings, there has always been that sensation of cold. He is very good at bringing me into damp and badly heated places. I will tell you about my weekend later on. That's why I'm here. Because it continues and it can no longer go on.

"I stared at him—his blond hair, against the light slightly, gave him a kind of halo. And those limpid eyes appeared lit from within.

"He ordered me not to look at him, to keep my head down. 'Open the zipper of your jeans,' he said. 'Yes, that's good: just open, not pull down.'

"He came back to me. He undid his belt, caressed my cheek with its leather. It was only at that moment that I realized I was literally drenched—it was pouring out of me, my belly was at melting point and I was terrorized."

"He finished undoing his trousers and slapped me across the face several times with his cock before forcing it in my mouth.

"He went in so far that I felt nauseous. He had a robust cock, rectilinear, wide at its base—thicker than my wrist. I started to go back and forth the best I could. I told myself I deserved to suck that big uncircumcised penis. It was like desired rape. I was suffocating slightly.

"It was the first time. For everything, by the way, it was the first time. Like when he went behind me and pulled my jeans down to midthigh. When he ordered me to lean forward, head in hands, buttocks offered. When he penetrated me with the tip of his fingers, testing the solidity of my hymen before plunging his fingers into my ass— three fingers, right away. It was just before he sodomized me—not for one moment, at that time, did I think he could take me any other way.

"And then words. When he told me to wrap my tongue tight around it, to go back up to the glans before plunging again, my nose in his pubic hair. When he came out of my mouth, he said that I was useless, incapable of making him come. He said it again when he came out of my ass: 'Incapable of making me come—what are you good at?' I crawled at his feet, told him I was sorry, I was going to make him come, I would be able to do it. He came back into my mouth—his penis had a bitter taste I learned to recognize, but again, he didn't come. He was doing it on purpose, of course.

"He finished undressing me, he made me walk up and down. We went into the kitchen, he made me lie down on the very cold white varnished wooden table. There were neon tubes on the ceiling and he ordered me to touch myself there, in front of him, spreading my legs wide. The idea that he was watching me made me come almost immediately.

"He told me off; obviously, that was the purpose of the game. I was panting, I had come so intensely that my thighs were soaked. He inserted himself between my legs, lifted them to place my heels on his shoulders. I wanted to look at him but I closed my eyes, because of the neon, and he deflowered me.

"Since I've known him, he has always liked to fuck me in harsh and at the same time gloomy lights, neon, bare lightbulbs, hanging on a wire. Stage spotlights. And on cold surfaces—lacquered woods, paving stones. Only once did we do it in his bedroom, but he had thrown some white sheets on the floor, which he'd carefully sprinkled with water, before stretching me on the damp material. He rolled me in it, only letting the part of my body he wanted to use show.

"I felt a brief, sharp pain, then my blood flowed, at least I thought it was blood. He pinched my breasts hard, and I came again. When he pulled out of me, he still hadn't ejaculated, and he said I was useless, I was good for nothing. He removed the belt from his trousers and hit me several times on the breasts and belly.

"I fell on my knees and took him in my mouth again. He didn't stop hitting me, on the back and buttocks, harder and harder, and I stopped sucking because I had come again."

I look at her carefully, straight into her face. She is not embarrassed, neither by recalling her memories nor by her use of the most precise words—it is plain that she takes delight in it. As if such a graphic confession was part of a protocol imposed by the master, and that, far from saying something on neurosis, it was part of its manifestation—

its complacency, I should say. Surely not. Judith uses those words because she thinks they are adequate—and I have a very brief flash, imagining her in class, in front of her bewildered students, with those same words, spoken in that calm, balanced voice.

"That's how our relationship started.

"He told me to get dressed, immediately, without having a wash, my panties sticky, the jeans stained with the blood, which still dripped. And the rest.

"I asked him where the toilets were. He took me there, left the door open, watching me with interest—delighted, without showing it, because of my confusion when the gush of piss hit the water in the bowl, like a heavy fountain.

"He gave me, in detail, the protocol of our meetings. The exact time. The way I had to always kneel down as soon as I entered. The underwear I had to wear from now on—or rather, not wear. He ordered me to go to a saddler to buy a crop for breaking in horses—specifying that the handle had to be metallic. 'What are you?' he asked me. 'I'm nothing.' 'No,' he specified, 'you're less than nothing, you're my slave.' 'I'm your slave, yes . . .'

"The next day, seeing him in class—I had sat alone instinctively, far away from him—gave me a shock. I had spent the night thinking it all over, trying to understand why, and my nerves were on edge, as if after insomnia. I looked for a long time at my skin, covered in red patches, the exact demarcation of the belt with which he had chastised me—that's the word I used spontaneously. Chastised for some fault—and each time I reached that point, I caressed myself and came, and the question disappeared—or rather, the eventual answer—but the question remained, burning, and I caressed myself again.

"Five days later, another meeting—just after class. I had brought the crop, spotted several days before and bought just prior to going to see him. The door was ajar, I entered and looked for him. He didn't seem to be home. I took my clothes off and knelt down in the middle of the living room, in front of a heavy, low table where I had laid the crop. He made me wait an extremely long time. He was there, of course, scrutinizing my submission.

"That day he just hit me on the loins, buttocks, and thighs, in neat parallel stripes. 'Count the blows' was all he said.

"At ten I thought it had to stop, he was doing it just to draw lines, I was not going to be able to refrain from screaming much longer. At thirty, I said to myself he will be fed up soon, the stripes are probably overlapping, forming a mesh, and it was no longer of interest, from an aesthetic point of view. I almost tried to get up, but he had stretched me over the lacquered wood, and bound my wrists to the legs of the table.

"He stopped at sixty, and I was nothing but pain—no, I was beyond pain. I had screamed of course, pleaded, cried, and still the leather rained down. I don't know when I thought, strongly thought, that I deserved what was happening to me.

"He stopped, caressed me with the metallic knob of the crop, which he pushed inside, in one orifice, then the other. 'You want it, don't you?' No point specifying what I wanted. 'Please, please . . .' 'Please what?' 'Take me, please . . .' 'Take me how, little slut?' I realized he wanted to hear the words, and I begged him to sodomize me, as deep as he could, to tear me apart. That pleased him, but he put his cock first in my mouth. My nose was stuffy with tears, and I was half suffocating while sucking him.

"That's it. It's been going on for five years."

She looked at me. Obviously, it could all be fake—all the more so for it sounded true. Psychopaths are good actors, when acting is part of their delirium. But at worst (was it then something worse than the suspicion that it could be true?), the narrative was there, and was telling something. And I felt something inside me, quivering.

* * *

"Other rituals were organized, over time. The uniforms he wore. That so-special sensation of rough material which grated against my buttocks when he fucked me in the ass. The weapons he made me lick, after having pushed them in certain orifices. The fiction of his 'army comrades' to whom he sometimes loaned me. But above all, that way to make me an enemy, the prisoner tortured to confess some unspeakable secret . . ."

I was listening to her, and I was no longer listening: there was something impossible in her story, but nevertheless I believed more and more in the reality of what she was narrating. Usually, and contrary to the old jokes on the subject, the masochist doesn't live on the same planet as the sadist. I would even say that they loathe each other. The idea that someone could sexually enjoy suffering, outside his own protocol, offends one extremely; the idea that the other could benefit from his own cruelty, canceling thus her own will, shocks the other. So Judith was suffering not in her flesh, but in someone else's—and that dirty perv who was making a martyr of her, was—grudgingly—the instrument of it.

"I'm coming to the point of that weekend," she said after a long pause. Her silence, after a few seconds, had respected mine, a rare thing with psychopaths, who love telling their story.

"I now live in Paris. I only go back to Laon for the ceremonies he imposes on me. He phoned me on Thursday—he was expecting me on Friday night, at the station.

"In the train, the man opposite me was nice, well-read, and frivolous looking. We chatted, and for the hour and a half our journey lasted, I had all that time, in my head, that second thought—I was once again going toward that horror, and my belly was all puckered with pleasure, and I didn't listen to anything that nice, handsome man was telling me. Something, insidiously, was cutting me off from the world. It's as if I'm in a camp—a private camp, for my sole use, where the world is no longer relevant.

"He was waiting for me. Our greetings have been reduced in time to the essential—an exchange of looks, I lower my eyes, mentally kneel down.

"Of course, I'm not fooled. In reality, he's a little lout who did his studies too. And who has guessed what I am since the beginning. Who has read me like no one else has read me. To be honest, I've already told this story two or three times—each time they looked at me, horrified, explained to me that I'm mad—so? I can diagnose that too.

"For a while I visited some specialized circles, or which pretend to be, anyway. Some *masters*, as they say, and *submissive girls*. Poor little men, poor little wankers, always so worried at the thought that one could enjoy suffering and humiliation . . . yes, able to elaborate a script of submission, minute by minute, where all the violations are codified and punished. But with no question, ever, as to the reason, or unreasonableness, which pushes the *submissive* to accept those games.

"We left for La Fère. Do you know it? It's a garrison town since time immemorial. One of the last places before the east. In crisis now that the armies are reduced.

"Whole army barracks are deserted, and that is where he took me. Empty huts, weeds everywhere, broken windows, abandoned dormitories, watchtowers without sentries. He stopped at the entrance. 'Step out, go to the middle of the courtyard and undress.' November in such a place is November twice over. It was cold and gray, I was already shivering in my coat, even more when I took it off. The rest followed, until I was naked in the middle of a paved courtyard, near a pole which, in the past, held a flag. Night was falling, he turned on the headlights of the car to cast light on me. The headlights were very white, dazzling. I heard the car door slam, I saw his shadow moving toward me . . . The taste for uniforms, you see: he was dressed like an SS officer, from cap to patent leather knee-high boots, he was holding in his hand a cosh—I didn't recognize him at that moment, he had become so much himself, the blond hair shaved on his temples, the ruthless, limpid eyes. '*Schnell*,' he shouted. I didn't even know he could speak German. '*Schnell, schnell!*' He lashed at my buttocks, while I stumbled along, moving toward a barrack hut in front of me, sliding on the wet paving stones, bent over because of the cold, the humiliation, too. I remember feeling embarrassed because of my hard breasts, the nipples stiff with cold, and arrogant. I was experiencing again the feeling I had earlier in the train, that foreknowledge of the horror—as if everything I had lived till then was only the draft for an ultimate show . . . I fell twice, sliding over the greasy paving stones. I had long streaks of mud all over my body.

"He made me enter an old dormitory, then a room next to the showers. He hit me behind the knee and I collapsed on the frozen tiles. He grabbed me by the hair, dragged me to a corner, and tied me with handcuffs to a leaking pipe. He hit me four or five more times, I was screaming, protecting my face. Then he threw his crop on the floor, took out a pair of scissors from his pocket, and started to cut my hair—I used to wear it medium-length till four days ago. The locks fell on my shoulders and belly—he was cutting it short, hacking at the mass.

"When I came back on Sunday, my head completely covered, when I undressed in my bathroom, and my mirror showed me that poor bungled head, with the white trace of his snips, I didn't recognize myself—no, it's not that, I recognized someone who was not me—who was me only externally, but in a few snips, he had made another woman come to the surface.

"He tied me up and left me there, all night. I didn't hear the car go. Night fell, I was alone, I ended up shouting, crying, there was just the sound of the wind, the cold, the damp. All night long. For a moment I was crying so much that I felt nauseous and vomited bile. No, that is not the right word. I was vomiting myself, that's it, myself.

"He came back in the morning, he was still speaking German. He told me I had to choose between absolute submission and immediate death. It was like lightning, you know. The feeling of recognizing a scene one has already lived. The other, in me—not me, for I would have preferred death—the other said she wanted to live, and that she would do what he wanted and that she would submit.

"He made her kneel down, while leaving her tied up—the hand-cuffs slid on the pipe, he opened the trousers of his uniform and forced his cock in her mouth. She sucked him as she could, awkwardly—as if all my science had vanished. After a minute, he kicked her in the belly, telling her she didn't know how to do it, that I couldn't do anything. That she was just good enough to lick his boots—he pushed her neck down, and I licked the patent leather. I still have the smell of polish in my head. Again he kicked me, she collapsed at the bottom of the wall, bent over. Something warm ran along my back, and I realized he was pissing on her.

"He untied her, dragged her around the whole camp. It was drizzling. She was frozen stiff and she was burning inside. A little later in the old kitchen quarters, he plunged two fingers into her sex—the leather of his gloves was frozen, but he plunged them effortlessly, so ready, open, and available she was."

She is silent. Is it my turn to say something? From the start I had created for myself an attentive mask, and slightly doubtful, too. The abomination of her story must not taint my listening. The purity of her story must not provoke my own desire.

"To cut it short," she resumes, "we stayed there for two days. He barely fed her, some filthy things thrown on the floor, that she had to lap up, her hands handcuffed behind her back. He penetrated her in every orifice, without ever coming. He hit her a lot, yes. He tortured her, in fact. It's incredible what a boy with imagination can do with needles, time, and alcohol. All the time he called her a filthy Jew—and it was a red rod plunging deep into her, each time, to touch the other, the one suffering inside her—not her, for she was in the ecstasy of a fantasy realized.

"She reminds me—this is going to make you smile, isn't it?—that she thought several times about her mother, that mother she never knew, thinking she is the one who should have expiated, but that she had passed to her the torch of guilt—and it's her she blamed for being a survivor, in that long female filiation, since her grandmother, who had done what was needed to survive, in the past, and didn't talk about it, and the whole story was coming out now, and it was her shouting the shame of survival, under a low sky . . . At three in the afternoon, on Sunday, it was almost dark, and there was that sudden storm. He left her in the middle of the courtyard, chained, with rusty old chains, to the pole in the middle, like a fallen flag. Washed by the rain of her stains. He left in his car, he looked at her from far away, she could see the smoke of his cigarette coming out of his open window. He turned the headlights on, like on Friday night, to illuminate her ruin."

She is silent again.

Looks at me.

"You have some doubt," she says.

I don't know if I doubt her. I no longer know, in reality. She has that characteristic of the perverted, she knows the cause of her delirium, she has explored in detail the transferred guilt, the unbearable survival. Fifty years after the end of the war, it's still there, the memory passed on like an inheritance.

She stands up suddenly:

"You have some doubt," she repeats.

In a few quick movements, she undresses. Her body is a wound, covered in bruises, gashes, cuts, and scabs. And I look neither at the dried blood nor at the traces of blows. Only at that milky skin, or what's left of it, the very dark triangle between her thighs, then her face again . . . Time stops.

"Kneel down," I say. "Head down, come on, will you never learn?"

Of course, and as every time, I plunge deep into her mouth, up to the hilt, as far as her glottis, until she has tears in her eyes.

"You told our story really well!" I say.

And as always, for five years, it's only when I remember her story that I manage, finally, to come.

THE HUT IN THE JARDIN DU LUXEMBOURG

Régine Deforges

Stretched out in her usual place, on the grill of the Métro, the woman drank her rosé wine straight from the bottle. She put it down next to her, made a face, and shouted abuse at a well-dressed young man who looked like a dynamic executive. Startled, the poor guy hastily stepped from the pavement and was nearly run down by a 63 bus. That provoked hysterics of laughter from the woman, who stood and slapped her thighs. On the other side of the street, behind a café window, he could read the word "Shame!" on her lips. The young executive told the passersby to look at the drunk woman laughing like a kid, head thrown back, her mouth with barely a tooth in sight.

"It's a shame, isn't it?"

The passersby shrugged their shoulders and kept walking. As the cars stopped at the red lights, they blocked the scene. He stood up for a better view.

The woman had another swig, then lit a cigarette. A child, running past, stumbled over her outstretched legs.

"Get lost, little shit!"

The boy stopped and looked at her closely.

"You want my picture, asshole?"

"Just look at yourself, old cow," he said, and dodged the bottle, which shattered on the road, showering a couple of German tourists who retreated at the abuse.

Still grumbling, the woman lay back down, rested her head on her folded arm.

"Come summer, or winter, she's there," said the waiter, noticing his interest in the woman. "For the ten years that I've been working here, I've always seen her. She's part of the decor. When it's very cold the boss has a coffee or a soup taken to her. Never as much as a thanks, she'd rather say fuck you. In ten years, she hasn't changed much. Life on the street must preserve you. Occasionally she's picked up by the police, enough time to delouse her. Two days later she's back at her spot. Must be malice that keeps her alive, the other tramps are afraid of her. They try to coax her with those dainty little bottles of alcohol they steal from the local supermarket. It works for as long as the drink lasts."

A funny customer. For a week he had been sitting in the same place every day, had ordered half a pint, then a second, and a third, which he drank without taking his eyes off the sidewalk opposite. He was a handsome young man, not at all the depraved type you might imagine would be interested in old sots. Not a foreigner, either. A normal person!

To get rid of the waiter, he ordered another half, which arrived immediately. The conversation would have resumed if the boss hadn't called him from the other side of the counter.

"Maurice, you're wanted in the kitchen."

Maurice left, and he immersed himself once more in his contemplation of the woman. Still lying down, she had lifted her knees. As always, his penis started to swell. He rubbed himself through the pocket of his linen trousers. Beneath her dirty old skirt, the woman hid a plump and hairless pubis, a slit with a thin red line. That sex had obsessed him since that day the previous week when, waiting for the green light, he had had all the time in the world to contemplate it. No woman's sex had ever had that effect on him. It was enough for him to remember that sex any time of day, in any place, to have an erection. He would have given a fortune to lick it, to make it gape gently. She probably had a round crimson clitoris that would swell when stroked. His erect cock seemed on the verge of exploding. On the other side of the street she rose, leaning on a window.

He dropped a handful of coins on the marble top of the table and hurried along behind the woman. As if she were royalty, she crossed the Boulevard Saint-Germain to a chorus of horns and screeching brakes. Indifferent, she dragged her feet up the Rue de l'Odéon and stopped before a gateway where she pissed, standing up. After a good shake, she resumed her wandering. In front of the theater, she seemed to hesitate, and then went to the left of the building and into a café at the corner of the Rue de Vaugirard. She bought a packet of cigarettes and ordered a glass of white wine. He followed her in.

When she took a cigarette from her packet, he offered a match. She gave him a nasty look before accepting it.

"Half a pint," he said, turning back, mainly not to scare her away.

"You buying me a drink?" she asked.

"What would you like?"

"Same as you. I've the feeling I've seen you somewhere? . . . It's not you who eyes me from the other side of the street? . . . You find me attractive perhaps? To your taste?" She laughed obscenely. "You know you're not the first? . . . Men are such pigs! You saw my pussy, didn't you? . . . That turns you on, the pussy of an old tramp like me? . . . Hey, I was right! . . . Look here, ladies and gents! . . . Look at the handsome guy who gets a hard-on for me!"

"Hey, old bag, stop bothering the customers. Finish your drink and out. Should gas them all, those animals."

Without thinking, he threw his fist across the counter. The blow went straight to the boss's nose. He started to squeal like a pig, holding his face. Blood poured between his fingers.

"Pay up and let's get lost! I know him, he'll call the cops."

They left to the insults of the boss's wife.

"Bastards! Thugs! Murderers!"

They entered the Jardin du Luxembourg breathless and collapsed on the chairs near the Médicis fountain.

"Well, well, my boy, you packed a good punch. He's going to have a nose like a tomato for weeks. Why'd you do that?"

"I didn't like the way he talked to you."

"Shouldn't worry 'bout it, I'm used to it. Got a light?" she asked, taking out her packet of cigarettes.

For a moment they smoked in silence.

"Tell me if I'm wrong, it's my pussy you eye every day?"

"Yes."

"You like it?"

"More than that."

"You'd like to see it properly?"

"Yes," he said in a whisper, tightening his fists.

"Come on then."

They crossed the whole garden. Behind a mass of blooming privets there were toilets and a hut in which the gardeners stored their tools. The door was locked with a heavy padlock. From the pocket of her skirt, she extracted a key that fit perfectly into the lock.

"In exchange for a few goodies, the gardener lets me sleep here from time to time. Come in."

The light was coming through the disjointed planks. On the hard mud floor, some burlap bags provided bedding on which the woman stretched out. She raised her skirt and spread her thighs. Her sex appeared white and plump. It seemed as if the small hut was lit by it. He fell on his knees. With slow, tender movements, she opened her labia. It was wet and red.

"Do you want to lick it?" she asked softly.

"Yes," he replied in a hoarse voice.

His tongue slid into the unctuous slit and moved up to the clitoris, erect like a tiny penis. The woman moaned and her thighs trembled and spread further. He opened his fly and took out his bursting penis and masturbated it gently while his tongue dug deep into the gaping pussy on offer. The woman came, with little spurts of come that he swallowed voluptuously. He was not going to be able to hold on much longer. His face smeared, he pulled himself up and pointed his cock into the beckoning hole and came in long spurts. The woman came again, emitting little cries.

Without any hurry he tidied himself. The woman seemed to sleep, her limbs splayed, her little girl's sex gleaming with sperm. In the semidarkness she was as beautiful as a young bride.

Without making a noise, he closed the door to the hut behind him.

ABOUT THE CONTRIBUTORS

FRANÇOISE ALLAIN
Françoise Allain is a doctor and sexologist in her fifties who has extensive experience of masochistic relationships, having once been a submissive and now switched to being a dominatrix. She has written about her personal life in her first two books, *Début* and *Suite*.

CALIXTHE BEYALA
Born in Cameroon, Calixthe Beyala has lived in France for the last thirty years. She is highly active within the French black community, and has published twenty or so novels, including *C'est le Soleil qui m'a Brûlée*, *Le Peti t Princ e de Belleville*, *Femme Nue*, and *Femme Noire*.

MARIE BOMAN
A math teacher, Marie Boman came to writing late in life. She reveals that she often writes in a trance, allowing her feelings to take over and explore the hidden depths of sensuality, emotion, and excess. Her novels have found a large audience: *Impulsion*, *La Dernière Heure*, *Huit-Clos Impertinent* . . .

SOPHIE CADALEN

A forty-year-old psychoanalyst and writer, Sophie Cadalen has succeeded in blending the rigor of her professional life with the compelling attraction of literary erotica. A specialist in the treatment of sexual deviance, she made a big splash with her first novel, *Le Divan*, which has since been followed by *Tu Meurs* and *Les Autres*. Now based in Paris, she often appears on television as an expert on abnormal psychosexual pathology.

LAURE CLERGERIE

Laure Clergerie is thirty years old. She teaches literature in western France. Her first novel, *La Phaetonne*, is a striking, no-holds-barred tale of sexuality at its most raw.

VALÉRIE CLO

Valérie Clo was born in 1970. A full-time novelist (*Encore Un Peu de Patience*, *Papa Bis*), she also writes film scripts and plays, and runs writing workshops.

JEANNE DE BERG

Catherine Robbe-Grillet was born in Paris in 1932. She published her first novel, *L'Image*, as Jean De Berg, and, later, *Cérémonies de Femmes* as Jeanne de Berg. A fascinating figure on the Parisian cultural scene, Jeanne de Berg has also appeared in some of the films of her husband, Alain Robbe-Grillet.

JEANNE DECIZE

Jeanne Decize is the pseudonym of a thirty-year-old Lyon-based journalist. She loves writing fiction and has published a handful of erotic stories.

RÉGINE DEFORGES

Born in 1935, Régine Deforges has been a bookseller, a publisher, and an author. Her Blue Bicycle series was an international bestseller, translated into twenty languages and filmed. She was the first independent female publisher in France, and set up her company L'Or du Temps, specializing in erotic literature, in 1968. Her own erotic books have all been incredibly popular and include *Contes Pervers*, *Lola et Quelque s Autres*, and *L'Orage*.

FLORENCE DUGAS

The mysterious Florence Dugas is an emblematic figure in French literature, where she both shocked and fascinated readers with her BDSM trilogy (*Dolorosa Soror*, *L'Evangile d'Eros*, and *Post-Scriptum*) and became a veritable icon of the erotica world. She teaches theater in western France and has recently retired from writing, in the belief she can offer no more of herself.

KARINE KELLER

Karine Keller is a thirty-five-year-old Swiss journalist who enjoys blending Eros and Thanatos in her erotic stories, in which she invites her readers to enter the mysterious and disturbing world of fantasies.

MARIE L.

One of the most daring French erotic authors, Marie L. is on a self-consuming quest for the absolute and explores all aspects of erotic pain, not just in her writings but also in her life, as a striking book of self-made photographs, including mutilation and self-modification, once shockingly demonstrated. Her autobiographical books, *Confessée*, *Noli Me tangere*, and *Petite Mort* have had a similar impact.

BRIGITTE LAHAIE

The high priestess and star of many classic hard-core films of the 1970s, Brigitte Lahaie is also a writer and the presenter of a major radio talk show that is followed every day by thousands of listeners. A major advocate for erotic writing, her stories are both tender and explicit.

CAROLINE LAMARCHE

Caroline Lamarche was born in 1955 in Liège. She began her writing career in 1995 with the novel *La Nuit l'Après Midi*, which was acclaimed by both reviewers and the reading public. Her exploration of sadomasochistic relationships and the sheer quality of her writing make her a leading figure in female erotica. Her most recent novel Carnets d'une *soumise de province*, was a big success.

MICHÈLE LARUE

Author, journalist, and filmmaker, Michèle Larue is an important figure of the Parisian BDSM scene. She is a leading advocate for sexual rights and the casting aside of all forms of sexual taboos. She also writes as Gala Fur, unveiling the secrets of her own life as a dominatrix. Many of her stories have been translated into English and published in a variety of anthologies.

SANDRINE LE COUSTUMER

A comedy actress in her thirties, Sandrine Le Coustumer is particularly attracted to women's intimacy and her relationship with her own body. Her lighthearted style allows her to approach women's most taboo secrets.

MAÏNA LECHERBONNIER

Maïna Lecherbonnier is thirty-two years old. Writer, businesswoman, model, and management consultant, she enjoys exploiting her sexuality in her everyday life. Her first story collection, *Exercices Sexuels de Style*, was a major bestseller in France. She is currently working on a guide to the art of erotic *savoir vivre*.

NATHALIE PERREAU

Not just a writer but also an actress (*Jo y à San Francisco*), Nathalie Perreau enjoyed bestsellerdom with her autobiographical novel

L'Amour en Soi, in which she revealed her taste for submission and multiple partners. She died tragically at the young age of thirty-five in a car accident in 1993, along with Vanessa Duriès, the pioneering author of *Le Lien*.

FRANÇOISE REY

A teacher of literature in the Beaujolais region of France, Françoise Rey created a mighty splash with her first novel, *La Femme de Papier*, in 1989. She is now considered to be one of the leading figures in contemporary erotica and has published another twenty novels, including *La Rencontre*, *Nuits d'Encre*, and *La Brûlure de la Neige*.

ALINA REYES

Alina Reyes is fifty and was born in Bordeaux. Her first novel, *Le Boucher*, published in 1988, was a major success and turned her into a prominent figure in erotic literature. Together with Françoise Rey, she has been instrumental in increasing the genre's popularity and reputation from the ghetto into which it had fallen since the publication of *Emmanuelle* in 1974. Alina Reyes has published over thirty books, including *Derrière la Porte*, *Satisfaction*, and *Corps de Femmes*.

SONIA RYKIEL

A world-famous French couturier, Sonia Rykiel enjoys a wonderful reputation for her clothes and designs worldwide, and her thirty-year career shows no signs of slowing down. She has always been attracted to the shape of women's bodies and the amorous impulse. As a writer, her tales are like sketches in which she captures all the movements of passion.

JULIE SAGET

Actress, songwriter, and singer Julie Saget enjoyed fame in the 1960s. She discovered erotic literature under the wing of famous actor

Michel Simon. Her first erotic book, *La Maison de Repos*, explored the theme of sexual dependence with great subtlety.

ASTRID SCHILLING

A Belgian author and scriptwriter, Astrid Schilling lives in Paris. Now forty-five years old, she has published over twenty books on subjects as varied as feng shui, meditation, and healthy well-being. She has always been fascinated by eroticism as a source of life, and explores its margins in *L'Homme de Gand* and in numerous erotic short stories.

FRANÇOISE SIMPÈRE

A science journalist, Françoise Simpère has made a name for herself with a series of novels in which sexual relationships are clearly free of morality and possessiveness. In comparison with Françoise Rey, she flies the flag for a joyful and liberated form of eroticism that banishes all guilt. Her books have all proven very popular, and include: *Des Désirs et desHommes*, *Le Jeune Homme au Téléphone*, *Les Latitudes Amoureuses*, and *Aimer Plusieurs Hommes à la Fois*.

JULIE TURCONI

Born in France just over thirty years ago, Julie Turconi lives in Montreal where she writes and explores madness, lust, and the anatomy of desire. She also organizes a reading series.

AGNÈS VERLET

Agnès Verlet is thirty-four years old. A literary journalist and author, she lives in Paris. She is fascinated by the erotic power of words, and has published several erotic short stories.

CLAIRE YENIDEN

Now in her fifties, Claire Yeniden has published only one novel, *Lettres du Désir*, but it has made quite an impact and been translated in five countries. Her treatment of erotica is both refined and powerful, with all moral parameters suspended, thus providing the reader with an unusual thrill.

GERALDINE ZWANG

Geraldine Zwang is a journalist who lives in the South of France. She worked for many years for sex magazines, mainly *Union* and *Couple Magazine*. She strongly believes that in order to write erotica you must not allow any self-censorship to slow you down, and her sometimes brutal stories are evidence of this.